Eartheart

Finally, The Orchid Valley

Rose Mallek

Gotham Books

30 N Gould St.
Ste. 20820, Sheridan, WY 82801
https://gothambooksinc.com/

Phone: 1 (307) 464-7800

© 2023 *Rose Mallek*. All rights reserved.

No part of this book may be reproduced, stored in a retrieval system, or transmitted by any means without the written permission of the author.

Published by Gotham Books (August 01, 2023)

ISBN: 979-8-88775-367-6 (H)
ISBN: 979-8-88775-365-2 (P)
ISBN: 979-8-88775-366-9 (E)

Because of the dynamic nature of the Internet, any web addresses or links contained in this book may have changed since publication and may no longer be valid.

The views expressed in this work are solely those of the author and do not necessarily reflect the views of the publisher, and the publisher hereby disclaims any responsibility for the publisher hereby disclaims any responsibility for them.

Contents

Prologue of Eartheart 1
Synopsis of Eartheart 3
Chapter One Strange Visitors 13
Chapter Two The Orchid Valley 30
Chapter Three The Maze 40
Chapter Four The Strange Dream 55
Chapter Five Behold The Whisper! 73
Chapter Six A Visitor From Below 86
Chapter Seven Under The Sea 98
Chapter Eight The Song of the Whales 118
Chapter Nine Farewell to the Whisper 133
Chapter Ten Alone in the Mural Forest 147
Chapter Eleven Strange Omen of the White Owl 160
Chapter Twelve The Council Decides 173
Chapter Thirteen Tragedy at Weneslydale Gorge 185
Chapter Fourteen Into Maudland 200
Chapter Fifteen Captive in Maudland 207
Chapter Sixteen In the Black Willow Keep 216
Chapter Seventeen Urage Returns 230
Chapter Eighteen With Old Friends Again 243
Chapter Nineteen Into The Spirit Valley 256
Chapter Twenty Into the Valley of Orchids 272
Chapter Twenty-One Into the Lion's Lair 288
Chapter Twenty-Two The Wedding 304
The End 306

EARTHEART

Prologue of Eartheart

Judd Gardener straightened up and lay his fishing rod across the gunwales of the canoe. He shaded his eyes as he stared across the small lake. The morning sun had already begun to break through the stand of balsams near the shore line and glance off the still surface of the lake. Judd sighed momentarily regretting the swift passage of time. It seemed to him that he had been only fishing a short while, when in fact he'd been on the lake since four that morning.

Reaching down, Judd picked up the thermos from floor of the canoe. Just time for another cup of coffee before he'd have to start thinking about hauling the canoe out of the water and loading it back on the roof of the station wagon. Judd's thoughts were interrupted with the sound of the water breaking behind him. Turning slowly, he expecting to see an otter or a beaver. The thermos slipped from his hands and landed with a dull thud on to the floor of the canoe and his mouth dropped open, as right in front of his astonished eyes, a woman looking perfectly dry, rose up from the middle of the lake. Judd's sensible face puckered in confusion as he gaped at the woman wading to the shore. As he watched her mount the grassy lake bank he ran a hand nervously through his thinning gray hair and squeezed his eyes open and shut a couple of times, hoping that the strange apparition would disappear. But when he opened them she was still there.

The strange woman stood on the lake bank looking around for a few moments. She looked to Judd, almost as though she was searching for something. She was middle aged, heavy set and wearing an odd sort of period costume with a white kerchief knotted beneath her plump chin. In her arms she was carrying what looked like a bundle of clothes. Still transfixed with amazement, Judd watched the woman walk toward an old hemlock tree. Stooping down she carefully lay the bundle under the tree. He watched her closely as she stood for a moment looking down at the bundle. Then she turned and stared across the lake at Judd. Caught on unaware, he took a sharp breath inward as her eyes met his. Her face was immobile and her eyes were dull and expressionless. She looked almost as if she were in some sort of trance. Then without warning the woman turned away from Judd and began to head back into the water. Aghast and at a loss at what to do, Judd watched incredulously as the she disappeared beneath the surface of the lake as quickly as she had risen. Still was still

EARTHEART

staring at the sport where the woman had disappeared, he was trying to decide what to do when a small frantic cry echoed across lake. As Judd turned and glanced back at the bundle under the hemlock tree a look of comprehension dawned on him.

EARTHEART

Synopsis of Eartheart

Arliss lured from the safety of her home in the predawn hours is set upon by Urage and the Carnumbra. Mallwynn and his companions arrive in time to drive off Urage and his Carnumbra before they do Arliss any real harm.

With Urage out of the way, Mallwynn tells Arliss about her true heritage and tries to convince her to return with them to Eartheart.

Before Arliss can even absorb Mallwynn's incredulous tale, Urage returns with reinforcements. She has no other choice but to flee with Mallwynn and his men.

Clad in a faded chenille robe and tucking her cat Kipper under her arm she makes a hasty departure with the wizard's party through Shadow Lake into the vortex of the well between the worlds.

They reach Eartheart just moments ahead of Urage. Mounting waiting horses they tear hell for leather up the steep slopes of a valley, in a desperate bid to reach the only pass out before Urage.

Mallwynn, the last one through, raises his staff and calls down a shower of tumbling rocks and boulders. In less than a blink of the eye the pass is completely closed.

Grateful for their narrow escape, the party waste no time in putting distance between themselves and Urage. Riding most of the night they reach the edge of Wailingdell Forest just after dawn.

As Mallwynn, Arliss, Striker, and Farin enter the forest they hear the rustle of leaves and the sound of soft whispering voices. Mallwynn noticing their look of alarm softly reassures them, "don't be frightened it's only the trees talking."

Arliss watches wide eyed as the trees now all whispering at the same time, bend first in one direction and then in another as their voices in soft rustling waves spread throughout the forest.

"The trees welcome all of us into the forest. " responded Mallwynn softly, to their quizzical glances.

After awhile they no longer noticed the whisperings of the trees. Arliss would occasionally feel the soft brush of a leaf against her cheek

EARTHEART

and she would smile as she knew it was a friendly gesture from the tree almost like a favorite aunt's kiss. In a few hours they came close to the center of the forest. Ahead of them the trees cleared and the land sloped down into a sunken meadow. In the middle of the meadow they see what looks like a huge hedgerow fortress so tightly pruned that the walls are as smooth as stone.

"What can that be?" frowned Striker eyeing the fortress with more than a little awe.

"It's the maze" murmured Mallwynn with a satisfied. But before anyone else spoke there rose caphonynious din as the trees, their leaves and branches shaking and trembling undulated as one body like waves across a stormy sea. A terrible howling keening moan blew through the entire forest. It was the most unnerving sound that Arliss had ever heard. The horses started to prance nervously and let out fearful neighs, It was all Arliss could do to keep her seat on the saddle and still hold on to Kipper.

"Urage has arrived" pronounced Striker grimly. Mallwynn had already turned his attention back on the maze. "Come while there still time!" he cried taking off at a gallop. Following close on Mallwynn's heels they come to halt outside at the high green wall of the maze.

Arliss wondering how they are going to enter the maze is disappointed as she searches the smooth greenery hoping to see a shadow or any indication of and entrance.

Mallwynn on her right muttering in a low voice to himself, didn't appear anxious. In response to his strange words began to shimmer and a door appeared in the maze.

They are in the maze several days before Urage finally gains entrance. The party is forced to escape through a subterranean tunnel hidden in the center of the maze.

They follow a luminescent lit tunnel, as it runs for miles through limestone caverns and passed underground rivers and lakes until at last they find their way out onto the sandy shores of the Cascall Sea.

Boarding the enchanted schooner The Whisper they set sail across the Cascall sea. One night, after they'd been at sea a couple of days a strange slightly slimy visitor steals quietly on board the Whisper.

The polite and dignified creature calls himself Whapper, and explains that he is a Cascallanian, an ancient race of aquatic people who live in clans in the coral caves outside the underwater kingdom of Emeridion. He says that he's been sent by the royal family of the City Emeridion to extend an invitation to the party to return with Whapper to Emeridion for a visit.

Mallwynn mentions to Arliss, Striker and Farin the existence of distant relatives living in the underwater Kingdom of Emeridion, who may be able to offer them aid, and prompts the party to accepting the invitation.

A day or two before the Whisper reaches its destination where they will meet the Emeridion escort, Mallwynn's announces his intention of leaving them saying simply that he has pressing business elsewhere. That day Mallwynn vanished before their very eyes.

Proceeding on without the Wizard they pull in at a small atoll where they're met by an escort of Emeridion's riding manatees.

The people of Emeridion call themselves The Children of Emer after their father the sea god Emer, in contrast to Whapper, look much like their land cousins except that their skin and hair is extremely light, almost transparent.

Arliss and the King's men are given fish shaped arm bands by Gilden Tidewater leader of the escort, them to allow them to breathe under water.

Riding manatees the party is taken beneath the sea. Amber globes filled with florescent material trailing on long hemp ropes that are attached to the manatee's saddle, light their way through the dark briny waters as they head for Emeridion.

Once arriving at Emeridion the party is taken to the palace where a feud is going on between Queen Amarin and her younger sister Elsaroth. Amarin is an intense young woman of little humor, who takes her role as the Queen of the Children of Emer very seriously. She will allow absolutely nothing, to come between her and her duty as Queen.

Amarin has little tolerance for Elsaroth's willful, highhanded, frivolous ways. The conflict between the sisters has escalated to such a level that the Queen mother fears that disaster is eminent for both her daughters and the kingdom.

The Queen mother entreats the party to take Elsaroth with them. In return for this she pledges her help in securing the Orchid throne for Arliss. Whapper is sent along with Elsaroth to "look after her." Used to the Emeridion Court dress of diaphanous gowns, feathered capes and bejeweled shoes, Elsaroth, refuses to travel without at least some of her wardrobe.

Despite her promise only to take the bare essentials Whapper, uncomplaining is bent almost in double with weight of Elsaroth's luggage. His fin like feet make sucking noises in the wet sand as he heads slowly toward shore. Cautioning him to be careful with her things Elsaroth strides blithely ahead of him shading her pale skin with a parasol that matched her gown.

Back on the Whisper they raise anchor and are soon underway plotting a course for the Orchid Coast. They make land fall the next morning sailing into sheltered cove the tie up at a small dock. his friends Davit and Darrah Drummond and their children.

The party is warmly welcomed into the home of the Drummonds. Despite curious glances and a few raised eyebrows the Drummonds say nothing about Whapper's fish like appearance. They pretend to see nothing unusual with Elsaroth in their small fisherman's cottage dressed in matching silver tiara, gown and slippers.

After an enormous supper they join the Drummonds and their small children around the hearth. As they warm themselves at the fireplace, Farin relates to Davit and Darrah the tale of their adventure.

Arliss stifled a yawn as she stretched her out her stocking feet toward the warmth of the fire. Breathing in the aroma of the burning apple wood her face grew warm and her eyes heavy. She must have dozed off because the next thing she knew there was a sudden knock at the cottage door. Arliss's eyes flew open in time to see the Drummond's big hounds skitter across the polished wood floor growling as they approached the door.

Davi, already on his feet, and wondering aloud who could be calling so late. With Striker and Farin, weapons drawn, peering over his shoulder, he cautiously opens the door.

The delighted cries of the men bring Arliss running to the door to welcome Mallwynn's return. Arliss's elation slipped away as she notices the anxious sober look on Mallwynn's face. A hush came over all of them as Mallwynn's began explaining that he'd come to warn them that Urage knew where they were and was already bearing down on the cottage.

Just moments before Urage and his Carnumbra arrive Arliss and the others manage to barricade themselves in the cottage. Urage and his guard surround the cottage and hold a siege long into the night.

EARTHEART

As Urage frustrated in gaining entrance, prepares to torch the small cottage, but Mallwynn is successful at luring him away.

A spell cast by the Wizard causes the schooner which is secured at the small dock with no one aboard, to hoist its sails, raise its anchor and slip silently across the cove.

It wasn't until the schooner is almost out of the cove, did Urage notice its departure.

As the schooner speeds swiftly toward the open sea, Urage and his men scramble to pursue it.

Mallwynn and Arliss and company take leave of the Drummonds at first light. Traveling by horseback they make their way upland to the edge of the Mural Forest.

Giant balsams inhabit the mural forest. The trees identical to one another in height and shape grow in long straight lines. The distance between each tree is so precise, it is almost as if it had been measured out by an overly exacting gardener.

They are only in the forest a short time, when Arliss chasing her cat Kipper, is separated from the rest of the party, and becomes hopelessly lost.

Trying to find her way back Arliss wanders for days alone in the forest until she is set upon by gypsies.

Back at the gypsy camp Arliss is questioned closely by the medium Minera, who is the overbearing mother of Janos the king of the gypsies. Minera eyes widen as she inspects the Emeridion band and an amulet given to Arliss by Mallwynn.

The Janos and the gypsies intend to rob Arliss of her jewels and steal her horse but Minera insists that they set her free. .She warns them not to take the girl's jewels or horse, because any harm done to the girl, will bring a curse down upon the entire camp.

Arliss promises the gypsies a reward if they can track down her traveling companions.

Janos and his gypsies set out to find the wizard's party.

They come upon Mallwynn, Striker, Farin, Elsaroth and Whapper just as they 'they are overtaken by Urage and his Carnumbra. The wizard's party is trapped on a narrow rope bridge spanning a deep gorge.

From the safety of the cover of the forest the gypsies and watch in alarm as Urage suddenly starts hacking away at the ropes that anchor the bridge.

Cries of shock and horror fill the air as the bridge gives away plunging all upon it into the deep chasm below.

Janos and his men return to the camp, and recount to the camp what they witnessed at the gorge. Arliss is desolate, but has little time to mourn as the caravan is soon overtaken by a company of Urage's black guard who are lead by a sadistic man by name of Klick.

Klick and the black guard rounded up the gypsies and question them as to whether they had come across a young girl traveling on their own. The gypsies tell Klick and guard that they've seen none on the road. Then as the gypsies are held at sword point their caravans ransacked and searched one at a time. The gypsies watched in silent outrage their all their worldly possessions are torn broken or scattered out onto the muddy road side.

Arliss, disguised as a gypsy slips through Klick's hands unrecognized.

As the blackguard is patrolling all the roads leading away from Maudland, Janos leads his caravan of gypsies over the zig zagging second Demon Bridge into Maudland, Urage's stronghold.

Arliss is reluctant to travel into Maudland but realizes she's safer with the gypsies than on her own.

While on the Second Demon Bridge Arliss has a vision that shows her the whole history of Eartheart since the beginning of time all in a single moment. Arliss admits to herself for the first time that she's changing drastically. She doesn't understand why it is happening but somehow she is becoming more sensitive and aware of the unseen.

At first glance the prosperous Maudland seems a model kingdom, with no sickness, poverty, or crime, but Arliss will soon find out she the true nightmarish nature of Maudland.

Desdemone, Janos' jealous and slightly deranged fiancee schemes with her ne're do-well brother Malcazar to get rid of Arliss.

They kidnap and drug Arliss and sell her slave traders.

Arliss's to finds herself in the slave yard of the Blackwillow Keep, where she is triaged and branded along with hundreds of other slaves by Master Kopter the slave master.

Arliss is relieved to learn that Urage isn't even in his keep. He still rides abroad seeking the elusive Glasstarr princess.

Winter is fast approaching when Arliss learns of Urage's eminent arrival at the Keep. The same day she is also learns to her immense relief that she and the other garden slaves, the very next day are to be sent up into the mountains to work for the winter in Urage's weaving sheds, but she just as she is about to leave the keep she is informed that she's to stay behind and work for Bree Filowdie, the Blackwillow Keeps eccentric and demanding chef.

On the eve of Urage's return while Arliss's is polishing his huge baronial table when she sees a face of a hag mirrored in the wood. The table is made from a single willow tree that grown on the grave of Urage's mother, Mardylla.

Arliss has a strange experience on the ramparts as she is confronted by a Carnumbra. She discovers that she has the ability to make herself invisible to the Carnumbra.

For weeks Arliss is able to avoid recognition by Urage, until one evening she lets down her guard and is recognized by the sadist, Klick who immediately sounds the alarm. Urage, Klick and the Carnumbra give chase to, Arliss as flees up onto the ramparts.

As Urage and his minions close in on her Arliss is left with little choice but to risk a jump from the ramparts into the sea. Closing her eyes tightly with a determined leap she launches herself of the ramparts just as she is airborne a gloved hand grab hold of her arm and then grips tightly as she and her captor plummet into the roiling Fane Sea.

It was only after she hit the water did she realize that her captor was none other than Striker! He slips an Emeridion band on her. Together they swim to the Whisper anchored just over the horizon.

Mallwynn, Farin, Elsaroth, Whapper, and Janos warmly welcome them aboard the Whisper. Arliss is speechless with joy. Tears run down her face as she grips each one of them, even Elsaroth, in a fierce bear hug.

Arliss and her friends exchange tales well into the evening until Mallwynn reminds them that they set sail at first light.

After a day and a half of hard sailing the Whisper pulls in at Looking Glass bay, an inlet near the great wilderness. The party makes its way overland stopping the night at the mysterious Wilderness Inn deep within the woods.

Their host at the inn the inscrutable Gramiel and Tharrin give the party a fine meal. After an exceptionally good nights sleep the party bids Tharrin and Gramiel good bye and sets out to try to reach the Orchid Valley the seat of government of Eartheart.

Urage is guarding all the entrances to the Orchid Valley save for the old Western Fairy Gates, which have been locked for over three hundred years. Mallwynn is certain that he can conjure up a spell to unlock the gates.

Arliss and her companions cross over the Fifth Demon Bridge and follow a narrow river pathway, a remnant of what's left of the ancient Fairy Road down into the Spirit Valley. They follow the path as it wound up the steep slopes of the Orchid Mountains right to the Western Fairy Gates.

Mallwynn after several hours of trying spell after spell is still unable to open the Western Fairy Gates. Mallwynn is perplexed as to why the gates won't open. The distant thunder of hooves and the baying of hounds remind them all of the urgency of unlocking the gates. At that same moment a light came into Mallwynn's eyes and he glanced at all of the with excitement, "Why of course only a Glasstarr can open these gates. Come on Arliss you must try." Urged Mallwynn.

Arliss guided by Mallwynn in casting the spell felt a little silly at first as she was having a hard time getting her tongue around some of the words, but she couldn't help but notice that once she said the words, they seem to ring and vibrate in the air. Even before she'd finished the incantation the gates swung open.

Without out any hesitation Arliss and her companions surged through the gates. The Gates closed slammed locked behind them barring Urage and his minions from the valley.

As they rode quickly down the Fairy the West Gate road toward the ancient City of Orchids the fabled horn of Gaelin sounded sweetly as had been prophesied, across the valley announcing the return of the Glasstarr heir. Arliss is welcomed jubilantly at the palace and quickly recognized by all as the Glasstarr heir.

Only a few days Arliss and her companion's lead the small army back out the West Gate he Orchid Valley. They head into Maudland. All of the towns and villages they pass through seem desolate and empty save for the occasional twitch of a curtain in a passing window. Along the road they encounter no black guards and meet with no resistance all the way to gates of the Blackwillow Keep. In fact the whole land seems unusually quiet.

On their arrival at the Blackwillow Keep, it too looks deserted, but the sound of beating drums draws their eye up to the ramparts and the little army steels it itself as a ripple of shock passes through its ranks as suddenly Urage surrounded by hundreds and hundreds of the Blackguard appear out of nowhere.

Drawing back to a nearby hill the Arliss the Wizard's party and the little army made camp. For days and nights on end the armies watched each other. From the ramparts Urage continually tries to engage Arliss into conversation with him. He calls out to her constantly, at first he is charming and persuasive and when she fails to respond he begins taunting her and the little army. After several days it's plain that Urage's constant barrage is having its desired effect on the little army as daily its morale slips.

Resorting to desperate measures, Arliss, Mallwynn and her friends come up with a bold plan to engage Urage in a face to face battle.

Ignoring the fervent protests of Mallwynn, Arliss, sets out with Striker and a small party of men and a few of Mallwynn's acolytes, to enter to the Keep under the cover of darkness through the postern gate located on the seaward side.

In a tower of the Keep where Urage has his apartment the party comes upon his private library filled with documents and records of the results of decades of Urage' breeding programs. They had only been in the library a short time when they are is surrounded by Urage and his men.

Arliss's expecting to be killed on the spot by Urage is calm and composed as she awaits her inevitable fate, but her composure quickly turns confusion as Urage reveals that he never had any intention of killing her. He reveals to Arliss the shocking truth as to how he had bred her specifically to be his wife.

Arliss, devastated by Urage's revelation, is held in a thrall as the matrimonial ritual presided over by Master Kopter commences.

Striker, his men and the two acolytes watch helplessly on as Arliss, with Klick holding a sword blade at her throat hesitantly begins to say the wedding vows. Urage quietly says his vows but is unable to hold back a smug smile of triumph as he awaits Kopter's pronouncement.

No one notices that the spirit of Mardylla has entered the body of one of the young acolytes. In the acolyte's body Mardylla brings the wedding to halt as she confronts Urage calling him a traitor. Urage with a patronizing look of concern starts to explain his motives to his mother but before he can say two words Mardylla stoops and seizes something from the ground. There is a sudden flash of metal immediately followed by a blood curdling scream as she runs Urage through with a sword. Then as spirit of Mardylla abandons the young acolyte, she collapses unconscious on the floor.

Klick raising his sword over the young acolyte's head and prepares to strike but Farin's arrow plunges into his heart causing him to drop the sword harmlessly to the floor.

Master Kopter grabs for Klick's sword but Striker is too fast a toss of his war ax slices off Kopter's arm as it still grasping the sword handle.

Master Kopter attempting to take a hostage lunge at Arliss. She sides steps him and he tumbles off the tower's low parapet wall impaling himself three stories below on his own branding irons.

Arliss and the Orchidians return victoriously to The Orchid Valley, where Arliss is crowned of Eartheart. Her coronation marks the beginning of the second millennium of peace and prosperity for Eartheart.

Chapter One
Strange Visitors

Arliss's spare frame was neat and lithe as she sprinted up Library Hill through the rain. She took the shallow granite steps of the library two at a time. But just as she shouldered open the library door, a rumble of thunder overhead caused her to stop in her tracks and turn. That's when she saw it again, illuminated in an oddly silent flash of lightening, the ancient yellow VW.

The tiny car had pulled up directly across from the library. The three large men inside dwarfed the car and made it look like a toy. Arliss shivered as a vague sense of uneasiness swept over her. She had first noticed the car when she had paused on Main St. to pull up the hood of her slicker. And now here it was again.

Turning quickly away, Arliss swung into the library and dumped a pile of books on the circulation desk. The thin lipped woman, sitting behind the desk, glanced up curiously as Arliss crossed quickly to the window.

The librarian's eyes returned momentarily to the pile of books the young girl deposited on the desk. It certainly was Arliss's usual fare, the strange bizarre and supposedly true tales of mystery, magic and myth.

"What rubbish!" she clucked disapprovingly to herself. Frowning as she wondered not for the first time, why an such nice quiet and otherwise sensible girl, like Arliss Gardener would fill her head with such strange stories. The librarian sniffed as she glanced at a particularly odd title and muttered to herself, "It's a wonder that she can even sleep at night." Her thoughts were interrupted as she heard a loud Pssst.

"Gladys! Over here!"

The librarian glanced up with a quizzical look at the girl still standing at the window.

"What's the matter, Arliss?" she asked the inflection of her voice rising as she got up from behind the desk.

"Has there been an accident?"

"No. . . nothing like that," murmured Arliss as she absently pushed a few damp strands of wheat colored hair back from her face. The rain still ran in rivulets down her yellow slicker beading into tiny pools on the parquet floor beneath her.

"Look out there." directed Arliss in an urgent whisper as Gladys joined her at the window.

"No! Not like that, they'll see you! she cautioned as Gladys started to push apart the wide slats of the venetian blinds.

"Oh, you mean that little yellow car?" whispered Gladys, as she contented herself with angling the slat slightly to get a better veiw.

"Yes." nodded Arliss, her steady gray eyes still fixed speculatively on the car and its occupants as she shrugged open her slicker.

"So...?" asked Gladys, her pencil line eyebrows raising in inquiry. "I think that car has been following me."

Gladys's eyes widened at Arliss's reply and her thin face began to twitch ever so slightly as she stared more intently out of the window. Then remembering the kind of books Arliss liked to read, the librarian's face hardened into a look of skepticism as she asked "What makes you think it wasn't just going your way?"

"Oh I did think that at first...," admitted Arliss hesitantly, still considering that possibility. "But they've been following me at about five miles an hour from main street to Library Hill."

"That is odd." agreed Gladys slowly as she peered more intently out the window.

"Oh look Arliss! One of them is getting out of the car!" exclaimed the librarian in surprise.

The man who got out of the car was a hulking figure. He was swathed in a voluminous black mackintosh. On his head was a black fedora with the brim slanted downwards, casting most of his face into deep shadow.

"That's the dark one." murmured Arliss. "He got out of the car on the high street. He used that phone in front of Preston's bakery. I think he must be foreign, because he had to ask someone how the phone worked."

They watched silently as the hulking figure stared up at the library.

"The other two are getting out to join him." said Gladys her thin face flushing with excitement. Then her eyes widened in surprise as she exclaimed, "They're all dressed exactly alike! How queer!"

Arliss and Gladys watched anxiously as the three men stood in a group talking and pointing up at the library. Then much to Arliss's relief the mysterious strangers got back in the small yellow car and drove off slowly into the night.

Arliss turned away from the window feeling a mixture of relief and embarrassment. Gladys on the other hand looked almost disappointed by the car's departure. The prim woman sighed in resignation, as she took her seat again behind the circulation desk.

Arliss had already turned the corner of the stairs when she heard the door of the library swing open. She paused as she heard, Gladys' voice. She was too far away to hear clearly what she was saying but as she listened closely she could make out a muffled male voice. Arliss suddenly gasped as she heard her own name mentioned. The men in the yellow VW must be back! she thought with alarm as her heart began to hammer in her chest.

Without stopping to hear any more Arliss started back up the stairs at a run. She reached the second floor in record time. Glancing quickly around she found to her dismay that there was no one else in the reference section. Running quickly into the stacks, she took refuge in the low numbers of the Dewey Decimal System. Leaning heavily against a bookcase, while she caught her breath she listened intently. She could hear the rumble of distant thunder outside and sound of the rain beating rhythmically against the library windows. Then her heart quickened as she heard a pair of heavy shuffling footsteps begin to mount the stairs. The footsteps paused as they reached the top of the stairs. Arliss, allowed a sigh of relief to escape her as she heard the footsteps moved off to the other side of the room. But it was only a second or two before the footsteps retreated back in her direction.

She was trying to decide whether to take a chance and make a run for the stairs, or head back further into the stacks. The decision however, was made for her, when out of the corner of her eye, she caught sight of the dark shape of a man rounding the corner into the aisle. The man was between her and the stairs. She decided that the best thing to do was to elude him until she could get the chance to double back and make a run for the stairs. Without hesitation, she took off deeper into the stacks.

As Arliss raced frantically down the narrow aisle she became aware of a low ominous rumble of thunder overhead. The thunder sounded so close, she was sure it was right over the roof of the library. She could almost feel the floor vibrate beneath her feet as she raced hell for leather down the aisle. She could hear and feel the rumble grow in strength and intensity until at last in a mighty cataclysmic boom it erupted, tearing open the skies overhead. And as lightening flashed through the tall windows, the lights of the library suddenly flickered went out. Arliss found herself plunged into a complete vacuum of darkness and silence.

Halting in her tracks and stood for a brief moment listening intently and her heart quicken as she heard once again the approach of heavy shuffling footsteps from somewhere behind her.

Taking off like a rabbit, Arliss was oblivious to everything, except finding her way out of the stacks and down the stairs to safety. As she raced through the darkness she suddenly felt an ice cold hand brush against her in the darkness, she opened her mouth to scream, but no sound came out. Panic gave wings to her feet as she bolted on down the aisle and out into the study area of the library. Deftly in the dim light from the window, she made her way between the rows of tables and chairs. Then as behind her she heard the sound of the footsteps almost upon her she ducked under one of the tables.

It seemed it was only moments later, that Arliss heard the footsteps weaving in and out between the tables. Her heart pounded as the footsteps drew closer, until finally they were directly in front of her! Holding her breath Arliss watched nervously as for a moment the footsteps remained perfectly still as if their owner were listening. Still holding her breath, she could feel her heart hammer in her chest as the feet begin to move again, back and forth in front of the table. She let out her breath and felt a surge of relief as the feet began to move away.

But then to her horror the unthinkable happened. She sneezed!

For an instant nothing happened, but before her brain could tell her body to move the feet were back again in front of her, and a grotesque head swooped down, and peered at her under the table. A scream left her lips, at the very same moment the lights of the library went on. She could still hear the echo of her own scream as it bounced off the high ceilings and walls of the library.

"Reverend Sykes!" gasped Arliss, finally recognizing the upside down face. His hands were clasped over his ears defensively, and his face was scrunched in pain.

"Gladys told me I'd find you up here." growled the reverend with a look of annoyance as he removed his hands from his ears.

"I didn't know it was you, Reverend!" apologized Arliss with embarrassment as she emerged from under the table, her eyes still squinting against the sudden bright light.

"Evidently." sniffed the reverend, still looking none too pleased, as he swept his sparse hair back into place on his dome shaped head.

"Is everything all right up there?" called Gladys anxiously, from the foot of the stairs.

Arliss still speechless stared blankly at Reverend Sykes.

"We're just fine thanks, Gladys." returned the reverend then he added as an afterthought, "Arliss was just a little startled."

Fixing his attention once more on Arliss, he asked "Did you know that I've called on you several times this week?"

"No. answered Arliss slowly frowning in surprise, "I had no idea."

"But you were never home." said the reverend crossly as at the same time he gave her a look as if she had been deliberately avoiding him.

Arliss felt absurdly guilty at this unspoken accusation and blurted out without thinking, "But Reverend, if I'd known you were going to call, I would have been home."

His eyebrows shot up at this comment but he said nothing.

"Arliss, a man has been making inquiries at the rectory about you," he said getting quickly to the point.

"Really!" exclaimed Arliss, her embarrassment giving way to her curiosity. "But why? What did he want?" she asked her eyes narrowing in bewilderment.

"I'm not quite sure," admitted the reverend frowning." but he was a very strange man, I must say. "

"Did he give you his name?"

"No he didn't, at least not that I can remember, but he did say he was a relative of yours and there was a slight resemblance, admitted the reverend gesturing to his eyes. But he wasn't fair like you. In fact his hair was very dark and wavy." he observed unconsciously patting his own mostly bare pate.

"He was quite tall I believe, and dressed in a dark cape. I think..." "A dark cape!" echoed Arliss incredulously.

The reverend nodded solemnly and for a moment a look of embarrassment crossed his face as he admitted, "Well, I can't really be certain that it actually was a cape, but I do know that it was something quite theatrical. Then he added slowly, "It's strange really. I don't remember this man's name, nor am I really certain of what he was wearing. He had the most odd effect on me.

"He rang the rectory bell about ten PM" recalled the reverend.

"It's unusual for me to get a caller that late, but I thought maybe one of my parishioners was sick. But then it was this strange man just standing on my doorstep. He stared at me without saying a word. I wasn't going to ask him in at first because he had such a peculiar look in his eyes. It sort of unnerved me and made me feel like he was reading my mind, but then my good sense got the better of me and I decided that he was probably here to see me because he had had a recent shock and that's was probably why he looked so odd. So I ask him in. Just as he crossed the threshold he gave me this queer smile, almost like a smirk really, it was as if somehow he had just cheated me or pulled the wool over my eyes or something like that.

Before I could open my mouth he took over the conversation. He questioned me about how long I'd been in the parish and I don't even remember how your name came up first place," admitted the reverend with a sidelong glance Arliss," but when it did, he became very interested and before I knew what was happening, I found myself telling him all sorts of things about you.

After he left, I felt terribly uneasy.

"What did he want to know about me," asked Arliss perplexed.

"He ask in particular if you had a certain piece of jewelry. An amulet I believe he called it. A star shaped thing he said it was with some sort of jewel in the center."

An odd disquiet filled Arliss.

The reverend noticing her the apprehension on her face said kindly, "Arliss, I have no wish to alarm you. Maybe I am making more of this than needs be. It was very late that night and goodness knows, I'm not getting younger, but still...it was a strange encounter. I'm telling you so that you'll be on your guard."

Arliss hesitated for minute her gray eyes wavering. Then reaching deep into a canvas purse slung over her shoulder, she pulled out a heavy silver pendant with a crystal star in its center, suspended on a thin silver chain and said, "I suppose you could call this an amulet."

The reverend's eyes widened in surprise.

"Dad gave me this a few days before he passed on. he said it was an heirloom from my natural parents."

She handed the pendant to him to examine. Looking closely at the piece of jewelry as he turned the amulet over in his hands and looked closely at it. He was surprised by the quality of the pendant. He'd only seen jewelry of this kind in museums. It was made of solid silver and quite heavy. The workmanship of the piece was excellent. The star in the center of the pendant was made out of some sort of unusually clear rock crystal that had been cut into many facets which sparkled brilliantly.

The reverend looked more perplexed than ever as he asked, "do you know who your natural parents were?"

"No. I was a foundling," answered Arliss shortly as she returned the amulet to her bag.

Glancing at her the reverend was suddenly struck by how alone she was. With a look of kindly concern as he advised, "You ought to tell your boss Frank Brown, to give you time off, from that two bit rag of his, so that you can go off to college and be with other young people you age. You certainly have the brains for it."

Blushing at the unexpected compliment Arliss, smiled shyly and said, "Maybe some day I'll do that."

The reverend glanced down at his watch and said "I've got to be off now. Can I give you a ride "

Since the rain showed no signs of letting up, Arliss accepted gratefully. Reverend Sykes swept her out of the library, and into his dilapidated chevy station wagon. The yellow VW was nowhere to be seen.

EARTHEART

Arliss was grateful that the reverend kept up a steady stream of conversation, about town affairs, so there was little response required her part. She spent most of her time thinking about the strange visitor to the rectory and wondering if he was in anyway connected to the men in the yellow VW. Her reverie however was broken when the reverend mentioned another strange occurrence in the town.

"The whole town is buzzing about the fact that Jeb Jones claims to have seen some strange fellows dressed in Halloween costumes, coming out of the woods around Shadow Lake. He apparently was out in his cow barn with a calving. On his way back to the house he saw them. A lot people are surprised to hear Jeb admit to story like that. He is normally such steady man and sensible man. But then his wife is the one telling everyone. Jeb's been extremely clam mouthed about the whole affair."

Then glancing thoughtfully at Arliss, the reverend admitted, "Personally, I think there's a lot more to this story than meets the eye. Now, Shadow Lake that's not too far from your place, Arliss?"

"Just over the rise", nodded Arliss, wondering now if the reverend thought there might be a connection between what Jeb saw and the visitor to the rectory.

The reverend was silent for a moment as if he was trying to make sense of it all.

"I'll let you know if I hear any more of our mysterious visitor." said the reverend as Arliss stepped out of the car. Then he bid her goodbye and warned her to be careful.

It was strange coming back into the darkened house. It had been still light, when she left, so she hadn't bothered to leave a lamp on. Reverend Sykes waited until she was in the front door, before he turned his car around in the driveway and drove back down the cove road.

She had barely closed the front door behind her, and when the marmalade cat, Kipper, wrapped himself around her ankles, purring like an electric motor.

"And I suppose as usual you're hungry? How is it you only have time for me when you're hungry?" she demanded of the feline with mock indignation. She shrugged off her wet slicker and hung it on a peg in the hall. The cat continued purring and circling her legs a she drew the living room drapes closed. For a brief moment she thought she saw a shadow cross the lawn. She moved quickly to the front door and flicked on the porch light, and she peered nervously out the window, but she saw no signs of an intruder.

That night as she slept, three dark figures emerged from the woods, and approached the darkened house. One separated from the group, and without hesitation walked across the lawn, and reached under a planter on the back porch, and retrieved a key. Beckoning to the other two, who joined him on the porch. They silently opened the back door and slipped into the house. On their entry into the house there was a sudden brief wild yowling and then silence. The men went from room to room, efficiently and silently, opening and closing drawers and closets. It was the wee hours of the morning, before they found what they came for, by this time, Arliss had begun to stir in her sleep and for awhile she lay in that twilight state somewhere between sleep and wakefulness. As her mind cleared, she became aware of the soft murmuring of voices. She strained to hear what they were saying, but the words were indistinct. Then she heard footsteps, that seemed to constantly approach the bedroom, but somehow they never arrived. She felt very strange, her mind felt quite clear, but it was as if her body was still asleep. Her legs and arms refused to budge. She couldn't even open her eyes. Strangely enough she didn't feel frightened just an odd sense of anticipation. She drifted off to sleep again but just moments after the strangers left the house, she awoke with a start. She had the distinct feeling that someone had just called her name. She knew suddenly that something was different. She sat bolt right up in bed and glanced at the clock. It was just past four in the morning.

It was far too quiet! She thought with surprised. At the same time her heart began to beat faster.

Where was the cat?

Kipper was her self appointed bodyguard. He nightly patrolled the perimeters of the bedroom leaving the area only when in hot pursuit of some wayward field mouse who had found his way into the house. Arliss grabbed her old blue chenille robe from the bottom of the bed and wrapped it tightly around her. Then she walked from room to room flicking on the lights and calling for the cat.

She knew that something was different. It wasn't just the quiet, it was more than that. The whole house looked as though something had just happened to it but Arliss wasn't quite sure what. She wondered what it could be as she moved from room to room. It was small things really like the fact she could have sworn the chair in the living room had been moved

EARTHEART

and as she pushed open the closed kitchen door she was almost certain that she had left it opened the night before. And her cat was still nowhere to be seen.

Arliss stood absently in front of the kitchen window sipping a glass of orange juice wondering what could have become of the cat. She was beginning to think that maybe she had left a window opened and the cat had decided to take a stroll. But that was extremely unlike him.

Then suddenly from outside of the window, she suddenly caught sight of a black shape out of the corner of her eye at the same time as she heard an incredibly loud thundering noise, so loud that it made the house shake. It sounded like the cavalry had just passed the house. Something clicked in Arliss's head as she found herself irresistibly drawn to investigate the noise. Setting her juice down so quickly that it splashed out of glass, she bounded to the back door and tore it open and crossed the porch and ran down the steps on to the lawn.

She could see that the sky overhead had lightened considerably, and dawn was only moments away. As she looked around in the gray light, at first she could see nothing but then as she glanced down at the grass she spotted fresh hoof prints.

Arliss turned around quickly looking in the direction of where the hoof prints led, where the land rose steeply just before the woods began. She caught her breath as she saw outlined against the ever lightening sky, four horsemen clad completely in black. They were poised on the rise looking down at her. Even in the murky light she could see that the figures were hooded. In their hands they carried long handled axes. Shocked by the sight, Arliss stared at the horsemen unable to believe her eyes. Then as she was suddenly reminded of the four horsemen of the Apocalypse she felt the hackles of her neck rise up.

Suddenly without warning, the horsemen launched themselves at her. They came thundering down the hill, bearing down on her brandishing their axes. Gasping in fear, Arliss broke into a run. She was only a few feet from the porch when the horsemen caught up with her. She was grappled by the collar of her old chenille robe and lifted into the air. The grass whizzed under her at an alarming speed. Without thought of harm or injury she tugged desperately at her robe until she managed to wriggle out of it. The ground rose up to meet her with a terrific smack knocking the wind completely out of her. Before she could recover her senses a shout went up, and she glanced up in time to see the horsemen wheel around and head back in her direction. As she watched them bear down on her for second time she had a sinking feeling in her gut, that told her this time they were not going to bother to stop to pick her up.

Suddenly there was a commotion behind Arliss and as two headlights flashed on, she realized it was the sound of a car engine. Glancing behind her and she was astonished to see coming at her in the predawn light, the little yellow VW! It came right over the back lawn. She shielded her eyes as the high beams were flipped on, blinding her and then she felt a rush of air as the VW roared by. The horses reared and screamed as the VW approached. Then there was the sound of the VW's engine being cut as the car stopped just short of the horsemen. The car was between her and the four horsemen.

Arliss immediately recognized the three large men who jumped out of the little yellow car as the men who had followed her to the library yesterday evening. To her amazement the elderly one with the shoulder length white hair reached into his mackintosh, and drew out a sword and held it high over his head.

Arliss watched in astonishment as his two younger companions also drew out swords. The three men approached within a couple of yards of the horsemen. Arliss's watched nervously as the four horsemen raised their axes in menacing manner. She was close enough now to make out their features to her horror she saw that three of the four horsemen's eyes had a red glow to them. The fourth 's head was still hooded.

"Urage! Keep away from her!" cried the white haired man ignoring the flashing axes which looked on the point of being launched.

The hooded man laughed harshly as he said, "Why old man? What can you do to me? Turn me into a frog?"

In less time than it took to answer that question a flash of blue light shot out from the old man's hands changing the war axes into huge frogs which croaked hoarsely as they leaped out of the surprised horsemen's hands.

Nonplussed, the four men turned their horse's around, and headed quickly back up the hill disappearing into the thick woods. Urage still hooded turned in his saddle and gave Arliss a final piercing look as he cried out, "I'll be back for you."

Arliss felt a chill go through her as she watched him disappear into the woods. The three men turned away from the departing horsemen in time to see her crumble in a heap on the ground.

Arliss heard their voices before she saw them. At first it was an annoying rumble in her ear, then the words became almost distinct she remembered thinking how strange their accent was. It was not from any country or region that she was familiar with and it was not as though they were speaking English as a second language.

When she finally opened eyes she found herself in her own living room. She was propped up on the old chintz settee. The morning sun was streaming in the window. A man's face was hovering over her. She recognized the stoic face immediately as belonging to one of the three men in the VW. He was the dark one. His skin was the color of warm amber. His thick glossy black hair lay straight and even, on his broad shoulders. He had a deep scar down the left side of his face. A thick fringe of hair framed his slightly slanted hard green eyes.

He was studying her face with a detached interest. Arliss hadn't made up her mind whether she liked the looks of the him or not. Making a move to sit up, she winced in pain as suddenly reminded of her bruises.

"Oh it can't be as bad as all that now surely? You only took a little tumble," said the dark haired stranger not bothering to hide the look of disapproval on his stoic face.

Arliss was so angry she that she was lost for words, so she just glared at the him instead. She could see the other two looking on. They had taken off their fedoras. The man with the white hair could have been any age from fifty onwards. The blonde wiry haired man beside him like the dark haired man, looked considerably younger. Perhaps only a few years older than Arliss herself. As she met the white haired man's gaze for some reason she was struck by a feeling of familiarity. He reminded her of her father, although he looked nothing like him, and she had this odd irrational feeling of remembering, sort of like déjà vu, except it was much stronger.

The white haired man's face had an ascetic look to it. His features were well defined with a narrow nose, and a strong chin. His forehead was high and his shoulder length hair was unusually long for a man of his age.

Without warning, Arliss had a brief visual flash of the white haired man hovering over her, except he looked much younger and he appeared much larger, and he was actually smiling. He was juggling tiny silver stars and crescent moons, that glittered like jewels, as they spun in the air. The mental image only lasted a few seconds, but it was very vivid.

Arliss was taken back by the recent events, which now found her rescued by three rather odd looking strangers, from four maniacal horsemen.

"My dear, please allow me to introduce myself and my companions," said the white haired man looking at her closely as he spoke almost as if he could see right through her as he announced, "I'm Mallwynn Darrowglyn."

"Are you some kind of wizard or magician or something," asked Arliss wondering just how he managed to change the axes into frogs."

"A wizard is what I am," admitted Mallwynn nodding as if he understood her curiosity." And I don't use any mirrors or any other rubbish like that."

A look of surprise crossed Arliss's face and before she could say a single word more, Mallwynn retorted sharply," And don't even think of asking for a demonstration. I don't perfume silly circus tricks to amuse idiots or children."

Looking past Mallwynn, Arliss's eyes lit on Striker. Just they way he stood annoyed her. He was leaning casually against her fireplace mantle with his arms crossed just like he owned the place. Mallwynn noticing her interest in the golden skinned man said, "That is Lord Strongforth. He answers to the name of Striker.

Striker's hard green eyes narrowed as he grudgingly nodded in acknowledgment to Arliss. He looked as though he hadn't quite made up his mind about her either. Arliss gave him a dirty look which seemed to surprise him.

The man with the wiry blonde hair stepped forth from the shadows where he'd been standing patiently taking everything in and bowed diffidently to her in an old world militaristic manner.

"This is Sir Farin Woodrow, you may call him Farin" said Mallwynn. As warm smile spread across Farin's expressive face. Arliss despite herself spontaneously returned the smile. Taking her eyes of Farin for a moment she spied her blue chenille robe at the end of the couch. Reaching down she grabbed the end of the robe and pulled it toward her. Except for a few grass stains it looked none the worse for the wear.

"I found it on a bush. It looked like it might have belonged to you." grinned Farin.

Arliss nodded her thanks as she slipped into the robe and wrapped it modestly about her.

Swinging her legs off the sofa, she stood up and tried to gather up what was left of her dignity. Mallwynn seemed to be in charge, and it was to him she addressed herself.

"Everyone seems to know what's going on except me.

Mallwynn didn't respond right away. He seemed as if he was listening for something as he walked over to the window and glanced anxiously out. Arliss thought he had chosen not to hear her, and she began to feel very annoyed. After a moment or two of Mallwynn ignoring her she was unable to contain herself longer as she sputtered indignantly," Well are you, or aren't you going to tell me what's going on here?"

Mallwynn taking off guard by her directness turned to her with a look of surprise.

Arliss sat back down on the chintz couch again suddenly feeling very tired as she asked this time," Who are those people and why did they try to hurt me? Who is Urage?" she asked with her gray eyes fixed on steadily on Mallwynn.

"I will tell you everything you want to know as soon time permits." he promised. Then as he noticed a doubtful look crossed Arliss's face the wizard added firmly, "You have my word of honor on that score."

From her position on the sofa, Arliss had an obstructed view of the dining room because the tall reed like figure of Mallwynn blocked the way, but at the sound of a loud angry hiss, Mallwynn stepped back giving Arliss a clear view of Kipper as he stalked into dining room. He looked like he was walking on his toenails and his back was arched with his tail rigid and held high. He looked quite menacing, until he lurched a little. Then suddenly as if all the starch had suddenly left him he staggered forward in the direction of Arliss. She scrambled off the sofa and flew across the room and sweeping the cat up into her arms. Holding the limp animal in her arms, Arliss turned angrily and confronted the three men.

"You did this to my cat. What kind of people are you she demanded?"

Striker appeared not to have heard Arliss, as he continued leafing through a book he picked up. Farin blushed and stared uncomfortably at Mallwynn, as if he could rectify the situation.

"Your cat will be all right," asserted Mallwynn quietly. "He is just recovering from the effects of a mild sleeping draft. He'll be as right as rain in no time."

Arliss reluctantly allowed Mallwynn to remove Kipper from her arms. Holding the cat carefully, Mallwynn deftly examined it and then handed it back to Arliss. As Arliss held Kipper in arms Mallwynn opened a vial that he had removed from his pocket and allowed a few drops of its contents to flow into the cats mouth. Kipper responded immediately, shaking himself as if he had just awakened. He sprang out of Arliss's arms and landed with a plop on the floor where he began to eye the strangers with a sort of befuddled suspicion as he thought he was not quite sure what happened.

Arliss still pondering her situation edged back on to the sofa glancing from time to time up at the wizard's aristocratic face. Kipper abandoning his surveillance of the strangers sprang up beside her, and within moments was comfortably dozing. Giving Arliss a long speculative look, the wizard took a seat in the rocking chair next to her. Drawing out from his cloak a clay pipe which he didn't bother to light, instead he sat with it clenched between his teeth as he regarded Arliss expectantly. Striker was exploring the room. He spent a lot of time looking at the photographs on the mantelpiece and reading the titles on the spines of the books on the shelves around the room. He even had the gall to go into the heated sun porch where she did most her writing, and although he didn't touch the word processor, he leafed boldly through her notes and research material, inspecting everything very carefully. Farin on the other hand was spinning the dial of the television set in the kitchen, with the channel changer and from what she could hear, he had mastered the channel rebound function and was flipping between news channels. Arliss wondered not for the first time of the possibility that she had jumped from the frying pan into the fire, but her instincts told that what ever these people had in mind, they had no intention of harming her, then as an after thought she amended at least not on purpose.

Arliss was getting more and more annoyed about all the brazen nosing and poking around that was going on. She would have thought that they'd have seen enough of her house last night when they searched it from stem to stern.

"You searched my house my house last night" she said pointedly. "Yes," admitted Mallwynn quietly.

"Why?" asked Arliss, not really expecting an answer. "

"Because I needed proof. "replied Mallwynn slowly as watched her face closely.

"Proof?" repeated Arliss, now more confused than ever. "Yes, of who you really are."

"But I already know who I really am." said Arliss puzzled, though even as she said it something was opening up inside her, a rising excitement and an acknowledgment of all the questions she never dares ask her parents because they had made her feel afraid of the answers.

"I found these small handmade infants blanket in your attic. "said Mallwynn as he pulled out a small embroidered blanket from the pocket of his mackintosh. "

"That's the blanket my dad found me wrapped in by the Shadow Lake. "My daughter made this blanket. "said Mallwynn simply, as he suddenly looked very tired.

Arliss was speechless.

"I am your Grandfather," admitted Mallwynn, softly as though not to startle her.

Arliss was silent, at first she didn't think she'd heard right but a glance Mallwynn confirmed that she had. "No. You can't be my Grandfather. You're making a mistake." she said shaking her head in disbelief. But even as she denied the wizard's words, she couldn't deny the feeling of familiarity that filled her when she looked at him. He looked enough like her, despite his age to be her father. It wasn't just the way he looked, it was the way he moved and the way that he spoke that was some how familiar.

Quickly and smoothly and without warning a dark shadow slid over the sunlit room followed instantly by a flash of lightening and a rumble of thunder. For a few heart beats everything and everyone in the room was still as a tableau. Then Farin sprang into action racing to the front window while Striker headed toward the rear of the house. Arliss lit a lamp as outside it had grown dark as the darkest night. It had begun to rain hard. The wind picked up and began to blow, whistling through all the nooks and crannies of the house. Arliss shivered as much from fear as the sudden cold.

"They are on their way back," cried Striker racing into the room "I can see them moving in the shadows of the trees. They are using the storm for cover. Mallwynn turned to Arliss by way of an explanation and added, "Carnumbra are not able to travel in daylight."

"Carnumbra!" breathed Arliss, blanching. Now she had a name for the nightmarish axed horsemen.

"Quick, we must leave immediately." ordered Mallwynn.

"Leave...? Leave now?" repeated Arliss helplessly. Mallwynn raised his hand to halt Striker as he swiftly bore down on the frightened girl. Farin had left through the front door and she could already hear the VW's engine revue up.

"I have more proof that may convince you" said Mallwynn.

"What could you possibly have" sighed Arliss, knowing now that she would be forced to go with the strangers convinced or not.

"I have this" said Mallwynn as he reached into his pocket and brought out dangling on a thin silver chain, a pendant. It was an almost exact duplicate of the pendant her father had given her on her sixteenth birthday. Her hand went to her chest, she could still feel her own pendant beneath the flannel of her nightgown. The pendant Mallwynn held was slightly larger than hers but it had the same ornate design with the crystal star in the middle. As the light caught the pendant's crystal it blazed with fire.

Chapter Two
The Orchid Valley

Arliss had only time to throw on her yellow slicker and grab the cat. Farin had already brought the car around to the front lawn. Striker and Mallwynn hustled her out the door. Farin had the car already moving before she got in.

The car wheels spun in the mud and came to a complete halt. Cold sweat ran down in rivulets from Arliss's forehead as Farin rocked the car gently back and forth in reverse and drive trying desperately to get some traction to get out of the mud. Arliss could feel the earth begin to shake as the four horse men approached in her panic she became suddenly inspired with the obvious, "We need to get out and push!"

Arliss took Farin's place behind the wheel while he and Striker leapt out of the small car and began to push. The little car quickly surged forward and when it reached the black top Arliss paused just long enough for the men to get back in. To her surprise and annoyance Striker got in on her side and effortlessly shoveled her over to the other seat. He quickly put the pedal to the floor and the four horsemen rapidly disappeared from view.

"Take this next right. It will take us on up to old logging road that goes to Shadow Lake," said Mallwynn over the rustle of the ordinance survey map. which he had spread over the back of the front seat. Arliss squirmed and moved forward to avoid the stiff edges of the map from tickling her neck. As she glanced out the window it did not surprise her that they had met no one else on the town roads. At this time on Sunday morning the towns people were usually still asleep. As they raced through the quiet streets. Arliss gazed with longing at the quiet houses of her sleepy neighbors. She envied their normality, which only a few hours ago, had been hers also to take for granted.

"Why are we going to Shadow Lake," asked, Arliss wondering uneasily what the old wizard, Striker and Farin could want up at a remote woodland lake. But before anyone could answer her Farin cried out, "Look behind you. They're coming!" Arliss spun around in the tiny car seat and craned her neck to look out the dusty window of the car. Her eyes widened in astonishment and she drew a sharp breath inward as behind them in the distance she saw what Farin had seen. It was a large dense cloud of darkness the size and shape of a small three story building. The dark massive cloud hugged the ground as it moved with great speed in their direction.

Striker once again put the accelerator to floor and the little car trembled and shot forward and before long the strange blackness disappeared as they rounded a bend in the road. Further up the road they took a fork onto the logging road.

The logging road took them up only the part of the way. They had to leave the car where the logging road ended. As she got out of the car Striker grabbed her roughly by the arm and pointed up the woodland trail that lead to Shadow lake. Run Arliss! he commanded and then with a grim look he added "if they catch us they'll kill us all."

Arliss didn't need to be told twice, still clutching Kipper in her arms she scampered up the trail. On and on she sprinted nimbly avoiding the deep ruts, tree roots, and loose rocks on the trail. Surprisingly her chenille robe didn't to slow her down too much, except when occasionally the trail narrowed and she snagged or caught it on burrs or tree branches. Behind her she could hear Striker and Farin as they half carried and half dragged Mallwynn. The old wizard kept demanding that they go on without him.

"I'll hold up the rear while you two take Arliss through the well" he insisted breathlessly. The two men continued carting him up the trail pretending they didn't hear a word he was saying. Arliss's chest burned with the exertion of the run and she was finding Kipper harder and harder to hold onto. The poor cat had no idea what was happening. Alarmed and frightened he longed to be set down so that he could scuttle into the safety of the dense underbrush. Fearing he would be forever lost, Arliss held the cat firm as he wriggled and squirmed digging his claws into the shoulder of her robe. But just when she thought she couldn't go any further the woods began to thin and she came at last to the shore of Shadow Lake. For a few moments she stood catching her breath as she gazed across the mirror dark. She'd been up for hours but the morning sun was still low in the eastern horizon. Behind her she could hear Mallwynn, Striker, and Farin crashing through the undergrowth. The din grew louder until at last the three men emerged from the forest and joined her by the lake side. Arliss had barely time to greet them when a without warning a dark shadow came over them.

"The Carnumbra!" exclaimed Farin. Arliss turned and gasped in horror, as the dark dense cloud which had been following them on the road began to descending rapidly over the woods.

Mallwynn, with his breath still labored from the run, took Kipper from Arliss. As she began to protest he drew her up short with a severe look, and said simply, "Trust me."

The woods were now in totally enveloped in the blackness. The air around them grew suddenly cold.

"Quick, Striker!" cried Mallwynn. "Take Arliss, through the well. Farin and I will be right behind you. Go quickly now before it's too late!" urged the old wizard.

Striker didn't hesitate for a moment springing into action, he grabbed hold off Arliss's hand he pulled her along with him further up the shore of the lake to where a thick clump of reeds grew. He bent down and pulled up something silvery that caught the light. It looked like an elaborately decorated silver t- handle of a shovel. It was attached to what at first glance Arliss had thought was fishing line attached to a loop on the t-bar handle. But as she looked more closely she saw it was a silver cord. It was as thick as a jump rope and it pulsated with light all along its length. Her eyes followed the pulsating cord across the lake to where it disappeared into the center of the lake.

"Hold on tight, Arliss your going for a ride." instructed Striker his hard green eyes flitting down the shore to where the black cloud was beginning to pour out of the woods onto the shore. Now you've got to hold on very tight. If the centrifugal force should rips us apart you'll die in the vortex." he warned gravely.

Arliss blanched but complied immediately. She could feel the buttons of Striker's mackintosh dig into her cheek.

"When we hit the water You'll have to hold your breath for a moment or two. You may feel for a moment like you are going to drown, but you mustn't panic and let go. Do you understand, Arliss?." asked Striker quietly, his green eyes fixed on her.

Unable to speak as her mouth was so dry from fear, she nodded her assent."

"Let's go." said Striker looping his arms through hers and grabbing the t- bar. Then taking a broad stance and braced himself and gave the silver cord a quick tug. Almost immediately the cord grew taut pulling them both headlong into the water. She and Striker were swept off in a spray of water with great speed across and down into the center of the lake. Arliss got a lump in her throat as she heard Kipper cry out from the shore in a plaintive yowl just as her head went under water. She had to concentrate with all her might just to hold onto Striker, as they down, down down into the center of Shadow Lake.

They were in a whirlpool of black water, spinning, spinning, around and around. Arliss wondered grimly how much longer she could hold her breath. Another moment or so and she was sure her chest would explode. Then they began to whirl faster. The centrifugal force became so great Arliss was certain she would be ripped apart from Striker and perish. The roar of water ceased and the pressure let up of her chest. She still held her breath but somehow it didn't feel as uncomfortable. The blackness had been replaced by a sort of twilight blue and they were no longer traveling through water but through emptiness. They were in a void. She and Striker were linked together spinning in a curious waltz through space and time. Behind them in the distance she could see two shining spinning bodies. She surmised with detached interest that they must Farin and Mallwynn. A warm pleasant feeling engulfed her, filling her with peace and serenity at the same time she felt a strong urge to let go, but she knew that if she did she would perish in the void. This realization should have terrified her, but somehow as the warmth and peace had wrapped around her a dangerous indifference had also taken hold of her.

As suddenly as she and Striker had entered the void they were pulled out of it again into icy cold wetness. The shock caused her to loosen her grip on Striker, but as she started to slip away she felt his hold on her tighten in response. Then all at once they stopped moving forward. Arliss saw the silver T- bar fly up through the water as Striker let go of it. For a few seconds it seemed that they were stock still in the water, but then they were propelled upwards until they broke through the surface of water.

Gasping for breath, Arliss treaded water as she looked around her. They had emerged into a pond in a huge limestone cavern. The pond water was as still and as black as ink with clouds of pale algae floating on the surface. The limestone roof was partially opened to the sky. Overhead the dying embers of a setting sun began to sail across the pond in a shimmering veil of red light. Arliss glanced around her. Reflected in the pond waters was a stand of ancient copper beech trees growing in a small pocket of earth next to the pond.

Arliss felt a sudden chill on her face as a stiff breeze whispered down the cavern and through the copper beech trees making the sound of a thousand pages turning quickly. Under the branches of a beech tree that overhung the pond she caught sight of Striker. His eyes were fixed on a pulsating cord of silver that stretched tautly from the cavern wall into the pond. As Arliss looked on there was a splash and spray of water as the handle of the cord erupted onto the surface of the pond. Then with a sudden whoosh and whirring the cord and handle were retracted quickly into a deep crevice in the cavern wall. Moments later Mallwynn and Striker broke through the surface of the water. Arliss was very pleased to see that they had both made it through the well but she couldn't help feeling bad about her poor old cat Kipper and as she did she felt the hard lump in her throat again. She knew now that there was no way the cat could have made it through the well.

Even as Striker was helping Mallwynn out of the water the old wizard was urging them all to hurry as he warned, "Urage, could be right at our heels. "There are many places in these caverns that he could use to travel back from Shadow Lake."

Taking only a moment to wring as much water out of their clothing as they could. They quickly made their way to the mouth of the cavern where they had stabled their horses. Arliss saw a different side of Striker as he greeted his coal black steed Eagliss warmly as if it were just an enormous puppy dog. He scratched the horses affectionately behind the ears and offered it a dubious looking carrot from out of his saddle pack. Eagliss gratefully accepted the gift, First nibbling daintily on the end of the carrot. Then skillfully drawing the carrot into its mouth with its velvet lips.

"This is Targus, the horse you will be riding," said Striker giving the horse next to Eagliss a friendly pat. Lost for words, Arliss stared at the big powerful stallion. It was black and about the same size as Eagliss, but unlike Eagliss it had a thick silver gray mane and tail. Arliss intimidated by the size of Targus was silent for a moment.

Farin, was mounting an unusually copper red colored horse he called Rubicon. He smiled at her reassuringly and said, "Targus is a fine horse. Mallwynn chose him especially for you. He's got great heart and common sense. You'll get on well with him."

Striker held Targus steady for Arliss to mount.

"Do you need any help?" he asked giving her a measuring look as if to assess her skills. Not wanting to give him any satisfaction by admitting she hadn't ridden anything other than a pony at the county fair when she was eight, Arliss said casually, "No thanks. I've ridden before." Feeling Striker's eyes on her she tightened the belt of her blue chenille robe which was still damp. She and hitched it up slightly and approached Targus in a relaxed confident manner. But as she patted the horse on the neck the same way she had seen Striker do, the horse's eyes swung side ways in its socket giving Arliss a leery look and snorted loudly. She quickly withdrew her hand. Striker was grinning widely. Arliss pretended not to notice his amusement as she put her bedroom slipper foot in the stirrup. The grabbing hold of the saddle she heaved herself up and swung her leg over the saddle with as much dignity as she could muster. She was still trying to figure out what to do with the reins when Mallwynn, appeared suddenly in front of her. "I think that I have something that belongs to you," he said.

Arliss watched curiously as the wizard drew open his wet cloak and took out what appeared to be a cinched oil cloth bag. Then as he shook the bag it began writhing wriggling on its own accord as if it were filled with snakes.

Arliss's dared not to hope what she was hoping but she couldn't hold back the smile of anticipation from her face as she watched the wizard untie the oil cloth bag and reach in. As Mallwynn drew out the large disheveled marmalade cat, Arliss's eyes widened in delight. Kipper. blinked incomprehensibly the sudden light. At first sight of Arliss he fixed her with a look of desperate entreaty and let out and an almost human cry. Arliss laughed and gave the wizard a look of gratitude as she leaned over and scooped up the anxious cat.

Arliss watched as the wizard reined his huge golden charger Leonis alongside a particularly old and gnarled beech tree. She watched with curiosity as the wizard reached up into the beech tree and draw down what appeared at first to be a loose branch of the tree but when she looked at it more closely she could see that it was a cane of some kind. But it was far longer than most canes she'd seen before. It was made out of straight branch of beech wood. The cane was highly polished and had a crooked neck. It was knotted and twisted into a spiral as if at some time a vine had grown tightly around it. and polished with a crook neck. Mallwynn noticing her interest held up the cane and said, "It's my staff. I felt lost without it as I use it as a focus for my power. I couldn't take it through well so I left it here for safe keeping."

When the wizard and his party left the cavern chamber they found themselves in a deep broad valley. This is the Valley of Creation," explained Mallwynn gesturing with his staff. "As long as time is remembered, this has always been a sacred place for all the inhabitants of Eartheart. The cavern we just emerged from is one of the Krippner Caverns. They are thought to be the birthplace of all Eartheart." Mallwynn pointing up to the steep mountains that ringed the valley." Those are the Umbrial mountains. The only way over them is through a narrow pass. If we can get through the pass we stand a chance."

Darkness was descending as they journeyed across the valley to the foot of the mountains. The ascent up the narrow winding mountain trail was slow and difficult. It required all of Arliss's concentration just to stay on the horse so she hardly noticed the discomfort of her wet clothing. They were riding single file on the trail. Kipper, had taken an immediate liking to Targus. The cat looked perfectly at home lolling across the front of Arliss's saddle playing with the horse's mane, but when Striker, who was ahead on the trail gave the signal to halt, Arliss, in her inexperience, reigned Targus in so abruptly that the horse stopped short in his tracks, very nearly causing Kipper to be tossed from his precarious perch.

"Looks like Urage, has caught up with us already", said Striker grimly, as he glanced sidelong at Mallwynn and Farin."

Arliss turned in the saddle and followed the men's eyes as they looked down into the valley. She saw a line of smoky torches snaking quickly across the floor of the valley. The wind gusted up from the valley and bringing with it the rancorous odor of smoldering rags and animal fat and the sound of a hunters horn. Just down the trail from them they heard a single wolf like howl.

"Quickly," roared Mallwynn, "He's sent the hell hounds as the vanguard, "We must make haste, or they'll be upon us in no time."

Stones and rocks tumbled down the trail behind them as they raced blindly up the mountains. The horses sensing the closeness of the hell hounds, desperately forged ahead. The din of their strident howls and barks rang across the valley sending shivers up Arliss's spine. Targus's main was drenched with sweat Arliss suspected that it was a much from the fear of the approaching hounds as the effort of the arduous climb. Arliss was having a difficult time just keeping her seat. She expected at any moment to be pitched off. Kipper, was faring much better he was bracing himself with horses mane. As the mountain trail changed direction Arliss caught sight of the smoky column of horsemen as they swept up the mountain. She was shocked by the speed at which they were advancing. She could already hear the faint rumble of their hoof beats. It didn't seem possible that a lone horse could move that fast never mind an army. Targus's ears started to twitch nervously as the soulless howling of the hell hounds sounded so close that it seemed it would only be moments before they were upon them. Up ahead at the base of the summit they could see the pass, a narrow notch cut out of the mountain. Arliss holding on tightly to Targus, chanced a look over her shoulder, she blanched as she caught her first sight of the hell hounds. The pack flowed up the trail with a single purpose, like living river of undulating flesh and muscle. Their slick black bodies gleamed in the moon light Their enormous heads seemed unnaturally disproportionate to their bodies. They were salivating lather from their massive jaws.

The wizard and his party reached the summit of the mountain with the pack of hell hounds closer than ever still in hot pursuit. They were almost on top of the pass. Farin was through first. Striker was by Arliss's side urging Targus on and Mallwynn was following close behind her. They had almost reached the pass when all at once one of the hell hounds broke from the ranks and tore past Mallwynn and cannonballed in between Striker and Arliss. Before anyone knew what was happening, Arliss's horse Targus let out a blood curdling scream, and reared up in the air. Arliss was so suddenly airborne that she didn't know what was happening until just seconds before she landed on a clump of scrub yew that grew at the edge of the trail. Collecting her wits quickly she rolled further off the trail out of harm's way and looked up in time to see Targus rise up in the air again. She watched in mute horror as the horse tried desperately to drive off the hell hound which was snarling and snapping as it ran in between the horse's legs. Just as the horse managed to get hound out from under its legs the hell hound in a sudden bound launched itself with gaping jaws at the horses face. The horse screamed and reared up frantically, clipping the hound on the side of the head and rendering it senseless. The hound had no sooner hit the ground when an arrow whizzed through the air from Farin's bow piercing it through the eye and killing it instantly.

The rest of hell hound pack had reached the base of the summit and were now upon them. Following quickly on the hounds heels was Urage and his Carnumbra. Their smoky torches lit up the mountain with an eerie light. The pack of hell hounds spotted Arliss almost immediately, lying at the side of the trail, just short of the pass. They swiftly bore down on her. Panic stricken, she hauled herself to her feet and stared with abject terror at the fast approaching horde. Then all at once she heard her name called and she glanced up in time to see Striker swoop down her with surprising speed and strength and hauled her up in front of him like a sack of turnips. Striker wheeled the horse around and headed into the pass. Farin on Rubicon, with Targus by his bridle rode through the pass just ahead of them. Arliss sighed with relief as she noticed a large ball of golden fur attached to the base of Targus's mane. Mallwynn with his staff held high stood in the middle of the pass urging them on. They tore past the wizard and out the other side of the pass. They swung their horses around in time to see the wizard holding his staff out toward the steep walls of the pass. There was a crackling noise as white shards of light shot out from the staff and on to the walls of the pass. The light seemed to bounce, ricochet and splinter off in many directions. Then as the ground rumbled beneath them, Arliss watched in amazement as the walls of the pass began to shatter open spewing out huge boulders that within a very short time completely blocked the pass, leaving Urage, the Carnumbra and hell hounds on the other side. As they watched the final boulder come to a rest, they were all stood quietly for a moment savoring their narrow escape.

Heeding Mallwynn's warning that it would be only a short time before their pursuers found a way around the blocked pass, the party quickly set off. They left the trail and picked up speed cantering down a grassy meadow until they reached a stream. In an attempt to get the hounds off their scent they entered the water.

The moon had risen high and its pale light lit their way as they made their way upstream. Arliss could smell the musky scent of damp vegetation. She could hear all around them the quiet rustle and movement of unseen nocturnal creatures in the trees and under growth along the stream. Choirs of peepers from nearby swamps competed with the crickets to make the night air sing. Moonlight through the trees made lacy shadows in the stream. The water swirled and eddied around the horse's legs, the hooves made sucking gurgling sounds going in and out of the water. Her robe had at last dried out and she finally felt dry and comfortable. She soon became lulled by the gentle sway of the horse and the murky light soon lost track of time and distance. She vaguely remembered passing a fork in the stream. The trek through the stream seemed to go on forever.

It was almost dawn when they came at last to a steep waterfall. To Arliss's amazement, instead of leaving the water at this point as the way was clearly impassable. The wizard continued on, passing through the curtain of water with apparent ease and disappearing completely from sight. Nonplused as Arliss was she only hesitated a moment before following Mallwynn through the falls and into a deep low cave. Arliss was glad the brief moment under the water fall had only left her a bit damp.

The horses hooves echoed deep and hollow on the floor of the cave. Just as Arliss's eyes were getting used to the darkness she noticed a gradual lightening of the dark. Soon the whole cave was illuminated in curious warm light. Arliss couldn't say at first where the light was coming from. Then as she glance glanced around she noticed that the golden light was emanating from a rock on the cave floor.

When the light was at its height, their eyes were drawn to the ceiling of the cavern as overhead there was what sounded like the rustling of a thousand leaves frantically brushing against each, and the sound of high pitched squeals. From the various eaves and pockets in the upper reaches of the cavern bats poured out in a seemly endless number. Striker drew his sword and held his hand up to his face while he brandished the sword in the air. He was muttering something under his breath that Arliss couldn't quite make out. They all watched transfixed as the bats swirled up a chimney hole in the cavern roof and disappeared from sight. Only the cat which had taken up the stance of a hunter on the saddle seemed disappointed by their departure.

After feeding and the watering the horses they settled down on the cave floor in a semicircle circle to sleep. Arliss curled up in the heavy warm cape Mallwynn had given her from his saddle bag watched in fascination as Mallwynn tapped the glowing rock with his staff. Immediately the rock began to dim to a soft glow. Arliss was soon sound asleep. Kipper tapping one of her closed eye lids with his paw seemed satisfied that she was settled for the night. He then took up a positioned at Arliss's head in folds of the hood of her cloak. Kipper then puffed up his fur and burrowed into Arliss's long thick hair for warmth. Through slitted eyes he watched the chimney hole of the cavern waiting and hoping for the bats return. But it had been a long tumultuous day for the cat, and despite his best efforts and before long he too was asleep.

Chapter Three
The Maze

The sun was at its zenith, by the time they left the cavern under the falls. The early autumn sky was deep blue, and across it moved large fleets of white billowing clouds. Proceeding on their journey, they entered the stream above the falls and continued upstream as before, riding single file.

After the cool dampness of the cave, the sun felt pleasant to Arliss as it warmed on her head and shoulders. She could hear the breeze sighing through the heavily leafed trees which still hadn't changed their color. She buried her hands in Targus's gray colored mane, it felt silky and at the same time coarse. She was getting used to Targus's horsey aroma and didn't find it too unpleasant. It was a warm musky smell mixed with the scent of damp hay and just a faint whiff of dung. It was impossible not to let her spirits rise. She knew she hadn't seen the last of Urage, but somehow in the light of day he had lost his power to frighten her. He seemed so far away almost like a childish nightmare.

As they had traveled upstream for a few miles, the woodland began to change. Now, on both sides of the stream grew nothing but oak trees. Soon the oaks began to thicken until at last they were so dense, that it was impossible to tell, where one tree left off, and the other began. There were small chinks in the wall of trees, maybe just big just enough for a small adult or child to slip through, where a little light could be seen, as if inside the woods the trees grew a more natural distance apart. It was as if the trees at the edge of the wood formed a wall around the forest. On the other side of the stream, there were far fewer trees. Beyond these trees, Arliss could see miles of rolling meadow stretching out as far as the eye could see. The land continued on like this for several miles, but before long they came to a stone bridge. It was the first sign of civilization, that she had seen since entering Eartheart.

The stone bridge arched gracefully over the water. It had a pillar on each of its corners. The pillars were carved out of granite in the shape of hooded grim faced sentries gazing off with sightless eyes in either direction of the bridge. As she looked at the stone sentries, Arliss felt a faint stirring of unease inside her. At first glance Arliss had thought that there wasn't a break in the wall of oak trees by bridge but when she looked again she saw a narrow entrance into the dense oak wood about the same width as the bridge. On the other side of the bridge, was a thin ribbon of a road that ran through a grove of trees into across the meadow and eventual disappeared over a distant hill. "That's the old Fairy Road," said Mallwynn as he noticed Arliss looking at the road. "If you were to follow that road due west for a couple of days it would take you right past the north gate into the Orchid Valley."

"Are we going that way?" asked Arliss looking off in the direction of the road.

"No we're going to go through the Wailingdell woods said Mallwynn nodding in the direction of the entrance to the woods. "Unfortunately, the old Fairy Road will be too well watched.

"I've heard," said Striker looking across the meadow to where the road disappeared over the hill," that the old Fairy Road though it narrows in some places to a mere pathway will take you into the Valley of Spirits and all the way to the stairway of the Fairy gate."

"Yes," agreed Mallwynn.

"The Fairy gates have been locked for centuries," commented Striker, taking his gaze away from the road to look toward Mallwynn.

"Yes, that's true" nodded Mallwynn, not saying any more but there was a look on is his face as if he held something back.

"I remember the old legends and songs about the gates." mused Farin softly."

Mallwynn was looking intently at Striker as Farin's voice trailed off. Arliss saw a look of understanding flash among the men. This troubled her, it reminded her of all the questions that she wanted answered. Then as if he read her mind, Mallwynn said, "Before we sleep tonight I will tell you as much as I can."

Then as Mallwynn turned Eagliss in the direction of the entrance to the woods, he said, "Urage will be expecting us to take the old Fairy Road. That is by far the quickest route to the Orchid Valley."

The wizard and his party headed over the bridge into the dense woods. Inside the living wall of oak trees the woods changed. There seem to a very fine mist in the air that somehow caused the colors of the forest to be sharper and richer. They didn't see many animals, but those that they did seemed oddly sentient. The normal sounds of the forest were absent, instead the animals seemed to call to each other, as if they were passing along some message and most unnerving of all they could hear drifts of whispered conversation, carried in the air. At first they couldn't make out what the words were, then they recognized the word strangers and then Arliss thought she heard the name Mallwynn.

As Mallwynn noticed Arliss's unease in the woods he said, "There are many things are strange in these woods, but none that will do you any harm. These woods used to be the home of a people who called themselves the Druids. They came here through the well between the worlds a very long time ago."

"Were they wizards like you," asked Arliss hoping to get Mallwynn to talk about himself. She was curious about him and what it must feel like to be a wizard. But she would never had dared asked him anything so personal."

"No, not at first. They were just ordinary people. But they had great empathy for all living things. This understanding eventually gave them great knowledge and powers of discernment over plants animals and people."

"What happened to them," ask Arliss.

"They're still here." admitted the wizard glancing sidelong at Arliss." Arliss had a strange prickling sensation at the back of her neck at Mallwynn's words and she was suddenly aware that the woods had grown very still. It was almost as if everything in it were listening to intently to Mallwynn's words. She could tell that Striker and Farin who were riding a few paces ahead had also noticed the odd quiet as they had become very alert and watchful with their hands within easy reach of their weapons.

"So they're still here," said Arliss glancing warily from side to side, half as if she expected a druid to jump out into the path in front of them.

"Yes, very much so. But not as you might think. You see they loved this wood much that they had an almost symbiotic relationship with it. The longer the druids lived in the Wailingdell woods the more like the trees they became. The spirit of the trees entered the Druids and eventually the Druid's spirits entered the trees until there was no boundaries between them and that's how they are now."

Then as an after thought the wizard added, "There is druid blood on the Darrowglyn side of the family."

Arliss grew quiet as she tried to imagine what these strange people were like.

The wizard and his party rode single file on the narrow path through the woods. The woods were no longer still. The whispered conversations and watchfulness from the creatures of the woods carried on as before. Arliss was growing used to it. The whispering she realized was just the creatures of the woods sharing their interest and curiosity for strangers. If she listened carefully she could understand a lot of the comments that were made. It seemed that all the creatures recognized Mallwynn. They realized that Striker and Farin were the Old Kings men. There were many comments about how she and Mallwynn resembled one another. There was a lot of speculation at to who she was. They creatures of the woods were very proud and excited about Mallwynn's visit but they were also worried because they could tell that there was some kind of trouble afoot.

The little party continued through the woods in companionable silence. It always seemed to Arliss that the path ahead would end over the next rise or just around the bend but strangely enough it never did. She at first thought it was an illusion caused by the odd murky light of the woods. Arliss stopped to unhook the end of her cloak which become caught on wild rose bush that grew along the path. Hearing a faint rush of air behind her, she turned in the saddle and stared in amazement. The path behind them was being quickly filled in with trees and vegetation just as if it had never been there at all.

Mallwynn who had stopped a few yards up the path to allow her to catch up. As he caught a glimpse of her surprised face he said "Wailingdell woods has chosen to extend a pathway for us. Hopefully it will lead us to a sanctuary."

"Will Urage be able to enter these woods," she asked as she caught up with the wizard.

"Yes, I am afraid so, "sighed Mallwynn, "Wailingdell won't welcome Urage, but he and his minions still have the power to pass through. Wailingdell is helpless to stop him. Urage wouldn't think twice, before setting the entire woods and all the life in it down to the ground."

Suddenly all the trees around them began to sigh and moan. There was cracking and whining sounds as the trees began to twist and bend sending a shower of green leave all over the path.

"Stop this silly nonsense right away. If you lose many more leaves you'll make yourselves sick." said Mallwynn sternly.

The trees responded immediately, straightening up and becoming quiet, while Mallwynn glared up at them. Arliss watched in amazement. It probably was a trick of the light but she could almost make out expressions of fear and anxiety on a few of the trees, but most of them looked embarrassed by Mallwynn's rebuke.

In a more kindly voice Mallwynn said, "I'm sorry. I really didn't mean to frighten you. I was mainly illustrating to my granddaughter here, the lengths that Urage will go to, to get what he wants." There was an audible sigh of relief through the trees.

They stopped after a few hours, for a meal of bread and cheese and some blueberries that they found growing along the pathway. They were the best she ever had, small perfect and sweet and at the same time tart on her tongue. They quenched their thirst with a flagon of cold apple cider that Farin passed around.

At last at dusk the pathway and the forest ended. They were standing on a rise and spread out beneath them was a vast meadow. In the middle of the meadow was a large hedgerow maze. From up on the rise there was still light enough to see the intricate labyrinth of hedges.

"This is Drudic maze," said Mallwynn, answering Arliss's questioning gaze, "One of many on Eartheart."

They rode down the hill into the meadow toward the maze there was no entrance in sight. Mallwynn seemed unperturbed by this. The maze he said was built by the ancient druids and would provide a safe haven for the night if they were lucky enough to figure out the entering spell.

They rode around the perimeter of the maze until Mallwynn picked a particular spot in the hedge that looked no different to Arliss from any other spot. The wizard shook his staff on the ground three times and in a deep mellow voice muttered an incantation under his breath and although she didn't understand the words, they were pleasant and melodious to her ear. She noticed as he said the spell not a creature stirred, all around them was a vacuum of silence. Exactly as his staff hit the ground for the third time there appeared a shimmering of light on the hedge in front of Mallwynn, and before there very eyes a narrow arch shaped doorway appeared in the hedge.

For a moment, no one moved then Mallwynn glancing at them said, "I think we'll be safe here for tonight. It's highly unlikely that Urage will dare enter the maze, and even if he does we will probably be all right." Then he warned them grimly, "But we must all be careful. It is possible to get lost forever in the corridors of the maze. Many have perished thinking salvation was just around the next corner."

They wizard and his party went through the archway into the maze. As soon as the last of them was through the door in the hedge vanished, as if it had never been there. The moon overhead cast light and shadows on the thousand year old hedgerows that made up the walls of the maze. Someone had gone to a lot of trouble to keep the maze up. The hedgerows were tightly pruned with sharp edges and corners as smooth as stone. Arliss reached out and touched the springy dense growth just to reassure herself that it was living hedge. The passageways of the maze seemed endless. A lot of care had been given to keep the maze interesting. Along many passageways niches had been carved out in the hedgerows and furnished with stone benches, bubbling fountains and statuary depicting woodland themes. There was topiary pruned into the pillars, archways, windows and even stairways which led nowhere to lend architectural interest to the maze. Arliss noticed that the main passageways always seemed to have more than one passageway leading off, and often as many as three or four. Sometimes they would travel down a what looked like a promising passageway to take them into the center of the maze only to find it ended in a blind loop. At first they didn't mind getting constantly lost constantly, in fact they found it amusing. But after a while it got to be tedious. They were tired and hungry and aware of the fact that even in the maze they weren't safe from Urage. Striker said frowning, "I think we've come down the same pathway four times."

"How can you tell," shrugged Farin, "They all look the same to me."

"I know because I've seen that statue of a toad stool at least four times." replied Striker crossly.

"Are you sure it's the same toad stool." asked Arliss reasonably, "I've noticed several different statues of toad stools."

Striker looked on the point of saying something back to Arliss but thought better of it.

Mallwynn appeared lost in thought and his lips moved as if he were counting under his breath. Finally, he seem to realize that they were waiting for him to say something. They were all stunned when he turned his horse Leonis around and started off at a quick trot calling for them to follow him..."

Nonplussed they exchanged surprised looks as the followed obediently behind Mallwynn. He seem to know exactly where he was going. Without hesitation he led them through the passageways of the maze, choosing the correct turn every time and constantly weaving inwards until they reached the center of the maze. They ask latter how he was able to figure out the way in to the center of the maze. He gave a pleased smile and said, "It's well known that druids enjoy puzzles, hence the maze itself. So I guessed the puzzle might be some kind of repeating number pattern.

"Take the third turn left in every fourth passageway. Is that the sort of thing you mean," asked, Striker with an impressed look.

"Exactly," replied Mallwynn with a modest smile.

The center of the maze itself was a wide open grassy square with pathways leading to a center dais.

"I think we'll be safe here for the night," said Mallwynn as he slipped off Leonis to have a closer look at the dais.

"Runes," said Mallwynn thoughtfully, tracing them with his fingers. Then softly to himself he said, "This maze may have yet more puzzles worth solving." Kipper, delighted to be able to stretch his legs again, scampered off as soon as Arliss set him down from the saddle. When she last saw him he was stalking the inner wall of the maze, hoping to find a field mouse hidden in the gnarled inner branches of the hedgerows. They unsaddled the horses, and allowed them to graze freely in the center of the maze. They made camp on the dais, and sat around on leaning back against their saddle packs. It was a clear windless night starry night. Arliss thought that the stars seemed so close that if she were to climb a tree she would almost be able to touch them.

Farin passed around some more of the bread and cheese they had earlier and some tart sweet apples. They washed it down with water the had collected from one of the fountains in the maze.

Arliss hadn't realized how tired she was until after they had eaten their meal. She felt her eyes grow heavy and begin to close, but as she noticed Mallwynn's steady gaze on her she quickly shrugged off her sleepiness and sat up and leaned forward with anticipation. Striker and Farin were also watching the wizard intently waiting for him to speak.

And although Mallwynn's voice creaked with age it still had a strong and authoritative timbre and his eye took on a faraway look in them as he began telling the strange tale. "Eartheart for more than a millennium and up until the late king's recent demise has been ruled by an unbroken line of Glasstarrs, whose seat of rule was the Orchid Valley. All during the Glasstarr, reign both Eartheart and the Glasstarrs themselves have enjoyed peace and prosperity. However about a hundred years ago, things suddenly changed. Prince Darl was hunting with some friends near the Maudland border. Maudland at that time was then a part of the great wilderness. The king specifically warned Darl not to venture into Maudland because it was an evil and dangerous place. But the lure of plentiful and exotic game was too much for Darl to resist. So he persuaded a few friends to come with him across one of the Demon bridges over the spirit river into Maudland. There he fell foul of the powerful sorceress, Mardylla of the house of Black Willow."

Mallwynn paused here and took out a pipe from out of his cape and proceeded to fill it with what looked like flower petals from a leather pouch. When the pipe bowl was filled. He tamped it down well with the pad of his thumb. Then he drew out a flint box and lit the pipe, in a few moments he was completely engulfed in an aromatic cloud of pipe smoke. Then he was finally ready to begin talking again.

"Mardylla was the last of a line of sorcerers, and necromancers. What we people in the Orchid valley refer to as a general bad lot. Well what happened was that somehow Darl was separated from the rest of his hunting party, and Mardylla who was already several centuries old at the time, but very well preserved mind you, stumbled upon him in the woods. She was struck by how unusually handsome he was and quickly became obsessed by him. She lured him back to the Black Willow Keep. Enamored as she was first by his good looks, she also became captivated by his wit and charm, which she could not fully enjoy, as long as he was ensorcelled. The truth of the matter was that her pride got the better of her. She wanted Darl to feel the same way for her as she did for him. Finally she found herself with child and she decided that it time to lift the spell. She had convinced herself that the obsession was mutual.

Young Darl was bewildered when he came to his senses in a dank and dark keep in the company of a beautiful dark haired lady. Mardylla spun him some tale about nursing him back to health after finding him in the woods close to death. Darl quickly became fascinated with Mardylla, but just as rapidly he found himself repulsed by her and her dark ways and soon could barely look her in the face without cringing. He was horrified by his predicament. Finally after many days, he managed to escape the keep. Mardylla was outraged and began to plan a revenge, which ultimately was to be carried out by Darl's own son which he had no idea existed. Mardylla wanted the retribution to be slow, sweet and certain.

Darl returned to the Palace of Orchids. Where all were relieved and elated at his return having long since feared him dead. He related to his family the events that led to his capture and ensorcellment by Mardylla. He begged the king, his father for forgiveness for his disobedience into trespassing into the great wilderness. The king, who had for many months now, mourned Darl, happily forgave him and warmly welcomed him home again. The incident was quickly forgotten by all, save the arch wizard of the court, Astarian my father. He knew Mardylla to be a formidable and wicked sorceress. He had concerns which he expressed to King Fallard, but the king dismissed them as unnecessary worries. But the king's words, didn't put my fathers mind at rest. He still felt uneasy.

Sure enough, nearly six months after Darl's return, the king's family suffered a terrific tragedy. All five brothers and sisters died mysteriously on the same day, one by one, of a strange malady that overcame them quickly, causing a high fever, with death ensuing soon after.

Darl was the only one of the king's six children, who was spared. No one else in the palace, was affected with the strange illness. And unbeknownst to Darl, the King, or the Queen, that as the little four-year old princess Ansid, the youngest child, laid her feverish brow, on her mother's breast, and took her last breath, Urage was born. A gloom settled over the Orchid Valley, and Astarian's suspicions grew. But he had no proof so he began to quietly, and diligently search for answers. He made many forays, into the wilderness, in and around Maudland. He searched through his own tomes, until he was certain of the spells she used.

It was less than a year since the day of the death of the King's children, that Astarian brought him proof of Mardylla's guilt, and sorcery in the death of his children. The king was outraged, he immediately ordered his army to go out into the wilderness, and surround the Black Willow Keep and bring back Mardylla for trial. The keep was empty, Mardylla and he young son were gone. Astarian blamed himself for not acting more quickly.

It was obvious to Astarian that Darl was still held firmly by strong threads of sorcery. Darl refused to wed and beget an heir. He said that the guilt and grief were too much for him. Astarian knew the only way that the threads of ensorcellment could be broken were to bring back the witch try and execute her. For the next fourteen years he dedicated himself to this cause. He traveled to all parts of Eartheart in search of Mardylla. At last he found her deep within the Krippner caverns in the Valley of Creation.

Capturing Mardylla and her entourage was difficult, and many of her minions escaped, including young Urage, who followed his mother all the way back to the Orchid Valley and witnessed her trial and execution.

The death of Mardylla was like the lancing of a boil, healing began to take place. The gloom lifted. Darl at long last married. A year later, Kallin a son was born, and laughter was once again heard in the palace. The tragedies of the past became a dim memory."

Mallwynn's voice trailed off and he was silent for a moment. His eyes had a faraway look to them. Arliss began to fear that he had said all that he was going say and she would be left now, with even more unanswered questions. She could hear Striker and Farin stir beside her as she asked, tentatively, "What happen to Urage"

With a start, Mallwynn roused himself from his reverie at her words and he said, "Urage moved back into the Black Willow Keep on the Fane sea, which he renamed the Maudland keep. There he brooded, and watched and began to plan. It was often rumored that Urage had learned the black arts at his mothers knee and was particularly gifted. For forty-five years, until his death, my father Astarian, watched Urage closely. He grew to manhood, a bitter cold and ruthless man. He began to turn the wilderness, around the keep, into farmland. He set up a scheme that brought settlers, into the fertile land. The settlers thought some of the requirements for the land grants odd and foolish. Urage became known as Urage the Mad. Many people were turned down for the land grants for no apparent reason and many who were chosen weren't sure why. They felt uneasy, but the gift of free and fertile land was irresistible. The land around the keep prospered and became known as a good place to live and except for the exacting of certain odd and strange laws, Urage was thought to be fair even if a little eccentric and foolish."

"My father Astarian," said Mallwynn, "continued to watch Urage all the while he wondered about the rhyme or reason for Urage's strange laws. Many years passed by and eventually the King passed on and Darl took the throne. He proved to be a good and wise king." Arliss noticed a certain heaviness enter Mallwynn's voice. "Kallin, Darl's son took the throne after Darl passed on. King Kallin's heir Balsarrian eventually married my only child Kyrianna. They were your parents, Arliss." Mallwynn said glancing pointedly at her.

Arliss listened keenly as Mallwynn carried on. "The beginning of the end came when King Kallin, Balsarrian's father was on a long planned visit to a neighboring kingdom attending the summer games. All our best men were competing The Hibilian games are only held once every ten years. It is a much looked forward to event held always on the fields of Gramatian in the kingdom of Thallsparr. Of course, as always, there was a big attendance from the Orchid Valley of every able bodied man, woman, and child, who could get to Thallsparr by wagon, foot, or on horseback. A few days before the games," recollected Mallwynn his eyes fixed on Arliss. "Your father Prince Balsarrian, injured himself in a very unusual accident. He was an excellent swordsman and he had planned to compete in the games so he was sparring with a man, who had only recently joined the ranks. This man was from a distant far off land. No one knew much about him. His name was Brassar Forbitts.

Why he was allowed to spar with the prince I will never know, except maybe for the obvious reason, that he was a remarkable swordsman, being nimble strong and accurate. The Prince was glad to have him to practice with. The Prince was a soldier and he did not let fear hold sway over him. On the very day, before they were about to leave for the games," said Mallwynn his voice now hard and cold.

"The Prince's sparring partner's blade slipped, clipping the Prince heavily on the thigh, with such strength, it shattered his bone. Well, while it was not unusual for a soldier from time to time sustain a small injury, it is indeed inherent in the skill of sparring and generally no one is held accountable when this happens. But right away, the captain of the arms, who had witnessed the accident, felt something was amiss.

When it was apparent that the injury was serious. There was quite a scuffle with people running for the court physician and other people with good intentions getting in the way. The Prince's sparring partner seemed deeply contrite, and steadfastly refused to leave the Prince's side and refused to go to the games.

It was only on the orders of the Prince himself who told Brassar Forbitts that since he himself was unable to compete, he was their best chance to bring back the much coveted prize, the silver sword. This was presented to the finest swordsman at the games. Brassar Forbitts finally relented and left for the games with the rest of the army.

Sometime during the games, Brassar Forbitts, disappeared, having not competed in any of the events and he was, never been seen nor heard of again."

Mallwynn stopped talking. He felt his mind drift back to the morning he left the valley for the games. It was had been an unusually warm summer morning. He'd seen them for the last time in the palace garden. Balsarrian and Kyrianna were so busy cooing over the baby they hadn't even noticed him come into the garden. He had stood watching them for a moment touched by how happy his daughter looked. Despite their protest he had said his good-byes and left quickly not wanting to intrude. And that was the last time he saw Kyrianna and her husband alive.

It was an hour or two before the dawn that dangerous time near the end of the night just before the real certainty of sunrise. Those are the hours that are the blackest and the most treacherous on Eartheart. When the dark forces are at their strongest. It was at this very time that a lull came over the Orchid valley. The nocturnal creatures that usually thrived in the woolly darkness grew oddly silent. The void was filled by a feeling of dread that poured into the valley like thick fog. It hung heavy in the air thick and palpable.

Urage slipped the visor down of his black crested helmet finally satisfied that all things were ready and in place for his entry into the Valley. He didn't believe in leaving anything to chance. He passed with his dark legions silently through the north gates down the road toward the sleeping palace.

Og, one of Urage's captain broke from the ranks to join his master at the helm. Urage's seven foot frame towered above Og's. Only the Carnumbra could matched Urage's height. That was because their human bodies had been unnaturally elongated by the bestial spirits that invaded them.

"If this damn palace wasn't so ensorcelled we would have no need to come so close to the dawn," spat Urage to his captain.

Og, sensing his master mood remained silent for a moment before saying, "I don't think you need worry Lord, everything been prepared as you ask. My men know that they are to work with speed and no one is to be left alive in the palace. All evidence of our presence, will be erased, even the hoof prints of our men and Carnumbra."

Urage nodded his head with approval at Og's words. He knew Og was right he had no need to worry. After all he had the best army on all of Eartheart. He had genetically bred his regulars to be the finest fighting men in the world. And then he had swollen their ranks with his Carnumbra. His Carnumbra as far as he was concerned were one of his greatest achievements in the dark arts. He had separated out from his kingdom the most spiritual of men and offered their bodies to particularly bestial spirits. He had thought at first that hell's bottom feeders because of their baseness and tenacity would best suit his purposes.

These however proved too unruly, and simple minded for his use so he turned them out of their human vessels and began again. This time he chose from the horde at the upper levels of hell, the most savant and dangerous of the demons. With their master's approval, he provided six hundred and sixty six of these with the bodies of men.

It was deep into the night in the palace when the nurse Myrtle suddenly awoke. She was confused for a few seconds wondering what had awakened her and then she remembered the baby. She listened intently for a moment but heard only her own breathing. Then she heard the voice in her head again. She recognized that it was Kyrianna. Her voice sounded weak and frail. Myrtle calmed herself to try to make sense out of Kyrianna's words. "Myrtle, Urage is here."

Myrtle gasped.

Kyrianna's voice sounded strangely calm.

"Balsarrian is dead and I lie waiting only for you before I go and join him." Grief hit Myrtle full in the chest. Hot tears, ran down the old woman's face. Kyrianna's voice, now took on a more urgent tone "Please Myrtle, you must hurry now if you are going to save her."

The old lady needed no further prompting. She frantically got out of her bed and tore open her door, and was already in the nursery before she heard Kyrianna voice again.

"Careful Myrtle, even now they approach the nursery."

Myrtle scooped up the sleeping child and raced to the door. Quietly closing the door behind her, she slipped unseen out into the garden. Myrtle was shocked, when she entered Kyrianna's and Balsarrian's suit. As she took in the horror, she could smell smoke in the air. Prince Balsarrian lay deathly still on his bed, if it hadn't been for the ugly dagger buried to the hilt in his chest he would have looked as though he was sleeping, and somehow in death the years were erased from his face and he looked now like a mere boy. She heard Kyrianna before she saw her, the throaty rattle of her breathing. She lay only a few feet from the bed in a pool of dark crimson blood.

It was a long while after Mallwynn's tale before any one spoke. It was finally Arliss, who spoke first, with her gray eyes clouded and her face somber she said quietly, "So it was Myrtle who brought me through the shadow lake."

Mallwynn nodded. In a puzzled voice, she continued, "Why did Urage wait all this time, to come and get me?"

"Urage succeeded in destroying only a small part of the palace," said Mallwynn, "But Kyrianna and Balsarrian's suit and the nursery were in that part of the palace. So it was always believed that you had perished in the fire," said Mallwynn.

"What about Myrtle?" questioned Arliss.

"Poor Myrtle," said Mallwynn, "was found after the fire was put out, wandering aimlessly, a short distance from the palace. She had lost her mind and had to be cared for the rest of her life."

"King Kallin died last year, in the middle of the night," said Mallwynn, "I was with him, and just as the King passed over, there was a knock on the door and there was Myrtle completely lucid. She told me what had happened, and where she had taken you. Then without warning, she dropped dead on the spot."

Arliss, was silent a while, as she tried to take in everything that she had heard. At last, with a heavy sigh, she said, "Why does he persist so long in his revenge."

"It is not just revenge now," said Striker speaking for the first time. "He wants to be Emperor of Eartheart, and that is something he can never be, as long as your alive." Speechless Arliss, stared at Striker the suddenly she felt a cold shiver run up her spine as if someone had just walked on her grave.

Then from the woods on the rise came an inhuman chorus of shrill keening.

"Urage!" gasped Mallwynn as it dawned on him with shock that the sound coming from the woods were the trees protesting Urage's approach.

Chapter Four
The Strange Dream

In less than a heart beat, Striker, and Farin had crossed quickly to the hedge, and stood silently listening to the unearthly cries of the forest. As Arliss stood beside Mallwynn, on the dais, in the darkness, she drew her arms across her chest, and bit down hard on her lower lip, as with every eerie cry from the forest, she felt a new and stronger wave of terror sweep over her.

Then to her relief, the cries of the forest stopped, but then came the baying of the hell hounds. As she listened, she heard the sound of many voices rising and falling in unison, in a strange wordless chant. She could feel the short hairs all along the back of her neck, rise and stand on end.

"Mallwynn" she whispered, wanting to inquire as why the Carnumbra were chanting, but Mallwynn with his finger held firmly to his lips, cautioned her with a severe look.

Her eyes in the darkness remained fixed on Mallwynn, as she listened to the queer and sonorous chant. His facial expression now, gave her little clue as to the gravity of the situation."

But Farin already had an arrow in his bow with the string pulled taut, and was sighting an invisible target along the shaft of the arrow, aimed at the entrance to the center of the maze. Striker stood at his side looking deceptively casual, his sword withdrawn, but in the moonlight Arliss could see how firmly he gripped the hilt.

Arliss left the dais, and with trepidation withdrew Wingsinger, from its scabbard, and stood there, with Striker and Farin, poised for action. "At least I won't go down without a fight. "she promised herself grimly. Farin was right, she was glad she had Windsinger, she just wished ruefully that she had had the time, to learn how to use it."

The men and hounds were growing closer now. They were just outside of the maze now. Arliss listened she could hear Urage and his troops as they chanted and marched slowly, along periphery of the maze. She supposed that they were searching for the entrance.

They did one complete circuit of the maze, and Arliss began to feel her spirits rise, as it looked like Urage would be unable to gain entrance.

Then he and his troops started out again, on a second circuit of the maze. Arliss tensed and listened carefully as the chanting and marching became even slower. Then as it stopped abruptly and she realized, with a sinking feeling, that Urage had found the entrance to the maze. Mallwynn acted immediately, with Arliss, and Farin and Striker's assistance, he sent all the horses back out into the maze with a hiding spell, saying as he did so," If they stay here they will just be meat for the hell hounds."

Mallwynn returned to the dais in the hub of the maze beckoning to them to draw close saying, "If you follow my instructions we will still be safe from Urage and his minions." Arliss sighed with relief at Mallwynn's words.

"Now," whispered Mallwynn leaning heavily on his staff, and looking solemnly at her.

"No matter what you see or hear, don't utter a word or all will be lost. "Before Arliss could think about the meaning of the wizard's cryptic words, she heard a single hollow resonating voice, that broke the taut quiet, with a chant of an incantation.

A low rumble began, coming from the earth, and building in intensity until at its peak, the sky cracked open, with a brief and brilliant flash of light.

Then from nowhere the wind picked up in the maze, and began growing in force until it howled, and bent the trees down low with such force, that branches snapped, and leaves swirled everywhere. Mallwynn had maneuvered them, back onto the dais again.

"Join hands," he commanded, taking Farin's and Arliss's hands. Striker closed the circle as he took hold of Arliss's and Farin's other hand.

"Remember," said Mallwynn swaying with the force of the wind.

"Not a word and don't let go "He warned.

Arliss had strained to hear the wizard's words, which were carried off, in the wind that swirled all around them. She had returned the now miserable cat, to a deep pouch in her cape, but even with the weight of the cat, the cape along with her hair, still blew wildly in the wind. Then as suddenly as it began the wind died down and to her horror Arliss saw the maze hedges begin to shimmer again. Her first instinct was to reach for the hilt of battle singer, but she remembered Mallwynn's warning and gripped even tighter onto his and Striker's hands. The chanting started up again as the ranks of Carnumbra and hell hounds filed into the maze. She could hear the howls, of the hounds, and the sound of thundering hooves, and guttural voices all around them, growing louder, as Urage and his minions wove their way up and down corridors drawing ever closer to the center of the maze.

She could feel her knees begin to buckle with fright and her stomach cramp convulsively. Then suddenly, she noticed a tingling sensation. It traveled up from Mallwynns hand, surging up her arm and through all of her body, and then finally traveling down her other arm, to her fingers. She felt Striker jerk, as he too received the surge. It felt pleasant, She thought, like a positive or current. She still felt all her fear and dread, but now there was an almost intangible buffer of comfort and support around her.

The din and clamor of Urage's Carnumbra and hell hounds grew even louder, and the walls of the center of the maze shook, as riders swept passed outside the center wall.

All eyes were riveted on the entrance to the center of the maze. It was the hounds that first appeared, pouring from the entrance into the maze square, a frightening mass, of slick black bodies, writhing with their mouths slathering in massive heads. Arliss watched in horror, as the hounds flooded across the circular pathway, that rimmed the center of the maze. And like tarry black foam they churned down the pathways and over the grass making straight for the large dais, in the hub of the wheel. On the dais Arliss gripped, Mallwynn and Striker's hands even tighter.

When the hell hounds reached the dais, Arliss could hardly believe her eyes, an amazing thing happened. The hounds appeared totally unaware of their presence on the dais. Instead they circled the outside of the dais, forming a living undulating river of blackness. It was as if an invisible barrier surrounded the dais.

Then suddenly all the howls and barks ended abruptly, at the trumpeting of a lonely horn. And there at the entrance to the center of the maze, was Urage atop a huge black charger, the master of the hell hounds, with a hunting horn in hand. The hounds gathered around him, drawing close they were respectfully quiet and obedient.

Red eyed and wraith like, the Carnumbra broke ranks and filed past them, going in two directions around the outer circle of the hub of the maze. Again, as with the hell hounds, the Carnumbra were unable to see them.

Arliss watched Urage with anxious fascination. Urage's large charger pawed the ground impatiently, as he stared into the circle. He was extraordinarily tall, and he was handsome in a strangely elegant way. His body was clad from head to foot in black mail and leather. He wore his helmet low over his dark predatory eyes which now seemed to be looking with nonchalant interest in her direction.

He started forward coming directly toward them. Mallwynn squeezed her hand in warning. When Urage reached the rim of the circle, he raised his hand, and the Carnumbra came to a halt.

Arliss had just decided, that he probably couldn't see them. When she realized, with a start, that Urage was looking directly at her. She felt her heart begin to thump hard as he said, "Greetings kinswomen, at last we meet."

Then as if he saw her fear, he said firmly, "Don't be afraid. I have come to rescue you, from these buffoons and accompany you home to the Orchid Valley. He flashed a slick smile and raised an eyebrow quizzically." She bit her lip to hold back the anger that flared up in her, as she thought." He really thinks I've forgotten how he and Carnumbra nearly trampled me to death in my own backyard a few nights ago."

And then as if he read her thoughts, he said in a confidential manner, "Oh I know what you're thinking Arliss, and I can't say I blame you but you will see it was just a misunderstanding."

Then he paused and as he pushed his helmet back slightly, his eyes locking on to hers and he said "A couple of my men, who I sent to escort you back to Eartheart, were out of order and they got a little rough. I assure you the men have been dealt with severely, and it won't happen again.

Did he really think that she didn't know that he was there that night, he and his Carnumbra. That was him, wasn't it, she thought to herself as she suddenly realized, with a start, that this was the first time, she had really seen Urage up close.

That was him, who pursued them out of the Valley of creation, wasn't it?

Then as she felt her convictions begin to slowly erode, she felt another desperate squeeze, from Mallwynn. Urage turned from them, signaling one of the Carnumbra leaders to his side. After conferring with him, the Carnumbra departed the maze center taking with him the hounds, and the rest of the Carnumbra.

What now wondered Arliss. Urage now stood alone outside the circle. He paid them no further heed for the moment, instead he busied himself removing things from the pack on his horse. He preceded to casually set himself down on a blanket, and he took out a flagon of wine and some food and began to eat and drink.

The sun had begun to rise, and the gold shafts of light were quickly sweeping away all the shadows that lay in the maze. Arliss began to feel more than a little silly and looked first to Mallwynn and then at Striker and Farin. The latter two seemed to share some of her doubts and discomfort, as they each in turn raised their brows and shrugged their shoulders all the while not breaking the circle. Mallwynn merely shook his head gravely.

"Come and join me, and breakfast with me," urged Urage. Arliss glanced quickly at Mallwynn in confusion, he shook his head sternly at her.

"Come now, Arliss, don't be stubborn" pressed Urage, "more firmly this time, "You may even bring the addled old man, and his two misguided fools."

She was tempted to ask what he meant by that, and then she began to wonder.

Was Urage really as bad as Mallwynn portrayed, maybe the situation was really ridiculously over blown, after all, they only had the word of an insane woman, that Urage had killed her parents.

Despite her fear, Arliss found herself increasingly fascinated by Urage, and was embarrassed to find she couldn't take her eyes of him. His voice cloyed at her when she turned her eyes away.

With alarm Mallwynn broke the silence, and was speaking to her, but Mallwynn's voice seemed distant, and it took a lot of effort just to listen to him. It was much easier instead to look at Urage, and listen to the sound of his voice, go rhythmically up and down, she felt very relaxed. She hadn't realized how tired she was.

A bit of discomfort showed on Urage's face. This puzzled Arliss, as she could see no particular reason for it. She noticed absently beads of sweat forming on Urages upper lip.

Why was that she wondered idly, it was still quite cool. Her reverie was broken by the feeling of warmth on her chest. She glanced down and was surprised to see that the Glasstarr medallion was glowing. Suddenly she felt very confused, and alarmed as Mallwynn's voice, penetrated through to her.

"Keep your eyes away from him Arliss" he pleaded. "Your very life depends on it"? Then with startled awareness at her predicament, she tried to pull her eyes away and as she did so, she became abruptly conscious of a very palpable evil, emanating from Urage, like bad smell. She closed her eyes tight, in a desperate effort to block him out, and to her horror, even with tightly closed eyes, she could still see Urages face, smirking and grimacing before her with all look of casual charm gone, instead his eyes were filled with rage.

As she opened her eyes, she gasped in horror as she saw Urage again, now in front of her, laughing horribly. And then as a scowl flared across his face he said "You see Arliss you can't escape me" and then he roared with malicious glee.

Mallwynn shook with fatigue, the effort to maintain the protective circle, was draining him. He wondered, how much longer he could hold the circle intact. Arliss's horror slipped away as she felt the limpness in Mallwynns grip. It scared her his hand felt suddenly so cold as if all life had left him. Urage was watching her with frank enjoyment.

"He can't hold on much longer, can he Arliss?" said Urage with matter of fact satisfaction.

Then anger began to rise within her. "No" she thought, as she dove deep down within herself to drive Urage out. With all her strength and will she pushed mightily inside herself, and then felt something snap and give way.

The Glasstarr medallion burned on her chest, and then with a powerful psychic thrust, from an unknown place within her. She drove his image out and away from her.

The walls of the maze began to shimmer again, and the blue stones set in the spokes of the center of the maze began to glow. Urage screamed and his horse reared up in fright. He leapt on its back and drew his sword and leveled it at her and said "I will get you Arliss Glasstarr, and you may depend on that, and it will be all the worse for the waiting."

With that he bounded out of the maze like a retreating storm.

It was late morning before they stirred themselves from the dais. The horses everyone of them, had returned from their hiding place in the maze, and they now grazed peacefully on the grass in the maze square.

Farin had climbed an apple tree and wedged himself in the cross branches of tree, his perch afforded him a clear view over the hedgerows of the maze.

"There are no signs of Carnumbra and hounds. They have probably retreated for cover beyond the woods," he surmised looking down at Mallwynn Arliss and Striker on the ground. Returning his gaze to the meadow he announced, "There is no sign of their presence in the druidic forest, but we are however flanked on all four sides by Urage's regulars. I wouldn't think Urage and his Carnumbra could be too far away. I see some supply wagons rolling in and tents being set up. He paused with a sigh of frustration and speculated, "I think they intend to wait us out."

Striker and Arliss set off on horseback to explore the rest of the maze during the last of the remaining daylight hours. They left Farin in the apple tree as lookout, with Mallwynn pacing back and forth, underneath, fingering a string of beads, as Farin called down to him any new details. They found nothing of interest save a few fountains in niches carved into the hedgerows at various points. There were also stone benches along odd corridors. They found their way back to the center of the maze shortly before sundown without too much difficulty. They all sat in a circle together eating a small meal of cheese and bread with water from the fountain. They ate in companionable silence. The water from the fountain was curiously refreshing and it had a strange but pleasant bite to it.

Striker was the first to break the spell of peace and tranquility as he rose to return the leftover food to the saddle bags.

"How long do you think Urage will stay out of the maze?" He ask with studied casualness. Without looking up Mallwynn answered, "That is a difficult question," said Mallwynn, "But as you know, he was greatly weakened by entering the maze in the first place." Looking up now his clear steady gray eyes were sharp and focused. "This is a hollowed reverent place of the druids, "He continued. "And as such it has many spells and enchantments designed to discourage the ignoble from entering it. Although the druidic people have all but died out, their magic was very powerful and is still so today. I can't say for certain, when he will be back, or indeed even if he will be back, he may just try to wait us out."

Mallwynn had just taken out his beads and Arliss had been watching him as his hands were habitual running up and down their length, fondly fingering them. This was the first time she seen the beads up close. She was surprised at their beauty. There were tiny quartz crystal stars encapsulated in the tiny glass globes that interrupted lengths of swirling deep blue lapis lazuli planets.

It was on all their minds although no one would say the words Urage had them trapped.

Wrapped once more in the heavy green cloak with the cat curled at her feet. Arliss was soon deeply asleep. She had a very strange and vivid dream. She was walking through a tunnel of whirling wind, in the wind birds flew and sang a strange and haunting song.

As she listened to the melody, she could feel her heart rise, and her eyes began to tear with emotion and she saw a strangely familiar figure at the end of the tunnel beckoning to her, as she moved forward down the tunnel the form advanced keeping a distance ahead of her. She got up close enough to realize that it was a woman, but she was not able to see her face. She was tall and slender and wore a long pale robe. Her fair hair was long and heavy and she wore a gold circlet around it. She still couldn't see the woman's face.

Ahead Arliss saw the end of the tunnel. The woman quickly reached it and disappeared from sight. When Arliss reached the end of the tunnel. She found herself back in a corridor of the maze. It was nighttime and there was a full moon overhead. Just up ahead in the corridor, Arliss caught sight of the woman as she disappeared around the corner. She hurried to catch up with the woman, and as she turned the corner, she could see that the woman was up ahead waiting for her. Somehow, she could never quite catch up with the lady, as she followed her through the labyrinth of the maze. At last, she found herself at the entrance to the center of the maze, which was completely empty except for the mysterious lady.

She was standing in the hub, next to the dais, and she was looking directly at Arliss. Then as Arliss watched in astonishment, the lady knelt down on one knee, and began to trace the runes on the edge of the dais. Then an amazing thing happened, she stood up and there was a soft whirring noise, and suddenly the whole massive dais slipped silently to one side.

A black rectangular hole was revealed, and the lady quickly descended down into it. Even as Arliss ran to the dais, it had already begun to move back into place. She reached the dais in time to hear it click quietly into place. Stunned she stood in front of the dais looking down at the runes and patterns that decorated its top and edge facade, when from the corner of her eye she caught a glint, of something metallic lying on the ground. It was a silver bangle. She picked it up and in the moonlight she could see the runic symbols etched in the silver. There was a clear crystal in the center. Impulsively she slipped the bangle on her wrist. The moonlight caught the crystal and white light shot out of the stone and into her eyes blinding her. Her head started to spin and she heard the singing birds of the tunnel once again and then everything went blank.

It was still dark when she opened her eyes. She didn't remember the dream right away. It was only after a few moments had passed, that she wondered what it was, that had awakened her. Then she remembered with uncanny clarity, the lady of the maze, and the tunnel of sweet singing birds.

Startled by the vividness of the dream, she sat bolt upright in the moonlight, and strained to make out the sleeping forms of Mallwynn, Striker, and Farin as they lay undisturbed.

Was it a dream? She wondered silently, wishing she had the nerve to awaken Mallwynn. Then she sighed, as she decided reluctantly, It must have been a dream, but never the less, she resolved to tell Mallwynn about it in the morning, as it was a very strange dream.

She then gathered the green wool cape around her grateful, for its warmth in the cold night air, and lay down to sleep a little more, As she did so, she caught a flash of silver and with disbelief she sat up, and in the dim light she looked down at her left wrist. There was the silver bangle, with the crystal stone set in its center and the faint archaic etchings, traced into the silver. There could be no doubt, it was the one and the same of her dreams. She must have let out a sound as Mallwynn was sitting up looking at her bleary eyed and expectant and soon Farin and Striker were also awake and so she recounted her dream to them, in a matter fact voice as she tried to stem the rising elation that she felt. A way out! she thought, this may be our way out!

The men listened making no comment, and when the tale drew to an end, she pulled up her sleeve, and showed them the bangle. Mallwynn's eyes widened. Farin gasped and then a slow smile spread across his face.

Striker leaned forward, his face pensive, looking at the bangle hard, as if he expected it to vanish before his very eyes.

"Here she said," slipping the bangle from her wrist and handing it over to Striker who in turn passed it on to Mallwynn. Mallwynn looked at it carefully.

"I will be able to tell you more about this when we get to the Orchid Valley," he said as he studied the runes on the bangle...

"In my rooms at the palace I have many books", he said.

"That explain the purpose of these runes, and the origin of a charm or magic device such as this."

"If the dais does conceal an exit, "said Striker, studying the dais with speculation, "It could be the answer to our troubles.

"Come now," urged Mallwynn, and then he paused and his eyes moved back and forth, as if he was listening to a far away sound. Then he said, "We don't know just how long we've got before they return. We must make haste, to see if escape is indeed possible."

Quickly they gathered up their belongings and supplies, and leather flagons which they filled with water from the fountain. They packed them on the backs of the two sturdy pack ponies. They saddled up the four horses and in a short while they were ready to leave. They were just standing in front of the dais when to Arliss horror the walls began to shimmer. She thought at first she had imagined it, as it shimmered just briefly and went out.

Then the shimmering started up again only this time more strongly. In shock, for an instant, the four of them just stood frozen. Then with her hands flying to her face, she said, frantically "Why now?"

Unable to keep the fear from her voice. She glanced over at Mallwynn, and Striker and Farin and saw the same fear reflected on their faces.

Then with a frenzied rush the four scrambled into action. The ground trembled underneath them, as they sought to find the mechanism that would slide the dais open.

They inspected every inch of the dais and found nothing. Hearing the howl of the approaching hellhounds, Striker looked earnestly at Arliss and said with forced calmness, "Think Arliss, what exactly did the lady do before the dais opened."?

EARTHEART

Arliss with one hand on her brow, for a moment closed her eyes to try and bring back the image of the lady standing at the center of the maze, just before the dais slipped opened.

"This is what she was doing," said Arliss as she knelt down and began to trace the runes. Nothing happened, in desperation, she repeated the tracings, this time with more care and again nothing happened. The dais remained solidly in place.

"I am almost certain," she said with rising panic, "That I am doing exactly what she did."

Hearing the chant of the Carnumbra grow louder, she thought with certainty, "We're not going to make it out in time."

With her legs turning to water, Arliss strove to remain calm. as she began to rhythmically strike her fist into her hand attempting to dislodge some tiny detail of the dream.

"The bangle must have something to do with it." exploded Striker, "Of course it does "snapped Mallwynn angrily, his nervousness anxiety getting the better of him.

"But it may take us hours to determine, just what that." Mallwynn ignoring their surprised looks at his outburst, turned away and continued to examine the runes on the rim of the dais. Arliss nervously twisted the bangle on her wrist, The hell hounds were now only a couple of corridors away, when a strange thing happened, on what she thought was the third turn of the bangle around her wrist. the bangle began to glow, and white light shot out of the crystal into the center of the dais.

Then with whirring sound and a whoosh, the dais slipped aside to reveal a rectangular hole.

"Thank goodness," breathed Mallwynn, with a sigh of relief as he turned to them. For a brief instant the three of them stood staring transfixed, at the gaping black hole where the dais had been.

Arliss felt a chill go up her spine as she stared at the hole, it resembled a freshly dug grave. But as she continued to look in the darkness, she could make out the shape, of a ramp descending down into the hole. "Quickly lets make haste," said Mallwynn. One at a time they hurriedly led their horses single file down the ramp into a tunnel. Kipper had assumed his perch, on Targus, on top of the saddle bag. Farin and Striker raced out again to bring in the two pack ponies as Arliss watched the ramp. They were halfway to the dais ramp when the hell hounds burst through the entrance to the maze.

It all happened so fast she didn't have time to think. The air was filled with vicious snarls and ear ripping barks and deep throated malevolent growls, as the hounds moved toward them like fast moving shadows in the moonlight. She saw Farin, who was closest to the dais, attempted to shoot an arrow, while holding on to the reins of the pony. The pony screamed and reared at the sight of the hounds, entangling Farin his bow and the reins. Instinctively withdrawing Windsinger, she ran to help Farin, as the hell hounds descended upon him. Leaving the safety of the ramp before Mallwynn had chance to restrain her.

Striker was already surrounded by hounds, with his sword drawn he was just holding them at bay. As she got close to Farin a hell hound got between them, baring its teeth and growling and snarling menacingly at her." Go Back" yelled 'Farin above the cacophony of barking.

She was at a loss at what to do, but couldn't believe that it would end like this. The hound seemed aware of what it was doing, deliberately preventing her from getting to Farin. Then for no reason other than a desperate whim, she fixed the hound with an angry glare and focused every bit of anger she could muster on the hound, and to her utter amazement, the hound cowed down his enormous head between his paws whimpering, and slunk away on his belly, across the grass.

At the same instant, the other hounds stopped in there tracks, and ceased barking. They stood silent and confounded, their large heads cast downward, against the backdrop of the chants of Urages advancing troops in the corridors of the maze.

Farin stared at her with a strange look his face. She, returned his look with a mystified shrug.

Taking advantage of the hounds confused state, the three moved quickly and cautiously with the ponies, toward the safety of the ramp and the tunnel.

No sooner were they all in the tunnel, when the dais slipped back into place, with a hollow scraping whoosh, sealing the tunnel shut. Relief flooded through Arliss as they stood in the lit tunnel. They had made it, they were all safe.

Farin spoke for all of them, when he said, "We were very lucky, we escaped by less than a hairs breadth."

Mallwynn allowed them no time to contemplate their good fortune, instead he urged them on.

"We can't be sure we're safe, until we put some distance between ourselves and Urage." Taking heed of the wizard they quickly mounted their horses and were soon off.

The tunnel was wide enough for them to ride two abreast. It was lit by narrow luminescent bands of rock, that ran across the arched ceiling, of the tunnel. They were set at intervals of about eight feet.

The ghostly archways extended as far as the eye could see. The tunnel wound down deep into the earth. Conversation was difficult as their words were punctuated, by the hollow clip clopping of horse's hooves. Their voices echoed up and down the tunnel, making even the most mundane comment, seem rather odd and mysterious. There was a constant sound of water dripping in the tunnel, and occasionally they would come upon a large puddle.

Once in a while, the tunnel would branch off into a much narrower passageway. Mallwynn told them that these tunnels had been very useful to the druids as they had allowed them secret access and exits from many locations.

They traveled on and on for hours. Arliss had begun to think that maybe the tunnel would never end. She noticed too, that the others were also, were beginning to show signs of fatigue. In the dim light Mallwynn's face looked drawn.

It was a relief, when at last the tunnel widened into a circular chamber. It was about four times as big as the tunnel had been. Leading off the circular chamber, were two more passages. One appeared to be a continuation of the main, tunnel. The other passage was much smaller. Straight ahead of them as they entered the chamber, was an archway with a pair of rusted wrought iron gates. Striker slipped easily down of Eagliss back and tried to open the gates, but they were locked firmly.

"I doubt very much if these gates have been opened in the last few centuries," said Striker as he gave the gates another shake for good measure.

"Well then it's these passages we should take," said Mallwynn." Striker looked at Mallwynn quizzically.

"This passage," said Mallwynn, "Is our best chance of escape. If we are able to get through the gates, and lock them behind us. They will serve to slow Urage up, if he gets this far." Mallwynn then turned to Arliss and said, "Why don't you try the bangle again."

Shrugging back her flaxen hair, she nodded her assent. She got down of Targus, and went to the rusted gate and began to turn the silver bangle, on the third turn as before a shaft of white light shot out of the crystal stone into the rusted lock of the gate.

"Ahh," she said with satisfaction as with an achy metallic groan the gates swung open.

When they had all passed through the gates, they clanged shut again. They were now in a narrower passage. The tunnel immediately began to climb upwards. They got off the horses and led them to lessen burden on the beast's upward journey. Arliss's legs were killing her but she refused to give into the urge to stop and rest. She just kept putting one foot in front of the other.

Mallwynn was leaning heavily on his staff and his body seemed more frail than ever, as he shuffled constantly upwards. The younger men fared better, pacing one another they were some distance ahead, each trying manfully to look more nonchalant and energetic that the other.

Kipper was right at home in the semi-darkness, often padding some distance ahead, then rebounding back with a mad scurry in hot pursuit of some small subterranean creature. When at last it seemed that they could go no further the passage ended.

They found themselves in a huge cavern. The cavern was startlingly dark. "Dark as death, and just as cold, said Mallwynn grimly. There was a tiny pinprick of light in the distance, that Farin pointed out hopefully.

They huddled together in the passageway just outside the cavern until gradually their eyes became accustomed to the dark. The pinprick of light looked like a far off lone star in a midnight sky.

"We can't see more than a couple of feet in front of us," complained Striker, groping around. Mallwynn wordlessly thumped the ground with his staff three times, and the staff with a sudden flare lit up, illuminating a pathway and a large part of the cavern. Immediately there was a blood curdling din, of high pitched squeals and screes, swooping and flapping, as startled bats swarmed out of their dark eyries.

Having already been scared witless, several times in the last few days, Arliss was unmoved by the airborne havoc. Striker however, was quite forthright in his disgust, and distaste, for what he couched as, "Slimy, disease ridden, flying vermin."

Arliss remembered then, the cave under the water fall, and how strange Striker had looked when they saw the bats.

They cast huge shadows on the cavern walls as they followed the pathway further into the cave. Ahead now, in the inky shadows, they could see the light from the staff reflected on a huge body of water. It was a large underground lake, surrounded on three sides by sheer walls of smooth porous limestone.

Stalactites hung from the cavern roof, drooping in heavy fronds of ethereal veils. All around them were clumps of stalagmites, erupting in conical swells from the cave floor.

The limestone had an iridescent quality, shimmering in the light, with hues of pastel colors, splashed here and there, amongst the white. There was a myriad of limestone formations, of fantastic gossamer flowers and stars, clinging to the walls of the cavern. They found that merely brushing up, against these beautiful serendipitous formations, could cause them to instantly disintegrate, so they were careful to stick to the pathway.

High up on the cliff wall, they could see a dark shelf. That was where the tiny point of light was coming, from, and what they hoped was the way out.

After close scrutiny of the cliff walls, they saw a narrow path carved out of the side of the cliff. It climbed treacherously up and around the cliff walls and arrived finally at the high shelf. This was the path they would have to take to get out.

Striker gazed up at the steep narrow pathway and let out a low whistle which to his alarmed chagrin only served to get the bats going again. Arliss watched in amazement and Farin groaned with laughter as Striker with a grimace of disgust warded off hundreds of confused bats who continually launched themselves at him. When the clamor died down, and Farin had stopped laughing, they all became serious again, as they considered with trepidation, the steep and narrow pathway ahead.

They decided that despite their growing fatigue, to proceed ahead without stopping and get out of the cave, as soon as possible.

"The sooner we are out of here, the better," muttered Striker, with a wary eye cast toward the cavern ceiling."

Striker took the lead turning Eagliss, toward the cliff path. Mallwynn on Leonis, with his staff in hand, rode behind Striker illuminating the way. "Come on now, we'll be left in the dark if we don't hurry," urged Farin, as Arliss hesitated before the cliff pathway. The pathway, she thought, now that she was right up to it, Looked, even more impossibly narrow. She took a deep breath and nudged Targus forward onto the pathway. Farin followed on behind on Rubicon with the pack horses in tow.

As they made there was up around the sheer cliff wall, bits of debris and rocks spattered down into the lake below, causing haphazard ripples in the black still waters. The falling stones made hollow thonks, as they struck the water and the sound reverberated throughout the cavern.

At times, the path would become so narrow Arliss's leg would scrape against the sheer cliff wall. It was slow and agonizing going. There was an occasional yowl of protest from Kipper, as from time to time his tail got wedged between the saddle pack and the wall.

She could feel sweat trickle down her cold damp brow on to her face, as she tried not to look down at the cliff edge, with its abyss of water and darkness yawning up at her. Ahead of her Striker and Mallwynn were wending their way up toward the dark shelf.

As Arliss she neared the top of the cliff, Arliss felt a wave of exhilaration as cold air wafted across on her face and she realized that it must have come from the outside.

At last she reached the shelf with Farin following close on her heels. She paused for a moment, before following Mallwynn toward the light, and looked back down into the chasm of darkness from whence they came. She could hardly believe they had all had made it up here safely.

They followed the pathway in the cavern upwards through some giants crevices. They could hear the waves before they saw them, coming in rhythmic rushes of breezy air that grew louder, the higher up they went. Until finally they left the cave and came out into dazzling sunlight and found themselves on a deserted beach in a tiny rocky cove and beyond it as far as the eye could see was water.

"This must be the Cascall sea." said Mallwynn "We have come a long way indeed."

Striker shaded his eyes as he squinted and scanned the beach. Then he spotted a rickety dock a little way down the beach in distance.

As they drew near the dock, they could see that the dock, like the cove itself was deserted and showed no signs of recent use. Striker turned to Farin and said, "Let's go and scout around, there must be someone who lives nearby."

Turning to Mallwynn and Arliss, Striker said, "Why don't you two wait here and Farin and I will go and see what we can find out."

Arliss watched as Farin and Striker, headed away from the beach up a rise and into the woods and disappeared from sight. Turning away she began to help Mallwynn set up camp next to the dock. They unloaded the pack ponies and removed the bridles and saddles from all the horses allowing them to canter freely down the beach.

Arliss gathered flotsam and jetsam from the beach to make a small fire. She slipped off her leather boots and waded out to a group rock emerging from the water. She had a bag, Mallwynn gave her, slung over her shoulder. As she expected, as she searched low on the water line there were many tiny mussels clinging to the rocks.

Carefully, she cleaned and rinsed them in the tide scrubbing off their tiny little beards. Mallwynn meanwhile combed the fringe of the woods and came back laden with wild onions and mushrooms. They put all their ingredients into an iron cooking pot, they got from one of the saddle packs, but did not light the fire as they waited to be sure, from Farin and Striker that it was safe to do so.

It was a long time since Farin and Striker had left. Arliss wondered what had become of them. Mallwynn said nothing, but he paced back and forth in front of the unlit fire, anxiously looking inland, in the direction of the woods. At long last the men returned reporting that the saw no signs of civilization.

Long after they had eaten the mussel stew, and the sun had set over the sea. They sat around the fire in companionable silence. After the confinement of the maze, and the tunnel, and the cavern, the openness, and airiness of the beach, was deeply appreciated by all. And somehow, here on the beach under an enormous starlit sky, even Urage seemed insignificant. Arliss fell asleep that night, feeling, content and optimistic.

She didn't know how long she had been asleep, when she was awakened by Farin, whispering as he shook her, "Come on Arliss, you have to see this."

Still groggy she stumbled to her feet, while gathering her green cloak around her for warmth. They joined Striker and Mallwynn, who were already up, and standing in the darkness, near the edge of the shore staring out to sea.

She couldn't believe her eyes when she looked out at the sea. There sailing into the cove, lit up in the darkness and heading straight toward them was a ship. It was heading for the dock.

"It's a ship," she said with surprise.

"Yes, said Farin, "A double masted schooner."

Arliss watched in the moonlight as the ship drew closer to the dock, she could see on the ship's bow a figurehead. The figurehead was a woman leaning out over the waves with her finger held to her lips. "Very strange," said Mallwynn as he stared out at the schooner with a perplexed frown.

"This is not just a ship, this is a ship without a crew or captain."

Then finally as if he could not believe his own words, he said in amazement, "There is no one on that ship!"

Chapter Five
Behold The Whisper!

The mysterious craft pulled up to the dock. Arliss could now see the name written in silvery white letters along the starboard side of the ship, "The Whisper." She could now see up close the wooden figurehead of the beautiful lady on the bow of the ship, hushing some unseen speaker with her finger held to her lips and staring off in the distance with sightless eyes.

From down on the dock they could hear the groaning of the anchor being lowered, and the splash as it hit the surface of the water. Farin and Striker caught the coils of hemp as they fell unbidden from the ship, and tied the lines to the dock. Then as dawn light came over the distant hills on the other side of the cove, the ship's lights flickered and went out.

"Well what you think" asked Farin as he scrutinized the Whisper with eager curiosity." Shall we have look on board, she's riding low, she must be carrying cargo. "

Both men turned to Mallwynn who was still looking at the ship with wariness.

"By all means." said Mallwynn, "It's safe enough it's just so... unexpected." Arliss watched as, Striker and Farin swung themselves up onto one of the ropes. And with their legs wrapped around the rope, they proceeded hand over hand until they reached the deck railing where one at a time they swung themselves over lightly onto the deck and disappeared from sight.

Arliss stood on the dock with Mallwynn looking up at the ship as they waited impatiently for Striker and Farin to reappear. The ship looked ghostly in the gray dawn light, it stood tall in the water with lines and rigging hung from the twin mast, like ribbons around a may pole. A mild breeze billowed out the sails, causing the ship to rock and creak at anchor.

At long last Striker and Farin appeared on deck again, and lowered a gang plank down to the dock. Arliss followed Mallwynn up the gang plank onto the ship.

Striker and Farin had taken a cursory look around, and, as Mallwynn predicted the ship was empty.

On the after deck Arliss and Mallwynn followed behind Farin down the narrow dark companionway below deck. Striker was ahead of them, he paused to light a brass oil sconce with a taper from the lamp he carried. The light from the brass sconces, was reflected back softly on the mahogany walls of the companionway.

The first door on the starboard side in the after passage led into the captain's quarters, a sextant case was opened, and the instrument laid out on some charts that cluttered a small table. There were pencils and a compass beside it. Most peculiar of all was the captains log which lay open.

"Take a look at this," said Striker as he held the brass lamp over the book.

On the first page, Mallwynn read the entry aloud, "expected aboard the Whisper today, honored guest Princess Arliss Glasstarr, and her grandfather Mallwynn Darrowglynn Arch Wizard to the Orchid Court, Sir Striker Strongfourth and his cousin Sir Farin Woodrow. Long, live the Whisper and all who sail in her."

Mallwynn closed the book thoughtfully, and looked at them and shrugged, "It seems we are expected."

Arliss was unnerved by the emptiness of the ship. It wasn't just that it was empty, but that the ship had a very definite attitude of waiting for someone, who had just left and was expected back presently.

As if the same thoughts ran through his mind, with a look of unease Striker said, "I wonder what the meaning of all this is,"

He swung the lamp up and around while he surveyed the rest of the cabin…

"Not room enough in here to swing a cat o' nine tails," he remarked with a grin. and then he added "This takes me back Farin, to the isle of Dunlar.

"Aye." agreed Farin smiling.

"The Fidorian brothers had us crewing ships every summer while we were Windgarth Castle," explained Striker.

"Lets not tarry here," broke in Mallwynn," We must inspect the rest of the ship before we set off."

On the portside of the narrow after passage way, across from the captain's quarters was a tiny first mates cabin, and next to it was another cabin, in it were three narrow double decker bunks, against either wall.

"This is the sleeping quarters for the crew," explained Striker.

"This ship has been specially fitted, usually in any vessel I've been on the crews quarters are below the forward deck."

"That's true," agreed Farin.

A narrow after passage led from the sleep quarters, down a few shallow steps, to a tiny dining saloon. Everything in the saloon was compact and most of the furniture and fittings were built in. The ceiling was low and made of varnished narrow planking of white pine. Light filtered into the saloon from portholes on the starboard wall.

There was a deep low alcove to the right of the steps. The alcove was lined on either side by high-backed cushioned benches, with a long table in the middle. A wide brimmed copper shaded lantern swung gently from the dropped ceiling in the alcove.

They took turns peeping into the tiny narrow galley, next to the saloon, that was only large enough for two people at the most.

They explored the rest of ship, going up on deck again and going below through the forward companionway to the hold. There was a compartment in the hold that was used for transporting livestock. A couple of compartments were set aside for dry goods.

They entered another compartment and, it was filled with food stuffs and large barrels of ale and casks of wine.

After the ship had been inspected from stem to stern they made haste to shove off, as they were anxious to put some distance between them and the cavern tunnels. They loaded the horses and pack ponies on board along with all of their gear. Kipper had already installed herself in the crow's nest atop one of the mast, and bathed lazily in the morning sun. Only Mallwynn had expressed any reluctance to sail in the ship, as he explained he wasn't a particularly good sailor, but as he himself had pointed out that there were many means available to Urage, to discern their where abouts, and even now, he could very well be hot on their heels. They would be less easily tracked on water.

Arliss tried to keep out of the way as Striker and Farin hoisted in the anchor and the Whisper sailed resolutely out of the cove and into the Cascall Sea.

They began tracking due west hugging the Cascall coast. The ship responded like a living entity. When they would need to haul round to change tack, the boom would swing around and the sails would catch the wind just right, or furl or unfurl at the right moment, which was very providential as they could never have sailed her without a larger crew.

Arliss enticed Kipper down out of the crow's nest and stowed the cat and her cloak on the bunk in the first mate's quarters. Kipper was content for now to lay on the gently swaying bunk.

The water in the basin in the wash stand, was fresh from the galley, it was cold and she hadn't taken time to heat it on the stove, but never the less she felt pampered with the cake of lemon scented soap. She scrubbed herself vigorously all over, doing her hair as best she could. It had been just over three days since she left the Valley of Creation with Urage in pursuit, but it felt like a life time.

She gratefully changed into the soft fresh clothing that she had found laid out on the bunk. The white close fitting trousers, fitted her like leggings, and over the white short sleeve tunic top she belted Windsinger.

After she was dressed she braided her long hair into a tight pale rope and fastened it with a clasp. She slipped the crystal bangle back on her wrist and touched her tunic to feel the Glasstarr Amulet beneath it. Then She then went up on deck to see what she could do. Mallwynn looking a little green, and was standing stoically by the starboard railing. Striker instructed her on taking the wheel. It took a lot of concentration just to stay on course, so they frequently spelled each other at the wheel, as they tacked further up the coast.

Arliss was amazed at how fast the time sped by. She was quickly getting used to the roll and pitch of the deck. Even Mallwynn was more comfortable as he sat up by the bow, his eyes fixed in the direction they were sailing fingering his beads.

They were making good time and had come a long way, and now they were sailing directly into the setting sun. They weighed anchor just before the fiery red orb sunk into the Cascall sea.

Striker finished lashing down the rigging and went down the forward companionway, to the hold to check on the horses.

Farin and Arliss had raided the hold for provisions for supper, and they went below to the galley to prepare the meal.

They had a spread of cold sausage with herb biscuits and cheese and ale. They were famished and ate voraciously, especially Farin, who kept up his banter in between bites, a less loquacious Striker, merely nodded his head from time to time in agreement.

The copper lamp swayed gently to the pitch of the ship casting a warm glow that waxed and waned into the shadows. Kipper the cat was curled up between Mallwyn and Arliss. Arliss found it quite annoying that the cat had taken such a liking to the old wizard. She was sure he had put some spell on the cat. He actually seemed to talk to Kipper at times making these strange little shushing noises that oddly enough, the cat seemed to understand perfectly, and would respond to the wizard with a humming purr that was interrupted by a few well placed throaty meows.

When the meal was over, Striker frowned and said, "Mallwynn, who do you think is responsible for the ship"

Mallwynn looked up from the charts he had been studying, and said thoughtfully, "I really don't know for certain, but I expect that the help we have received, has come from some of the old ones, who went before us, and now live in the upper plains of existence, behind the mystic veil. Urage has shaken things up severely, on the upper plain. There are those who fear that the balance of good and evil may have been irrevocably damaged and unfortunately for us, and Eartheart, there are many in the nether world that would do much to help Urage.

Then Mallwynn sighed, and said, "I'm afraid Urage has amassed even more power, than I had realized. He won't be easily defeated if at all.

The mention of Urages name sent a chill down Arliss's back.

"Where are heading for" said Arliss, as she suddenly realized that in her relief at putting distance between her and Urage, she hadn't thought to ask where they were sailing to. At first no one said anything.

Mallwynn turned to Arliss taking out his pipe as he did so, and as he tamped the tobacco down into his pipe with his thumb he said vaguely.

"I should think we'll put in somewhere along the Orchid coast," looking at Striker and Farin, as they nodded in confirmation."

Arliss hesitated realizing something was being held back, "and then she said "Then what "

"Well then we must get you to the Orchid valley," said Mallwynn although his tone matter-of-fact his words seemed measured.

With a sigh of annoyance Arliss said "Why the Orchid Valley"

Slowly now and reluctantly Mallwynn said, "We will go to the Orchid valley because as it's been the seat of Eartheart since the beginning of time. There, Gailin, the ancient the Keeper of the Orchid crown will invest you as Empress of Eartheart."

"No," announced Arliss forcefully.

Farin looked bewildered, Striker's face was inscrutable only, his eyes betrayed his intense interest.

"No" said Mallwynn tilting his head to look at her.

"If I become Empress of Eartheart," said Arliss heatedly, "That means I'm never going home again."

Mallwynn sighed deeply and for a while they sat in silence, he had let his pipe go out and now sat fingering his beads.

Then finally he spoke, "Arliss I am going to ask you to trust me, and in return I promise you that in the end whether, or not you become Empress of Eartheart will be left entirely up to you."

A flood of relief washed over Arliss at Mallwynn's words.

"But," he continued, "If Urage has his way there will be no choice, he wants you dead, and according to ancient Orchidian law, Gailin the crown keeper will be forced to surrender crown and scepter to Urage, if the legitimate heir dies before investiture."

A vague feeling of dissatisfaction came over Arliss, and it must have shown on her face, because Mallwynn said."

I know you have more questions, but for now, I have no more answers, only suffice to say, our chief concern is to keep you alive, as long as your alive there is hope for Eartheart."

Sobered even more by his words Arliss grew silent.

Striker stood up and stretched, and Farin yawned, Arliss suddenly remembered her own tiredness, and was thinking about turning in for the night, when Mallwynn said, "Oh there is just one more thing..." As he paused they all turned to look at him.

"Before we head around to the Orchid coast since its on our way, there is one place I'd 'like to stop at, the city of Oceanus."

Striker's eyes widened in surprise at Mallwynn's words.

"Oceanus..." repeated Farin as if the sound of the word was strange to his ears.

"Yes Oceanus," said Mallwynn.

"Not the city of Oceanus," said Farin smiling in disbelief. As Mallwynn nodded his response, the smile faded from Farin's face as he gasped in surprised wonder "Oceanus!" he was now wide awake.

"The underwater city of Oceanus, there really is an Oceanus?" Striker stunned at Mallwynns words, stopped in his tracks, and slid back down into his seat, as Mallwynn nodding his head said, "Yes there most certainly is a city under the sea called Oceanus."

"What sort of place is Oceanus" asked Striker dubiously and then without waiting for an reply he said, "I had always heard of such kingdoms of sea folk in the old songs and poems, but I never believed such strange tales to be real."

"Oh yes indeed they are as real as the nose on your face," observed Mallwynn dryly.

"As a matter of fact Arliss and myself have kin there on the Darrowglynn side of the family."

Arliss who had been taking this all in a haze of disbelief suddenly broke in, "Who am I related to who lives under the sea"

"Hmm... actually," said Mallwynn, "A couple of third cousins."

"Oh this should be interesting, said Farin raising an eyebrow. "Well before I continue I must get something from my cabin." said Mallwynn as he slipped out of the alcove and shuffled down the corridor toward the sleeping quarters. The three were left pondering his words only a few moments before he came shuffling back, bringing with him a pentagonal shaped case. The outside was decorated with tiny sea shells and small fish and sea horses. Mallwynn sat down with the case in front of him and without saying a word opened the hinged box and drew out four gold bands. They were wide and flat with stylized enamel fish set in.

"These are Poseidon bands," said Mallwynn.

"They will make it possible for us to go underneath the sea and visit Oceanus, just as it enabled the wizard Bower Darrowglynn to forsake the land and join his true love under the sea.

"Where did Darrowglnn get the bands "asked Striker.

"The family story goes like this, and this is a very old tale, so I don't know how close to the mark it is." said Mallwynn , "But apparently Bower Darrowglynn searched high and low, for a very long time before finding them in a far off kingdom. He had been in love with Queen Kandra for many a year. He was wizard enough to make it possible for her to live on land. But she couldn't as she was the only daughter of the late King Olan and there was no one else suitable for the throne so naturally she could not leave her people. Then there came word of the existence of these bands. Well Darrowglynn didn't cease until the bands were in his possession and he was wed to the Queen, but that is another tale. Anyway, that started the long-standing relationship between our families."

"What about the bands? asked Arliss "How did they come into your possession."

"When Bower Darrowglynn passed on, his oldest son Krael was sent by his mother the Queen to bring the sad tidings, as the well as the bands." said Mallwynn holding up the bands.

Bower Darrowglynn had done much to enhance the lives of the people of Oceanus. They loved and admired him very much and along with the Queen greatly mourned his passing. While Darrowglynn lived in Oceanus, many times family and friends would visit, and he would meet them at the surface with the bands. After his death the queen following Bowers wishes sent Krael to return these bands to land and place them in the custody of my grandfather Bower's nephew, Declann Darrowglynn. We of course have visited back and forth over the years, but I have not been there in over fifty years. Mallwynn finished speaking and looked around at the three of them.

"Hmm...Well there is no time like the present," he announced as he slipped the Poseidon band on Arliss's arm.

"We don't know what's ahead for us, but you may as well get used to wearing the bands, and have a tool in case of unforeseen events. And when we reach Oceanus, it won't be so much of a shock," finished Mallwynn cryptically. He passed Striker and Farin each a Poseidon band. At the same time, Arliss gasped and her eyes widened, and with a look of Startled disbelief, she turned to Mallwynn and began to remove the band, as Striker and Farin watched warily with their own bands still held in their hands.

Mallwynn reached over and stopped her saying, "You'll grow used to it in time.... How else could you talk underwater?"

He then slipped on his own as did Striker and Farin, in wordless amazement The men reacted in much the same way as Arliss did.

Mallwynn's voice sounded tiny and far off in her head but as she focused in on him the contrast was striking, not only could she hear him clearly but she also understood him like never before. She felt what he was feeling when he spoke images rolled through her mind of things he spoke off she saw his world through his eyes. She felt his grief and his joy his strengths and his fears. The old man's eyes met hers then she blinked and once again he sounded very distant again, she concentrated and focused and she could hear him in a normal manner as if she wasn't wearing the Poseidon bands.

"It's just a matter of practice and control," he said. "In no time at all, it will be very easy to do."

As if in agreement they all disappeared from the saloon in separate directions and busied themselves with the various shipboard chores before turning in for bed.

The next few days they settled into a pleasant routine that kept themselves busy from sunrise to dusk, sailing the little ship through the fortunately smooth waters. In the evenings they would share a robust meal together, and after the meal they would go up on deck, bringing their mugs of ale, and while they mended the nets and sails they would take turns telling tales and singing Eartheart folk songs and sagas. Striker in evenings, would point out and name the stars and other celestial bodies to Arliss and he explained to her the use of the sextant and the night sky for navigation. Farin kept his word and instructed her on the use of Windsinger. For hours on end they would spar till finally, the sword seemed an extension of her arm.

A strange intimacy had settled among them. They didn't discuss the Poseidon bands in fact no mention was made directly of them again. Instead they were careful not to pry into each other's minds. They learned how to keep a psychic distance from each other, to protect their privacy. They however were very conscious of one another, it was as if there was a thin veil in between them.

When they were a few days under sail they noticed that they were being followed by a school of dolphins. These were quite tame and, in the evening, when they weighed anchor, they would come close enough so that Arliss could reach over and touch their smooth wet heads. They were playful creatures they frolicked amongst themselves, talking to one another in high pitched squeals. One dolphin in particular was very friendly and in the evening if Arliss wasn't up on deck he would squeal repetitively until she came up from below. She had taken to calling him scamp, the name suited him well. He was full of tricks, his favorite was sneaking up behind her when she was engrossed in some activity and spraying her with water. Scamp and the other dolphins were very good natured and they took it upon themselves to form an escort which followed the ship and could occasionally be seen driving off any unsavory aquatic types. They were also very helpful with the fishing.

They often fished with poles of the deck, in the evening, it seemed as if the dolphins rounded up the fish for them, as they hooked many more than they did before the dolphins arrived. What they didn't use or save for bait they tossed out to the dolphins who leapt gratefully in the air catching the fish daintily in their beak like mouths.

And so time aboard the ship past very quickly and according to the log that Mallwynn kept they had already been ten days out at sea.

On the morning of the tenth day they awoke to a strangely calm sea. The sky overhead was perfectly clear, and its color was a deep blue. The sun low in the eastern sky shot red gold bolts of light over an endless expanse of smooth sea. In the western sky, right at the bottom of the horizon was a faint patch of grayness really no more than a speck on the horizon All hands were on deck at sunrise.

"I don't think we will be going too far today," said Striker looking off at the western sky with, a frown of concern. "Yes." agreed Mallwynn, "We all should rest while we can, and try to prepare for what might be ahead."

"Look!" exclaimed Arliss. "The dolphins have gone!" "That's right, agreed Farin with surprise.

"What ever made them leave," he asked of no one in particular.

"Well by the looks of that sky," said Striker, "I would think it might be possible, that they are taking shelter closer inland, maybe in some cove or inlet."

"You may very well be right Striker," admitted Mallwynn.

"But There is no way of knowing at this point whether we are in for a bad storm or just a cloud burst, but let us prepare for the worst and hope for the best."

By midmorning they had finished getting ready for the approaching storm, which now loomed larger in the sky line. Everything was lashed down and secured. The small row boat was stowed in its berth on deck, and was stocked with emergency supplies in case of the worst.

The men were attending to the animals in the hold, making sure that nothing was left undone in preparation for the storm.

It was usual for Arliss to slip over the deck for a quick swim in the evenings, but because of the approaching storm, she decided to take her swim while she could.

She stood on the deck, poised to enter the water. After ten days at sea Arliss was deeply tanned, her flaxen hair was lighter than ever, beneath her short tunic her well muscled legs were bare. She wore a leather belt slung over her hips in which she kept a silver dagger, which Striker had given her. Her gray eyes were cloudy now, as she considered for a moment whether she had left anything undone in preparation for the storm. She'd offered to help in the hold, but Farin had said it wasn't necessary as they were nearly finished.

Satisfied that she had done all she could, she smiled with anticipation as she slipped silently into the water and then dove beneath the surface. In anticipation of the underwater journey to Oceanus, Mallwynn had encouraged the three of them to practice frequently, using the Poseidon bands underwater.

Although she had worn the Poseidon band, now for many days, she was still unused to the peculiar feeling of being underwater yet able to breathe, an odd sensation. The first few minutes she had to guard against the instinct to hyper ventilate, and it was many minutes before she could relax and become unaware of her own breathing.

She had never stayed below for very long. This was because of the darkness, the darkness of the night. Under the sea at night, was abysmally dark, like the middle of the longest night, yet because of the Poseidon bands she could see perfectly, not in the same way she would normally see things. It was a peculiar kind of vision really, it seemed almost like there were a hundred thousand different shades of darkness in the water and she could distinguish each and everyone.

This was the first time she had ever swam during the day. She felt unhurried as it would be well into the evening before the storm would hit.

After swimming underwater for a while, she returned to the surface, to enjoy the heat of the sun on her face, then after a few minutes, she again dove underwater. This time she swam down deeper and deeper, swimming constantly downwards toward the murky bottom. She stopped and looked back up at the boat. She could see the whole underside of the ship, its shape clearly defined in the water. She thought it looked, like a huge bird floating in a watery sky. All around the water was teeming with life. Tiny almost transparent fish swam in clouds past her. Plant fronds tickled her feet. Her hair fanned out from her head like some exotic aquatic plant or animal with a life of its own. Her eyes had gotten used to the dimness of the deeper water and she only hesitated a bit glancing up at the little ship before she continued her journey still further downward into the deepening murkiness. When she stopped once again and looked back up at the outline of the ship it was incredibly small and far away.

She was near the bottom now and the vegetation was much thicker.

There was still many of fish of all kinds and all shapes and sizes but in general they were bigger and fewer, than the ones near the surface. Sea creatures swam near her and around her peering at her curiously. She touched some as they swam near, some would timidly retreat swimming out of range and some would come even closer. She could barely see in front of her now maybe only a couple of feet. The light way up on the surface and being in the shadows of the deep gave her the feeling of being in a tunnel. Out of the corner of her eye she caught a glimpse of some sort of aquatic snake undulating through the water. She noticed that the fish seemed to have lost interest in her and now were rapidly swimming off. Then she felt her hackles rise as the dimness of the water suddenly became more intense. She spun around and found herself looking at the head of a huge octopus!

The scream was that of deep terror ripping through her chest, and was spewed silently out into the water becoming a muffled feeling that was no longer sound. At the same instant she was off. Soaring upwards toward the surface like a rock out of slingshot. Inextricably almost casually the moving tendrils wound up and cinched her in a loop of tentacle. The tentacle bound her arms to the side and now with wide eyed horror she watched herself propelled with great speed to the monstrous mouth of the creature.

Up on the ship, Striker was just finishing up with the horses in the hold stable. Mallwynn and Farin were still securing the rest of the hold compartments.

A feeling of dread overtook Striker, stopping him in his tracks for just an instant. And then a look of horror crossed his face, as he turned and ran up the forward companionway, He heard the thunder of footsteps behind him, he raced onto the deck. And as he ripped off his boots, he felt rather than saw Farin, follow suit. He launched himself in the water thrusting downward reaching pulling himself down through the water with all his might.

Chapter Six
A Visitor From Below

Down, down, down Striker swam, with Farin close behind him, as he searched the waters for Arliss, his eyes gradually grew more accustomed to the dimness.

Then his eyes widened in horror as below him, in a mass of frothing writhing water he spotted her locked in the tentacle of a huge octopus. It's head alone, must have been about fifty feet wide and a hundred feet long.

With a sudden spasm the octopus's tentacle tightened crushing Arliss. She felt queasy as the tip of the tentacle writhed and slithered around her ankles. She felt herself start to lose consciousness, but then suddenly the octopus slackened its grip on her, and for a moment or two, she felt hazy and confused, and then as her mind cleared, she felt her instinct to survive return.

As the coiled tentacle slackened some more she slid her hand over the hilt of the silver dagger and drew the flat side of the blade smoothly up past her stomach, till it rested just under her breast. Suddenly the loop of the tentacle holding her jerked closed again, jamming the flat of the blade deeply into her flesh. As she fought to remain calm she pried her hands up under the top of the blade angling the point outward toward the sensitive flesh of the underside of the tentacle. Using her left hand as a fulcrum she levered the blade of the dagger up, with her right hand, until it was just nicking the tentacle, slimy liquid began to ooze from the tentacle and run down her body.

Then with a mighty upward thrust she drove the blade straight through the octopus's tentacle, and with lightning speed it uncoiled and whipped her through the water. The tentacles churned all around her as she spun through the water.

She felt crushing pain as her body slapped hard against something rough and gritty. Then she blacked out.

She could feel the sway of deck beneath her. She opened her eyes. Her head and body hurt all over.

For a brief moment she wondered what she was doing lying on the deck of the Whisper.

Mallwynn's anxious face hovered over her

Then as he noticed her awake, he smiled down at her warmly and said in a grave voice, "You are certainly tough one, even for a Glasstarr."

He paused for a moment as he looked steadily at her. She frowned in confusion at his words. Then a look of understanding swept across her face as she remembered everything.

With a sigh of disbelieve Mallwynn shook his head and said, "After all of that, I can't believe that there is nothing more wrong with you that a few bumps and bruises. A little salve will soon put those right.

"With a skeptical snort Arliss glared at Mallwynn and said, "A few bumps and bruises! I've been wrung out like yesterday's wash!" Then she felt something rough and wet on her face and she turned her head, next to her on the deck was Kipper watching her attentively, his eyes narrowed to chinks and he let out as a solicitous yowl as he tilted his ginger head quizzically at her.

Standing beside Mallwynn was Striker. He was dripping wet, and in his hand was the silver dagger he had given her, the one she'd plunged into the octopus's tentacle.

With a look of respect, he caught her eye, and flipped the silver dagger in the air and caught it expertly by its hilt. Then as he leaned over and slipped the dagger back into its sheath on her belt, as he said, "Admirable performance Glasstarr, that Octopus must be at least three leagues away by now."

"And hopping mad," broke in Farin smiling as he stood soaking wet at the other side of Mallwynn.

Striker raising his eyes skyward said, "It's beginning to look very bad I think we had better get you below quickly and prepare to ride out this storm."

Overhead the sky darkened suddenly, and harsh fractured lightening flashed across it, followed closely by the ominous boom of thunder, which reverberated across the water.

As fat drops of rain began splattering down on the deck, Farin and Striker helped Arliss below to her cabin. Mallwynn from a pocket in his cloak gave Arliss an ornate crystal jar of salve, advising her to put it on all her bruises, and on the large circular welts where the octopus's suckers had been in contact with her skin.

The storm was fast upon them now, and except for Arliss, it was all hands on deck to manage the little ship. The craft rode the waves well, and as the wind whipped up the water the waves crested high over the ship, flooding the deck.

Sometimes the little craft would be picked up high in the air, and then in the next instant, plunged down with a towering wall of water to one side.

The men had tied lines to themselves to keep from being pitched over board. The rain continued to pour in sheets, onto the deck.

When the storm was all but over, Arliss came back on deck, fully recovered, even the sucker welts had begun to fade. Striker and Farin were amazed at her rapid recovery as were Arliss herself but Mallwynn who said nothing looked pleased with himself.

Then in the late evening, as rapidly, as it came upon them the storm passed and miraculously, they had suffered no damage.

That night in the tiny saloon they enjoyed a simple meal of biscuits and slices of hard cold spicy sausage washed down with ale. It had been many hours since they last ate.

The animals had weathered the storm well, and had already been fed and tended to, so after the meal, they all turned in for the night.

Arliss was exhausted it had been a long hard day, and as soon as her head hit the pillow she was deeply asleep.

She stirred briefly in her sleep, vaguely aware of some high pitched squeals.

"The dolphins are back," she murmured before sinking back into a deep sleep.

She slept on, unaware of the huge slimy form that lumbered over the rail of the little ship onto the deck. It shuffled across the after deck to the companion way.

The animals in the forward hold of the ship, whinnied warily, sensing the oddness of the movement on the deck.

The creature opened the companion way door and silently disappeared below.

Arliss found herself wide awake and not knowing why. She caught her breath as she became aware of a shuffling movement around her room.

As she lay stock still in bed, she became aware of snuffling wet sounds, waxing and waning at regular intervals. Her heart began to pound hard, when with horror she realized that it was the sound of someone or something breathing.

Then the shuffling movements stopped.

Hardly breathing, Arliss lay rigid in bed. From the sound of the wet breathing, she could tell that the creature was at the foot of her bed, right in front of the cabin door.

As cold sweat began to run down her back, she quietly drew her knees up and pressed the damp palms of her hands down on the mattress behind her, then with lightning speed she sprung quickly upright on the bed, and launched herself at the shadowy hulk at the foot of the bed.

Striker awoke in alarm to the sounds of a ferocious scuffle coming from somewhere down the after passage. He sat up so quickly in his bunk, that he smacked his head on the cabin ceiling.

"Quick Farin there's something wrong!" he cried as he leapt out of the bunk and slid to the floor. Farin was behind him as he tore open the door and ran into the after passage. Both men were joined by Mallwynn as they sprinted towards the only closed door in the after passage.

In the darkness, she grappled the slimy cold creature with three of her limbs and repetitively walloped it with the fourth. The creature tried to pry her away with his finlike fingers. They fell to the floor, her lithe agility enabled her to roll on top and seize the opportunity to place her feet on each of his upper limbs effectively pinning him to the deck. All this happened in a matter of seconds.

The creature was letting out awful wails now, and Arliss would have felt sorry for him and let him go, if she hadn't been so frightened. Behind her, doors were being thrown open and there was a clatter of running feet and voices raised in alarm.

Mallwynn and Striker and Farin were not prepared for the sight that met their eyes when they opened the door. Illuminated by the lamp that Mallwynn held over head, was Arliss perched an enormous fish like man who was desperately howling.

"Hold on a bit there Arliss," cried Farin "Give the poor beast some breathing space."

Arliss looked up in surprise and then back down at the creature and seeing that his expressive green face was filled fear. She let go of him and stood up.

They all stood around the odd looking creature, who made no attempt to get up. Kipper the cat for some strange reason seem to like the beast and was licking his face. The creature's face looked quite comical as his mouth formed into a strange smirk trying fastidiously to avoid the cats roving tongue.?

He wore a short purple tunic with an emblem of a dolphin on it. His feet were nothing more than flippers and big ones at that. He has regular legs and arms, but his hands were finlike and he had six fingers on each hand. His head was pretty normal, but Arliss thought that his lips were definitely fishlike. His nose was flattish and his eyes were too far apart, positioned almost on the side of his head.

"Hey fellow do you have a name?" demanded Striker his face hard an expressionless.

Then in a very dignified voice that was at the same time childlike, the big creature answered, "I am Whapper, of the clan of Sidmore."

He had drawn himself up off the floor and now was standing at his full height of seven and a half feet. His hands reached out to grasp Strikers hand in greeting. Striker returned the shake firmly. Still gripping Whapper's hand Striker, gave him a hard penetrating look and said coldly, "How do you explain you presence here?"

Whapper looked taken back by Striker intensity, and before he could answer. Mallwynn broke quietly," I recognize the emblem its the Oceanus secret service."

"The secret service hmm..." said Striker noncommittally as he finally released Whapper's hand.

"That is true," asserted Whapper in a sincere voice.

"I am here on official business."

Whapper then turned quickly to Arliss and said Your highness, I meant you no harm. I have been charged with escorting you to the home of a relative of yours."

"This is too strange not to be true," said Farin with a perplexed look, as he swept back a lock of his wiry blond hair. Whapper sniffed at Farin's words and looked deeply offended.

"Who is this relative?" quizzed Mallwynn, looking terribly uncomfortable now,

Whapper answered, "The lady Elsaroth Darrowglynn Madenwater, Queen Amarin's sister."

"Ahh" said Mallwynn nodding with understanding "That explains the subterfuge."

Three sets of puzzled eyes turned toward Mallwynn.

"This is just the sort of thing Elsaroth would do, intercept us on the way to Oceanus and divert us to the dowagers palace. Thus creating an embarrassment of protocol and making Amarin squirm." One look at Whapper's face confirmed Mallwynn's words.

"But surely your a traitor to your queen!" said Farin in a shocked voice.

"Not so at all, I'd sooner die than be a traitor to my queen!" cried Whapper staunchly. Then with less heat he explained with a look of distaste that he had been assigned into the service of Princess Elsaroth for life or as long as she tolerated him.

"But how did Elsaroth know of our coming" asked Striker, with a glint of doubt still in his eyes.

"No one can approach Oceanus and the children of Poseidon," said Mallwynn, "Without their being aware of it. It would not surprise me at all if your disappearing friends the dolphins, when they left us headed straight for Oceanus to report to Queen Amarin."

With an embarrassed look Whapper nodded his head in confirmation saying, "I was dispatched immediately to bring by whatever means, Princess Arliss to the dowagers palace."

"I do not appreciate these devious pranks of lady Elsaroth's," chastised Mallwynn sharply as his face puckering with annoyance.

"I assure you that neither lady Elsaroth nor myself wish to harm anyone, our only wish is to bring you to Oceanus as an honored guest."

At last satisfied with Whapper's answers, they all decided to get some more rest. Striker and Farin took Whapper with them into the crew's quarters, where they could take turns keeping an eye on him.

The next day dawned far too soon for everyone as the interrupted night's sleep left them all fatigued. After breakfast Mallwynn shocked and surprised them all when he announced that he would leave them that day and he expected them to carry on their trip to Oceanus without him.

Striker and Farin looked worried but said nothing. Arliss was at first speechless. When she at last recovered herself, she said, "You can't mean that Mallwynn, what will we do without you..."

Mallwynn interrupted her with a sweep of his hand, and as he addressed himself to the four of them, he said "I must prepare to leave in the next hour. I have no doubt you will manage admirable, without me, after all now you have Whapper Sidmore as a guide and ally."

Whapper with a look of pride, drew himself up a little taller at Mallwynns words.

Striker's face was inscrutable and there was a certain hardness about him that wasn't usually there. The light went out in Farin's open friendly face and his look became guarded.

As if he noticed nothing, Mallwynn continued. "These releases me to attend to some very pressing matters, which, need my attention in the Orchid Valley."

The announcement of Mallwynn's departure was so shocking to Arliss that she hadn't until now considered by what means his departure would be made.

She would have asked him but she was peeved at him. He had sounded quite pleased about leaving. Arliss found that very annoying. So she would just have to wait to see in what manner he would take his leave.

Arliss did not have long to wait before the hour was out Mallwynn asked them to gather in the hold of all places.

Mallwynn raised an eyebrow when Arliss drew him aside to a quiet corner of the hold. She inquired delicately of Mallwynn as to whether their underwater relatives resembled Whapper in anyway.

"Not that it would make any difference what they looked like," she asserted, "It would just help if I was prepared, after all this was not the time to offend anyone."

Mallwynn studied her keenly for a moment then said,

"It is pleasant to see that you are concerned with diplomacy and well you should be, as much may depend on it now. You have no need to be concerned on that score however, as our relatives are really quite ordinary, and wouldn't turn many heads, if they were to walk by".

They were all gathered around, Mallwynn stood in the middle of the compartment that served as a stable. His horse Leonis was at his side.

He turned to them and said "Use your head and follow your heart. I will meet up with you somewhere between Oceanus and the Orchid Valley,"

He then raised both his hands above his head, then lowered them in an arc to his side, and in a split second he and the horse was gone leaving the air shimmering briefly in the spot where he and his horse had stood.

It still was only the middle of the morning when they raised the anchor and set off. If they made good time that day, Whapper said that they would probably reach Oceanus by noon the next day.

The ship board chores kept them all busy. Whapper proved to be a willing and able hand. Where he had learned the above water skills he did not say. Whapper found the ongoing banter between Striker and Farin captivating but confusing.

"Why do they smile, while they are being insulted," He asked Arliss.

She explained to him that they were joking. He didn't understand what joking was after trying several times to explain it to him.

She decided that Striker and Farin were not very funny after all and she agreed with Whapper it was strange to smile while your were being insulted.

The day quickly wore on. There was more than enough chores to keep them all very busy.

It was early evening just at twilight when they weighed anchor.

Whapper refused to take an evening meal with them as had to return to the sea for a short while to replenish himself as he was not used to being, out of water, for such an extended period of time. He said he would return in a short while.

With the arrival of Whapper and Mallwynn leaving the mood had changed aboard the Whisper. As they sat around the table in the saloon, even with Whapper gone, the intimacy of the past days was gone. Striker was distracted and on edge even Farin seemed gloomy. The next morning everybody was topside early. Now that they were so close to their destination, the time for Arliss seemed to drag on, she spent a lot of time wondering about Amarin and Elsaroth and what Oceanus would be like.

As Arliss stood at the prow of the ship, looking down she could see the wooden lady, speeding over the water, with her carved tresses spilling out behind her and her eyes constantly seeking out something in the distance. Arliss too, had been gazing out to sea, anxiously anticipating the first sighting of land.

From behind her Striker said, "We're just about an hour away from the island of Thalassa."

"Good!" said Arliss with growing excitement.

"There we will dock the ship and bring the horses ashore?" she asked.

"That's right," confirmed Striker as Whapper joined them.

"From there it is but a short journey to Oceanus," said Whapper.

A while latter they sighted the tiny island of Thalassaa tiny speck in the distance. And a short while later, they were in front of the entrance to a strait, which was cut into the chalk cliffs of the island. The strait was so narrow, that they almost missed it. There was barely enough, room for a single ship to pass through it.

"This is called the King's gate," said Whapper.

At either side of entrance to the strait, cut into the chalky cliffs were huge carved statues.

On one side was a stern faced man was sitting on a throne with a crown on his head, his stone eyes regarded them coldly, he was carrying a trident in one hand. "That is Poseidon, the ancient King of the sea," said Whapper reverently.

"Do you see those metal rings driven into the side of the cliff," asked Whapper pointing to either side of the entrance to the strait.

"In my great grandfathers day, there used to actually be gates that hung from the cliffs, that could be locked and unlocked, they have disappeared long ago, no one knows where."

Opposite Poseidon on the other side of the entrance to the strait, were a pair of beautiful girls, whose bodies were half covered in scales, instead of legs they had tails. The girls appeared to be feeding a pair of dolphins who were carved in the process of leaping out of a small stone fountain.

As fantastic as the scene was, Arliss thought it had an odd realism to it, she could almost swear she saw a small fish drop from one of the girls hands into the dolphins mouth. That couldn't be, she thought and yet if she blinked and looked again she could swear there was something different about the tableau. As they glided past on the Whisper they all became silent.

The huge statues at the entrance to the strait, seemed to have a strange effect on all of them and all eyes turned to catch a last glance, as they sailed on into the narrow strait.

The white striated cliff walls towered on either side of them now, leaving just a narrow runner of vivid blue sky above them. Arliss shivered at the sudden drop of temperature. She felt chilled and confined as, she could almost reach out, and touch the cliff walls as they sped by.

At last with a blast of warmth and light they sailed out into a tiny cove with a natural harbor. There was land on three sides and chalk cliffs with the narrow strait on the fourth side.

The water was very blue and as they skimmed across the still waters, straight ahead of them, green meadows ran down to the waters edge, and beyond the meadow in the distance Arliss could see hills and forests.

On the far side to the right of them as they came in the harbor was another steep chalky cliff. On top of this cliff was a white marble temple with columns.

"That's the temple of Poseidon," said Whapper following Arliss's gaze.

She could see a steep stairway carved into the chalk cliff, it zigzagged up from the waters edge, to the temple at the very top of the cliff.

They carefully navigated the ship, toward a rocky beach with a dock leading out from it, opposite the cliff, with the temple of Poseidon. Here they dropped anchor and tied up at the dock.

So used was she, to the pitch and roll of the ship, that the first time on land after ten days at sea, Arliss's legs felt strange and clumsy.

They quickly unloaded the horses and brought the animals off of the ship and walking them up the beach to the meadow. There they allowed them to graze freely . Arliss left Kipper in the meadow with the horses.

The weather was midland there was plenty of field mice available. She knew that he would fend well for himself, as it was not uncommon at home for Kipper to disappear for days at a time and to return from his adventures with nothing worse than a few burrs stuck to his fur.

Kipper however was not too keen on the idea of being left with the horses, and he showed his disapproval by tilting his head up and fixing Arliss with a frosty stare and letting out a loud bad tempered yowl.

They took the time to leave the ship in good order, coiling lines, furling sails, and stowing away gear, cleaning out the bilge and battening down the hatches to secure the ship against any inclement weather while they were gone.

They were finally ready to leave just at sunset. Arliss felt a certain regret at leaving the ship, as it had been her home for almost two weeks and Camden cove seemed a world away, which it was. The four of them got into one of the ship's small rowboats. And as the oars dipped silently, through the water, the full moon rose over head. Swiftly they glided over the water back toward the entrance to the strait.

Then suddenly Farin pointed up toward the chalk cliff as he cried out in surprise," Look up at the temple! "

Arliss and turned quickly and looked up toward the temple, it was engulfed in white light, and it stood like a large square beacon on the top of the cliff.

"How can that be, the Island is inhabited," said Striker mystified as he gazed up at the temple.

Whapper without breaking the rhythm of his rowing, turned and looked upwards toward the cliff, and said, "Poseidon's temple has eternal lamps that come on at dusk. The lights can be seen for miles around."

A few moments later as they neared the strait entrance, Arliss looked ahead, through the strait to the King's gateway, where she could see the profiles of the chalk statues, of Poseidon, and the mermaids, and dolphins, outlined in the moonlight against the navy sky. Then suddenly without warning, Striker lifted his oars out of the water, and gestured for them all to be quiet. In the sudden intense silence, the little boat continued to drift into the shadowy entrance of the strait.

As Arliss listened intently, she became aware of a faint far off rhythmic creaking, that grew steadily louder, and another sound, like the distant wailing of the wind. But as the wailing grew louder, Arliss with a hollow sinking feeling in her gut, realized that the wailing had an awful familiarity about it.

Then her heart quickened, and she caught her breath, as she with sudden alarm, she knew without doubt, that it could only be, the chant of the Carnumbra!

In the same instant, a tall black shadow slid across the King's gateway, and a serpentine prow of a dark galley appeared in the gateway.

"Urage!" gasped Arliss in horror.

Chapter Seven
Under The Sea

There was a moment of stunned horror in the little boat, as the terrible name that Arliss said, still rang in the air. Urage had finally caught up with them, and now that it had happened, it seemed that it had been inevitable, but On the Whisper, with miles of open sea in every direction, Arliss had been lulled into a false sense of security, and the cloying pervasive dread, that she had felt since her first confrontation with Urage, had finally left her. But now in a sudden rush, the dread once again engulfed her, this time more strongly than ever.

Speechless she watched as Striker, with beads of sweat coming from his upper lip, pick up his oar as he cried, "Quick Whapper, let's get this boat turned around and head to shore!"

He then began swiftly digging his oars back into the water. Whapper had blanched and there had been a sudden wild look in his eyes, when he had heard Urage's name, but he complied immediately with Striker's command and, although there was a fine tremor in his legs as he rowed, his stokes were smooth and powerful.

Farin looked shaken, as he said ruefully, "How could he have found us so quickly, the Cascall sea is vast."

Striker glanced up toward the lit temple and said bitterly "They've been drawn here, like moths to the flame."

As Striker and Whapper furiously rowed the little boat out of the strait, and back into the cove, the dark galley entered the strait.   Arliss cringed, and felt her flesh crawl as the inhuman chants of Carnumbra bounced like an unholy litany, off the steep walls of the strait. "Our best chance is to try to make it to the cliff shore below the Temple," said Striker, his voice straining as he rowed hard. Whapper grunted in agreement, and said "If we go up the steps to the temple, we can enter the water on the other side." "Why can't we ditch the boat and swim underwater through the strait" asked Farin with his eyes riveted on the entrance to the strait." "We could do that." said Striker hurriedly, as he glanced nervously over his shoulder while he rowed," But I think we would be taking a great risk getting that close to Urage with a Poseidon band on. He already has great powers of discernment and we are even more open to him, with the

Poseidon bands on." The chants now echoed loudly out, from the strait across the still waters of the cove. Numb with terror, Arliss was afraid to look behind her, for fear of what she might see and despite the speed at which they sped across the water, she feared they wouldn't make it to the shore in time.

It seemed an eternity, when at last, they reached the base of the chalk cliff. With almost frantic speed, they jumped ashore and tied the boat up at a small jetty, in the shadows not the cliff stairway. Just as they were heading for the stairway, Farin, whispered urgently," Look here it comes!" Awestruck, Arliss stood, with Striker, Whapper and Farin in the shadows of the stairway, and stared in fascination, as the long black galley drifted out of the strait into the moonlit cove. Long oars, on either side of the ship, dipped and pulled through the water in unison to the Carnumbra's chants. The galley had one mast with a single large black sail, and at the top of the mast, flew a pennant. "The black heart with the flame in it, how fitting." said Striker sardonically.

The long boat glided into the center of the cove. Smoky torch light burned on the deck, and standing at the helm was a dark figure. '

Arliss caught her breath, "It was Urage!"

"Get down! warned Striker, as Urage, raised a spy glass to his eye, and began scanning the temple and the cliff walls with it.

For long seconds Arliss lay face down in the shadows, not daring to raise her head. Then the chanting stopped, and from the galley, a cry went up and Arliss held her breath.

"They've spotted the Whisper," said Striker softly.

"While they are distracted, we've got to make our move. Now when I 'give the signal head for the stairs."

"Now!" whispered, Striker urgently, as he rose up from the shadows and sprinted toward the stairway.

The others were quickly behind him as he took the cliff stairs two at a time.

The steep cliff stairs smelt musty, and were damp and slick underfoot. Arliss could hear Whapper's feet slapping against the steps, as he quickly though awkwardly mounted the stairs behind her. Already Striker had reached the first landing of the stairway with Farin just a few steps behind him. As they both crouched down behind the solid stone railing of the stairway, Striker signaled down to Arliss and Whapper, who were still flying up the stairway, to drop down behind the railing out of sight.

Keeping below the railing, Arliss and Whapper continued their ascent, until they at last reached the first landing. Exhausted with the steep sprint, Arliss slumped gratefully down behind the stone railing next to Farin. Her chest burned with pain and the backs of her legs ached and as the thudding of her heart slowed, she heard from down on the water, a few strident voices calling out to one another.

Then there was for a moment perfect silence and then what she thought was Urage's voice, she couldn't be sure because it had a hollow quality, as it bounced across the water.

"They have pulled up along side of the Whisper, on the other side of the cove." said Striker quietly, as he peered down over the railing.

Then from across the cove there was the sound of running footsteps on the galley deck, and then heavy metallic clanging and groaning, punctuated finally by a sudden big splash.

"The anchor," said Striker softly.

Then as he peered again over the side of the railing, he said. "They're off loading their horses and hellhounds. Some of the Carnumbra are already mounted and are heading inland." said Farin,

"If they make search of the other side of the island, it should give us time to make our escape."

"Don't forget though," warned Striker," That there is a pathway that leads around the cove up to the temple."

Arliss cautiously knelt up, and looked over the stone railing of the landing, down across the cove at the galley. There were many of the Carnumbra milling around the deck, and she caught her breath when one of them turned his red eyes in their direction. She ducked quickly down, and when she looked a moment later he had turned away. "Come on now, we have to hurry!" urged Striker as they started up the stairway again.

They kept low as they flew up the steps, reaching the second landing, they paused for a brief rest. The stairway again had changed direction, and as they were just about to start up the last flight of stairs, a shout went up, from down on the water, stopping them in their tracks, Striker groaned and said grimly, "It looks like we've been spotted."

Farin was the first to move as he ventured a look over the railing. He jerked head back down almost instantaneously as he gasped

There are mounted Carnumbra heading up toward the temple, but not only that, they've launched a dozen long boats, manned with more Carnumbra, and they're heading straight for the cliff stairway. They're going try, and cut us off before we get to the water!"

"Come on lets go!" urged Striker as he grabbed Arliss's Hand, and began taking the stairs two at a time again.

Farin was right behind poor Whapper spurring him on, with lurid descriptions of what Urage would do to him, if he caught him.

When they at last reached the top of the chalk cliff, Whapper's breath was coming out in funny honking rasps and he looked paler in the moonlight, as if he had lost some of his greenness.

Arliss felt as though she was breathing fire, her whole body was heavy and numb with pain. She just wanted to lie down and rest, but on the signal from Striker and Farin, she and Whapper both sprinted behind them, across the grassy plateau, and into the shadows of the illuminated temple. Then they all raced silently down the slope, toward the water.

Arliss stood along side of Striker and Farin, at the waters edge still catching her breath. She looked nervously behind her back up the slope toward the temple, she wondered what was keeping Whapper. He was just standing there by the shore's edge, with his chest still heaving from exertion, looking expectantly out to sea. When suddenly he cocked his head to one side, and his eyes shifted back and forth, and a then look of recognition flashed across his face as he glanced back toward them and smiled and said," The Children of Poseidon are on their way."

As Arliss stared out across the sea, she saw in the distant darkness the soft glow of yellow lights. At first she could barely make them out, but as they came closer and the lights got brighter, she saw a small group of pale haired, light skinned men riding strange sea creatures. They rode in formation, undulating with an odd rolling movement quickly toward them.

She could see now, that the strange sea creatures were manatees. They were silvery gray in color, with soft loose snouts, and they created a fine spray as they sped rapidly through the water.

Whapper called out to Children of Poseidon, in an odd musical language. It surprised Arliss that such a pleasant sound could come from Whapper.

"Whapper, who are these people," asked Farin, "Surely not Elsaroth's men?"

"No, they are the Queens royal guard,"

A strong faced man at the head of the formation, raised his voice in a commanding manner. Whapper gestured toward him, and said, "That's Gilden Tidewater...Lieutenant Tidewater."

As they drew closer, Arliss noticed that Gilden Tidenwater's eyes were odd, they were the palest blue, she'd ever seen. His thick shoulder length hair was so pale that it was transparent.

Two of the royal guard had moved out of formation, apparently in response to the command, Gilden Tidewater gave.

Whapper watched impassively, as the guards approached him, then Arliss saw a brief flash of silver, as they descended on him in a sudden rapid movement and restrained him, and as she heard the finality of the snap, and click of silver cuffs and chains, there was not one single word of protest from Whapper.

"Now just a minute," said Striker in alarm, as he moved toward Whapper" there is no call for that!"

"I expected this much." said Whapper shrugging his shoulders in resignation.

Addressing Gilden Tidewater, Arliss implored, "Please, can you set him free of the cuffs. This has all been a misunderstanding..."

Her words were brought to an abrupt halt, with an exclamation from one of the royal guards, who was pointing upwards toward the top of the slope. When she turned to look behind her, she gasped. There poised alone, at the very top of the slope, in the shadows of the temple, was Urage!

He was mounted on a massive black horse. His face was clearly illuminated in the flickering light of the torch he carried. But even if Arliss couldn't have seen his face, she would have recognized him anywhere, as his bearing of "brooding power was unmistakable.

As Arliss stared in horrified fascination, an aura of smoky torch light rose up in the darkness behind Urage, as swiftly and silently, the Carnumbra, and hell hounds joined him at the top of the slope. Then suddenly from the top of the hill, came a single inhuman whoop, that shattered the taut silence. It was immediately answered by a chorus of shouts, cries, and howls as Urage and his minions, began flooding rapidly down the slope toward them.

Then in a sudden forward thrust, Urage broke away from the ranks of minions and hurtled at breakneck speed toward Arliss. A dark scowl crossed Urage's face, as he locked eyes with Arliss. The hot burning of the Glasstarr amulet on her chest, finally broke the thrall and she was still in the act of turning, when she was not too gently grabbed, from behind, by Lieutenant Tidewater, and heaved on the front of his manatee. In a matter of moments, she was heading rapidly out to sea, held fast by the leader of the royal guard.

A torrent of flaming arrows whizzed by them as Arliss as she cautiously ventured a glance over her shoulder, she was relieved to see Striker, Farin, and Whapper, were each mounted behind a royal guardsman only a short distance behind her.

When at last they were out of range of the flaming arrows. Gilden Tidewater brought his manatee to a complete halt in the water, and they waited while the other guardsmen caught up with them. Then Gilden Tidewater uttered a few staccato sounds, and immediately all the guardsmen fell into rank behind him. Then moving up ahead, he issued another command, and then tightening his grip on Arliss he made a clicking sound with his tongue and immediately they dove beneath the surface of the water. Suddenly they were rushing down, through cold murky water. It was so abrupt Arliss had to fight back the panic she felt, and allow herself once again to grow used to the Poseidon band. Her legs felt slippery, on the creature back, a sudden turn would have been enough to unseat her, so she was grateful for Gilden Tidewater's steady grip holding her securely on.

It had been another close call with Urage, she thought as they sped deeper into the sea. She couldn't get his face out of her mind. That twisted leer or how his eyes bore through her, seeing every flaw and every weakness. She was out of his reach for now, but for how long How long would her luck hold up.

A pleasant melodious voice sounded in her head interrupting her grim thoughts. "My name is Lieutenant Tidewater, at your service Princess Arliss,"

She was again taken off her guard and she said, "I wasn't sure we would be able to talk to each other as you were speaking a different language on the surface.

"The Poseidon band that you are wearing, it's power is more concentrated in the water, so you can even understand the language of the people of the city of Poseidon."

Glass balls of different sizes, and encased in net and filled with yellow light, were attached by strings to loops in the saddles of the manatees. Gilden Tidewater referred to them as float lights. They illuminated their way ahead for a good distance.

"Are we far from Poseidon asked Arliss."

"Not far," replied Gilden Tidewater, "Poseidon is only an hour away.

Down, down they went, scattering schools of curious fish that were attracted by the float lights. Arliss was getting used to the ride on the manatee and had relaxed her hold on its back.

At last they reached the sea floor, large shadowy fish had drawn near them and moved silently around them as they rode along the sea floor. As Arliss strained in the dim light, to make out the fleeting shadows of the fish, that brushed lightly against her, away in the distance darkness, she saw a violet haze rise suddenly up from the sea floor. When they drew closer she could see that the violet haze was taking shape.

"So this is Poseidon!" thought Arliss as she gazed in amazed wonder at the cluster of huge translucent violet domes, that rose up from the sea floor, with the largest of the domes, at the very center of the cluster. It reminded her of a huge upside down pudding mold.

Within a short while they reached the outside of Poseidon, and Gilden Tidewater swung quickly down toward a gateway, that was cut into the base of the outside wall of one of the domes. He said, "They are expecting us at the main water lock at the portico gates. "Schools of sculpted metal dolphins decorated the two large grid iron gates, that swung silently open, at their approach.

Arliss hung onto Gilden tidewater as he urged the manatee through the grid iron gateway, into a wide stone waterway. The waterway, was lit in a soft shadowy light that gave everything a violet gray cast. They swam rapidly through waterway. Then abruptly Gilden Tidewater reined the manatee upwards and they broke through the surface of the water into a large rectangular pool.

There was the sound of running feet and the clamoring of a bell nearby. And behind Arliss and Gilden Tidewater, the float lights popped up through the water and bobbed on the surface, as the royal guard continued to surface in an orderly fashion. Arliss noticed that their clothing, when they surfaced was perfectly dry. The water just beaded off 'the material of their uniforms.

Arliss let out a sigh relief when she spotted both Striker and Farin surfacing one after the other behind their riders.

A dusky purple sky glowed softly overhead as Arliss pushed back her wet hair, and looked around her. Low buildings on three sides of the pool along with a portico gateway, formed a grassy quad. Ahead of her, in the twilight, across the expanse of smooth lush lawn , and beyond the iron portico gates, was a dark rolling meadow through which a broad empty road cut a swath through, as it rose steeply, to meet the purple horizon.

As Gilden Tidewater nudged his manatee up along the edge of the pool, he said "This is the main portico water lock. If we had gotten to Poseidon before dusk, we could have gone straight through to the palace water lock. But every water lock in the city closes at dusk and won't open again till daybreak."

With ease Gilden dismounted and he turned and gave Arliss a hand as she slipped of the manatee onto the grass.

Striker and Farin had quickly joined her, and like her they were both soaking wet. Striker looked ill at ease, and out of his element. He said nothing but, Arliss noticed that his hand was never far from the hilt of his sword and he watched Gilden Tidewater very closely. Even though Farin, smiled at Arliss, his eyes looked guarded and then without looking at her, he said under his breath, "Be on your guard, keep wind singer ready, who knows what kettle of fish we've wandered into."

The three of them watched as Whapper was quickly led off. Arliss, shivered as the cool night air chilled her. She wondered, nervously, what would become of Whapper. They had tried to intervene with Gilden Tidewater, but he merely shrugged and said it was out of his hands.

As Whapper was hurried across to the grass to the barracks to the right of the pool, he turned quickly before he disappeared through the barracks doorway, and caught Arliss's eye and winked.

"We don't get too many visitors from above the sea." said, the royal guardsman, as he led them into a long low fieldstone lodge that was opposite the portico gate.

The inside of the lodge reminded Arliss of an old English inn, it was dimly lit with dark polished woodwork and paneling against whitewashed walls.

They were each given dry bundle of clothes and a place to change.

Arliss donned the simple soft blue riding habit. that she'd been given, and pulled on a pair of soft silvery gray riding boots. The texture of the leather of the boots had felt strange to her, it was unlike any leather she had seen before, layered and brittle and opalescent. At last dressed, she returned outside, grateful to be warm and dry again.

She found Striker and Farin waiting, they were dressed in dry tunics and cloaks. Farin was scrutinizing the gray boots he wore they looked very similar to the ones that she had on. When he saw her he glanced up and grinned, then with a twinkle in his blue eyes, he pointed down to the boots, "They're not leather, you know."

As she responded with a quizzical look. He said," They're fish skin I think, and they're really quite comfortable."

The three of them quickly mounted the horses that had been brought around to the front of the lodge.

Moments later, Gilden Tidewater rode up, with a small number of mounted royal guard behind him and as he drew up alongside of Arliss he said." Princess, If you're ready we will go up to the city."

He gestured toward the portico gateway and said "The Queen anxiously awaits your visit."

Striker's face had hardened on Gilden's appearance. Arliss flashed Striker a look of inquiry he turned and glanced at Farin and then gave her an almost imperceptible nod.

With a dark purple sky overhead, they set off through the portico gates up the narrow road toward the city at first they could not see anything, except the dark road ahead. Gilden said the city lay over the next hill.

When they reached the summit of that hill, Arliss stopped in her tracks, as before her, in the distance rose the walled and terraced city of Poseidon. The city was lit up, and it sparkled like a jeweled crown in the night.

Upon seeing Arliss's amazement and wonder, Gilden Tidewater smiled and drew his horse up alongside of her, and said, "Poseidon is not unlike many Eartheart cities above the sea. Legend has it that a long, long, time ago, before written memory, Poseidon too, was a city above the sea on a small isle not unlike Thalassa where Poseidon's temple is, and that it sank into the sea after a black day when Eartheart trembled.

He then pointed straight ahead in the distance toward the highest point of the jeweled crown, "That's Castlehill, the highest point in the city," he said smiling at her look of amazement. As she looked toward the top of the hill of the city. She could see rising high above the rest of the city a castle with soaring turrets.

"Come, the queen awaits." said Gilden as he urged his horse forward, and they all followed quickly behind him, as he began to canter quickly down the road toward the gates of Poseidon.

A short time later they arrived outside the two large studded oak gates of the city of Poseidon. The purple dome overhead had deepened and darkened now to an almost blackness.

"Pull those hoods up and keep your heads low," ordered Gilden as he knocked on a small door cut into one of the bigger doors. Striker's face, it looked like thunder as he hesitated briefly before he complied to Gilden's order.

"Who goes there" came the voice of the sentry. Upon Gilden identifying himself, the small door was immediately flung open. Once through the gate, they found themselves amongst a throng of milling people.

"This is the lower city," said Gilden, as they began riding up a torch lit street, that rose up steeply toward castle hill. The lower city, although crowded and somewhat seamy in places, but had a decided cheerfulness about it. There were many narrow streets and lanes with rows of tiny stone houses intermingled with many little shops and taverns and a few dilapidated inns.

The streets themselves were filled with hawkers and peddlers. And as they rode by, carts piled high with warm floury loaves of bread, and carts with smoked fish hung on strings like elongated gold medallions. The savory faintly sweet aroma. suddenly reminded Arliss how hungry she was.

She had noticed, that there were few people, like Whapper, amongst the crowds. When she ask Gilden about this and he said, "Whapper, as you probably know, is from a very ancient race of people called the Cascallanians. It is said they were here long before the Children of Poseidon. They live for the most part outside of the city in extended family tribes, in nearby coral caves. Their society is different from ours, some say better than ours, more in concert with the sea. Over hundreds of generations, our races have become interdependent. Most Cascallanians enter the city only on market day, to ply their wares and purchase supplies, but many like Whapper, have made their lives in the city."

The gate into the middle city, swung open at their approach. It was obvious that they were expected. The neighborhood past the second gate was a striking contrast from the bustling vibrant and somewhat seedy lower city, instead once past the second gate, there were lovely mansions set back on beautifully kept lawns. There was not too much foot traffic up here, just the occasional carriage or so. The road now had become extremely steep as Castle hill drew closer.

As they neared the top of the hill Gilden frowned as he reined his horse in front of a particularly elegant mansion which in contrast to the houses around it, was in complete darkness. Looking at the house speculatively he said, "That's the Dowagers house, home of The old queen and Princess Elsaroth."

As Arliss stared up at the darkened house a feeling of uneasiness swept over her. As the torch light from the street reflected on the windows she thought she saw a shadow move away from the window, but before she could say anything, Gilden had again nudged his horse forward.

"Its probably just my imagination," she thought as she followed quickly behind him.

At last they reached the top of castle hill, and Gilden Tidewater reigned his horse where the road ended in front of a wide moat as the drawbridge in the curtain wall of the castle lowered.

The high curved castellated wall with turrets, extended on either side of them, as far as the eye could see.

Arliss felt a surge of excitement rise up in her, as she rode over the draw bridge and through the curtain wall, and out into a broad meadow.

There in the darkness, on a rise stood the palace. It took her breath away, as she gazed at the tall graceful facade. A light burned in every window of the palace. Clusters of long elegant towers with spires rose above a tall steeply slanted green tinged copper roof piercing the velvet darkness of the purple domed sky.

As they approached the entrance to the palace dozens of liveried footmen poured out from the entrance.

Once in the palace, Arliss got only a fleeting glance of the vaulting marble foyer, with its grand staircase, as they were led quickly into a drawing room to await the Queen's arrival. Here Gilden Tidewater, bowing low, politely and formally took his leave. "Arliss," said Striker frowning as the door closed behind Gilden. "I have grave reservations about coming here. I don't think Mallwynn could have known how tense things are here, or I think he would have advised against our coming."

Striker rose to his feet, and began pacing back and forth and as he paused for a moment in front of them, he said, "If you ask me we were practically smuggled into Poseidon."

"Yes," said Farin thoughtfully." The usual pomp and formality was noticeably absent."

Arliss who had said nothing hesitated and asked, "Do you think this a trap we've wandered into."

She remembered how she had thought it strange that Gilden insisted that they keep their heads lowered as they came through the lower city. But there had been something forthright and honest about Gilden that had made her comply without question.

"No," said Striker firmly, "Mallwynn would have had an inkling if the Children of Poseidon had planned to betray us. I don't think Amarin would dare to cross Mallwynn, but what I am afraid off, is getting in the middle of Amarin and Elsaroth, and I think we should watch our step, very carefully to avoid that. Its my guess that their rivalry knows no bounds and has reached a critical point. That stunt that Elsaroth tried to pull off, sending Whapper to waylay you, may have been the last straw for Amarin."

Striker then lowered his voice to an emphatic whisper, and leaning forward he said, "Whapper said that there were rumors that Amarin was planning on banishing Elsaroth from the city and all who sympathized with her. This could be the start of a civil war in Poseidon."

Before Arliss could take in the full significance of Strikers words Farin had sprung to his feet, at the same time the drawing room door swung open.

An old man wearing a long gray robe with a shock of white hair and twinkling blue eyes entered the room.

"Lathain Ballaster, Queen's equerry, secretary and all together general dog's body," he said with a smile as he reached down and shook Arliss's hand and at the same time taking in Striker and Farin with his penetrating glance.

"Please call me Lathain, Madam, I am here to see to your needs, and those of your men," he said as he gave Striker and Farin a second, more measured look.

Then Lathain straightened up and stood before them with his hands clasped, and for a moment he said nothing as restlessly he wove his fingers in and out, as three pairs of eyes looked on. Just as Arliss was beginning to feel uncomfortable at the lengthening silence, he spoke.

Looking at their expectant faces and gesturing with his hands, he said "I suppose you are wondering about all of this." Without waiting for a response he went on. "Princess, I assure you first of all, that Queen Amarin welcomes you as honored guest. She also offers you her profound apologies.

She regrets that your welcome into the city of Poseidon was not more fitting to the future Empress of Eartheart. The queen has asked me to tell you, princess, that it was concern for your safety that prompted her to take measures, so as not to draw attention to your arrival."

Lathain looked relieved as Arliss nodded in understanding. He then excused himself from the room. They were only alone again, a few moments when the drawing room doors, again swung open and as the Queen entered flanked by guards on either side, they quickly stood up.

The small dark haired woman stood still for a moment, and she frowned and her cool blue eyes narrowed as, she appraised them with one long inscrutable look. Then she reached over and grasped Arliss's hand firmly in hers, and her quiet face broke into a warm smile.

"Princess Arliss, I am so glad that you have come to Poseidon." Still smiling she turned to Striker and Farin and bade them welcome. Arliss noticed that Lathain had quietly entered the room again and at the Queen's signal he approached her with a message, which he gave her in soft whispered tones.

For an instant anger flared across the Queens smooth face, but she quickly recovered herself nodding her head in an accepting manner.

Amarin addressed them again, she said, "You are welcome to remain in Poseidon as long as you like. I know vaguely of your difficulties, we will talk in detail about them later."

Even as Amarin spoke they could hear raised voices in the hallway.

"Right now however," she said dryly, "We will be treated to the unexpected company of my sister,"

The doors of the drawing room were flung wide open and in the doorway under Amarin's pained gaze, stood a tall statuesque blond woman, she stood absolutely still for a few seconds.

Arliss suspected that this was so they would all get the full effect of her entrance. She was dressed completely in pure white and silver. Her skin was white and pink and ethereal, her fine silky hair was gathered up in a silver clip, and it cascaded down her back in loose curls of silver.

And as if she needed any more ornamentation, she wore on her right cheek a small silver starfish that was made up of lots of tiny little diamonds.

"Greetings dear sister I do hope you haven't started the festivities without me." laughed Elsaroth as she flung open her silver lame' cloak with a flourish, revealing beneath it, her lush figure, draped in a diaphanous gown, that was caught at her tiny waist with a silver girdle. And then without batting an eye or turning her head, she shrugged off her cloak. Her man servant must have been used to this habit of hers, as he was in just the right spot to catch the cloak.

Then drawing them up in her gaze, Elsaroth's pale blue eyes widened and she said with just a hint of sarcasm, "So this is our future Empress and her valorous knights."

Under Elsaroth's scrutiny, Arliss felt her face grow hot as, she suddenly felt very shabby and foolish.

"Sister please introduce me to our honored guest." said Elsaroth, Introductions were icily made by Amarin.

It was after a strained supper and well into the evening before Elsaroth finally took her leave.

By firelight in the queens study they had told Amarin their tale. Amarin's quiet face clouded with concern, as she listened without comment. And when at last they finished the tale she said, "Here in Poseidon, we've known of the unrest above the sea, for quite awhile. However it sounds much worse than we expected, and although Urage cannot at this time directly effect us. I find it disturbing that he continues to delve more and more into the black arts, not only because this disturbs the balance on the mystical plane and could cause havoc above and below the sea. But Urage's delving in black magic presents another more immediate danger to the Children of Poseidon, this I will speak of later. "

Then Amarin paused a moment and regarded Arliss thoughtfully. She thought Arliss attractive, maybe even pretty, but the girl was much too lean and angular, to ever be considered beautiful in the classic sense. But there was a keenness in those steady gray eyes that Amarin hadn't expected. There was something very unusual about this girl. She had a strange energy about her, the kind of energy that makes things happen.

Then Amarin's face took on a shrewd look as she said, "Arliss Glasstarr, I think you'll will make a fine Empress. I would like to offer you my allegiance and any assistance that you might require"

Arliss was surprised and flattered by Amarin's comments, and she felt guilty because she had no desire at all to be empress of Eartheart. But perhaps Amarin could help them defeat Urage. Because now she realized, that until Urage was dead she would never have any peace, and with a guilty second thought neither would Eartheart, and it seemed that even down here in Poseidon people were threatened by Urages evil.

Throwing caution to the wind with the decision to be blunt Arliss inquired, "What kind of assistance can you give us," at the same time, she caught Striker's eye, he looked surprised but he gave her a nod of encouragement, and Farin who was beside him, smiled at her with approval.

Amarin too, seemed surprised at Arliss's directness and for a moment or two she was silent. Her eyes clouded with thought, and then she said, "I must of course talk with my councilors, but within our natural limitations, anything you need to fight Urage is yours." "What about men?" asked Striker.

"Can The Children of Poseidon stay on land long?"

"Indefinitely," said Amarin, "With Poseidon bands."

"Oh...," murmured Farin, "And I don't suppose there's many of them laying around."

"Actually," said Amarin, "We do have quite a cache of them, that Bower Darrowg lnn found and brought down to Poseidon with him"

"I thought that there were only a few of the bands," said Arliss.

"Bower never revealed that there were as many as there were. They obviously had been made in ancient times, by a trollish people with the help of a powerful wizard to fight an war between those who live above and beyond the sea, the Children of the Sun, and the Children of Poseidon. There are enough bands for a small army. Enough so that sun children could march on an undersea city such as Poseidon.

There has been no conflict with the Children of Poseidon and the Children of the Sun, in many millenniums. We believed that this is because we exist for most Children of the Sun as mere legends, and myths. Had it been possible for great numbers of sun children to come to Poseidon or cities like Poseidon, there would have been many wars. Queen Kandra swore Bower to secrecy to keep the Children of Poseidon a myth and thus to keep the peace."

Amarin paused for a moment and sighed, and said, "But now I fear that peace may well be gone from Eartheart forever if Urage has his way."

Arliss frowned and said, "do you really expect to be affected by Urage's foul schemes down here?"

"Yes, I think it's only a matter of time," sighed Amarin, "He has known of our existence for some time now. But what he doesn't know yet, is that the wizard who made the Poseidon bands, many millenniums ago, was non other than Erskillon of the house of Black Willow, Urages's great grandfather, who was perhaps the greatest wizard that ever lived.

Arliss gasped as Amarin continued, "The secret to the bands is in a book of magic somewhere in the Black Willow keep. It is well known that Urage is obsessive in his quest for knowledge of the black arts. It is only a matter of time before he stumbles upon the secret of the Poseidon bands.

Seeing the looks of shock and dismay on their faces, Amarin said, "So you see I must do all I can to help you defeat Urage and if I could get my hands on that book it would mean a lot to the Children of Poseidon. I'm going to send with you a special ambassador. This ambassador will be fully authorized to request immediate aid from Poseidon.

Upon receiving word from this ambassador, we will muster any troops or supplies swiftly to any location requested. In return we want the secret of the bands destroyed or put in a safe and neutral place."
"Something in Amarin's tone of voice made Arliss wary of the offer of aid, even though the reasons Amarin gave were sound and reasonable, something wasn't right? There was just something odd in Amarin's manner.

Then without thinking Arliss said, "Just who is this Ambassador?" Lathain who was still at the Queen's side, at this point broke into a coughing fit and had to excuse himself from the room.

There was a moment or two of uncomfortable silence as they waited for Amarin to reply.

Arliss glanced over at Striker he had a distinctly suspicious look on his face.

"My sister Elsaroth, whom you met this evening," answered Amarin finally with a challenge in her eye.

Then turning quickly away from them, she said hurriedly, "I can't think of anyone in my entourage more suitable or in fact more deserving of the honor."

It was Striker who broke the stunned silence of the three.

"I am afraid," he said in a faltering voice, "That a trip of this nature would be far too arduous for .... erh... ahh... so delicate a creature as your sister, if not physically impossible," he ended lamely.

Amarin was silent for a moment while she considered Strikers words. She frowned and her blue eyes narrowed as she again studied Arliss.

Arliss blushed as she realized that a comparison was being drawn.

"Princess Arliss seems to manage," said Amarin at last.

"Princess Arliss," said Striker very carefully, "Didn't have much choice, her life was threatened."

"I agree with Striker," said Farin, "We wish to travel unnoticed. A large party would put us at greater risk of being spotted."

Amarin nodded her head in understanding, but said, "There would be no large party just Elsaroth and her man Whapper."

Amarin's blue eyes became frosty and her voice had a hard edge to it as she said," You need allies against Urage. So of course my sister will accompany you."

Arliss glanced at Striker who's face hardened as he shrugged with resignation.

"All right." said Arliss curtly. Amarin's eyes widened at "the sharpness of Arliss's reply. Arliss felt her body tighten in anger as she looked down at the floor. She bit down hard on her lower lip.

They were in a tight corner with Urage and although Amarin may have ulterior motives sending Elsaroth with them. She had almost as much reason to want Urage defeated. They could not afford lose Amarin as an ally.

Arliss let go of her anger and with a strained smile she said in a conciliatory voice, "Of course your sister will be welcome to come with us."

A warm smile broke across Amarin's face as she said," I have under estimated you Arliss Glasstarr."

Arliss looked at Striker and said "How soon Can we leave?"

"Well," he said, "I think we should make haste as things continue to brew above water. I'd say we could be ready to leave tomorrow after lunch."

Lathain had entered the room once again and was having a long whispered conversation with the Queen, upon it's ending she turned to them and said, "Lady Elsaroth will meet you at the Portico gates tomorrow after lunch."

Amarin rose abruptly nodding her head to them, concluding the audience. She then turned on her heel and quickly left the room.

As the doors closed behind Amarin, Lathain crossed quickly to the wall next to the fireplace and gave the bell pull a tug, which immediately summoned a bevy of house servants.

Arliss, Striker and Farin were led out into the vaulting marble foyer and up the great stair case, up several flights of stairs and down a spacious hall, and as Arliss was issued through one of the many of the identical doorways in the hall, she saw Farin and Striker led off further down the hall and she was suddenly filled with an uneasiness and a longing to be above the sea once again.

The suite was beautiful, even sumptuous. The walls and ceiling were covered in shimmering iridescent mother of pearl. Arliss couldn't help but reach out and touch the pearly smoothness of the walls. Her eye was caught by a large intricately woven tapestry rug, with aquatic designs in soft colors of the sea, that covered most of the room. In the middle of the room was a huge bed, carved in low relief, with sea creatures. Slick dolphins nosing upwards formed the four posts of the bed. Suddenly Arliss realized how weary she was, it had been a very long day.

Violet light drifted in from the tall windows, which over looked the city. Arliss crossed to the window and looked down over the curtain wall, onto the terraced streets of the city. Immediately below the castle, she could see the middle city. There were a few house lamps lit up outside the prestigious manor houses, on the stately upper avenues. Only a little light carriage travel was coming through the gates from the lower city. There were a few foot soldiers patrolling on top of the wide ramparts of the walls that divided the middle city from the lower city.

As she looked further down before the city tumbled down into the farm belt, she could make out the sparkling lights of the lower city.

She was surprised at the longing she felt to go down to the lower city. It had been a long time since she had fun. She pulled herself away from the windows and inspected the rest of the room. At one end of the room there was a deep wide alcove lined with many floor to ceiling glass doors. Outside of the doors was a balcony.

The alcove itself was furnished with a couple of overstuffed couches, and tables with a couple of flickering lamps hanging overhead. At the end of the alcove were two heavy paneled doors.

Arliss tried the handle of the first one and found that it was locked, but the second one swung inward noiselessly, revealing a beautiful cream marble bathroom.

Arliss was aware of a rustling behind her and she turned quickly and saw a large buxom rosy cheeked woman.

She was wearing a crisp white apron over her long blue frock, a white kerchief covered all but a few strands of her silver gray hair. She was carrying a small tray with a covered jug and cup and saucer. She set the tray down on one of the tables in the alcove, she then turned to Arliss and said, "My name is Strezia and I'm here to draw your bath milady."

Then without stopping to draw her breath she continued,

"Your a right pretty young thing, milady, if you don't mind my saying so, have a seat now and I'll draw your bath."

EARTHEART

Arliss undressed and to got into the steaming tub full of silken scented water.

Strezia's motherly running commentary, as Arliss bathed didn't seem to require much in the way of a reply, other than the odd smile or nod of affirmation on Arliss's part, and for this Arliss was grateful as she was exhausted.

After helping her into a long white nightgown, Strezia hustled her into bed like a dawdling child.

Strezia then poured steaming liquid from the covered jug on the end table, as she handed the goblet to Arliss, she said "Now drink this milady."

"What is this?" inquired Arliss." as she sniffed the spicy mixture curiously.

"This milady, is good for what ails yea."

Arliss looked at her quizzically as she held the cup in front of her.

"It's a travelers tonic milady, you know, to revitalize you, for your long journey ahead. Now drink up milady."

Arliss did as she was bid as Strezia looked on with approval. She then showed her the bell pull by the bed for her to ring if she should need anything, and then she left as suddenly as she had come.

Chapter Eight
The Song of the Whales

Arliss lay in the big carved bed, and tried in vain to fall asleep. She missed the gentle rocking motion of the ship, and the sound of water lapping up against the sides of the Whisper.

After tossing and turning for a long while, she abandoned all attempts of sleep, and instead, she began reviewing the events of the last couple of days. She wondered what Mallwynn would have thought of his kin Amarin and Elsaroth, and the fine kettle of fish she and Striker and Farin had landed in.

Where was Mallwynn was now, anyway and what business could he have, that was so important, that he couldn't be with them now, when they needed him so much. Arliss missed Mallwynn very much, she had to admit that, she had found his odd mystical presence, strangely reassuring.

She hoped that where ever he was, that hadn't come to any harm and that it wouldn't be too much longer before they met up with him again.

In the maze Arliss had learned to build a wall to shut Urage out. She had steeled herself not to look at him, and not to listen to him, and above all, not to think about him. But as she lay in that big bed on that strange lonesome purple night, the wall began to crumble and unbidden thoughts of Urage flooded into her mind, and even as she recoiled in fear, for a moment or two, Urage's face loomed before her. And as her guts twisted into a rock hard knot, her mind's eye seemed to draw back and she saw Urage aboard his galley looking through a spy glass, across a dark and empty sea. Instinctively she knew then, that Urage waited for her somewhere above Poseidon City!

With a gasp her eyes flew open and she sat bolt right up in bed. The sound of her heart hammering in her chest, blocked out any other sound in the room. As she put her hands to her face her skin felt cold and damp. She shivered as she felt the bumpy goose flash on her thin cold arms. As her heart beat slowed she reached over in the darkness, fumbling as turned up the flame of the glass lamp on the table beside her.

After several long moments of consideration, she decided, that the "vision" was far too disturbing to leave until to the morning. As she got out of bed and drew on a wrapper over her nightgown, she wondered if Striker and Farin were still awake.

Crossing the room to the door she was surprised to hear the low murmur of voices, outside the door. Hesitantly she opened the door in time to see, the changing of the guard, that had evidently been posted outside her door.

"Does my lady require anything," asked the older of the two relief guards, a grim unsmiling man. Despite the politeness of his words, there was something vaguely threatening about the tone of his voice. Arliss had the feeling that she was expected to go back into her room and behave herself. Feeling a bit foolish as suddenly somehow her "vision" didn't seem as urgent as it had been only moments ago. She was just about to excuse herself and go back into the room, when suddenly she was seized by a wave of dizziness. And as she felt herself sway she put her hands on the door frame to steady herself.

The older guard's grizzled face mellowed, and crinkled with concern as he said, "Are you all right madam,"

"Of course I'm all right I am just a little dizzy, but I really need to see my friends," she slurred indignantly.

The two guards led her back into her room and put into bed, as the guards faces danced before her eyes, she said very deliberately and carefully, "I musth insisth on seeing my friendths right away !"

Then she sunk into black oblivion.

She heard her name being called in the distance. It was too much effort to listen, but the voice intrusively battered at her consciousness. The voice was joined by other voices calling her name imperatively. She opened her eyes and Striker and Farin's faces floated in front of her. Bitter liquid was forced between her lips. Immediately her head began to clear and she recognized the third voice as being that of Lathain Ballaster. She looked from face to face.

"What happened"

"You were slipped a sleeping potion," a very strong one said Striker.

"Nothing dangerous, my lady, just a harmless sedative." broke in Lathain "For which I have the antidote, you were never in any real danger."

"It was the spiced tonic," said Striker.

"We were also given some but fortunately Lathain got to us before we could drink it."

"Did Amarin do this!" asked Arliss incredulously.

"But why" she demanded, as their faces affirmed her suspicions.

"Please don't think ill of Amarin," pleaded Lathain.

"She did this to make it more difficult for Elsaroth to spirit you off during the night."

"I don't Know which I understand least," said Arliss mistrustfully," Why Amarin would drug me or why Elsaroth would want "spirit me off" Its all beyond me."

"I've known these ladies all their lives and I still haven't sorted out all their tangled schemes. But in the interest of time let me explain as simply and briefly as I can. Elsaroth's only chance of escaping her impending banishment from Poseidon city is to prevent Amarin from making the official announcement tomorrow of the Glasstarr heir's visit to Poseidon and the expectation that Elsaroth will accompany her back to the Orchid Valley on state business. Amarin couldn't make this announcement, if in the morning it was discovered that the Glasstarr heir was no where to be found in the palace, and had in fact been spirited out of the city. and worse still, as only a handful of the queen's trusted servants even know you are here, and there is yet no official record of your arrival. The queen would be unable to redress the matter."

Sighing deeply and shaking his head, Lathain finished, "Yes, it would be a very difficult situation indeed."

"And what is your role in all of this," said Arliss icy."

"The Queen mother, is my dearest friend. She asked me to arrange a meeting with you. She wants to meet the long lost Glasstarr heir, the young woman who will be traveling with her youngest daughter."

For a moment Lathain said nothing but just looked at Arliss with a look of entreaty in his eyes.

"And as I am sure you know, a mother's request is hard to refuse" he finished lamely.

It was clear that Lathain was not going to reveal himself any more than he had already done so, but it was also clear that he cared about all three women. Arliss glanced at Farin and Striker and realized that they were all of the same mind, so she shrugged and said, "Well when do we go"

Lathain let out a large sigh of relief and said," Right now, the Queen mother is waiting."

Quickly Lathain led them out through the glass doors onto the balcony. It was cold outside. Arliss shivered and drew her dark wool cape more closely around her. Their suites were at the rear of the palace. There were several stories above them and beneath them. Arliss glanced over the balcony, far below she could see a hodgepodge of tiled roofs jutting out from all angles at the rear of the palace.

"Such a difference," she thought, "From the front of the palace, which was so streamlined and elegant. Then again," she sighed "Nothing here in Poseidon City is what it seems to be."

They followed Lathain single file through the purple shadows as the balcony wound around to the front of the palace.

Above their soft muffled footsteps Arliss heard the distant hum of crickets within the curtain wall of the castle and the soft rustle of the wind through the trees.

They exercised caution as they passed many windows and doors on the balcony, but fortunately all the drapes were drawn and they passed by undetected.

When they reached the front of the palace they moved with more caution, perchance a soldier should glance up and see them and sound the alarm. On the front facade of the palace the balcony was interrupted by a series of three turrets, that were on either side of the entrance to the palace.

As they drew near the first turret, Arliss saw a tiny narrow arched door almost concealed in the curve of the turret. The door looked big enough only, for a child to squeeze through.

She and Striker and Farin waited in the shadows, while Lathain jiggled the door handle, but the door remained fast.

"Its locked." muttered Lathain under his breath as he began searching through the chatelaine that hung at his waist. He drew out a large skeleton key which he inserted into the lock and the little door slowly groaned open.

"Whoa! said Farin straightening out his large boned frame. He was the last one through the tiny door." I thought I might have to grease myself up to fit through."

The turret tower was pitch dark and smelled damp and musty. Lathain paused just inside the doorway to light a lantern. He held it aloft and led the way down a spiral staircase. The lantern lit up only a few feet in front of them as they felt their way cautiously down the staircase, with their feet treacherously dipping into blackness reaching blindly for the angled treads.

From narrow slat windows in the stone wall of the turret they could see over the curtain wall of the castle, to lights twinkling all the way down in low town.

When at last they reached the bottom of the staircase, there was door directly ahead of them, but instead of leaving through that door Lathain brought them around and under the staircase, where bending over, he held a lantern close to the fieldstone floor and pressed the floor in several places. Then as Arliss watched expectantly a large section of the stone sunk down slightly and slid away with a whoosh. Before them was a entrance to a tunnel system that ran under the palace and to several points in Poseidon City. Lathain told them that the tunnels had been in Poseidon City probably from the very beginnings of the city. They were built to allow the royal family, to move in and out and within the city in secrecy, when times required it. The tunnels were so ancient that many of the entrances had been long forgotten.

They quickly descended into the tunnel and made their way down a narrow passageway. Lathain explained in his soft steady voice that his father had shown him the tunnels when he was still a boy. He told them that this particular tunnel was a known only to his family. Generations of the Ballaster family had served the rulers of Poseidon City, and the secret tunnel entrance was passed down from father to son.

They had been traveling for quite a long time, and all the while, the tunnel had sloped more steeply downwards, until at last they reached a door in the tunnel wall. The door was bolted and chained shut but Lathain soon had it opened. The lantern lamp shone in on, what looked like a small windowless room.

A dungeon really, thought Arliss with a shudder. Then she saw the metal rungs imbedded into the wall leading up to a hatch in the ceiling. Arliss followed behind Lathain up the rungs He opened the hatch upwards and disappeared into the blackness. When she reached the top rung, Lathain reached down out of the blackness and hoisted her up the rest of the way. She now found herself in a shed of sorts, with a high ceiling and a cobblestone floor.

She smelt the acrid smell of gun powder, at the same time she heard a rat or a mouse skittering across the floor away from the light. She fervently hoped it was a mouse. When they were all through the hatch, Lathain closed it behind them and because the lid of the hatch was covered in cobblestones, when it was closed, it was invisible to the eye. And unless you knew where to look, you would never guess that it was there. "

"Where are we," asked Striker.

"We're in the lower wall of the city, in an old munitions storehouse for the Poseidon City army, this particular one is no longer used regularly."

"I would think it would suit your needs to discourage use of this store house." said Farin looking around at the few aging boxes stacked haphazardly against the wall collecting dust.

Moments later they were outside in the cool night air, and after traveling down a few alleyways they reached the main thoroughfare of low town. Lathain made them wait at the end of an alleyway, while he made his way through a throng of people in the busy street and rapidly disappeared into the shadows of a nearby building.

Farin muttered under his breath, "I hope that we are not jumping from the kettle into the fire, we have only this fellow's word on his good intentions."

"True enough," agreed Striker.

"But I think its in Lathain's interest to keep the balance of power in Poseidon City, and smooth over any rough edges."

"Yes I agree," said Arliss." And I don't think Lathain would allow any harm to come to us."

The passersby paid little attention to the three of them as they waited in the shadows of the alleyway. There was quite a mix of people in low town, there were beggars and prostitutes soliciting anyone with the least interest. There were also a few minstrels singing and playing some stringed instruments. Off duty soldiers could be seen in small groups looking surprisingly fresh, and awfully young for the hour of the night. An occasional carriage thundered through the street, scattering crowds of people to either side, 0f it, as it rumbled by. The people then flowed immediately back into the middle of the street behind the carriage, like the "back wash of a fast moving boat. They watched and waited anxiously until at last, Lathain suddenly broke through the crowd, accompanied by a small shabby man with a pinched face. He gestured for them to follow him.

They made their way through narrow streets to the central market square. In the center of the square was the low town water gate, the largest water gate inside the walls of Poseidon City.

Arliss had noticed that there were many small groups of Cascallians in the crowds that filled the street around the water gate. She was reminded of Whapper, and she looked forward to seeing him tomorrow and wondered, not for the first time if he was being treated well.

They crossed the market square to a small tavern. A chipped blue sign, swung just above the doorway, announcing, The Flying Fish Tavern. The tavern was between a fishmonger's shop and a greengrocer's shop. The greengrocer according to the hawker outside, was offering a special sale today only, on dulse and fresh aquatic amaranths.

They followed Lathain and the shabby man with the pinched face man into the tavern. The inside was dim and seedy and there was the smell of stale ale and tobacco smoke.

The shabby man with the pinched face strolled up to the barkeep, who was engrossed in polishing some streaky looking glasses, and whispered a few words in his ear. The barkeep immediately glanced up at the four of them, then with a look of recognition, he nodded an acknowledgment to Lathain.

Then he fixed his small shiny black eyes, on Arliss and then with a toothy smile he leered and said, "What will you ladyship be imbibing in tonight."

Before she could answer, Lathain broke in "Just a small brandy for the lady, and ale for the rest of us," and then he added acidly,

"And clean glasses this time." Latvian's nose wrinkled in distaste, as he fastidiously examined his gloved hand which he had ran along the bar. The toothless barkeep didn't appear in the least annoyed even as Lathain remarked, "We should all be thankful, that disease and pestilence has a devilish hard time surviving in ale and spirits."

They stood at the end of the bar sipping their drinks while the roar of conversation rose and fell in the tavern. The barkeep disappeared for a short time, only to be replaced by a younger - not - so - toothless version of himself, who must have been his son.

Clouds of blue gray tobacco smoke hung heavily in the air over the tavern tables. Crackles and ripples of loud raucous laughter rolled around the room. After a short while the barkeep returned and nodded in their direction for them to follow him.

They followed him through a maze of tables and up a steep narrow stairway, up three flights of stairs and down a narrow hallway, into a shabby sitting room. There was a fireplace at one end, and a bay of windows at the other end.

Several trestle tables and benches had been pushed up against the wall. On one of the tables was a stack of grayish white table clothes. Another trestle table was piled high with chipped mismatched crockery.

Over by the bay of windows, looking out, was a small but regal figure. Beside her, in chairs by the window were two plainly dressed women engaged in needle work. They didn't even look up when Arliss and the men came in, but the figure who stood by the window, turned immediately. Arliss was momentarily startled by how much, the Queen mother resembled Elsaroth, except she was older and more soft and faded looking. Her skin was creamy and paper thin and creased around her eyes and mouth. Above her high cheek bones, her blue eyes were astute and genial.

"Princess!" cried the Queen mother in a quavering voice as she opened her arms out toward Arliss. Arliss instinctively stepped forward to embrace the Queen mother. After a moment she pushed Arliss away and took a good measuring look, then she smiled and said in her quavering voice, "My! You are truly a wonderful looking young woman."

Then a strange look crossed the Queen mothers face as she continued to look at Arliss. Then she frowned and sighed, "Its plain to see, that the blood of the old ones runs thickly through your veins, my dear. Your eyes see more than most and your heart feels more than most."

She reached over and grasped Arliss's hands and said emphatically, "Please take care my dear! You will be in grave danger until you have asserted your birthright and gained the Eartheart throne.

Then she faltered and said almost as an afterthought, "Please take care of my Elsaroth." And then she added with a bitter sweet smile, "If she will let you."

They all remained silent for a few moments, as no one wanted to put into words their fears of the dangers that lay ahead of them once they left Poseidon City. And no one mentioned Urage.

Their reverie was broken by a sudden clatter, as one of the Queen's lady's-in-waiting, sewing basket slid off of her lap, and unto the floor, spilling out skeins and spools, of brightly colored thread onto the floor.

The Queen mother watched the ladies-in-waiting scramble to pick up the contents of the spilled basket. After they had gathered up all the contents of the sewing basket, they took their seats and quietly resumed sewing as if nothing had ever happened.

A keen look came into the Queen mother's eyes as she said," I have only limited influence with both my daughters, so except for my hopes and best wishes, the outcome of this, -is entirely out of my hands. The conflict between my girls, grows more deadly day by day. My only consolation is, that with Elsaroth out of Poseidon City, my girls will at last have a chance of avoiding certain catastrophe. Elsaroth's departure from Poseidon City is out of my hands, but be assured, in me, you now have a strong ally in Poseidon city will serve as a daily reminder to my daughter the Queen, of our kin and allies in the Orchid valley. Whatever Poseidon City can do for you, I will see that it is done as long as I have a) breath left, of that you have my words." Arliss thanked the Queen mother, and said with sympathy," Lets hope that when Elsaroth returns again to Poseidon City, things will be different between her and queen Amarin. Then a strange fleeting crumbled sorry look passed quickly over the Queen mother's face, and Arliss knew then, that the Queen mother never expected Elsaroth to come back to the city of Poseidon.

Sounding more confident than she felt Arliss said, "I am sure that it won't be long before we defeat Urage, and we will do our best to ensure that your daughter comes to no harm."

Arliss knew it was wrong to give the Queen mother false hope, but a piece of her believed the words, and still another piece of her didn't see the point of adding to the Queen mother's pain by being bluntly honest about their chances.

As the Queen mother took her leave she gave Arliss some final words of gratitude. Arliss couldn't help but feel a wave of guilt.

How was she going to keep herself alive let alone Elsaroth!

As soon as the Queen mother had gone they left the rooms above the tavern.

They returned to the palace without detection, the same way as they had left it. On the way back to the palace, Arliss had recounted to Striker, Farin, and Lathain her "vision". And she was relieved when Lathain without the least doubt of the veracity of her "Vision", assured her that he would see to it, that a decoy party, would be sent out from Poseidon City, to lure Urage off of their trail.

Arliss had just gotten into bed when she heard the bedroom door open. She feigned sleep, forcing herself to breath slowly and regularly. Through her eyelashes she recognized Strezia's form approach the bed. She collected the empty cup that had held the spiced tonic and left the room quietly.

The fatigue that Arliss held off so long finally caught up with her and she soon found herself plunged into a dark and dreamless sleep.

The public announcement of Elsaroth's departure was made the very next day, and although the Queen in her announcement had made it clear that they would leave with all possible haste. It was not until several days later, that they were actually ready to go. There had been trouble and confusion as to whom would accompany Elsaroth, but Amarin held firm against Elsaroth's wishes, that for now only Whapper would accompany her. She would be given an escort to where the water and land met, but after that they would be on their own.

Amarin had said, that it was much too soon and too politically dangerous for the Children of Poseidon to make any show of force on land. Ignorance of the existence of the underwater kingdom and their people, helped preserve the centuries of peace between them and the men of the land. Amarin had no wish to needlessly jeopardize that.

Although the atmosphere was tense and at times draining, their extended time in Poseidon City provided the party with much needed physical rest. They saw the Queen mother again, but only formally, and no more private conversations took place.

They attended dinner parties, and gala balls, in Poseidon City, and everywhere they went, they were greeted politely, but with much curiosity and a little suspicious reserve.

Arliss was relieved when the day of departure at last arrived. The jealousy and intrigue, that was always just beneath the surface, had grown over tedious.

They were given a formal sendoff from the market square, down in low town at the water gate, Elsaroth put on a good show smiling radiantly, as she opened up her arms magnanimously, to the crowd, the cheers were deafening.

As they approached the water gate. Elsaroth positioned herself just ahead of Arliss and Farin and Striker and made sure she was the first one to mount her manatee. And as she quickly dove through the subterranean gate, there was an even more deafening roar from the crowd. In the palace courtyard they had, had, a more personal send off, from Amarin and the Queen mother. The Queen mother had clung to her composure, her face was smooth and tranquil. The only the telltale signs were, her red rimmed eyes, and the nervous twitching of her hands.

Elsaroth had glared at Amarin and icily refused her proffered hand.

Instead as tears began to roll down her pale painted face, she moaned," Momma...!" and threw her arms around the Queen mother. A deep rendering sigh escaped the queen mother as she crushed her youngest child to her chest.

Elsaroth had quickly recovered herself, brushed away her tears, and had set to work concentrating on giving Amarin, plenty of angry hostile looks. Amarin had appeared unaffected by both Elsaroth's imminent departure and her angry looks.

Whapper had waited for them down at the low town water gate. He had had a guard on either side of him and he was still wearing handcuffs. When he saw Arliss he flashed her a brilliant smile.

He still appeared unperturbed by his situation. Arliss noticed that he, like Elsaroth, was wearing a Poseidon band. Arliss had once again, asked the guards to release Whapper from the handcuffs, but she was informed politely but firmly that on the Queen's orders they were not to release him until the sea met the land. Arliss didn't press the issue any further.

They were accompanied through the water lock, and out into the sea by a small battalion of men.

It took a while before Arliss's eyes became adjusted to the dimness of the water. The drop in temperature was very perceptible but strangely enough not uncomfortable.

Behind them, the city of Poseidon City grew smaller until it disappeared completely from sight. The glow lights, lit the way ahead as the manatee rapidly drove through the water.

With her hair streaming behind her, Arliss clung to the reins and leaned forward on the saddle of the manatee, and hugged the silvery beast's flanks tightly with her knees. She was enjoying the ride, now that she had decided that she probably wouldn't fall off after all.

After a while, they began traveling upwards toward the surface of the sea. When suddenly they came upon a large school of whales. Gilden Tidewater motioned for them to stop. They reined the manatees and pulled them off to the side and watched in fascination, as the majestic creatures slowly sailed through the water. As they slid silently past them like huge living walls of shadows. Arliss could almost reach out and touch their sleek bodies and although they were so close, the whales did not acknowledge their presence.

As she watched in rapt pleasure she could not comprehend fully the scale of the magnificent mammals. They were larger than anything else in the sea and she suspected, larger than most things on Eartheart. Then above the soft murmur of the people around her she heard the rise of a harmonious heart sweet song, picked up and returned by many deep hollow voices. It was the whales!

They were singing to each other, Arliss was astonished, and when she glanced a Gilden Tidewater, he just nodded knowingly. The haunting melody had a powerful effect on her, she got a lump in her throat and her chest felt tight and filled with a strange joy.

She glanced at Farin his eyes looked glassy, but when he noticed her looking at him, he stared intently downward. Striker was leaning over his mount with his chin resting in his hands, his fingers spread out shielding most of his face.

Arliss was surprised to notice that even Elsaroth's face had softened a little from its usual haughty skepticism, but it was she who broke the thrall, when with her voice heavy with sarcasm, she said, "Well are we going now, or will we wait until the fish stop singing."

"Mammals," said Arliss automatically.

No one appreciated Elsaroth's remark but they did get back rapidly underway.

Arliss had wrestled with herself not to wring Elsaroth's neck," At least not right now," she told herself, "We don't have the time." They quickly sped through the water and before long they neared the place where they had first entered the water.

Arliss began to worry about Urage, had he been lured off by the children of Poseidon or would he be waiting for them when they emerged from the water.

"Don't worry," said Whapper, it would be very unlikely for Urage to wait for us on the island on the off chance that we would return for the ship and the horses."

Arliss felt herself color up as she realized Whapper had read her thoughts. Realizing his gaff, Whapper smiled sheepishly and said, "Sorry."

She then vowed to shield herself more carefully in the future, "It was bad enough that Whapper was picking up on her thoughts, but she damn well didn't want Elsaroth the princess of pandemonium sharing her thoughts."

Then without warning a smirking voice insinuated itself into her mind, she recognized Elsaroth, as she taunted, "Your just not that interesting, terranean, so don't fret."

Repelled by the intrusion, Arliss instinctively reached down within herself and thrust Elsaroth's presence forcefully out, as the Glasstarr amulet glowed hotly on her chest, until it almost burned her.

Elsaroth's body recoiled and her head jerked back and in a breathless shriek she cried out, "Mercy! I was only jesting, please stop!" Arliss drew herself back inwards.

Arliss felt all eyes on her now, she wished that she could take back that moment with Elsaroth. She saw fear in the eyes of the others that looked at her. She noticed several of the soldiers taking a step backward, even Striker and Farin looked nervous. It was Elsaroth herself who broke the tense silence.

"What a headache I've got," she said clutching her head looking respectfully at Arliss, and she said, "Does Urage know you can do that? Then without waiting for a reply she, said, "Perhaps we have a chance after all."

They finally emerged from under the sea into the warm mid day sun. For Arliss it was almost like being born all over again as she took her first breath in days. She breathed deeply savoring the moment, but for a while afterwards she felt uncomfortable as she became hyper aware of every breath she took, and at one point she began to worry if she didn't think about what she was doing, that maybe she would forget to breath and then she would drop stone dead, which would certainly please Elsaroth no end, as she would then be free to go home to Poseidon City and torment Amarin. She was very much relieved, when a minute or two later, she finally forgot about remembering to breath and breathed anyway.

The sudden bright light had been blinding but the warmth felt delicious as it hit Arliss's body. She was amazed at how vibrant all the colors looked to her now. The sky was a deep azure blue with a butter yellow sun at its midpoint. There were a few streaks of white at the edge of the sky but other than that it was perfectly clear.

Thera, lay dead ahead, a chalk and green Isle on a smoky green sea.

Within a few minutes they had reached the shore. Here Gilden, at last removed the handcuffs from Whapper's hands. Whapper rubbed his wrist and chuckled with relief. They dismounted from the manatees in shallow water and said their good-byes to Gilden and his men.

They had been given supplies along with Elsaroth's belongings in oil cloth bags. They all carried these bags except Elsaroth.

As Whapper waded to shore, his web feet made loud sucking sounds in the wet sand. He had a look of resignation on his face, as he carefully balanced a small tower of oil cloth bags. "Careful now," warned Elsaroth as she waded alongside of Whapper,

"Some of my finest costumes are in those bags if you drop them I will. have your guts for garters! Mind the shoes haddock head, they're in the top bag! Now just what am I to do if they get wet!"

"Enough!" commanded Striker in a voice like steel.

Elsaroth looked nonplussed, and her pale blue eyes widened in surprise as she gazed up at Striker. She opened her mouth to say something but thought better of it and said nothing.

As Arliss stood on the beach. She heard what she first thought was the rumble of thunder. Her eyes were drawn high up to a sand dune an instant latter Targus appeared up on the crest of the dune. Then moments later more of their horses appeared alongside of him.

"It's strange," thought Arliss," It as though the horses expected them."

As the horses cantered eagerly down the sandy dune slopes toward them, Arliss could see that they were all there, including the pack ponies. They must have fared well on the island as they were all clear eyed and glossy coated and they even looked as if they might have put on some weight.

She shaded her eyes with her hand, and squinted in the bright midday sunlight, as she scanned the beach. The cat, Kipper, was no where to be seen.

She stifled a sigh of disappointment,

"The cat will turn up when he's good and ready. He's probably still annoyed at me for leaving him on the island."

When they came within sight of the dock everyone let out a collective sigh of relief. The small ship was still anchored and tied up at the dock. They were soon aboard the craft and had stowed away their gear. Elsaroth took Mallwyns old cabin, but not without first logging a good few complaints about the smallness of the vessel, and the dearth of creature comforts.

After consulting some charts it was decided that they would sail at dawn the next day. The rest of the afternoon was spent preparing the ship for its final leg of it the journey. They expected to reach the Orchid coast in two days time.

Chapter Nine
Farewell to the Whisper

"Well it's about time you showed up!" said Arliss, laughing with relief, as a loud plaintive yowl, came from down on the dock.

The old orangy gold cat, looked cool and composed as he sat on the rickety dock. The black ticking on his fur gave him a decided exotic look. He was not your everyday tabby, at least he didn't think so. He was sort of a toy version of an extra furry Bengal tiger, except he didn't like to see himself that way. As a toy that is, he preferred instead to see himself as an important beast. Maybe not so ferocious as his jungle cousin, but certainly no less dignified.

As he held his ringed tail behind him, it constantly formed and reformed itself into a loose question mark. Arliss watched, as the cat made a few fruitless attempts, to climb up on the taut line, that secured the little ship to the dock, but the rope was far too narrow for even a cat to walk on.

Arliss put her hands on her hips, and tilted her head to one side, as she looked down at the cat.

"Now what are you going to do You didn't expect the gang plank to be pulled up. Did you know, we are sailing at day break." The cat's eyes narrowed to slits, and for a moment he looked inscrutable.

"And I suppose you expect me to come down now, and hoist your fat carcass back on board."

The cat answered with an affirmative loud throaty meow. Arliss laughed, but she was not yet finished with the culprit.

"What would have happened to you now, if we'd sailed off without you I don't suppose you'd thought of that now, had you the cat now was deliberately ignoring her, he'd turned his complete attention to the task of smoothing the fur on his front paws, with his pink tongue, so that it lay, just right.

"You probably would've had to become one of those lonely feral cats, who live off the land, with no home, no family, and no kibble."

The cat apparently had, had enough of the lecturing, as he got up abruptly from where he was sitting, and began, hissing and stalking up and down the dock.

"All right! All right!" laughed Arliss,

"I'm coming down to get you right now, I promise!"

Later that evening, Arliss made supper with Whapper, he was relieved to be out from Elsaroth's clutches. He told Arliss, that he was tired of being treated like a wardrobe mistress.

They had found a smoked ham hanging in the hold. Which Whapper sliced very thin and fried it in herb butter. Arliss watched in amazement as he expertly measured out whole wheat flour, salt and baking powder and buttermilk. Then dividing the mixture, he kneaded it into several loaves of bread.

"Whapper! where did you learn to do that," asked Arliss, "I never realized that you could cook"

"Well my repertoire is limited to just a few simple things. Most Cascallians can't cook, nor would wish to, we prefer our food fresh and living, when it can do us the most good."

In response to Arliss's squeamish look, he continued,

"Not that we would eat any thing, that you yourself wouldn't eat, but we simply prefer our food alive. Not that I can't eat dead food," he said wrinkling his nose in distaste.

"But it certainly wouldn't be my preference. I'll go over the side later on, and get myself a few fish or something."

"He stopped and took a breath and said, "My mother you know was the Queen mother's cook."

A look of surprise and interest came over Arliss's face. Whapper took this as signal to continue.

"Since I was little, my earliest memories are of the palace kitchen. It was the warmest most comfortable place in the entire palace. From I was a small child, I helped my mother in the kitchen, and worked at other small jobs in and around the palace."

Arliss listened intently, as she as stirred a bowl full of eggs, to make scrambled eggs. Whapper had gotten the whole eggs in their shells out of a barrel of gloppy liquid in the hold.

She looked over at Whapper as he slid thick slices of cooked potatoes into a skillet with more of the herb butter. He cleared his throat and continued. "Few Cascallians hold as elevated a position, in Poseidon City as I do or rather did before my current trouble," shrugged Whapper with a look of regret.

"I was able to get on, "because I had learned to read and write. I was given this opportunity by Elsaroth."

As Arliss's eyes widened in surprise as Whapper continued.

"You see when Elsaroth was a child, she refused to attend school without a manservant, which she decided was going to be me. She could see no reason, why I should be able to hang around a warm kitchen, while she was confined to a drafty school room, burdened down with arduous academics."

He paused as he carefully turned the potato slices over in the skillet to brown on the other side. "By the time the novelty of having me in the classroom had worn off. I had begun to enjoy learning, The challenge of it pleased me. When Elsaroth realized that I actually enjoyed the classroom, she began to blackmail me. She threatened to have me thrown out of the classroom forever, unless I obeyed her every whim and told no one."

Here Whapper paused with sighed and rolled his eyes upwards and said with a wry grin, "So, as you can imagine I've done a lot of disgusting, embarrassing and silly things."

Arliss helped Whapper bring in the laden steaming plates, and they all sat down together, even Elsaroth who had finally emerged from out of her cabin at the sound of the dinner gong. She looked as if she were dressed for a state dinner, she wore a silver beaded gown cut low with a black feather boa.

Arliss glanced down at herself to remember what she had on. They ate the meal with relish, washing it down with pitchers of ale and cider.

Despite her slim and delicate appearance Elsaroth ate like a ditch digger. After everyone had ate their fill even Elsaroth and everything was cleared away, except the ale and the cider, they began to discuss their plans.

"As you know," began Striker, "We'll hopefully reach the Orchid coast the day after tomorrow, that is barring any foul weather."   Farin looked thoughtfully at Striker and said, "Once we hit land, we'll be more vulnerable to Urage than ever. "

"That's true," agreed Striker, glancing from face to face.

"That's why I am proposing this plan, which I think will confuse Urage."

Then he unfurled the rolled up map that had been at his side all during dinner.

"On this map as you see," said Striker," Pointing to a position in the Cascall sea.

"We are right here now, and in two days time, we should be here."

He said pointing now, to the Orchid coast.

"The Orchid coast is one of the most indented coastlines on Eartheart, it's full of small harbors and tiny coves. If we were to stretch out straight this hundred mile section of the coast, it would be well over five hundred miles long."

Elsaroth's eyes began to glaze over as she stifled a yawn.

"Well let me get right to the point," said Striker glaring at Elsaroth who by now had abandoned any pretense of interest.

"Urage will be expecting us to dock here at this small village of Cundracarne. Its a small fishing village. A few miles inland from the village is the most direct route up into to the Orchid mountains from the Cascall sea. Here in Cundracarne, is where I am sure Urage will be waiting for us. I propose that we land fifty miles to the north of Cundracarne and make our way in a more indirect route up into the Orchid mountains."

"This Village of Skeghaddie, "said Farin, pointing to a spot on the map, would be ideal."

"Skeghaddie? Isn't that where Davain Drumner was from?" asked Striker. "Yes, that's right. Davain was in my set at Windgarth, but he left early because his father, was suddenly taken ill."

"I remember him," said Striker as he stretched back in his chair and as he did so he noticed Elsaroth's eyes fluttering shut, and a soft, almost imperceptible snore kept time with! the rise and fall of her chest. Striker's forehead furrowed in annoyance, then a mischievous gleam came into his green eyes as he moved closer to Elsaroth, and then suddenly without warning, he slapped both his hands down hard, on the slick mahogany table.

Elsaroth jumped about a foot in the air and let out a shriek as her eyes flew open and her arms jerked inwards.

"Oh did I startle you," asked Striker innocently.

"Sorry."

And then as though nothing had happened, he continued, "Wasn't Drumner's father a ship wright"

"Yes, I believe so." said Farin," I think Davain took over the ship wright concern when his father died."

"Well," said Striker tentatively, "If we could get Davain to find a small crew to sail the Whisper down past Cundracarne and arrange to be seen from the shore. Which shouldn't be too difficult, as I am sure that Urage will have many lookouts posted."

"Yes, I think we can be sure of that," agreed Farin as he leaned back against the alcove seat with his hands clasped behind his blond wiry hair.

"Then I suppose," continued Farin thoughtfully, "They could land the ship in some remote cove and then high tail it back to Skeghaddie overland."

As Arliss studied the map, she glanced up and said, "Wouldn't the crew on the way back to Skeghaddie encounter Urage and his Carneghouls"

"If the decoy works," nodded Striker," That may well happen, but I think their true identity would allow them to pass by the ranks of Urage and his Carneghouls unnoticed."

"That reminds me," said Farin, as he turned to Whapper, "We're going to have to get you rigged out in something that will hide your...ahh, unusual appearance." said Farin tactfully, as Whapper held him in his steady trusting gaze."

"A hood should do it, for your head," said Farin as he "gave Whapper an apologetic look.

"And the clothing should take care of the green skin, But I don't know, what we're going to do about those." sighed Farin looking down at Whapper's feet with a perplexed look of despairing.

"We could try a pair of clown shoes," said Arliss 'struggling to keep her face straight.

"What... said Farin not understanding what she said.

"Oh the cloak will cover up his feet," growled Striker impatiently.

"Anyway, no one ever looks at feet."

"That's not true at all, said Elsaroth shaking her head adamantly.

"I look at feet all the time, you know to see whether someone is well heeled or not. You can tell a lot by someone's' shoes."

"Well he's not going to afternoon tea or a cotillion, so we are not going to worry about his feet," finished Striker dryly.

Arliss lay awake long after they retired to bed. She replayed over and over the evening's conversation. The ragged Orchid coastline had become etched on her brain. For the first time, she realized, that instead of fleeing from danger they were now heading toward it. After a sensation of falling she jerked down into the abyss of sleep.

At sunrise the ship was underway, and they passed out through narrow straight, through the king's Gates back out into the Cascall sea.

As the ship drew away from the isle of Thera, Arliss's eyes were once again drawn to the temple on the cliff. She frowned as she realized that she knew no more about it now, than when she first laid eyes on it, a couple of days ago.

Yesterday afternoon, she had asked Elsaroth innocently what was in the temple, Elsaroth's face had grown suddenly very pale. "Don't ask such questions here!" she had said sharply.

A short while later Arliss had overheard, Striker and Farin talking about going up to explore the temple.

"No! No! No! you mustn't do that, "Whapper had said emphatically.

Then as he glanced up nervously toward the temple, he said, "It is taboo for terranean to enter the temple!"

Striker had looked puzzled by Whapper's reaction, but never the less he said slowly, "Well then we will stay away from the temple, we have no wish to offend our new allies."

And that was the last thing said about the temple.

The two days on the ship sped by rapidly. Arliss and Striker and Farin were kept busy with the shipboard chores, as was Whapper when he wasn't holding Elsaroth's head as she, hung seasick over the side of the Whisper.

They arrived in Skeghaddie late afternoon. They had lowered anchor just as they neared they dock, and pulled into a mooring alongside of a small fishing boat. Farin jumped down lightly onto the dock and tied up the Whisper.

The fishing fleet had left Skeghaddie early that morning and, were not yet back, so there were only a few boats tied up at the dock and most these were deserted.

A cold wind blew off the water buffeting Arliss's face. Seagulls circled high overhead waiting for the next bail of chum to be tossed into the sea. Their screes and cries echoed across the harbor.

From the deck of the Whisper, Arliss could see Striker and Farin further up the wharf, engaged in a conversation with a bent looking old man with white hair and a beard, who was carrying a large hank of rope. She saw the old man turn and glance with interest at the Whisper and then he turned back to Striker and Farin and pointed across the harbor.

A short while later they were tied up at a small dock in front of the neat well kept two story house with front porch. The house was covered in cedar shakes, that were bleached and worn a silvery gray from the sun and the wind.

There were four large sheds off to the side of the house. Outside of these sheds were a few small ships and boats in various states of repair.

Farin rang the bell that was mounted on a post on the dock. As the bell clanged, the place seemed to come to life. Two big black hounds, who must have been sleeping in the shade of the porch resurrected themselves, and came bounding off the porch down the beach toward the dock barking furiously, with their tails wagging all the while.

One of the wide double doors of the shed nearest the house swung open, revealing a tall copper headed man with a small boy at his side, with the same copper hair.

Up on the porch stood a pretty young woman with a baby in her arms. A few seconds past, as the people from the shore, watched the people from the ship. Then sudden recognition dawned on Davain's face. He yelled, "Is that really you Farin Woodrow" as he swept his child up into his arms and strode quickly down beach toward the dock. "Yes, its me Davi," Farin yelled back, grinning from ear to ear," In the flesh."

Farin had already swung down the gang plank and was on the dock with Striker a few steps behind. Arliss hung back with Whapper and Elsaroth.

"You remember old Striker here," said Farin as he mounted the beach toward Davain, "You know he was a year ahead of us at the castle."

"Yes I of course I remember Strongforth. Farin bring yourself and Striker and all your crew up to the house," said Davain smiling broadly and then we can make proper introductions.

Davain glanced down at the young boy in his arms, and over toward the porch where the young woman with the baby in her, arms, stood smiling expectantly out at them.

"As you can see I have folks of my own to introduce, so bring yourselves up to the house, and we'll have a bite to eat, and afterwards a few pints of ale and a good chin wag."

"This is my wife Darrah," said Davain as he led them into the silvery gray house.

"And this one here," said Davain as he tousled the coppery hair of little boy who was stills in his arms.

"We call Young Davi, he just turned four last spring."

The young boy looked first to his father and then to the strangers which he regarded with a steady solemn look.

"Now that's our youngest, Lerona, born this time last year. Gets her good looks from her mother, "smiled Davain as he nodded to the child in Darrah's arms.

Farin briefly introduced Arliss, Elsaroth, and Whapper. Whapper was wearing a very long cloak with a hood that kept most of his face in darkness.

If the Drumners thought them an odd bunch, they hadn't said so, save for the raising of an eyebrow or two at the scarlet sequined gown with the jet black boa that Elsaroth had chosen to wear. It contrasted greatly with the simple blue and white, long gingham frock and white apron that Darrah wore.

Arliss herself wore a mid length green velvet skirt, and matching jacket, which Amarin had made for her, when she had heard that Arliss had come through the well between the worlds with nothing but the clothes on her back.

But both Darrah and Davain eyes had definitely widened when Whapper, upon a nod from Farin, lowered his hood.

Davain made no comment but steadfastly bid them to save their chat until after supper.

Before long they were seated around the Drumners big round table, in front of a deep bow window, that looked out into the harbor.   It wasn't long before Darrah set steaming crocks of savory fish stew down on the table in front of them. In the middle of the table, she put a loaf of farmhouse bread along with a pot of butter, and a block of sharp pungent cheese, and a jar of pickled green tomato relish. Davain eyed Whapper, curiously between spoonful's of fish stew. At last his curiosity got the better of him and as he was about to bite into a liberally buttered slab of bread, he said, "You're not from the south, are you"

After a considering pause, Whapper answered carefully. "The south of What"

Davain looked surprised, and he murmured, "Never mind we can talk about this later."

Arliss watched, as Davain's eyes rested on the slim gaudy form of Elsaroth, who was already on her second bowl of fish stew. Which she ate with a strange mixture of gusto and finesse.

As Arliss felt Davain's gaze on her, she felt the heat travel up her neck till her whole face burned. She bit her lip and looked downwards. Against the backdrop of the very normal Drumners, they must have looked like a troupe of traveling circus performers.

When she looked up again she found Darrahs friendly eyes on her.

"You must forgive my husband's rude stares," he said as gave Davain a playful cuff in the arm. He responded by throwing up his arms in mock terror and cringing.

Trying to keep a straight face Darrah said, "You see Arliss some of us here, don't see anything other than fisher folk."

After the meal was over, the table cleared, and everything was put away. They retired to the parlor which was at the rear of the house. The sun was had set and as darkness gathered around them, there was a chill in the air. Davain built a large fire in the fireplace that warmed the whole room.

Kipper had followed them from the boat up to the house, walking boldly past the two black hounds, straight into the house, where he settled snugly, into an out of the way corner by the fire. Only once Darrah managed to draw him out for a short while, with a little dish of scraps from dinner.

Darrah was putting the baby up to bed. Young Davi had already been bathed, and was awaiting his mother. Arliss was surprised to see how well Elsaroth and young Davi took to one another.

His serious blue eyes were fixed on Elsaroth in fascination. She spoke to him as if he were an adult. And from the snatches of conversation that Arliss was able to hear. Elsaroth was telling young Davi about the court parties that she attended and the clothes she wore. Elsaroth was pleased with her audience even if it was a small one and as for young Davi, Elsaroth's stories were as good as any fairy tale he had heard.

When Darrah came to get her son, she found the four year old curled up beside Elsaroth, fast asleep with his thumb in his mouth. When Darrah returned to the parlor, they all drew their chairs up around the fire. In low voices, Striker and Farin began to relate what had happened to them, since they had left Windgarth Island, and returned to the Orchid Valley.

They had been called to court because the old king was ailing, and it was expected that he would die soon. And with his death they feared, Urage would lay claim to the Orchid throne, and overrun all of Eartheart, with his demonic wizardry, and his army of the undead, the Carneghouls.

The old King had lay on his death bed, the old nurse, Myrtle had suddenly appeared at his door and in one single moment of lucidity, in over twenty years. She told the old King and Mallwynn, that their granddaughter, the Glasstarr heir still lived and where she was.

The king was overjoyed, the pall that had lay on heart for over twenty, was at last lifted. As the king breathed his last breath, he made Mallwynn and Striker and Farin swear a solemn oath, to find her and bring her back, to take her place as Empress of Eartheart.

So they had set off with Mallwynn on a quest to bring the Glasstarr heir. When they came to this part of the story, Davain spoke up and said "I thought that the last Glasstarr died when the old king died."

"We found that not to be the case," said Striker looking meaningfully at Arliss.

Davain let out a gasp of surprise. Before Davain or Darrah could say anything, Striker continued. "It would be safer for the princess, if you were to carry on as before treating her, as just an ordinary girl. Farin and I were charged with this quest by the old King and this is what we deem to be the safest way to bring the heir safely back to the Orchid valley.

It was growing late in the evening when they had reached the part of the tale, where they had landed on the island of Thera. When suddenly, outside, the Drumner's hounds began to bark. As Davain rose to his feet to see what was the - matter. The hounds abruptly stopped barking.

Then there was a hollow rap at the front door, clearly startled, they looked at one another in surprise.

"Who could that be?" asked Darrah nervously looking up at Davain as he started toward the door.

"I don't know he said as he glanced over at Striker and Farin," No one knows your here right"

"No one," mouthed Striker softly, rising at the same time, as he put a his finger over his lips and signaled for them to be quiet. He silently drew out his sword and Farin followed suit. They both crept down the hallway ahead of Davain, and positioned themselves on either side of the door while Davain called out, "Who is there?" "Mallwynn Darrowglynn, Archwizard and head of the kings council of the Orchid Valley."

Upon hearing Mallwynn's voice, Arliss sprung up and ran to the hallway in time to see Davain pull open the door. And there in the doorway stood Mallwynn. His face looked tired and drawn, and his spare frame looked leaner than ever.

"Mallwynn!" she gasped, "Your back!"

Then suddenly shy she was lost for words.

"Yes, I am back," he smiled, with his gray eyes twinkling uncharacteristically in his ascetic face.

Arliss always thought that the smiles of those didn't smile much, were so much more brilliant than regular smiles maybe it was because it took a whole lot more to make them smile.

Striker and Farin, after sheathing their weapons stood in the hallway, saying nothing, their faces beaming. Mallwynn seemed as pleased to see them as they were him. Even Kipper roused himself, from his snug corner to come out and greet Mallwynn, wrapping his thick furry body around Mallwynn's boot leg as he purred constantly. Mallwynn didn't seem surprised, by the presence of Elsaroth and Whapper. He nodded courteously to Whapper, and made polite inquiries of Elsaroth, about the health and disposition of her mother and sister.

Arliss could tell that the Drumners were very much in awe of Mallwynn. From the moment he arrived they could hardly take their eyes off of him, and when they were introduced to him. They looked shy, and unlike their usual selves they were at a loss for words, and barely managed to mumble out a few words of polite welcome.

Farin had once told Arliss that there wasn't anyone on Eartheart who hadn't grown up hearing songs, poems, and stories, about the legendary Mallwynn. Arliss, Striker, and Farin, had many questions to ask of Mallwynn, but he refused to answer any of them, insisting instead, that they continue with their own tale which had been interrupted by his arrival.

With Kipper comfortably ensconced on his lap, Mallwynn drew out his pipe from his cloak, and was soon puffing away on it, as he listened intently, to their tale, only interrupting to ask an occasional question.

Very conveniently, they were at that part of the story, just after Mallwynn left the Whisper, so that he was quickly filled in on their trip to Poseidon City.

When at last the tale came to an end with their arrival in Skeghaddie, Striker began immediately to outlined the plan to send the Whisper down the coast further to the south.

Mallwynn, his pipe in one hand nodded with approval and said, "A very good idea and if my guess is correct there will be no need to risk manning the Whisper on its journey to the south."

Striker was just about to ask Mallwynn a question, when suddenly, Mallwynn stopped him with a raised hand. Then with an agitated look on his face, he sprang to his feet. Staring off into space, he then tilted his head to one side, in a listening manner.

Then a grave look settled on his face, as he turned back to them and said, "Come we have no time to waste because even as I speak, Urage and his minions draw near!"

Suddenly the room flashed with harsh white light and, there was a rip and a clap of thunder.

"Hurry," implored Mallwynn, "He drives the storm before him."

Grabbing cloaks and putting on boots they all except Darrah, who stayed behind to look after the children, followed Mallwynn out of the house down onto the dock. The animals had already been unloaded and were comfortably installed in the Drumners stables. Darrah had taken the hounds into the house. They lay in front of the fire, where they held an uneasy peace with Kipper, who had settled himself up on a high shelf and was pointedly ignoring them.

Before they boarded the Whisper, Mallwynn instructed them to take only those things that they absolutely needed, and to leave everything else in good order.

It had begun to rain heavily, within moments they were all drenched. Davain came aboard to help carry out the supplies, they would need for the next leg of their journey. In a short while, all their personal belongings, which they were taking with them, lay in a small heap on the dock along with the supplies and riding tack that they would need for the trip.

Then Mallwynn instructed them to unfurl the sails and to lift the anchor. Farin was the last to leave the ship he raised the gang plank, and jumped lightly from the deck railings down onto the dock. The boat was still tied up at the dock and was bobbing and straining furiously as the wind caught the sails. The old dock groaned and threatened to give way and sail out to sea with the Whisper.

Mallwynn signaled them all to be quiet and he said, "I can feel Urage, he is very close."

With that, there was another crash of thunder this time directly above them and the skies were torn open, with the momentary glare of white light. Mallwyn raised his arms with his staff in one hand skyward, and began to utter an incantation. It was difficult to hear what he was saying as the wind was blowing so hard. Overhead, fast moving islands of blackness swept across a huge silver moon.

Farin had tossed the line on board after untying the whisper from the dock.

Mallwynns voice rose over the wind, and he brought his arms down in a wide arc. Again from his Staff, blue light shot out and encircled the small ship, until the whole craft, for a few moments was bathed in blue light. Then the blue light faded a little, and then diffused into the air, until it was completely gone. Then Arliss heard Davain gasp suddenly, as every lamp on the ship lit up at the same instant. The ship then rocked a bit and shuddered, and then on its own accord, began to draw away from the dock, and head out of the harbor into the Cascall sea.

Chapter Ten
Alone in the Mural Forest

As they hurried back up the beach to the house there was a sudden sibilant sizzle, as the rain began hammering down on them, in hard stinging beads.

When Arliss reached the shelter of the porch she turned, hoping to catch one last glimpse of the Whisper. She could just make out the ships lights, far out on the dark sea, shining like small blurry stars. She sighed as the tiny specks of light disappeared over the horizon, with the Whisper gone, she felt even less safe.

Mallwynn urged them quickly into the house. Arliss slipped off her cloak, and turned around in time to see Mallwynn, disappear back out the door.

With a look of inquiry she glanced over at Striker. He frowned and shrugged.

A few moments later Mallwynn returned.

"There in no time to flee! "he said as he slid the bolt across the door.

As he turned toward them, the look on his face, caused an intense feeling of dread to rise up inside of Arliss. His eyes had a kind of desperate look, and he shook his head, as if he could hardly believe his own words.

He looked Davain hard in the eye, as he said, "It is of the utmost importance, that no entrance into the house be left unsealed. No opening, no matter how small or inconsequential, must be overlooked."

Pale and shaken, Davain nodded his understanding and he then began leading Mallwynn from room to room.

The night chill had deepened, as they congregated in the parlor around the fire. As the rain beat a steady rhythm against the glass, Darrah drew the curtains, shutting out the foreboding blackness, that pressed relentlessly against the windows.

The easy carefree mood of the early evening was gone, instead a tense silence reigned, broken only intermittently by the eerie echoes of Mallwynns voice as he laid the sealing enchantment on every window and door in the house. The parlor was lit only by the light of the blazing fire in the hearth. Dark dancing shadows played over all their faces. Making them in the dim light, look almost unrecognizable to each other.

Darrah had brought the children back down to the parlor. They were both sleeping soundly, in a warm corner of the parlor, one at each end of a settee.

Mallwyn entered the parlor with Davain trailing behind him. Arliss was shocked to see, how exhausted and drained Mallwynn looked. The sealing ritual must have tapped an enormous amount of his strength. Arliss crossed the room going quickly to his side to help him.

"Over there," he muttered weakly gesturing to the chair nearest the fire. When he leaned his frail body on hers for support, she was surprised by how light and fragile he felt. The vitality that he usually radiated from his face was gone. He looked diminished as if he had lost some of his essential substance.

"Urage will try to gain entry anyway he can," said Mallwynn his voice unsteady.

Then he hesitated taking a deep breath in and said, "I think the sealing spells will hold."

Arliss felt another wave of dread wash over her, and as her gray eyes met Strikers, she knew that he too, hadn't missed the note of doubt in Mallwyns last few words.

Mallwynns eyes unfocused, flicked back and forth as he continued speaking as if he were thinking aloud.

Arliss strained to hear what he was saying above the rising wind, which now gusted strongly, outside.

"The demon will have to decide, whether to go after the ship while, there is still a few hours of darkness left to travel with his Carnumbra, or to stay and try to break the mystical seals that prevent his entry into the house. If he stays he may lose his chance to catch up with the ship and capture the Glasstarr heir. If he abandons the house to go after the ship, he may well have let the Glasstarr heir slip through his fingers again."

Mallwynn was silent a moment or two. Then he gave them an ironic smile and said, "Right enough though, its the old shell game. Is the Glasstarr princess, in the house or on the ship. That's what Urage must decide."

Then Mallwynn let out a weary sigh.

"I must rest now," he said his face gray and, his voice just above a whisper and as it trailed off his head dropped forward limply onto his chest.

Arliss gasped, and her eyes widened. She knelt quickly down beside Mallwynn. His face looked slack and sunken and as she held his limp ice cold hand in hers, and as she glanced anxiously up at Striker and Farin, she said with a tremor in her voice, "Mallwynn looks almost as if he may have died."

Farin looked stricken.

Striker leaned over and put his ear close to Mallwynns chest, after a moment of listening intently he let out a relieved sigh as he said, "He's just deeply asleep."

Farin propped Mallwynns head up while Arliss covered him with a blanket.

The trees outside the house creaked and groaned as the wind began to comb roughly through them. And as the wind gathered up even more power, it gripped the little house and held it tight and just as they thought the house would give way from the pressure of the winds grip. The wind would release the house, and then the house would shake and shudder, until a moment later when the wind took hold of it again.

Arliss stood by the fireplace. She couldn't seem to get warm, she felt like the cold and damp had penetrated her very bones. As the wind grew in intensity, she watched the flames flicker down and flare up again, as the wind howled down the chimney. She had just become aware of a certain familiar hollowness rising up from her stomach, the feeling she got, when there was there was something important left undone.

Something.

What was it?

With a gasp she remembered.

She hadn't even realized that shed let out a sound until all eyes in the room, turned suddenly toward her.

"What is it," demanded Striker, with his voice much sharper than he intended. Arliss looked at him and then with a shrug of disbelief, she said very softly, "Did you notice, if Mallwynn sealed the fireplace"

EARTHEART

Arliss could hear the clock ticking clearly on the mantelpiece as six sets of eyes stared at her in horror.

Then the sudden silence was broken by Elsaroth, who let out a low gut wrenching wail that rose quickly to a crescendo, and ended abruptly when a reptilian hand fastened over her mouth.

Elsaroth wild eyed and struggling as Whapper held her in his grip.

Whapper then put his wide green mouth close to her creamy shell like ear.

"Have you no shame! He demanded in a loud whisper his voice laden with amazed disgust.

Then turning her head carefully, in the direction of the sleeping children. Much more of that nonsense, and you'll wake the children!" he warned fiercely.

Elsaroth voice was muffled as she muttered something over and over again.

"What's she saying?" asked Farin frowning.

And then with one eyebrow raised he said "She going to fry...?" Elsaroth with a maniacal gleam in her pale blue eyes ripped back Whapper's fingers. Then remembering the sleeping children, she caught herself as she clenched her teeth and hissed.

"Die, you idiot! I am going to die! Your going to die! We are all going to die! And a lot sooner than we expected!"

Speechless Farina was aghast at Elsaroth's vehemence. It almost seemed to Arliss as though his wiry blonde stood on end, as he shrank back from Elsaroth.

Darrah and Davain were sitting pale and calm next to their sleeping children. Davain's large callused hand tightly gripped his wife's small hand.

"I've tried to awaken Mallwynn," said Farin a few moments later, having recovered himself, although he still gave Elsaroth a wary glance from time to time.

"He doesn't stir. His breathing is so shallow that you have to put your face to his lips to feel it."

Arliss looked over at the slumped figure of Mallwynn in his chair next to the fireplace. The fire in the hearth blazed brightly. Then above the wind, they heard the hackle raising sounds of discordant voices, and the thunderous rumble of scores of hooves as Urage and his minions approached the house.

Then the storm died down precipitously, leaving a dramatic quiet. Arliss held her breath as she heard footsteps mount the steps onto the porch and stop just outside the front door.

All there eyes were on the front door.

Darrah, held her hand to her mouth, her eyes were wide and staring.

The children slept on.

The two big hounds lay prostrate on the floor whining softly. The cat up on the shelf was poised to spring.

Then suddenly the door shook with a loud insistent rapping, followed by short a interval of silence.

"That's enough Klick,"

There was no mistaken Urages gravelly voice. Arliss watched in horror, as the door knob turned, at first cautiously and tentatively, then upon meeting resistance, the door was yanked in its frame. It was yanked so hard the glass in the door began to rattle but it did not break.

"Klick try the other windows and doors, quickly now! Get some men to help you!"

All over the house they could hear heaving, pushing, pulling, shoving and ramming, but nothing gave way. Urage still out on the porch began to roar and they could hear Darrahs window boxes and potted plants, being shoved off the porch and crashing to the ground. "This is that silly old mans idea of a trick... a misdirection."

There was a long pause.

"He's on the ship with her, while we storm this ramshackle cottage. We're wasting our time here!".

"Sir," said Klick, his voice deadly casual, "Shall I torch the house."

"No... leave it, if they are on the ship I don't want them to realize we are this close to them."

"Sir, just let me try one more thing, there's smoke coming out of the chimney, let me send a couple of men up on the roof and have them throw a couple of pots of boiling oil down the chimney. The smoke will either drive them out or the flames will take care of them inside."

There was a long pause.

The baby stirred fitfully in her sleep, and she raised her thumb to her mouth and began to suck it. Darrah scooped her up into her arms, and began quietly rocking her.

"I'll just give the orders Sir..."

"All right, Klick do it."

Klick sniffed at the same time his lips curled into a satisfied grin.

"Wait a moment Klick, on second thought, we've already wasted enough time here. The entire house is ensorcelled," said Urage decisively, as he glanced up at the roof.

"Come, now we've already wasted enough time."

"Ready the ranks Klick we going to follow the ship. They'll have to land on shore sooner or later," said Urage grimly.

"And when they do, we'll be waiting."

They could hear footsteps go down off the porch and away from the house. They only heard one set of footsteps leave. Urage still waited and listened outside the door. He wasn't completely satisfied that they were out on the ship. After many long agonizing moments, he finally strode off the porch in a resolute manner out into the night.

It was only moments after the sound of hoof beats had died away, that Mallwynn woke up from his deep sleep. He heaved himself out of the chair by the fire and as he leaned on his staff he muttered a few words under his breath and then there was a sudden blinding flash of ice blue light, that disappeared up the chimney. Then he turned from the fireplace and looked purposefully at all of them. "I didn't forget to seal the fireplace, rather than compromise the strength of all the other seals, I took a gamble that Urage would overlook this one. If not I would hopefully be recovered sufficiently to defend this one breach, hence my post next to the fire."

Turning to Darrah and Davain, still looked shaken as they sat with their still sleeping children. Mallwynn said gravely, "Your home is now completely sealed, no one may enter it, unless invited by you, and evil may never enter it."

By late the next morning they were all packed and ready to go. They said their good-byes to the Drumners. Davain said, "Good luck and goody for now. I am sorry that I can't come with you," he said as he put a protective arm around Darrah.

"Not this time anyway, but I can see that a time will soon come, if this beast has his way, when we will all have to take up arms against him or perish."

"Unfortunately, Davain you are correct," said Mallwynn, his voice solemn.

"Eartheart as we now know it, will never be the same again, if the Orchid Valley falls,"

When they set out that morning, the air was cool and crisp, and slightly tinged with the smell of smoke. Overhead the sky was a brilliant blue and the red leaves on the maple trees along the road out of Skeghadie, made a whispery papery sound as the wind crept through them.

They rode hard that day on a path that drew them away from the coast, upland in a northwesterly direction. Mallwynn told Arliss that they were heading up into Mural forest, which was at the base of the Mote mountains. Once through the Mural Forest, they would come to the Great Maudland road. This road ran up and over Mt. Sedwick, the largest of the Mote mountains. They would travel along the it, only to the point where it crossed the North Gate road. This road would lead them straight into the Orchid Valley and the city of Orchidia with the palace of Orchids.

"The Great Maudland road...," said Arliss slowly and then she asked hesitantly.

"Doesn't Urage live in Maudland?"

"That's correct," said Mallwynn nodding his head.

Arliss frowned and bit her lower lip and then with a look of askance said, "This road runs straight into Maudland, where Urage lives."

"Yes, the Great Maudland road is the main road in and out of Maudland. It runs past the northern gate of the Orchid Valley, all the way down to the banks of the Spirit river and the first of the ancient Demon bridges. At this point road crosses into Maudland and runs through center of Maudland all the way to the Fane Sea, to the seat of Urages government, the Blackwillow Keep."

Arliss shivered and drew her cloak closer around her.

"But aren't we taking a big chance, that well meet up with Urage along the Maudland road "she said unable to keep the apprehension out of her voice.

"Of course there is always that possibility," said Mallwynn.

"But I don't think Urage would ever expect us to be so bold as to try to enter the valley by the Northern gate. We will not travel on the road itself, but through the woodlands that runs alongside of the road. That should provide us with plenty of cover."

It was nearing nightfall when they at last reached the Mural forest. Approaching the forest from a distance away, Arliss had noticed nothing unusual about it, but as they drew closer she saw that the forest was enormous. Not only were there a tremendous amount of trees, but the individual trees themselves, were huge. At any moment Arliss would not have been surprised to see, huge squirrels and rabbits, suitable to the scale of the forest, spring out, and pounce on them. Fortunately that did not happen.

Mostly evergreen trees grew in the Mural forest there were many different kinds of pine, balsam, hemlock, juniper, and spruce trees. There muted green color provided a cool contrast to the fiery vermilions of autumn.

They quickly set up camp in a clearing at the edge of the forest. After having ridden all day without stopping they were hungry and bone weary. They ate cold chicken, apples, and bread and washed the meal down with ice cold cider that had been given to them by Darrah and after their long fast it was like a feast.

Arliss lay a bed of soft needles, beneath the huge branches of a hemlock tree. She breathed in the deep heady sharp scent of balsam, that wafted through the forest on a breeze. As wrapped comfortably in her heavy green cloak, she settled down to sleep, and just as she was nodding off, Kipper came up to he and began rubbing his cheek against her face. As she protested mildly, close by she heard the soft nickering of one of the horses. They now had two more horses, mares, that Davain had lent them from his stable, for Whapper and Elsaroth to ride.

Arliss had wondered what Elsaroth would think of her first night sleeping without the benefit of a bed. She had found out when they reached the forest. When Striker had suggested that they stop here for the night and Elsaroth had said blithely, "I think that's a splendid idea!" Looking expectantly around again, she hesitated and said, "Is the inn nearby"

Arliss was just getting up the nerve to answer her, when Elsaroth's smooth delicate face puckered with suspicion as she took them all in with her angry glare.

"There is no inn is there? Am I supposed to sleep out here like some sort of wild beast?" she demanded Angrily.

Elsaroth would have undoubtedly carried on in that manner for some time, only she was stopped dead in her tracks by a heated glare from Striker.

It was doubtful that night after they had settled down as to whether Elsaroth realized just how lucky they were to have the comfortable shelter under the trees but in the weeks to come she would look back and long for just such a place.

Feeling a little stiff and sore they set off through the forest soon after sunrise. The mural forest had another peculiar trait, which certainly made riding through it easier. All the trees were evenly spaced apart and looking past a tree in any direction was like looking down a huge evergreen corridor. The forest floor was springy to ride on and had a sweet musky smell.

Arliss held Tarsus's reins lightly in he hands, it hadn't taken her long to get used to riding him again. As she smoothed his mane, with her hands, his ears twitched responsively.

All around them, the forest was teeming with life. Birds twittered high overhead, and unseen animals scrambled through branches overhead and occasionally in tall evergreen corridors Arliss could see movement out of the corner of her eye and she would turn just in time to see a deer disappear out of sight down another corridor.

Arliss was never quite sure how it happened.

It was twilight and long shadows were growing in the forest. She was trailing a little behind the others. They had been riding all day long now, and she was beginning to feel very tired, as well as hungry. She wondered if they would be stopping soon.

Kipper had been comfortably perched in front of her on the saddle. When suddenly a hare appeared in front of them, it was sitting motionless in the middle of the pathway. Kipper in a flash sprang up on the saddle, poised for action.

Alarmed, Arliss quickly reached forward to grab hold of the cat, but before she could do so, the hare sprang to life and bounded off the pathway, and out of sight, down one of the evergreen corridors. At the very same instant, the big ball of orangy gold fluff was airborne.

Arliss saw it all, as in slow motion. As Kippers hind paws hit the ground first, absorbing the shock of his landing and at the same time, using the power of the impact to push himself forward, as he sped quickly after the hare, looking more like his jungle cousin, than the domestic tabby he was.

At this point Arliss should have called up ahead to Whapper, who was just a little bit in front of her. But in a split second decision, which she would have a long time to regret, she chose instead to pursue the cat.

She felt embarrassed that this had happened, and realized that she should have secured the cat to the saddle with a harness or a collar. As she nudged Targus on quickly after the cat. She reasoned it should be easy enough to catch up again, in this orderly forest. It would just be a matter of remembering the turns she took.

It was only a few moments later when she caught up with Kipper, he was sitting in the middle of an evergreen corridor nonchalantly grooming himself. The hare was no where to be seen. Arliss slid down of Targus, and gathered the cat up and within moments, she was back in the saddle and had turned, Targus around, and was heading back, to where she thought she had left the trail. Nervously she realized for the first time how similar all the well ordered trees were. She had turned right at a balsam but there were several balsams growing in a row.

Which one had she turned at? They all looked identical. So one after the other she began to explore down each corridor that turned off a balsam in the direction of which she came. Until before long, she was hopelessly lost.

As the twilight deepened. She felt panic rising inside her.

She called out several times.

She strained to hear an answering call, but she heard nothing but deadening silence.

The forest had become strangely quiet. Her voice sounded small and wavery in the vastness of the night.

Then off in the distance she thought, she heard voices calling her name, but it could have been the wind, which was now starting to rise.

In waning light, she headed Targus off in the direction of the could-be- voices. She called out again at intervals and occasionally, she thought she heard voices again, but they were always coming from a different direction.

She realized after a while, that she was not going to be able to find her way in the darkness, toward the voices. She would have to wait to sunrise. The prospect of spending the night in the forest alone, did not appeal to her, but as she reasoned to herself, in the morning when the sun rose, she would be able to guide herself with the position of the sun in the sky, along the general route which the party had planned to take. Sooner or later she was bound to meet up with them. She hoped.

Arliss curled up in her cloak, under a giant pine tree, and tried to calm herself enough, so she could sleep but, every time a tree rustled or a twig snapped, she stiffened and listen in terror, for the approach of some wild beast. She kept sitting up and staring into the darkness, straining to see some imagined lurking form, and then she would listen hard to hear above slow chirps of crickets, and the cool wind stirring through the evergreens, almost certain she had heard a far off chant of the Carnumbra. It felt like she was awake most of the night when finally, exhausted she fell into a heavy sleep.

She awoke to sharp spears of light piercing the darkness of the evergreen branches.

She pushed back the tree branches and was alarmed to see, it was well past sunrise. She knew Mallwynn and the others would have been up at dawn searching for her. They might have even passed this way already. She may have missed them. She glanced down at the trail and noticed no hoof prints but then she supposed that on the springy surface of the trail with its thick layers of pine needles, it might be possible that no hoof prints would be left. So that told her nothing. The cat was impatiently padding back and forth, he looked relieved to see her up and showed his pleasure by wrapping himself around her leg and purring.

She quickly gathered her things together and threw the saddle back on Targus and tightened up the girth and was ready to go in a few moments.

She glanced up at the crisp blue sky and decided that if she followed the path of the sun that it would take her in a westerly direction which would follow the projected route that the party had intended to take that day. So she set off growing more confident the further along she got. The cat was firmly situated in front of the saddle. She had constructed a makeshift harness for Kipper and had secured it to a loop on the saddle, suffice to say that the cat, wasn't very pleased with this arrangement.

The land began to sweep steeply downwards and in the far distance she could see it rise again. It was slow and difficult going, as Targus picked his way carefully over the gnarled tree roots which were more pronounced on the slope than they had been on level ground. Arliss suspected that this was due in part to the downward erosion from the rain and other elements, but the forest still maintained its amazing geometric shape, and the massive height of the trees continued to inspire awe in her.

She had been riding for several hours. The sun was now well into the arc of its westerly descent. She had reached the valley and was now starting on the uphill journey. She wondered what she was going to see when she got to the top of the slope. She hoped that she would leave the forest and enter the open fields that Mallwynn had said crawled up the sides of Mt. Sedwick. She knew she had to be careful as Mallwynn, had said that it was at this point the Maudland road, began its climbed over Mt. Sedwick.

It was nearly dusk an hour or two later, when she reached the top of the hill, and to her disappointment, instead of the rolling fields of Mt. Sedwick, there were just more of the same, and by this time monotonous, giant trees, spread out in long infinite corridors. She had no idea when the forest would end as the ground was level and she couldn't see above the trees.

It had been a very long time since she ate and she was past the point of even feeling hungry anymore. Instead, she felt light headed and dizzy. Her spirits had started to sag at the prospect of spending yet another night alone in the forest.

She had just decided, that she couldn't feel much worse, when with a sudden ominous roll of thunder, heavy rain began to fall. Arliss quickly sought shelter under the canopy of one of the giant fir trees. Its branches were just high enough above of the ground to provide her with a perfect view of the downpour.

As she leaned against a sunken hollow in the tree trunk. She watched as Targus from the shelter of the tree nibbled at a nearby clump of grass. Kipper was stretched out idly on a branch overhead. She shivered and pulled her woolen cloak more tightly around her. Then feeling very lonely, she said Kippers name aloud, softly, just so she could hear the sound of her own voice.

The cat sprang lightly down from the branch overhead and stood on his hind legs as he rubbed his face under her chin. As she patted him and felt the buzz of his throaty purrs, she resolved that tomorrow she would climb a tree and figure just where they were. The rhythmic sound of the rain mercerized her as it fell in wavering sheets of silver. Soon she let go and gave in to the sleep, which wrapped around her as comfortably as cotton wool.

When at last she awakened the night was full upon them and in the distance she could hear the far off hooting of a lone owl. As her eyes adjusted to the darkness, she could see the dark form of Targus restlessly swishing his tail, while his ears, twitched back and forth as if to catch a distant sound.

The cat was carefully grooming himself, he looked up and when he saw that she was awake, he yowled plaintively.

"What is it puss!" said Arliss in surprise. Then she heard it, away in the distance. Music!

Chapter Eleven
Strange Omen of the White Owl

As Arliss nudged Targus forward, she watched his ears flick back and forth in response to the distant music, she reached past the cat, and threaded her fingers through his coarse silky mane, and whispered. "That's right boy, its music."

"Come on boy, let's find the music," she encouraged softly. As she rode through the night, she matched her own rhythm with the horse's gait, and before long she lost her sense of time as she rode through the endless shadow filled corridors of evergreens.

The pathway ahead was splashed with dazzling white moonlight, but the trees themselves were so dark, that it seemed to Arliss almost as though they sucked in the darkness, a deep dark textured darkness.

Suddenly above the slow hum of the crickets, she heard an owl hoot. Startled by the strange half human call, she caught her breath and pulled back hard on Targus's reins, bringing him to a abrupt halt. Then for a moment, she listened carefully in the darkness.

Targus snorted impatiently and she was just about to urge him on, when suddenly without a single sound, a white owl swept down through the darkness, coming so swiftly toward her, that she didn't even have time to raise her arms up, to ward it off. For an instant the owl's face seem to hover before her, fixing her with a look of such intensity that it unnerved her, and just when she thought it would collide with her, it swerved, flying so close over her, that she could feel the air move.

Restraining the belatedly alert cat, who was now poised to pounce, she turned in the saddle to watch as the owl lit on the pathway for a brief moment before it took to the air again, carrying off with it, a hapless mouse. Then suddenly without understanding why, she knew that seeing the white owl had been a bad omen, and as she set forth again, she worried not for the first time that she might be heading into even more danger.

As she drew nearer the source of the music, she recognized, strains of lively fiddle music, and the high sweet sounds of flutes, along with many voices raised in song and laughter.

Then leading the Targus by the reins, with the cat slung under her arm, she crept closer to the music. Suddenly, she stopped dead in her tracks, as for a moment she had the distinct impression, that she was being watched.

Then as she peered hard into the shadows and saw nothing she dismissed the notion as mere nerves. The music was now so clear and sweet that she found herself moving in time to it. It was hard to worry about murder and mayhem, when there was fiddle and flute music. Then as she began looping Targus's reins around a branch of a huge pine tree two shadowy figures emerged from behind the tree and descended on her like a black cloud.

She panicked and lost her breath and screamed a silent scream, as behind her, at the same time she heard Targus's frenzied squeals as he reared wildly up and down.

Then a gag was tied so tightly over her mouth, that she felt sure, that she would suffocate, and her arms were roughly pinned behind her and bound with a thin cord that cut deep into her flesh.

Once she was restrained, the hands that held her, released her so abruptly that she stumbled and fell, and when she felt strange hands reach out to her, she began to kick frantically.

In the darkness a hand grabbed hold of her and dragged her to her feet. "So the ganja wants a fight, ehh Well I'm just the man to give him one!" cried an irate male voice as a hard fist slammed into the side of her head.

Stunned, she swayed in the darkness, as she heard another male voice cry out.

"Easy Gerico! Enough of that! Can't you see he's only young lad!"

Then as a strong smelling cloth was forced under her nose, she sank into a pit of a thin endless darkness.

When Arliss awoke sometime later her head ached and she felt sick to her stomach. She was lying face down on damp grass. As she rolled over and began to rub her face, where the grass had made it itch, she was surprised when she touched her face how painful and swollen it felt. Then when she tried to open her eyes, she found that one of her eyes was swollen shut, and the other one felt sticky.

Alarmed and confused she tried to remember what had happened. She raised her head to look around, but almost at once everything went black, and she sank back down into oblivion.

Awaking again a short time later, she managed to open her sticky eye long enough to realize, with a start that she was finally out of the Mural forest, as above her hung vast acres of navy sky, dotted with many tiny white stars, and a moon that seemed to her, strangely over bright.

Abruptly she remembered everything, the music, her capture in the woods, and her face grew hot as she realized what easy pickings she had been.

As she caught a sudden whiff of smoke, she propped herself up, on one elbow, and saw a large campfire nearby that had almost burned down. Then as she looked beyond the campfire, in the distance, over a rolling hill, she could see the edge of the Mural forest. Even from this distance the huge trees, made her feel small. And then as her head began to swim, she slumped back down again, and retreated into the darkness.

As she drifted in and out of wakefulness, sudden breezes would bring a little of the fire's warmth her way, along with gusts of thin smoke that encircled her in a light smoky veil, perfuming her hair with the scent of burning balsam. She had no idea how much time had passed as she lay in that haze, somewhere between sleep and wakefulness. Then she raised herself up again and looked in the other direction, at first she didn't know what she was looking at. There were many large wooden wagons, with curved roofs, all gathered in a semicircle. She realized, with surprise, that they were gypsy caravans. The wagons had doors and windows and even in the semi- darkness, she could see that the wagons were painted many different colors.

The moonlight cast a light on a prancing horse that was painted on the side of the only caravan that had lights on. Arliss could hear the low murmur of voices as they drifted her way in the smoky breeze.

Beyond the caravans she saw a broad white ribbon of a road winding up a gentle slope toward a distant mountain. The Great Maudland road, she supposed sleepily as she yawned and lay back down and began to drowse off again.

A moment or two later she became immediately alert, as she heard the door of the lit caravan creak open, and the sound of several people coming out of the caravan and approaching the campfire.

"Oh Janos, if only you hadn't let the horse getaway," a woman's voice complained bitterly.

Arliss opened her good eye just a slit and watched from beneath her eyelashes.

There was a heard a hiss and yowl as the large woman lifted Kipper out of the basket that lay near her feet.

"And you bring me, back a cat! A cat of all things!" said the woman her voice rising with indignation as she held Kipper high the air.

"A worthless cat!" she spat.

"This I need" she said rolling her eyes with a cluck of disapproval. "Minera," said a male voice quietly.

Arliss recognized the second male voice from the woods. "So suddenly the King of the Gypsies has no mother?" said Minera tartly.

As Minera spoke her whole body shook. She wore a long red satin dress that was drawn tightly across her hips, and had hundreds of tiny mirrors sewn on to it, and Arliss watched in fascination, as the mirrors sparkled in the moonlight and as Minera's hips shivered and rippled, almost as if they had a life of their own. Her hair was coal black, and she wore it neatly knotted at the nape of her neck, and as turned her head in the moonlight, Arliss noticed that her ears appeared to be pulled down, by the weight of the earrings she wore, they were large hoops with rows of tiny silver bells that jingled softly as Minera moved her head.

Arliss could see from the distance, that the brothers resembled each other, they both had mustaches and wore wide brimmed hats. Even so she knew immediately which one was Janos. He was such a contrast to his brother as he stood absently tugging on his gaudy tattered waistcoat his hooded eyes fixed anxiously on Minera, who still held the cat.

Gerico who looked quite a bit younger than Janos, appeared unaffected by Minera's words as he stood with an almost arrogant nonchalance, with his head bowed, and his hat covering most of his face, as with great care he thoroughly examined each one of his finger nails.

"Janos sometimes I wonder if you and your brother are not just plain stupid!"

"Mama, hold your tongue!" admonished Janos with annoyance.

With a wounded look, shook his head and said reproachfully, "Now is that a nice thing to say about your own sons?"

"What kind of an example are you setting for young Gerico here How is he supposed to learn to survive as a gypsy "

Behind her back, Gerico, mimicked Minera's look of disapproval and shook his head in mock disappointment at Janos. Janos responded with an exasperated glare.

As Minera bent over to return the cat to the basket. Arliss couldn't help but notice her generous backside, which would have been hard to miss on the best of days and as she straightened up and turned the mirrors of her dress caught the moon light and flashed like hundreds of diamonds.

"You let a magnificent horse get away and you bring me a cat and a gangly girl with no meat on her bones."

Then as an after thought Minera shook her head and said," What's this girl doing traveling alone, anyway Are you sure there are no others nearby"

Frustrated Janos took his hat of his head and gripped it in his hands. "Mama you don't listen long enough for me and Gerico to tell you anything. All the time you criticize," he said his voice rising with emotion.

He waved his hat at her as he said in anger, "We do nothing right for you Mama." I ignoring Janos's words, Minera shook her head sadly and said, "Tonight your father must be turning in his grave,"

Her voice trailed off as both men glared at her.

Janos had drawn himself up so that he looked even taller. He was calmer now, but he still used his hat as an extension of his hand. "Now you listen here mama," he said firmly.

"All the time you compare us to Poppa. Well Poppa's gone and I'm king now. Me and Gerico, we're sick of this constant nagging and criticism, we deserve better, besides it don't look too good in front of the other Gypsies. "

"What kind of gypsy lets a valuable horse go and brings home a cat," sniffed Minera with her voice now not quite so bold but determined to have the last word on the matter.

"All right. I am listening now," she said finally.

"Mama look," commanded Janos, "This is no ordinary girl."

"Janos is right, mama," said Gerico speaking for the first time.

"Why she's hardly more than a child," said Minera in surprise as she stooped to take a closer look at Arliss.

As Arliss felt their eyes upon her she forced herself to breathe evenly and feign sleep.

Janos stared down at the young girl. At first glance he had thought her a child, but then he saw that she was at least twenty summers. The quality of her clothing, marked her as one of the gentries, but her face and arms as brown as any farm girl. She was as lean and spare as a young boy if it hadn't been for that head of hair, long and thick, a lighter color than the silky floss of maize in the late summer, Janos would have sworn she was a boy.

"This girl is someone very important." said Janos with certainty.

"Just look at her jewelry, look at that bangle and the necklace with a star, "he said unable to keep the excitement out of his voice.

"And look at this!" said Gerico triumphantly as he held up the Poseidon band and its little octagon shaped case and the blue velvet bag that Arliss carried it in.

And as he spoke, he reached down and roughly pulled of the druidic bangle, from her wrist and without even bothering to undo the clasp he snapped the silver chain of the Glasstarr Amulet as he plucked it from around her neck.

Minera closely scrutinized the jewelry, that Gerico had handed her.

"Ohhh..." she said softly after a moment as her eyes widened and she smiled with pleasure.

"These are precious things," she pronounced with a look of respect.

Then she gasped and her face clouded over and she hesitated as she said," Oh this is not good at all! "

"What you mean Mama? What is this foolishness about now?" demanded Janos sharply.

Minera didn't answer instead she closed her heavy lidded eyes and began to moan softly. She held the jewelry in both hands up against her chest as her large body rocked rhythmically back and forth. Then a strange moan arose from Minera it sounded hollow and faraway.

"Is it Kamishka." asked Janos tentatively.

"Yes it I Kamishka, who else could it be" said the voice inside Minera with a strange ironic laugh.

"Kamishka what do you see" asked Janos with a slight tremor in his voice.

Kamishka let out another moan and said, "Patience please, Kamishka needs a chance to get used to being back in corporal form again.

"Its so exhausting for me."

There was a few moments when nothing was said then Kamishka began to speak.

"I see many thing.... Strange things. Things that I don't understand and a place so strange and far away that the old ways have long been forgotten as if they never even were. Can you imagine that!" said Kamishka as if she had "trouble believing her own words.

Then Kamishka let out a fearful gasp. "Oh what trouble I see! she said moaning plaintively.

Arliss felt the short hairs rise up on the back of her neck at the tone of Kamishka's voice. at the same time both men uttered a frightened gasp.

"I see a dark one. One with less than half a soul! He seeks the gadjah girl and he will not rest not until he finds her. A look of uneasiness played over both the men's faces as they stood silent not daring to break the thrall.

"You must let her go before she brings trouble down on everyone of you!" Kamishka said urgently.

There was a moment of tense silence. Then as if a veil had lifted from Minera, her eyes fluttered opened and she resumed her normal demeanor as if nothing had happened.

Minera listened without comment as Janos related to her what Kamishka had said. Then she looked once more at the jewelry this time she thrust her open hands forward displaying the bangle and the necklace and Poseidon band to her sons.

"Take a good look at these," she said earnestly. "See the marks of the old ones, look carefully for you may never see such markings again."

Gerico and Janos took the pieces and gingerly examined them handing them quickly back to Minera. Then Arliss heard the clink of the jewelry as Minera slipped it into her the pocket of her dress.

"Gerico put the gadjah in the vardo. We will get rid of her soon, somehow. She's no good to keep, she'll bring bad luck down on us all."

Arliss allowed herself to become limp as Gerico picked her up, and carried her over to one of the vardos. Pushing open a narrow creaky door, he stepped up into a darkened vardo and pushed aside a heavy beaded curtain and then dropped her unceremoniously onto a soft bunk.

As soon as the door slammed shut, Arliss opened her good eye and started to sit up, but as she heard footsteps again approach the vardo, she closed her eyes and lay still. The door opened once more, and she heard the knobby rattle of the beaded curtains being drawn aside, as amidst fierce yowls and hisses. Kipper was forcefully launched into the vardo, landing with a soft thud beside her on the bunk. The door was slammed shut again. This time the bolt was drawn.

Gradually Arliss's eyes became accustomed to the dimness. She could see Kippers dark outline as he sprang off the bunk onto a nearby dresser and she could hear his toenails, making hard clicking noises on the wood dresser top, as he paced back and forth, with his back arched, hissing with indignation.

She slipped quietly out of the wide bunk and made her way past the beaded curtain to the vardo door. She was grateful for the soft pile carpet beneath her feet as it muffled her footsteps. She gently tried the latch it of the vardo door, but as she expected it held firm.

She glanced hopefully over at the windows and crossed her fingers and hoped that there weren't locked from the outside. Crossing to one of the windows she looked out and was disappointed to see Minera, Janos and Gerico still gathered around the dying embers of the camp fire. Any attempt to leave the vardo by this window would be plainly seen by them. She climbed back onto the wide bunk, to try the other window, but her heart sunk, when she saw how crooked it hung in its frame. She heaved it open a crack, and gasped as it squealed so loud, that she was certain, that it could be heard from miles away. Her knees felt weak as she waited remaining perfectly still with her heart thudding loudly in her chest, until after many long moments, until she was convinced that she hadn't been heard. But when she attempted to heave the window the rest of the way open, it would not budge.

With a sigh of resignation, she closed the window again not caring this time, whether they heard her or not. She flung herself back down on the bunk and as she ran her hand over the silky counterpane, and as she began to think again of Kamishka's words a wave of fear swept over her as she realized that probably at this very moment Urage was looking for her. Pushing that thought out of her mind she wondered when the Gypsies would let her go and if they would give her back the charmed jewelry. She wondered where Mallwynn and the others were now. She hoped that maybe they were close by and she would meet up with them in the morning when the gypsies let her go.

For the first time, she allowed herself to think about what would happen, if she didn't meet up again with Mallwynn and the others. What would she do?

She couldn't wander around the Mural forest for the rest of her life hoping that Urage wouldn't find her and there was no point going back to the Krippner Caverns and trying to fathom out, how to travel down the well between the worlds. Even if she did succeed, Urage would only follow her home and kill her.

Then for the first time a curious thought struck Arliss. She knew that Urage wanted her dead because she stood between him and the Orchid throne, but suddenly she was convinced that there was more to it than that. Why did Urage bother to attack her, when she was with Mallwynn. If she had waited until after she had reached the Orchid Valley, when their guard was down.

A powerful wizard pitted against a lone girl, should have been no contest. She should have been only an inconvenience. She could have been done away with, the way he had done away with her parents Kyrianna and Balsarrian, or even by some internal machinations. Even Mallwynn couldn't watch her all day long, every day. But Urage wasn't taking any chances that she would even reach the Orchid Valley. In fact he would rather pit himself against an equally powerful wizard like Mallwynn, rather than allow her to reach the Orchid Valley.

She wondered why

She didn't know what the answer was, but she knew where the answer was, and that was the Orchid Valley. It was then at that very moment, that she made up her mind, that she was going to the Orchid Valley, with Mallwynn or on her own.

She had tried to stay awake, to check again if Minera and the men were still by the campfire, but unfortunately, she was still drowsy from the effects of the drug the Gypsies had given her, and before long, despite all her efforts she fell asleep.

She dreamt that she was in a strange forest, where the trees and grass were all black as coal. When she looked up at the sky, it was high noon, and sun was pale yellow in a clear blue sky. She glanced behind her, and saw she saw a black dot in the sky, which for some reason, made her very frightened. She stood paralyzed with fear as she watched the black dot grow larger, until finally she saw that the black dot was a bird, a very large bird. As it drew closer, she could see that it was an enormous white owl. The owl was heading straight for her, and as she screamed in terror, no sound came out. She broke into a cold sweat and started to run even as she did, she knew she could never out run the owl.

When the owl at last caught up with her, he dug his sharp talons into her back and carried her off, high up into the sky. Suddenly the owl began to rapidly shrink, until it was so small it dropped her and she plummeted down toward the ground. And just when she thought she was about to hit the ground, she jerked awake.

Her heart still raced, as she squinted her gray eyes in the light that was coming in through the windows of the vardo. As she turned her head she could see the cat complacently grooming himself on top of the dresser against the opposite wall. Outside of the vardo she could hear the hum of conversation and the sound of children's shouts and laughter.

"Come on, get up! already you sleep too much." said Janos smiling as he pushed back the beaded curtain.

Arliss sat up rubbed her eyes and looked at Janos in momentary confusion.

"You have slept nearly all day. It will soon be sunset." said Janos kindly as he saw her confusion."

"Oh." said Arliss in mild surprise, she had felt like she $¢had only been asleep a short time.

She was distracted for a brief moment as she noticed Kipper slink through the beaded curtain and out the door of the vardo.

"Come on you need to eat." said Janos nodding in the direction of the door of the vardo.

Arliss slid out of the bunk and onto her feet. Her head hurt and her knees still felt like Jelly as she followed Janos out of the vardo.

She wasn't exactly sure how it happened, but as she stepped out of the vardo, her foot must have missed the first tread of the rickety little ladder, and she let out a scream as she was pitched headlong into the air.

Janos, who was just a little ahead of her, spun around quickly and caught her in his arms.

Suddenly, for a long moment, there was complete silence, as Janos stood with Arliss in his arms, while the whole camp looked on. Arliss felt her face grow hot. There must have been sixty or seventy Gypsies, men women and children all staring at her and Janos. Then in the sea of strange faces she spotted Minera. Then a young beautiful woman standing next to Minera caught her attention, when their eyes met, she shot Arliss such an intense look of hatred, that Arliss was stunned. It happened so quickly that she was certain afterwards that she must imagined it.

Then the spell was abruptly broken, as a young gypsy man who had begun to laugh, called out.

"Janos has caught himself a pretty Gadjah!"

There was more laughter from the crowd as Janos quickly retorted.

"Oh be quiet Chenko. If only your brain, was as big as your mouth we'd all be rich."

Then looking up he saw that the crowd still watched them with intense interest.

"Don't gape like fools! Get on with your business," he chastised with irritation as he set Arliss on the ground.

The sun was just disappearing behind Mt Sedwick when Janos thrust Arliss down in the grass next to the campfire. The buzz of conversation from the women nearby had died down immediately and she found herself the subject of furtive as well as blatant stares.

Round dark pretty faces watched her with suspicion while older creased faces stared with open curiosity and even a little sympathy. They then passed looks among themselves and then resumed their conversations completely ignoring her until only the small children seemed aware of her presence.

There was a spit over the campfire. A wild boar had been trussed and speared with a straight pole. Beneath the boar was a bed of white hot coals which smoked and hissed every time grease from the boar dripped onto the fire. The aroma was tantalizing. Women and children were roasting apples on sticks over the flames and when they were browned and shriveled, they were pushed off the sticks onto a big wooden platter. It had been a long time since Arliss had eaten, and the smell of the roasting meat was almost more than she could bear.

Arliss had turned to watch as Janos threaded his way through a throng of people, at the same time she noticed the young gypsie woman again, as she separated herself from a group of women and approached Janos. She threw her arms exuberantly around him and, subtly turned herself in Arliss's direction, and gave her such a vicious hostile look, that Arliss was shaken. She realized then, that she hadn't been mistaken the first time. Janos was unaware of what had transpired between the two women.

Just then Arliss felt a hand on her shoulder and she turned to see Minera holding in her hands a plate full of food.

"That's Desmone," said Minera looking at Janos and the beautiful gypsy woman.

"She is engaged to my Janos. Pay her no heed, in some ways she is a little simple, she imagines that every girl in the camp above the age of thirteen and under sixty is scheming to run off with Janos." Then Minera sighed and said lamenting, to no one in particular

"My poor Janos what a time he is in for with that one."

Then in the deepening twilight beside the caravan with the prancing horse Minera spread a colorful shawl on the grass, and she gestured for Arliss to be seated.

"Eat," she said as she handed the steaming plate to Arliss and then as she sat down beside her large figure, spread out in soft mounds over the grass.

Minera called to a passing woman and directed her to bring Arliss over a mug of cider.

Minera studied Arliss closely as she ate. It had been over two days since her last meal and hunger had made her unselfconscious. She ate quickly, consuming roasted apples and pork, along with a thick slice of bread, washing it all down with the cold apple cider. When the very last morsel was gone, she glanced up and met Minera's look of approval.

"Your health must be good you have a fine appetite." she said.

"Thanks," said Arliss with a contented smile.

Kipper had sprung down from the roof of the vardo a few minutes after Arliss had begun to eat, and she had paused only long enough to toss him a few scraps of pork, which he ate with his usual persnicketies despite his obvious hunger.

"My my, oh my," said Minera, as she studiously inspected the cat. Holding him high by the scruff of his neck, with all four of his paws dangling and he hissed and spat in vain, as she held him just out of range. Arliss was on the verge of protesting when Minera handed the cat smartly back to her.

Almost immediately Kipper sprung out of Arliss's lap and she watched as he leapt lightly on to curved the roof of the vardo, curling up comfortably on the very top of the roof. Then taking on an inscrutable look, he rested his head on his paws and allowed his eyes to become slits as his ringed gold tail snaked through the air.

"Your cat is a beautiful animal," said Minera as she followed Arliss's gaze. Then she added slyly, "But I hear not as magnificent as the horse you were riding."

Arliss found herself shifting uneasily as she sensed the tone of the conversation had changed. She nervously brushed a few strands of hair out of her face. Then she blanched as Minera stared hard at her, almost as if she could see inside her.

Then with a slight edge of menace in her voice Minera said, "What's a young girl like you doing traveling all by herself in these parts, wearing charmed jewelry and riding great horse."

"Who are you anyway" demanded Minera with a voice as cold as ice.

Chapter Twelve
The Council Decides

For a moment Arliss was silent she was nonplused by Minera's directness. Thinking fast she decided to stick as close to the truth as she could without revealing too much.

"I was traveling with my grandfather and some traveling companions when we got separated in the woods," said Arliss carefully as she gestured in the direction of the mural forest.

Minera's eyes narrowed as she said with cool casualness, "Where did you come from, and where were you going to?"

Her eyes were fixed intently on Arliss.

Arliss was saved from answering these questions when Janos suddenly appeared at their side.

Looking hard at Minera, he said severely, "That's enough questions Mama. You forget yourself, it is the job of myself and my council to deal with these affairs."

Minera looked at first as if she was going to give Janos a good tongue lashing but at the last moment, thought better of it, instead she pursed her lips and rose with surprising grace, and silently began collecting the mugs and crockery.

With an inscrutable look on his face, Janos beckoned Arliss to come with him.

"We have business to take care of..." As Arliss followed Janos across the grass to the campfire, she wondered anxiously, whether she was going from the pan into the fire. Then as she glanced over her shoulder she caught a glimpse of Minera following behind them in the shadows. She didn't know if Janos had noticed her there, if he did, he said nothing about it.

The campfire was now almost deserted. All the women and children had left and now there were only men sitting around the campfire, many of who were elderly. Arliss recognized Gerico sitting among a group of younger men. He looked bored and complacent. When Arliss glanced around Minera had disappeared, but somehow Arliss knew, that she was watching and listening in the shadows. When she sat down on the grass the conversation, among the men, had come to an abrupt end, and then as she felt every eye turn her way, she lowered her eyes and nervously bit down hard on her lip, as all the men around the campfire blatantly sized her up.

"These are the members of my council," said Janos as he sat down beside her.

Some of the men nodded toward Arliss in response to Janos's introduction, but many of them continued to stare, at her, their gazes unwaveringly and their faces frosty and hostile. Then after a moment or two of uneasy silence, one of the oldest men broke the silence as he said, "So King, this is the gadja "

"Yes Uncle Chekof." said Janos nodding his head in affirmation.

"Are these yours ?" asked Chekof fixing Arliss with a penetrating look, as he held up the blue velvet bag.

Speechless Arliss nodded. Then the old mans eyes took on a gentle look and he said quietly, "You must be very frightened." Taken off guard Arliss remained silent. She felt her eyes well up and her throat swell with emotion. Passing her a large red handkerchief, Chekof said gently "Now just tell us your name and your business in these parts,"

Not knowing what to do she remained silent. A fine Queen I'll make, she thought ruefully as she wiped away the tears that had begun to spill down her cheeks. She was going to offer Chekof back his handkerchief, but she decided not to "after she blew her nose with it. "Listen young gadja,"said Janos kindly, " Its no good you not talking, we know that you are already in so much trouble that telling a few gypsies your tale, will not make a bit of difference."

She knew Janos was right, their was no point in remaining silent, so slowly and hesitantly at first, she began to relate her tale. When she told them that she was the Glasstarr heir that had been presumed dead since infancy, their was a sudden collective gasp, from those around the campfire and Minera emerged boldly from the shadows into the light, clearly not caring now, who saw her as she gazed at Arliss with such a look of surprised wonder that Arliss nearly stopped talking.

Arliss left out, the part of the story about her visit to Oceanus, not wanting to break the trust of the Children of Poseidon, who wished as few people to know about them as possible. All the while she spoke, the eyes of the gypsies, never once left her face. Only once was she interrupted when Minera broke in and said, "I've heard of the Krippner Caverns and the well between the worlds. It's been said that we Rom once came through the well. We can never go back though, we'd perish. It takes strong magic to survive the well."

When Arliss at last finished her tale she said, "I am sure my grandfather and the others are looking for me."

Then as looks of respectful awe from around the campfire gave her courage she said timidly as she looked at Janos, "Maybe you could help me find my Grandfather."

"Maybe." said Janos, ignoring the surprised looks thrown his way.

Janos's face took on a thoughtful look as he was silent for a moment, his eyes flicking back and forth as though he was listening to an inner voice and then after a moment he said, "I think that maybe we can help you, if you really are who you say you."

Arliss laughed with relief and said, "As far I know, I really am who I said I am."

Janos smiled at her candor and then he grew serious as he said, "The Rom don't usually don't mix in the affairs of gadjas. Their laws their kingdoms, their kings even their high kings have nothing to do with our life. We tolerate them and mostly they tolerate us."

There were audible grunts of agreement from around the campfire.

Janos said with a bite of bitterness. ,"If Urage should gain control of the northern kingdoms it would be doubtful, if it would have much of an effect on our lives. We Rom have been traveling northern lands and the kingdoms to the south and even across to lands beyond the Cascall sea, since time began and we will be still traveling when time comes to an end."

He paused here as if to gauge what effect his words had on her, then he continued, "But we don't side with Urage, usually we stay clear of him. We would never be this close to Maudland Keep if we hadn't heard that he was abroad in other parts."

He paused again and looked at her shrewdly and said, "I'm sure your Grandfather, the arch mage would be more than willing to pay a generous reward for your safe return along with your jewels."

A sudden disgruntled murmur rose from around the campfire, at the mention of the jewelry.

Janos looked around at the men's faces and said decisively, "The jewelry is no good to us, if we keep it, it'll only serve to bring Urage down on us." There were some nods of agreement from around the campfire.

"We'll help her find the Wizard and depend his generosity. It probably won't take us more that a mile or two out of our way."

Then one of the councilors spoke up, he looked to be the same age as Janos and Gerico. His face had a sulky look to it, that was even more pronounced because of the ugly scar that ran down the left side of his face. He said," I don't think we should keep this gadja with us any longer than we have to. We should take the jewels and send her on her way you know having one of these people amongst us will only cause trouble. I say lets get rid of her quickly. Urage won't pursue us for the jewelry he'll be too busy pursuing the gadja to bother with us."

There was a low rumble of approval at the councilor's words, that was quickly silenced when Gerico spoke up for the first time. "Ahh Malkizar," he snorted, "I see that your sister Desmone has been nagging you again. Is she afraid that the gadja with run off with her betrothed Janos?"

There were snickers and guffaws from the men around the campfire.

Arliss noticed then that Malkizar bore a strong resemblance to Desmone.

The men's laughter came to an abrupt end as Desmone suddenly sprang out of the shadows, and snatched the bag of jewels out of Janos's hands.

Demone's pretty face was pulled tight by an angry grimace as she shook the blue velvet bag at Janos.

"These are jewels are rightfully mine, they should come to me when we're wed. Janos, you have no right to give them back to this gadja."

"But Desmone..." began Janos his face a mixture of emotions.

"The Queen of Eartheart! HAH!" said Desmone as she turned and spat into the air in Arliss direction.

Then with her voice laden with disgusted incredulity, she said, "She'll be the Queen of Eartheart! When pigs fly!" Janos stood up quickly and grabbed hold of Desmone who began wildly waving her arms around in anger as her voice rose higher. Then as Janos forcefully restrained her, she cried out,

"Janos, you're hurting me, let go."

"Desmone, sometimes you drive me to the edge." said Janos with a voice as cold as ice.

Arliss watched in amazement as a strange transformation overcame Desmone. Although her eyes glittered with resentment, she became suddenly calm as she turned to Janos and she handed him back the jewelry.

"I'm sorry my love, I don't know what came over me." Desmone looked strangely pathetic as she walked quietly away into the darkness.

Arliss noticed a peculiar look on Minera's face as she watched Desmone walk away. It was a strange mixture between of disgust and admiration.

Except for Malkizar who shot Janos dark angry looks, the rest of men around the campfire avoided looking at Janos.

"We'll set out first thing in the morning," began Janos brusquely.

"We'll circle the forest on the old logging road and head in the direction of the Mote mountains. We can send scouts ahead to track them down, and then he added, "We'll soon run into them."

Looking hard at his councilors Janos said, "All who are in agreement with this raise their hands."

All hands went up, except Malkizar and the two men who sat on either side of him.

"Then that settles it." said Janos with a note of finality in his voice and a satisfied smile.

"The council has decided."

As Janos's rose again to leave the campfire. Minera intercepted him within earshot of the campfire. Her voice was charged with anxiety as she spoke. "You know Janos, I do not often interfere."

When Gerico glanced over at Arliss and rolled his eyes back, at Minera's words, she had to struggle hard to resist the urge to giggle, but her mirth was soon dampened as Minera continued talking.

"But you got to let the girl go right away, jewels and everything. Just let her go! If you keep her you will bring bad luck and trouble on us all. Urage will kill us all. "

"Mama," said Janos, "One more day a few more hour won't make any difference and it may bring us a huge reward. We can't afford to miss this chance. The council has decided We will leave tomorrow as planned."

EARTHEART

Janos turned on his heel and walked away.

A grim look was on Malkizars face as his eyes followed Janos's departure.

In the shortest time possible the scene around the fire changed dramatically, Arliss had expected everyone to retire to their vardos, but the reverse was true. People poured out of their vardos as if on cue. Someone must have signaled that the meeting was over, but Arliss didn't remember hearing or seeing a signal.

Soon many gypsies gathered in and around the campfire.

A small group of men set themselves apart and began to play music. They had fiddles and flutes and tambourines and drums.

A hush came over the crowd as they started to play a sweet sad dirge. When a circle was formed, Arliss was swept off to the side and gently shoved onto a makeshift bench by a motherly looking woman who didn't speak to her, but smiled a lot.

The song the musicians played was strangely familiar to Arliss although she could have sworn that she never heard it before. The sad high sweet strains of the fiddle music made her heart ache with emotion. She found her body slowly swaying to the rhythm of the music. Abruptly the dirge ended and almost immediately the musicians began to play a rollicking toe tapping song. Couples in colorful flamboyant clothes like pairs of tropical birds spun into the circle and began to dance. Someone handed Arliss a cup of wine. She sipped slowly on it as she watched the dancing.

Dark eyed men spun dark eyed women around, whirling them like colorful tops and catching them expertly again in their arms. Faces flushed and eyes sparkled as the mood heightened with excitement. Men began swinging the women up high in the air letting out whoops of pleasure and then swinging them back neatly onto the ground. The air around the circle grew warm with the energy of the crowd. As the evening wore on and more wine was consumed the mood became more feverish.

The circle widened and pushed back around a couple of the most expert dancers. Someone removed the door of a vardo for the couple to dance on. The dance rose to such a feverish pitch that the woman dropped out leaving the man dancing alone with his one hand held high above his head he brought his heels down so sharply and rapidly onto the wooden door that the wood began to splinter.

The Crowd cheered louder clapping in time to the music, and as the man continued to dance faster and faster. Cries of encouragement came From the crowd. Then as the man's dancing became more frenzied the door began to break apart. When at last the man finally dropped to the ground spent with exhaustion the door which he had danced on was reduced to pulpy shreds and shards of wood.

The music and the dancing continued far into the night long before the music ended Minera had taken hold of Arliss's elbow and led her back to the Vardo and bade her good night. As they stood by the door of the vardo Minera glanced back at the small group of night owls still dancing to the music of the dwindling musicians and said acidly, "Some people don't know when to go to bed. They haven't got the sense they were born with."

Kipper, with his unerring sense of timing slipped past Arliss, into the vardo as she closed the door behind her. Alone for the first time in many hours, she was suddenly aware of how tired she was. Her whole body ached with fatigue, and as she slumped back heavily against the vardo door she looked around and smiled. Apparently it had been decided that she should be treated as an honored guest. The lamp that hung near the back of the vardo was lit. The low flickering light gave the interior of the vardo a warm glow. The bunk that she had slept in earlier on had been made up with fresh linens and turned down, so that it looked soft and inviting. A linen shift lay over the chair with several towels, wash clothes and a comb and a brush and on the heavy bureau opposite the bunk, was a white enamel wash basin with tiny yellow and blue flowers painted on it. A thin ribbon of steam rose up from the matching jug that stood alongside of the basin.

Arliss shrugged off her riding habit and hung it on a hook beside her cloak. She poured the warm water into the basin and began to wash.

The cake of soap that was on the wash stand was so strong and sharp it made her nose sting and her eyes water, but never the less she was grateful for it. It felt good to wash. She scrubbed herself all over, even her hair. she rinsed the soap out of it as best she could with the remainder of the water from the enamel jug. Her hair still felt a little gritty, when she brushed it, sort of like she had spent the day at the sea shore, but it smelled lovely and clean.

Kipper had settled at the end of the bunk nearest the door where he kept watch through half closed eyes.

As Arliss drew on the fine linen shift, she couldn't help but wonder whose clothes line the gypsies had stolen it off. Then she slipped between the coarse linen sheets and as she drifted off to sleep, she could still hear the sounds of music and laughter and the sound of a nearby vardo door opening and closing.

She slept lightly and awoke briefly to the sound of voices raised in anger, a man and a woman voice, the man's voice seemed vaguely familiar. Then she lapsed back into a dream.

In her dream someone was having an argument with her. She could feel all the emotion and the heat of the spat but she couldn't see the face of the person she was arguing with Somewhere in the distance she heard hissing and spitting.

When she awoke in the morning she immediately had the sense that something was wrong. As she sat up she heard a muffled mewing sound and the cat was nowhere to be seen. She got out of bed and stood perfectly still and listened carefully. The mewing was definitely coming from the bureau!

The first drawer she pulled open, was full of colorful silk scarves. When she opened the second drawer Kipper sprang out!

Arliss sank back down in the bunk in surprise, as she wondered who would play such a strange prank. Why would anyone lock a cat in a drawer.

Why would they do such a thing?

The cat had come to no real harm, but it was a mean and cruel thing to do to an animal. She watched Kipper as he stalked back and forth hissing and spitting, she could almost swear that the fur on his back was standing straight up.

Then suddenly her attention was drawn for no apparent reason, to the wall hooks where her clothes hung. She noticed that her cloak and riding habit were hanging at an odd angle.

She got up to take a closer look, and was shocked to find that the cloak and riding habit had been ripped and torn to shreds, as if someone had taken a knife to them. She shivered involuntarily, as she realized with apprehension, what at first had seemed like an odd prank, now seemed to take on a more malevolent meaning. It was clear that someone wanted to frighten her, and it wasn't hard to guess who Desmone.

Just then a loud thump came to the door and before she could answer it the door swung open and there framed in the door way was Minera, not waiting to be invited in she entered the vardo, but upon seeing the expression on Arliss's face, she stopped short.

"What's the matter young gadja, you look like you've had a bad fright." Arliss wordlessly held up the slashed clothing.

Minera took the clothing from Arliss, and inspected it closely, her face grew hard and her eyes narrowed as she said, "Wait here I'll be back soon."

Then as she started to leave, she paused, as if she had thought better of what she was about to say, but decided to say it anyway.

"Don't you worry I'll make sure that you'll be no longer bothered by that young shrew who has more jealousy than common sense."

With no further explanation Minera breezed out the Vardo allowing the door to slam behind her.

When Arliss looked out of the window she could see Minera heading down the line of Vardos with a determined look on her face. A few moments later she returned to the vardo, with a bunch of garments over her arm, handing them to Arliss she said, "Here you'll find something to wear in this bundle."

Arliss silently accepted the clothing.

"We are heading out this morning," said Minera.

"We are almost ready to go, so get dressed quickly. You can ride up on the vardo seat with Janos."

Arliss drew on and fastened a deep blue wool skirt with crimson rickrack bordering the hem. She pulled a faded blue flannel blouse out of the bundle of clothing, and she was pleased that the blouse, like the skirt, fitted her perfectly. Then as she picked up a crimson shawl with a deep fringe, she stopped short in her tracks, as she suddenly remembered seeing Desmone wear a similar shawl. She groaned inwardly as she realized then just where Minera had gotten the clothes. Well Desmone is really going to love me now, she thought sardonically, as she tightened the crimson shawl around her shoulders.

From top of the vardo Arliss could see all around. Men were still putting the horses into the traces. She was in the lead vardo. There were a dozen or so vardos stretched out behind her. Four enormous horses stood already harnessed and yoked between the shafts of the vardo. The reins were neatly gathered up and fastened to a peg that was at the side of the seat of the vardo seat.

The size of everything made her feel very small, just getting up on the vardo seat was an ordeal. The steps were so far apart that she really had to haul herself up and she had no idea how she was going to get down. She wondered idly how Minera managed.

Janos climbed easily aboard the vardo and as he picked up the reins, he smiled at her and asked, "Don't you have a hat" himself was wearing his wide brimmed felt hat. "Your going to burn, by the middle of the day the sun gets very strong even this time of year."

Then he reached behind the backboard and pulled out a hat similar to his own and without ceremony thrust it on her head.

"Thanks," she said shyly.

The next while was taken up with a lot of activity. There were calls back and forth between vardos. Arliss couldn't make out what they were saying as they seemed to be talking in some sort of Gypsy shorthand. She was relieved, when the vardos did finally begin to roll. The sooner, that she reached Mallwynn and the others, the better. She had no wish to overstay her welcome with the Gypsies, but she was sure that as far as Desmone was concerned, she already had. And of course she knew that somewhere out there, Urage looked for her. She would feel much safer in the company of Mallwynn, Striker, and Farin.

They had been camped between the main road to Maudland and the Mural forest. The logging road that they were going to take, ran right alongside of the Mural Forest. They had to cross a meadow to get on to the logging road.

Arliss had to hold on tight as the vardo swayed from side to side, as they traversed the rolling meadow. Kipper slid and slipped on the curved roof of the vardo, at times sliding all the way to the very edge of the roof, hanging on by only the claws of his front paws, before he finally admitted defeat, and retreated to the middle of the vardo seat.

The ride became much smoother when reached the hard packed dirt logging road. The road immediately began to climb upwards. The vardos groaned and whined, with the strain of the ascent. The steady clip clopping of the horses was a mesmerizing comfort to Arliss. The road grew perilously narrow and still they continued upwards. Arliss tried not to look down, as when she did it seemed as though they were only a hairs breadth away from tumbling down into the gorge that ran along side of the road. Still they strained upwards.

They had to halt the caravan when the wheel of one of the vardos toward the rear of the caravan became stuck in the soft narrow shoulder between the road and the gorge. Arliss's knees had turned to water when Janos had flung the reins at her as he went to the back of the caravan to help push the vardo wheel out. Fortunately however, she needn't have worried, as the horses had no intentions of going anywhere until Janos returned.

When Janos returned to the vardo, he quickly got the horses and vardo moving again and they continued their upward journey. By early afternoon they had at last come to the top of the rise where the Mural forest ended and Mt. Sedwick rose another four thousand in the air.

The sky was a clear blue backdrop for the barren, craggy, slate colored mountain. The bare scrubby trees that clustered near the lower part of the mountain, reminded Arliss of a giant's rough unshaven beard.

The logging road curved up and around, then ran on a level ridge between the road and the mountain. This was a welcome change from the steady uphill toil. They had only traveled down the road for a short distance when Janos gave the signal for the caravan to pull off the road and on to a grassy slope between the road and the mountain. Here the vardos formed a semi circle with the open end toward the road facing the forest.

Janos jumped lightly down from the vardo, and turned and looked up at Arliss.

"I'm going to take some men and scout around in the forest."

Janos turned from her and he was silent as he studied the road up ahead. Turning away from the road his eyes keenly searched the edge of the great Mural forest, following, the huge wall of trees all the way back to where they stood.

He pushed his hat back and looked back up at her again, and said, "From what you've told me we should find the Arch Wizard and his party close by.

Arliss watched anxiously as Janos called a few men together, one who was Gerico, and they saddled up their horses, and rode across the hard packed dirt road and disappeared into the shadows of the Mural forest.

Chapter Thirteen
Tragedy at Weneslydale Gorge

A short way into the Mural Forest they had come upon the small stream of clear running water. Following Janos's hunch, he and his men rode along the banks of the stream, under the huge evergreen trees for several hours, hoping for a clue of the Arch mage and his party.

Janos had just to been ready to tell his men that they should head back to the road when Chenko had cried out excitedly, "Look King, Tracks! And they look fresh!"

Janos dismounted onto the damp muddy bank of the stream. Then as he knelt to study the tracks more closely, he gestured for his men to take a closer look as he said with rising elation," It certainly is the Arch Mage and his party."

Janos was relieved they'd found the tracks, it wouldn't have surprised him, if they hadn't, as the Mural forest was notorious for people losing their way and disappearing completely without a trace. legend had it, that the reason that the trees in the Mural forest were so huge, was that the forest itself was fed on the bone meal of lost travelers. The very thought of this, made Janos shudder. He was glad that the tracks seemed to be leading back in the direction of the logging road, he would be very glad to get out of this queer forest.

Janos and his men, like most Gypsies were expert trackers. From an early age they were trained to watch the roadways for signs of who went before them. They were easily able to follow the tracks, even after had become faint on top of the thick layer of evergreen needles.

"On to the bridge quickly!" cried Mallwynn, over the baying of hounds, as they galloped rapidly toward a narrow rope bridge, that was strung over Weneslydale Gorge.

Striker urged his reluctant horse onto the swaying bridge, the gorge was so deep and narrow, when he did looked down, he couldn't even see the bottom.

"I don't think the bridge will hold all of us!" he cried as he rode part way onto the swaying bridge.

"Here they come!" cried Whapper in alarm as from around the bend of the logging road appeared a dark swarm of hell hounds behind which rode Urages and his regulars.

They rode toward them at great speed, churning up great clouds of dust.

Mallwynn glanced over his shoulder at the advancing men and dogs and he hesitated for only the briefest of moments before crying out with a wild look in his eyes.

"The bridge will have to hold!"

Elsaroth's horse balked, refusing to go onto the swaying rope bridge, and all her cajoling was to no avail as the horse refused to move.

Farin rode quickly up behind her and slapped the horse firmly on haunches. The horse responded immediately, starting forward and stepping quickly onto the moving bridge.

Relieved, Elsaroth glanced back at Farin with a look of gratitude. Mallwynn had been the last one onto the bridge, and as it swung erratically from side to side, his horse neighed and snorted in alarm.

Striker was still only three quarters way across and already Urage and his men and hellhounds had almost reached the bridge.

"Quickly!" pleaded Mallwynn, over the cacophony of baying hounds.

Then as the hellhounds reached the gorge's edge and tried to funnel onto the narrow bridge, there were howls of terror as many of them slipped off the cliff's edge plunging into the gorge.

Still others followed them, like lemmings off the cliff to certain death. The hellhounds that did make it onto the narrow bridge, were immediately pelted with arrows by Mallwynn's party.

As Urage reached the bridge he took hold of the curved brass horn that hung on a leather cord from his shoulder and raised it to his lips and blew a strange and lonesome call.

The effect was immediate. The hellhounds stopped in their tracks and lay down obediently.

Urage signaled his lieutenant to take a sword to the ropes that anchored the bridge to the side of the gorge, but just as the lieutenant was about to hack into the thick roping, Urage stayed him with his hand.

"Halt!" he cried out.

"Not another step our my man Klick here will send you all lying into the gorge."

At the sound of Urage's Voice, Mallwynn glanced behind him, and when he saw Klick's sword poised on the anchor rope, he wheeled his horse around, as he cried out in alarm,"

"Stop! Do as he says!" Urage smiled smugly as everyone on the swaying bridge came to a sudden halt.

"That's much better old man. You do have a shred of intellect left in that addled old brain of yours, after all."

Then as Urage looked more closely at Elsaroth his smile of satisfaction abruptly faded as he said in disbelief, "This is not the Glasstarr princess!"

They had come out on the road a couple of miles up from the gypsy camp. Janos stood silently with his men in the shadows of the giant trees and watched with great interest as the scene on the bridge unfolded.

Above the groaning of the bridge, Urage called out, "Old man where is she" Mallwynn, took a deep breath in and set his mouth firmly as he shifted back in his saddle.

"Come on old man I don't have all day," said Urage with a dangerous edge in his voice. Then as if to underline his intentions, he gave a nod to Klick, who with a sudden flash of his blade expertly sliced halfway through the rope that formed one of the rails of the bridge. The rope at once began unraveling at an alarming rate.

Then Urage nodded again to Klick and as Klick raised his sword to slice into the anchor rope.

Mallwynn cried out, "No don't! Please wait."

"All right old man, I'll ask you one more time. Where is the Glasstarr Princess"

There was complete silence for a moment or two and it seemed that Mallwynn wasn't going to answer Urage, but finally he said, "I'm afraid I really can't tell you that."

At Mallwynn's words Urage's face darkened in anger. His command to Klick was short and sharp.

"Cut the ropes. Kill them all!"

This time Mallwynn didn't blink and his face was serene as Klick raised his sword, but just as Klick began to swing the sword downwards through the air. Mallwynn began to speak, his voice and manner, quiet and nonchalant.

"Hold it Klick," said Urage unable to resist hearing what the Wizard had to say.

"Look Urage it's no use killing us all." said Mallwynn reasonably, his face tranquil and composed.

"Let the others go or at least the young women and her manservant, they have nothing to do with this trouble."

"You're toying with me now, old man," said Urage coldly.

Then as his mouth tightened, he shook his head and said, "I wish that I had the time to play along with you for it pains me to see you die this quick and easy death. For the amount of bother you have caused me, you deserve infinitely worse."

There was only silence from the four on the bridge. It called Urage that there was so little reaction from Mallwynn.

"Sir." said Klick, with a strange gleam in his eye.

"We could take them prisoner, and ahh...interrogate them more, ahh... more thoroughly later on, Sir."

Interpreting Urages indulgent smile, as approval Klick pressed on.

"I mean Sir, if I may be so bold as to remind you, that back at the Black Willow Keep, we do have certain facilities that would perhaps make the ahh...interrogation of the old man and his party ahh...more satisfying, and who knows, he may even tell us where the Princess is." Urages folded his arms in front of him on his saddle and his mouth grew rigid.

"You'll never learn will you Klick."

Then he shook his head ruefully and said, "Now just pause for a moment, and take your mind off those delicious base things that bring you so much pleasure."

Klick's face reddened.

At the same time, someone coughed nervously and all of the regulars within earshot took a step or two backwards.

Urage slipped down from his saddle, and shrugged back his heavy black cloak. His hand was lightly poised over the hilt of his sword.

Klick swallowed hard.

Even though Klick was tall, Urage still towered over him. Urage began pacing back and forth, in front of Klick, with a considering glance from time to time toward the swaying bridge.

"Now my little man, just who would the princess be with, if she's not with Mallwynn" asked Urage as he gestured in an almost theatrically manner toward the bridge.

Then he stopped pacing and paused in front of Klick as he raised one eyebrow quizzically.

"Hmm? Any theories Klick?"

Klick's downcast eyes were shifting from side to side as he appeared to be trying to make himself invisible.

'Well let's think about this Klick." said Urage thoughtfully tapping his chin.

"Perhaps she's with the late King's right hand men, Strongforth and Woodrow?" said Urage raising his eyebrow quizzically at Klick.

Then Urage turned and gestured again toward the bridge. "But it appears that's not so, for as even you can see, the two fellows themselves stand here before us on the bridge." said Urage his voice heavy with sarcasm.

Striker and Farin doffed their hats at Klick.

"Even you Klick, with your limited intellect can see that this green chap and his mistress do not have the Princess either, not unless they're hiding her up under their cloaks, which I very much doubt."

Klick was busy studying his boots.

"Now, I know that the princess is not dead, and I know that she is not yet in the Orchid Valley. So where is she Klick?"

Klick mumbled something

"What was that Klick Speak up man."

"I don't know Sir." said Klick his voice just above a whisper as cold sweat began to pour of his brow.

"Pardon, still can't hear you old man."

"I DON'T KNOW SIR." said Klick his voice cracking.

"That's better." smiled Urage

As Urage he withdrew his sword his eyes were fixed intently on Klicks face and Klick blanched as Urage with 'both hands, leveled his blade at him.

"Let me tell you something Klick, something, which if you weren't such a half-wit, you'd have determined for yourself."

Then as Urage lightly caressed Klicks neck with the tip of his sword, raising fine lines of crimson blood, he said softly, "The reason why we don't see the princess before us, is because they've lost the her you fool!"

Then with almost manic glee, Urage laughed as suddenly and without warning, he spun around and sliced into both anchor ropes of the bridge.

There were sudden horrific screams, both human and inhuman as Mallwynn, Striker, Farin, Whapper and Elsaroth, horses and all plunged into Weneslydale Gorge.

A chill shot up Janos's back as he heard the screams and he could still hear them in his head, long after they had faded away.

His men looked shaken as they turned to him with looks of confusion.

"What will we do" whispered Gerico.

Janos pressed his finger to his lips and directed their eyes back toward the bridge.

Urage's men stood around him and watched in stunned as silence as he turned again toward the gorge and spat into it.

Then he turned back to his men, with a grim smile, and, he said, "Good riddance to all of them!"

Suddenly the soldiers began to cheer and clap, but when Urage raised his hand, the laughter stopped immediately.

"Klick I want you to send back to the Keep For reinforcements. I want you to immediately send men to fan out and search for the girl, lets start with the forest. That's a likely place."

Janos and his men rode their horses through the Mural forest at breakneck speed, hoping desperately to reach the gypsy camp before Urage's regulars did. In their haste they took a wrong turn, and lost precious time backtracking.

When Janos heard the hoof beats behind them, he wheeled his horse around and took a sharp breath inwards as he looked down the infinitely straight corridor of giant trees at a small contingent of Urage's soldiers riding rapidly toward them.

Janos swore under his breath.

"We'll never be able to outrun them."

As the soldiers approached Janos recognized the look of disdain on their faces.

"What's your business in these woods. scum?" said the sharp faced lieutenant.

Ignoring the contempt in the Lieutenants voice, Janos said easily, " A little hunting a little scouting," as with a slow grin, he held up a brace of jack rabbits that he caught as they'd rode along by the stream.

"Where are you camped" asked the lieutenant, his eyes narrowing as he scrutinized them.

"Over by the road." said Janos casually tilting his in the direction of the road.

"What's your business in these parts, Gypsy?" asked the lieutenant suspiciously.

Janos being a consummate liar had already thought ahead and anticipated the question so his answer came naturally and easy.

"We have heard that there is a shortcut over to Boggham moor, this way.

We're heading over to Milltown on Muskrat lake.

"Oh yes," said the lieutenant noncommittally. "Why are you going to Milltown."

"We're going to have a new vardo built at the Watrane mill. "

After a moment or two of consideration the lieutenant nodded and then as he watched the Gypsies closely as he asked," Have you seen a young fair haired girl in your travels, either alone or with others,"

Janos glanced quizzically at his men, then as they shook their heads, he turned and looked the lieutenant the eye as he said firmly, "No, we haven't."

Then before the lieutenant could ask another question Janos said, "Have you heard of the shortcut to Muskrat lake

"With the tables tuned on him, the lieutenant looked momentarily taken back, then he nodded grudgingly and said, "There is a bridge three miles further down the logging road, that leads to the road that runs down to Muskrat lake."

Janos noticed that the lieutenant said nothing about the rope bridge.

The lieutenant seemed satisfied and about to ride away when Janos spoke again.

"Why are you looking for this girl."

"None of your business Gypsy, and by the way, we've orders to search all the homes in the area, and that means your caravans. So you'll be seeing more of me later scum." said the lieutenant with supercilious smile."

Janos's face was sober as he watched the contingent ride off.

It was around dusk when Arliss watched the men approaching camp. She knew without having to be told that something wasn't right. Maybe it was the speed at which they approached the camp. It somehow seemed urgent or maybe it was the fact that the men were returning alone with no signs of Mallwynn or the others. Then as they drew closer she knew that she was not wrong the expressions on the men's faces were grim. They rode right into the midst of camp. Even as he dismounted, Janos was signaling the Gypsies to gather around. Arliss found herself at front of the crowd.

"What's wrong?" asked Minera her smooth wide face puckering with concern.

"Urage and his regulars are looking for the gadja, they are combing the Mural forest. They'll be heading this way soon!" said Janos urgently.

There was a collective gasp from the crowd. Janos's turned to Arliss with an apologetic look, and she knew he had more to tell her. "What is it" she asked uneasily.

Then Janos spoke so quietly and quickly that Arliss at first didn't think that she had heard him right.

"Now listen young Gadja the news is very bad. The mage and your friends they're all dead. Urage killed them. He cut the rope bridge that there were standing on right out from under them and they fell into Weneslydale Gorge."

"But they can't be dead!" gasped Arliss in disbelief.

Then Janos shook his head and sighed as he said with certainty, "No one could survive a fall like that. That gorge is so deep that when you throw a stone into it you'll never even hear it hit the water." Wide eyed with shock Arliss stared back at Janos with still not believing what she was hearing, but as she looked from face to face of the small scouting party, their expressions confirmed Janos's words.

"No!" she stammered, "That can't be! I would know."

Janos's eyes met Minera's as he shrugged helplessly. Minera cautioned him with a look to say no more.

Time and place stood still for Arliss, as she found herself in a strange cocoon of grief. Her chest filled up with sorrow, she heard a strident keening wail, it was many moments before she realized the keening was coming from herself.

The woman who smiled a lot, took Arliss back to the Vardo and sat with her while she wept.

Arliss was grateful that she said not one word.

"They know she's got to be nearby, and they won't stop looking till they find her." said Janos

Looking at Minera he said, "Can you find a way to disguise her. There could be trouble if they find her with us."

Malcizar pushed through the crowd. His face was pulled tightly into a scowl, "I don't see how keeping the gadja with us, one moment longer is going to help the camp. The Wizards dead and we've lost any chance to a collect reward for her.

Janos turned on Malcizar coldly," I will decide what is going to help the camp."

"Malcizars is right,"said Desmone angrily as she broke from the crowd, taking a place beside her brother. Her body was trembling with pent up rage .

"Why should we have to take on any risk to ourselves for this gadja Gadja's have never done anything for us except drive us from their lands. They hate us they say we're dirt. In gadja towns our children are teased and made to feel ashamed of who they are. And you are going to give her shelter!" Spat Desmone vehemently.

There was a ripple of approval from the crowd. "What are we going to do King" asked Chekof quietly.

"We will do everything, that we can do." said Janos firmly. "But we can't send her off on her own. It would only be a matter of time before they found her, and it wouldn't be too long, with their methods of interrogation, before they knew we had her all along. They would need less of an excuse than that to throw all of us into the keep dungeon, and make slaves of us and doghouses out of our vardos." Many of the crowd nodded in agreement with Janos words and fear and worry replaced the indignation on their faces.

"So King what now" prompted Chekof asking what was on all their mind. Janos didn't answer Chekof, instead there was a sudden flash of gold as Janos handed Chenko a few coins.

"Take Cosmos and head over to Milltown and order a new Vardo, tell old Hector at the Watrane Mill we'll bring the rest of the money in the spring when we come to collect the vardo, he knows we're good for it. We'll leave signs along the roadway for you to catch up with us."

Then astonishment registered on almost every face in the crowd as Janos took a breath inwards and said, "The rest of us are going to head into Maudland."

After the murmurs and grumbles died down Janos began to speak.

"Everyone who is traveling away from Maudland is going to be stopped and searched. Its very likely we're going be searched too, but if we're heading away from Maudland they are going to search us far more thoroughly and they may even detain us. Traveling into Maudland will make us seem less suspicious. In a few days all this will die down. Then we can slip out of Maudland with the Gadja. Once away from Maudland we'll set the Gadja free with us of course accepting her jewelry as payment for her escape from the devil man."

There were many rumbles of approval from the crowd at Janos's plan.

Cold rivulets of water ran down Arliss's back. as she sat up on the vardo seat, shivering, but inside she was numb, dead even. Her hair was still wet. Minera had colored it with walnuts and leeks. She didn't look like herself anymore. Even Urage wouldn't have recognized her. That thought should have pleased her but of course nothing could please her anymore. Minera had even darkened her brows and eyelashes with kohl and reddened her cheeks with rouge, she looked almost like any other gypsy girl except her eyes were lighter.

The trip back down the logging road was even more perilous than the trip up had been. Janos was tense, it took an enormous amount of concentration just to keep the vardo on the road. The steady downward progress was very hard on the horses.

It was nightfall before they reached the bottom of the logging road where the land leveled out, when the sound of the baying hounds and hoof beats behind them, brought on a new wave of terror that cut through some of the deadness in Arliss.

She had turned to look back up the logging road the direction of the approaching hounds and soldiers and as she turned back around her eyes met Janos's.

"Listen Gadja. Don't let me down now because now you are a Gypsy, and Gypsies spit on fear." he said looking at her earnestly.

Arliss took a deep breath in, and nodded her compliance. The horsemen and hounds caught up with them as they crossed back again, into the meadow along the Maudland road.

Janos signaled a halt to the caravan train.

Arliss's blood ran cold as she watched Urage's contingent approach.

The Gypsy horses whinnied and snorted in fear at #the approach of the hell hounds.

Then the brass horn was sounded and the baying stopped. And the hellhounds lay down at the edge of the meadow, and the Gypsy horses calmed down.

Arliss watched transfixed as the red eyed wraith-like beings separated from the regulars and fanned out, circling the entire caravan. She noticed for the first time, with a chill, that each of the Carnumbra carried a long handled ax. and as the moonlight glanced off of the razor sharp blades, her mouth became dry and her hands clammy as she realized with a jolt that there was nothing more concealing her, than a few ounces of vegetable dye.

"That's Klick, Urages right hand man." said Janos,

"I remember him from the bridge. "

Arliss took a breath in as she remembered it had been Klick who was with Urage at Skeghaddie.

"Its a good sign that Urage himself is not here," said Janos under his breath.

"Don't speak directly to any of the soldiers. it is not our way. They will speak only to you through me." said Janos tersely as he swung down from the vardo.

Arliss watched anxiously as he disappeared down the line of vardos in the direction of the approaching regulars.

From her perch high atop of the vardo Arliss could see all that was going on. Klick looked about middle aged, he was tall and powerfully built, in his hand he carried a riding crop. He and four of the regular began the search at the rear of the caravan. They made the occupants of the vardo line up beside it. Then as Klick along with two of the regulars questioned the occupants, the other two regulars began ransacking the vardo.

Immediately angry indignant protests broke out from the Gypsies. But this was to no avail as the regulars continued turning the vardo inside out, strewing its contents haphazardly out onto the ground, while blatantly pocketing many small valuables that caught their eye. When the roar of the protesters seemed to be getting out of hand, Klick unruffled, gave a signal with his riding crop and the Carnumbra responded immediately by moving forward and tightening the circle and at the same time, moving their long handled axes into an attack position. This had the instant effect of silencing the Gypsies and the search continued on, with them watching in resentful silence.

Arliss noticed, that it was as Janos had said, the women did not speak, but stood silently as questions were ask of the males. Many of the older women kept their shawls up over their heads loosely covering their faces.

Arliss worried about what had become of her amulet and the charms. Had Minera hidden them on her person in her own vardo, or had she hidden them in the vardo that Arliss now sat on, in either case, if the regulars found them it would be all over for all of them. Arliss held her breath when she saw the search had reached Minera's own Vardo. She watched as Janos helped Minera down from the vardo seat onto the ground. Minera was uncharacteristically quiet, as Janos answered Klick's questions and as the regulars searched and plundered through her belongings. Arliss suddenly knew then that Minera must have hidden the charms and jewels on herself. She was relieved when the search party finally moved on to the next vardo. The search proceeded up the caravan until it reached the vardo next to Arliss. Anxiety spread through her like wild fire. It was all she could do to remain in her seat.

As the regulars approached her she arranged the shawl over her head and face, the way she had seen the other women do and she averted her eyes downward. She could only see the approach of highly polished boots.

"Get down here now!" commanded Klick so suddenly and so harshly that Arliss was taken completely off guard. She hadn't expected Klick to speak to her as none of the other women had been spoken too.

Did he know who she was?

The thud of her heart sounded hollow in her ears, as she sat perfectly still, paralyzed with fear.

"I said, step down." repeated Klick, now there could be no mistaking the menace in his voice.

Janos moved quickly the side of the vardo and reached up and practically pulled Arliss off the seat and swung her to the ground. Her legs were so shaky that when he let go she felt sure that she would collapse in a heap on the ground."

Then as she glanced up furtively at Klick, she was surprised to notice a strange sort of excitement in his eyes.

Then as he looked closely at Arliss's face a look of confusion came into his eyes as if something just didn't seem quite right, and as he reached out to pull off her Shawl, Janos protested indignantly," Hey that's my sister! leave her alone."

And what happened next, happened so fast that Arliss wasn't quite sure exactly how it happened. She heard the crack of Klick's riding crop as it made contact with Janos's face and as she heard a gasp of horror from the crowd as blood spurted from Janos's face and he folded in two in agony, something snapped in her, and suddenly she was no longer afraid. She felt a sudden heat rise up inside her as she glared angrily at Klick, and her hand of its own volition, took flight, and delivered a hard resounding whack to his face.

For a moment Klick was stunned.

The sudden cheers of the crowd died as a slow grimace spread across Klick's face and his eyes hardened and suddenly without warning, Arliss found herself slammed up hard, against the side of the vardo, and as her head began to spin the ground sprang up to meet her. "Come on", we're wasting our time here there's nothing here but Gypsy scum," said Klick as he turned reluctantly away from Arliss.

"We've got a lot of ground to cover tonight."

As Klick turned and walked away he regretted having to leave the gypsy girl behind. It would have been such good sport to take her back and see just how hard he could make her scream. She looked so timid and frightened sitting up there on the caravan, he couldn't resist her, the thought made him smile as he indulgently forgave himself, his moment of weakness. But then he frowned as he remembered the way she slapped him and that angry defiant look she'd given him, that had really surprised him. Perhaps he was wrong about her.

Anyway it didn't matter as he couldn't take the risk of indulging his foibles now, as word would certainly get back to Urage. The very thought of that made him perspire as he knew well that he was on shaky ground with Urage as it was.

Arliss watched with relief as the black polished boots departed without even a glance in her direction.

Arliss had a yet another lump on her head, and there was an ugly welt across Janos's right cheek and nose but after he cleaned the blood up, he too seemed none the worse for wear.

The mood of the caravan was subdued. Janos had decided that they wouldn't linger in the meadow but instead take advantage of the darkness to try and move unnoticed into Maudland. Soon after they had set off on the Maudland road, it began to rain heavily.

To nervous to sleep, Arliss rode up on the vardo seat with Janos. She drew the hood of her cloak over her head to keep out the rain. Kipper was curled at her feet taking shelter under the folds of her cloak. She felt a great sense of relieve that Klick hadn't seen through her disguise. Janos had told her of the plan to go into Maudland, and although she wasn't happy about the prospect, she was tired of cowering fear of Urage. She promised herself that when they left Maudland and the gypsies set her free she would make her way to the Orchid Valley and somehow she didn't yet know how she was going to make Urage pay for what he did at the Wensleydale gorge, and for killing her parents those long years ago. She knew now without a doubt, that one day, she was going to stop him once and for all.

The road had been empty the first part of the night, as they road up and over Mt. Sedwick, but as they drew closer to the Maudland border they began to see more and more travelers along the road, and many of them rode in carts piled high with all of their possessions, fleeing the towns and villages along the Maudland border as news of the death of Mallwynn filtered through to them.

It continued to rain heavily as the steady exodus from the Orchidian border towns continued most of the night and there existed along the road that night a strange sort of camaraderie brought on by the foul weather, and the desperate circumstance, under which most had undertaken their journey, but never the less Arliss was surprised at how adept Janos was at striking up conversation with the travelers along the road, and finding out just what he wanted to know without seeming overly curious. People were stunned by the news of the death of Mallwynn. Many expressed fear and dread at the prospect of having Urage as King. Some thought it odd, and speculated as to Urage's involvement in the freak accident that not only took the lives of the Archmage who was the last link between the long lost Glasstarr heir and the old king, but also the lives of the king's right hand men, Sir Strongforth and Sir Woodrow.

They learned that Urage had blockaded the all the gates to the Orchid Valley, except for the eastern gate, which had been locked for hundreds of years. And now Urage was combing the land from the Mural forest all the way to the Cascall sea for what was rumored to be a pretender to the Orchid throne.

From up on the vardo beside Janos, Arliss listened quietly and she felt encouraged when many people in whispered tones expressed their curiosity about the, "Pretender", and still more hoped that there really was a Glasstarr heir. Janos told her that there had been for many years now, strange and dark rumors among the Ochidians who lived along the Maudland border, about the attractive, prosperous, well ordered towns and villages of Maudland. They seemed to many to be almost too perfect. There was something distressingly unnatural about them, sort of like a cloying sweet smell.

They had traveled along the Maudland Road for many hours and Arliss must have drifted off to sleep for when for when she awoke, the rain had stopped, and along the bottom of the horizon, dawn was breaking and ahead the Maudland road sloped steeply downwards to a dark stone zigzagging bridge, spanning what appeared to be a winding twisting river of mist.

She blinked in surprise. Janos turned and smiled.

"That's the Spirit river and the Fourth Demon Bridge. We'll cross over it into Maudland."

Chapter Fourteen
Into Maudland

As they headed down the slope toward the bridge, Janos began to tell Arliss about the strange bridge over the misty river. It was cold in the gray dawn light, and Arliss shivered and drew her wool cloak tightly around her as she listened intently to Janos.

He told her that there were five Demon Bridges in all and legend had it that they were built long before the Rom came through the Well Between the Worlds, when all of Eartheart was still the land of the old ones, long before they passed into the great wilderness.

Just beyond where the mist ended along the river banks on either side, ran ancient pathways. Strange and awful creatures were said to lurk near the banks of the Spirit and Nightshade River. It wasn't wise to walk too near the rivers, especially after dark as there were far too many reports of sudden and inexplicable disappearances. "I've heard a tale about Urage and the Demon bridges." he said grimacing as he mentioned Urages name.

Janos's face puckered thoughtfully as he said, "Long before even Minera mother's mother was even born, he built his great road to Maudland and he tried to build a bigger bridge across it, wide and straight like his great road. But he couldn't do it. Each time he built a bridge, not even a year would pass before it would crumble and fall into the Spirit river and be swept away. Urage tried again and again, he built bigger and stronger bridges but each time the same thing would happen, but the Spirit River beat him. At last he gave in and brought his great road down to meet the fourth of the Demon bridges."

The caravan of vardos rolled through the heavy veil of mist and onto the zigzagging bridge. The sound of the rumbling wheels echoed and reverberated ominously against the bridge's high stone walls.

As Janos expertly maneuvered the heavy vardo around the sharp angles of the zigzags, he told Arliss about the runes carved into the bridge walls that were so ancient and mystifying, that so far no one, not even Mallwynn nor Urage had been able to decipher them.

As Arliss listened closely to Janos's words, she peered hard through the mist, hoping to catch a glimpse of the strange carvings, but all she could make out, were vague shapes, but then as the vardo rolled past, she reached out and ran her hand along the wall. It's hard surface felt like no other stone she had ever touched before.

Then suddenly without warning there was a harsh crackling sound, and Arliss gasped, jerking her hand away, as a shaft of blue light shot from the wall into her hand.

Thunderstruck and wide eyed she turned to Janos, still holding her tingling hand.

His mouth had dropped opened as he stared back at her in shocked amazement, but he quickly recovered himself, and a look of curiosity came into his eyes, he called out the signal to halt the caravan. Almost immediately, the hollow, rumble of wagon wheels came to a halt.

Murmurs of surprised annoyance rose up from the Gypsies, who had no idea why Janos was stopping.

Without a single word to Arliss he leapt lightly down from the vardo and she watched as he crossed in front of the horses and moved a short ways back along the bridge to the where she had touched the wall.

She strained hard to see him through the mist as he ran his hand along the wall. There was no surge of blue light this time. Janos stood for a moment gazing thoughtfully at the wall before he beckoned her to join him.

Standing beside Janos she hesitantly reached out to touch the wall again. This close she could now see the strange symbols, and odd looking animals, carved deeply into the black stone. As she touched the wall, it began to crackle and she felt and saw the flicker of blue light again beneath her finger tips, but this time it didn't alarm her. In fact it was some how strangely familiar, and as she placed her other hand against the wall, the crackling subsided, and she impulsively moved forward pressing her face against the wall's cold rough stone and instantly her was mind filled with many vivid images.

She saw the Demon bridges as they were, down through the ages. She saw the bridges alter as the land changed. As the river narrowed, curved, and shifted so did the bridges. The climate changed and grew so cold, that the mist cleared and beneath the bridge the river froze like molten glass. All around were fields of hard blue and white ice. Then the sun warmed up and the ice melted, and beneath its soft damp veil, the river teemed again with rushing waters. Then the land flattened out and the sun baked it, burning off the mist and drying up the river. The trees and grass withered away, and armies of dust devils swept down through the dried up river bed, and under the bridge, and further on down the cracked and dried course, until finally leaving the river bed and whirling across the dry barren land.

Masses of people passed over the bridge, in a sudden flash she saw everyone of their faces. Then the scene changed, and she was in primeval stone forest and all around her the steep walls of a valley rose up.

She watched as strange long robed mystics hew the petrified trees, into building blocks for the bridges. Then water filled the valley, and the stone forest was completely submersed. The body of water was called the Meducin Lake. The water had magic properties and she saw pilgrims at its banks carry away phials of its precious water.

The lake dried up and the primeval forest reappeared but it was no longer stone, but a living breathing forest.

So many images filled Arliss's mind. She was remembering both backwards and forwards.

Filled with awe and wonder she slowly drew back from the wall. Overwhelmed by what she'd seen, it took a moment for her mind to clear.

She mustn't have heard Janos the first time he spoke as when she looked up he had an agitated look on his face.

"Are you all right," he asked as he looked at her closely.

As she nodded wordlessly, he gave he an odd smile.

Janos was silent and pensive as they crossed into Maudland.

Arliss glanced over her shoulder, she noticed uneasily, that the wall of mist on this side of the river seemed murky and somehow strangely menacing. Then as she realized, that the only way back across the spirit river, was over those strange narrow zigzagging bridges she was gripped by an irrational fear of being trapped, and she had to fight hard to ward off the impulse to jump off the vardo, and run back across the bridge.

As the morning wore on, Arliss noticed with regret that the comfortable easiness that had existed between her and Janos was gone. He now spoke to her very little and when he did he was overly courteous. Often she felt him glance her way as if to try and fathom out, what happened at the bridge. But he never asked her any questions, and she felt reluctant to talk of something that she herself didn't understand.

It seemed to Arliss that since they'd entered Maudland the light was subtly distorted in a peculiar way. It was almost like looking through a thin piece of clear crystal. And the air somehow felt thicker and heavier and when she breathed it in, it had a bitter metallic taste. The land along the road now was so choked and overgrown with trees and brush, that the trees that died didn't even fall to the ground any more, instead they just rotted away in place.

The trees thinned and the road dipped and bottomed out and parts of it were so soggy that the horses hooves made sucking and squelching sounds as they plodded along.

Before long they came upon a vast and rank smelling swamp filled with ghostly gray sugar maples that were stripped bare of all their leaves.

The swamp ran back from the road on both sides as far as the eye could see and they had almost past it by when Arliss started and gasped, as from out of the corner of her eye she saw the limbs of a tree bend toward her in an odd way almost like it was a human arm reaching out in supplication. But when she looked again the tree was perfectly still.

With a sudden shudder she glanced away, as she was reminded of a grim garden of lost souls.

There were many tiny towns in the distant rolling hills. Small farms cut up fields into regular patches of color ranging from the blackest black of moist new turned soil, to the fragile new born green of winter rye.

The country side seemed to Arliss to be unusually still and quiet, almost as if it existed in a vacuum, and the bleak far off caw of a crow only emphasized the deep silence of the land.

Janos told her that they would make camp that night at the market town of Blackheath.

"Its a fair-sized market town, so we shouldn't draw too much attention to ourselves. "He said with his eyes still fixed on the road ahead.

Then glancing her way he said by way of an explanation, "We usually go up to Rydale. That's one of the bigger market towns in Maudland, but we were there just there a couple of days ago, it would look queer if we went back so soon."

As the day wore on they met few people traveling along the road, most were from other parts of Eartheart and were hurriedly leaving Maudland.

The camaraderie, of the exodus of the previous night beyond the Maudland borders was gone. No one spoke to them, those who accidentally glanced their way turned away quickly, not wishing to make eye contact with strangers, particularly gypsies.

They encountered a few units of Urage's regulars along the road, heading out of Maudland, but much to Arliss's relief, they paid them little attention save for a few looks of disdain from individual soldiers.

The constant swaying and monotonous gritty rumble of the vardo made Arliss very drowsy and finally unable to resist it any longer she dozed off to sleep.

When she awoke it was already nightfall and moon had risen. They'd turned off the Maudland road and were heading down a narrow road to the market town of Blackheath.

They set up camp in a large meadow just outside the town. Arliss sat on the rickety steps of the vardo eating an apple she had left over from supper and as she happened to glanced up, she noticed uneasily that Desmone's brother Malkizar was watching her. He was standing a few vardos down from her, with another man, who Arliss didn't recognize. Even when Malcazar saw that she had seen him, he still continued to stare blatantly at her.

Then a scowl crossed his face as with his eyes still fixed on her, he began talking earnestly to the man who was with him. Embarrassed and uneasy Arliss, lowered her head and pretended not to notice him.

Janos had gone off, with Chekov to the tavern in Blackheath to try to get the lay of the land from any loose tongued locals.

Minera was receiving the few timid towns people that had ventured out to the meadow to have their fortunes told. Minera before she disappeared into her vardo earlier that evening had turned to Arliss frowning as she said, "I hate to tell these people's fortunes. Then as she twisted her pursed lips to one side as she said with disgust, "Never in my life, I tell you Gadja have I seen so many people smile alike and talk alike it's just not natural."

At the far end of the caravan lone fiddler began to play a soft subdued song. It seemed to reflect the mood of the camp as there had been no singing and dancing that night, and many of Gypsies had already gone to bed.

When Arliss looked up again, she was relieved to see that Malcazar and his friend had disappeared.

That night Arliss fell into a fitful sleep. She dreamt that she was perpetually falling down into Wenslydale Gorge.

As she plummeted down that dark deep chasm, large rocks stretched their sharp brittle spines up toward her, thirsty for her blood and guts, but just when it seemed certain that she would hit the rocks, her body was seized in a sudden tonic grip that was so strong it awakened her.

This happened over and over again during the night, until at last she was mercifully swept into a soft cottony blackness where she reposed for an hour or so until she gradually became aware of a repetitive creaking noise somewhere in the vardo. It probably came from the door.

The door!

Her eyes flew open and she sat upright in the bunk, peering into the blackness straining to see the source of the noise.

In the moonlight she noticed the dim outline of Kipper on the dresser where stood his eyes fixed on the vardo door. After a long moment or two of listening intently, she still heard nothing, nevertheless she swung her feet out of bed and moved softly to the door and listened quietly.

She still heard nothing.

Then as she crossed back to where her clothes lay. Her fingers fumbling nervously on the buttons of her blouse as she dressed quickly.

The strange unnatural silence persisted, but she knew someone was out there, and she knew instinctively that they were listening to her now as she moved around in the dark as they a decided their next move.

The creaking began again this time she could hear whispers outside the door and horrified she watched as the bolted vardo door begin to move in its frame. She made no effort now to be quiet now as she slipped on her boots and drew on her cloak. She toyed with the idea of crying out for help on off chance that someone would hear her, but she knew her voice would be far too muffled by the thick sturdy walls of the vardo. Her best bet would be to wait until they had the door opened and then she would scream bloody murder.

She looked around the moonlit vardo for something to use as a weapon, in a corner she spied a broom handle. She grabbed it up in both hands and held it like a lance.

At least she would not be taken without a fight she thought grimly as she watched now as the vardo door began to wobble loose tooth in an old hags mouth.

Then from behind her came the sound out glass shattering and Arliss spun around in time to see a dark shape lunge through the window.

There was the sound of the vardo door weakly giving way. She opened her mouth to scream, but before she knew what hit her. She was grabbed from behind and a damp strong smelling cloth was shoved up into her face. She choked as she breathed in. And her knees gave way as she sunk into a hole of darkness.

Chapter Fifteen
Captive in Maudland

When Arliss next opened her eyes it was dawn and she was on the floor of an open wagon with a florid faced man hovering over her.

For a moment or two she just stared up at him in confusion, trying to comprehend her situation.

A look of annoyance crossed his face, as he noticed she was awake, reaching down by his side he picked up something, heavy and metallic.

Her confusion turned quickly to alarm, as the man suddenly lunged at her, with what she could now see was a set of manacles in his hands.

She drew back and tried to roll out of his reach, but he was quick and managed to grab hold of one of her hands. Even as she continued to struggle, she felt the iron manacle being clamped down firmly on her wrist and snapped into place. But she fought harder than ever, twisting, turning, flaying out with her free hand, until she landed a smart whack on his face.

"Quick! Give me a hand over here! I need help! She's a demon!" he cried in disgust as he glowered down at her.

Amidst her struggle, she saw Malchizar's sharp narrow face appear over the side of the wagon, his feral eyes darting, furtively from side to side as he took in the situation. Almost immediately behind him was Desmone. Her eyes glittering as she watched Arliss struggle, her mouth widening into a smile of satisfaction. As Arliss writhed and kicked furiously, she felt the man's grip suddenly tighten on her as he scowled across at Malchizar.

"You told me you could keep her quiet," he said panting from exertion.

Smelling a sudden pungent bitter odor, she glanced up, and saw Malchizar pouring a phial of liquid onto a cloth.

Renewing the fervor of her struggle she began to fight with a fierceness she didn't know she possessed, and as she managed to prize her hand out from the man's grasp, she heard Desmone cry out, "Quick Malchizar hurry she's getting free!"

As Malchizar's hand came down quickly over her face she descended back into blackness.

When she next awoke, she was in a place so dark, that it could have been her grave, only the sound of her own breathing reassured her, that she was still alive.

Silently she cursed Malcazar and Desmone as she struggled into a sitting position and looked around in the darkness.

She thought maybe she was in a store room or a cellar, but then as she stared hard into the blackness, she made out a small faint square of gray light suspended in the dark, and as she looked harder, she saw a vague shape of a doorway with a small barred window.

Weighed down with heavy chains, she struggled, clinking and clattering to her feet, and hobbled with strange lopping gait to the dim doorway. As she had suspected, it was firmly locked.

"Malchizar! Desmone! Damn you! Let me out of here!" she cried, banging furiously on the door with her fist.

Then as she dropped her manacled hands to her side, gasping with the exertion, she listened intently, but all that she heard was the deep resonant silence of thick walls and stone floors.

Undaunted she drew back from the doorway and began hurling the chains up hard, against the cell door as she cried out Malchizar's and Desmone's names over and over again.

She was making so much noise that she almost didn't hear the still quiet voice that spoke from somewhere behind her.

"I wouldn't be making such a fuss, if I were you. It'll do you no good you know good Gypsy girl."

Arliss felt all her anger suddenly fizzle as she gasped with astonishment and spun around her chains rattling and clanking as they whipped around her.

"Who are you?" she blurted out, as she peered into the darkness searching for the source of the voice.

"Iver Kedwick at your service Milady," said the pleasant male voice.

Then with only the briefest of hesitations he added, "And please allow me to introduce, Mastrada and her brother Gasperon."

Arliss heard a male grunt and a nasal sounding, "Pleased I'm sure."

"Is there anybody else in here that I don't know about." asked Arliss crossly, for she was still embarrassed that she had been taken unawares, and she was sure that these people must think that she was some sort of mad fool.

"Not as far as I know on less of course you count the odd rat," said Iver cheerfully.

"I didn't hear a thing," said Arliss more to herself than Iver, wondering how anyone could manage to be so cheerful in a place like this.

"I thought I was in here alone," she admitted sheepishly.

"Evidently." he said dryly.

Arliss was glad that Iver couldn't see her face because she knew it was red. "Where are we anyway," she asked suddenly remembering her predicament.

"The Black Willow Keep." came Iver's immediate reply.

She drew in a sharp breath at the same time as a wave of nausea swept over her. She could hardly believe her ears.

How had this happened?

Had Malchizar and Desmone turned her into Urage?

Arliss's mind raced as she considered the possibilities.

"I gather you didn't expect to be here." said Iver kindly after a moment or two of silence.

"No." answered Arliss numbly, feeling suddenly more wretched than she had ever felt in her entire life. She needed to sit down. She moved awkwardly away from the door, with her chains clinking and rattling as groped her way along the dungeon wall and slumped down.

"Damnable thing this slavery thing, and I suppose it was this Malchizar and Desmone, who sold you?

"Slavery?" said Arliss softly not sure at first that she had heard right.

"I'm sorry," apologized Iver, "I thought you knew."

"Slavery" repeated Arliss to herself as she felt a tiny ray of hope rise up in her. Did this mean that Urage didn't know she was here in his keep.

"Are you sure "she asked cautiously not daring to allow herself to enjoy too much the feeling of relief that was quickly sweeping over her.

"Well, yes, you see, Mastrada and Gasperon are also slaves. I expect you'll all go up to the slave yard tomorrow together." "Pleased I'm sure!" agreed Mastrada.

Gasperon grunted.

"I presume you have a name young lady,"

"I do, but I'd rather not tell you what it is," said Arliss, taken unawares and not wanting to reveal her name.

"Oh I say! A bit of a mystery woman." said Iver amused by her candor. "Pleased I'm sure," agreed Mastrada.

Gasperon grunted.

Arliss giggled in spite of herself.

"Oh I understand old girl, better than you know, but a word to the wise, make sure you have a moniker ready for Kopter the Master Sorter, in the yard tomorrow, if he should ask, usually he doesn't bother.

"Are you a slave too?" asked Arliss suddenly wondering how Iver knew so much.

"I suppose we're all our slaves in our own way." he said obliquely.,

"Pleased I'm sure." commented Mastrada

Gasperon gave a derisive snort.

Arliss thought that Iver was going to evade her question, but he must have sensed her thoughts because he suddenly began speaking again.

"I'm here my dear, because I ran a bit foul of the Maudland law. Gambling. That sort thing." he said vaguely. Then he added almost as an afterthought. "It was a nasty business indeed."

"Pleased I'm sure." agreed Mastrada. Gasperon sighed loudly.

After a few moments of silence it seemed clear, to Arliss that Iver wasn't going to say anymore about how he got thrown into the dungeons of the Blackwillow Keep. She liked Iver Kedwick, but she just didn't think he was telling her the whole truth.

"Mastrada. Gasperon. Have you been slaves long asked Arliss politely, no longer able to contain her curiosity about them.

"Pleased, I'm sure," sighed Mastered.

Gasperon let out a soft moan.

Arliss had known that this was how they'd answer, but she couldn't bring herself to address her question to Iver, as though they weren't even present although truth be told, she hoped that Iver would answer her question.

"These poor wretches have been bred for slavery." said Iver quietly.

Then as if on cue, Mastrada said solemnly, "Pleased, I'm sure." And Gasperon Groaned.

Arliss was shocked and horrified, she had realized that there was something odd about Mastrada and Gasperon, but she thought maybe that they were perhaps just a bit slow. So among other things, Urage was a slave breeder!

Arliss was still reeling with shocked disbelief when she heard a far off a bell begin to clang.

"Looks like we're about to dine," said Iver his voice cheerful again.

"I wonder what fine cuisine chef has cooked up for us today. Yesterday he out did himself, there was actually meat on the plate. Although I must admit I was a bit hesitant as to inquire of the nature of beast, as there has been rather fewer rats around here lately." he finished solemnly.

Just then the cell door swung open and two burly men were silhouetted in the light from the hall. Arliss squinted in the sudden brightness and as she turned her head away, she caught a glance of Iver. He was sitting on a stone bench at the back of the cell, he wore manacles, and leg irons like her. He sported a thick mustache and had thick dark unruly hair. He was very thin and even though his clothes were tattered, he looked very gallant.

As their eyes met he smiled cheerfully and bowed low at the waist. Arliss found herself smiling in response to his warm greeting. Then as she turned her head slightly she caught a glimpse of Mastrada and Gasperon, sitting close to Iver. They were both stunningly attractive and didn't resemble their voices in the least way. They looked almost identical, extremely tall with light blond hair. Open mouthed with wide staring eyes, their faces looked almost childlike.

Then as the trays were slid roughly across the floor at them Iver inquired "I don't suppose Captain, that you've heard anything from my devoted brother, Braithly."

"That's Staff Sergeant, Kedwick and you know it," chuckled the older of the two guards. But none the less he looked flattered.

"Nah, we haven't heard anything from the Kedwick Estate yet. No word in the guard room that I heard of anyway."

Then turning to his companion, he said, "Tork, you haven't heard anything have you"

Tork shook his head and said grudgingly, not since this morning."

"Oh well," said Iver brightly, "Maybe they'll be something on tomorrow's post coach."

"Didn't your brother let you stew for three months last time," queried Morag.

"Something like that," admitted Iver.

"He can be a jolly unreasonable fellow when he wants to be." "He better not leave it too long, this time, "warned Morag.

"The Lord is not as lenient as he used to be even with gentlemen like yourself. You may soon find yourself in the slave yard."

"Yes, quite so, quite so, this is a devil of a predicament I'm in," mumbled Iver more to himself than anyone else.

Then as the light from the doorway shone on his face he shrugged as if to shake away his cares and he straightened up and began rubbing his manacled hands together briskly.

"I don't suppose you two fellows would see your way clear to giving us another blanket. It gets terribly drafty in here at night and that poor girl has nary a one." he said nodding toward Arliss.

Tork scowled and looked like he was about to say something, when Morag cut him off with a look and said, "Tork go see if you can find the Gypsy a blanket in the supply room she'll be just dog meat if she gets sick."

Arliss watched Tork retreat into the corridor as she tried not to wonder too much if Morag was being literal.

Iver's voice took on an conspiratorial tone as he said, "Come on Morag old man get these fetters off of us, and I'll see you right when Braithly comes, you know he always pays all my debts in full."

Then more softly he said with emphasis, " All of my debts Morag."

A certain greed lit the jailers eyes at the same time as his veil of disinterest slipped.

Iver alert to what was going on pressed his suit as much as he dared.

Oh come on Morag, Your in charge around here, you have discretion when it comes to us ragamuffin prisoners. .Mastrada and Gasperon wouldn't hurt a flea."

Behind Morag's back, Iver gave Arliss a conspiratorial wink as he said, "And the Gypsy girl is feeble minded, that's -probably why they sold her."

Morag swung his attention around to Arliss. She tried to look as dull witted as possible. Then as Morag turned away from her with a satisfied look nodding his assent to Iver, she thought dryly, I must have been pretty convincing.

Morag then took the keys from around his belt and unlocked all of their manacles and leg irons. The relief from pain relief was incredible, it was a pleasure for Arliss just to be able to stretch her cramped muscles without the weight of the heavy chains.

Tork, returned a short while later and tossed the blanket hurriedly into the cell. He didn't comment on the manacles and leg irons that lay in a pile by the doorway.

As Morag turned to leave he turned to them with his voice turning suddenly cold as ice as he said, "I'm leaving orders with the night crew, if there is any funny business at all in this cell tonight, your are all to be strung up."

Arliss shuddered as she followed Morag's eyes to iron rings located high in the dungeon walls.

"Even if they only THINK that something funny is going on in here they will be instructed to string you up, and as far as I'm concerned you can swing, till hell freezes over. Is that clear "

Looking from face to face Morag seemed satisfied. And as he turned to go, he locked eyes with Iver, as he said "Braithly's purse better be heavy."

Then as Morag turned to Tork, his mood was suddenly congenial again as he slapped Tork on the back.

"Tork, those wenches won't wait forever and I just heard the arrival of our relief. Come on I'll buy you an ale."

The two guards then left slamming and locking the cell door behind them.

Thank you very much." said Arliss as she rubbed her wrist where the manacles had bit into them.

"Think nothing of it, my dear. They're in a particularly jovial mood today. It's payday and they 've just received their wages, and they're looking forward to an evening of whiskey, wild women, and song and goodness knows what else."

Arliss had caught a glimpse of what was in the metal dish before the cell door had closed. It was a grayish lumpy substance, along with a piece of bread that felt heavy and damp. Suddenly not feeling hungry, she set the dish down.

Almost immediately Gasperon started grunting excitedly and Iver said, "I do believe that our friend here, Gasperon wants to know, if your not going to eat your supper, if he can have it."

Gasperon grunted wildly in confirmation.

"Of course he can." said Arliss.

Gasperon must have been able to see a lot better in the dark than she, because almost instantly she heard a few quick steps and a swooping sound and when she reached over to her surprise the plate was gone.,

"Swift, isn't he "commented Iver dryly.

When the meal was over Arliss could hear the sound of footsteps moving around the cell and then, Mastrada's beautiful face was suddenly illuminated, as she slid the trays through a slot in the bottom of the cell door. Arliss groped around in the dark and found the blanket which she gratefully wrapped around herself. And as she leaned back against the dungeon wall. She wondered where Urage was now, for all she knew, he could be walking around overhead this very instant, as here she sat down below in one of his own dungeons. The very thought made her shiver convulsively.

Then she suddenly thought of Kipper and she'd wondered how he was faring. She missed him, but she thought he was probably a lot better off where he was, than here with her in the Black Willow Keep Dungeon. Then she began to worry about tomorrow and the slave yard and the ominous sounding Master Kopter.

Arliss despite all her worries began to drift off to sleep. She didn't how long it was she slept before she was awakened with, what only could be described as the sound a well-bred pig might make if he snored, coming from Iver Kedwick's direction.

"Pleased I'm sure," spat Mastrada in annoyance her voice stern.

Gasperon whistled loud and shrilly.

With a few sputtering snorts the snoring came to an abrupt halt.

"That's quite enough now!" said Iver sharply, his voice still heavy with sleep.

"Now look here," he grumbled, stifling back yawn. "Every night I go through this same nonsense with the two of you."

Then he said firmly. "Now I want you to listen to me very carefully." "Pleased, I'm sure." said Mastrada timidly frightened by Iver's uncharacteristic sternness.

Gasperon snorted,

"I don't want a peep out of either you for at least a few hours.

"Plea...."

"Now I mean it! That's enough!" he warned.

"It's a wonder that I even have a mind left after being holed up with the two of you for a week." he muttered crossly to himself as he settled back down to sleep.

Strangely enough after that, peace reigned and not a peep was heard, not even the sound of Iver's snoring.

Arliss didn't know how long she'd been asleep when the cell door creaked open again, and an indifferent male voice said, "Look lively gypsy girl! Out in the hall on the double! I'll have the two savants out here as well."

Bleary eyed Arliss stumbled to her feet to follow Mastrada and Gasperon out of the cell, as she left the cell she heard Iver whisper, "Be careful gypsy girl! Keep your head and hold on! Things will change!"

The guards quickly slipped the shackles back on the three of them and led the up the torch lit corridor toward the slave yard.

Chapter Sixteen
In the Black Willow Keep

The guard threw open a set of heavy doors, and issued them out into a small courtyard milling with slaves.

Arliss was separated almost immediately from Gasperon and Mastrada, who were taken off in different direction.

"Wait here for Master Kopter," the guard ordered as he left her with a group of young female slaves.

The slaves around her murmured to themselves as they glanced her way curiously. She averted her eyes and drew herself in, and tried to look as inconspicuous as possible.

Some of the slaves resembled Mastrada and Gasperon. Like them they were tall and strikingly attractive and had that same almost placid vacantness about them. She assumed that they too, were the bred slaves that guard had called Slavants.

She noticed a tall thin man dressed completely in black moving through the crowd in a very methodical manner. She surmised that this was Master Kopter. She watched him as he moved from slave to slave, inspecting each one of them in turn as he made notes in a large black book which he carried.

Several guards followed behind him pulling a low flat wagon on which rested a smoking copper brazier with a number of metal rods protruding out of it. As she caught sight of a slave's face contorted in momentary agony, that she was sickened and horrified to realized that the rods were branding irons! It amazed her as she watched the grizzly proceedings that very few of the slaves cried out as they were branded, but instead bore it stoically as if a natural part of their existence.

The slaves were taken after inspection and branding, and loaded onto one of the many wagons that waited by the gateway of the slave yard. When these wagon's were full the gates were opened and the wagons driven out into the main courtyard, and out of the keep. Even as Master Kopter drew closer Arliss's spirits began to rise as she realized, despite the prospect of having to face the agony of the branding iron, that it was likely, that in a short while, she too, would be in one of those wagons, bound for who knows where, but definitely out of the keep and away from Urage. But then her excitement was suddenly checked, as she began to noticing that not all of the slaves that Master Kopter inspected were loaded onto wagons.

Near where she stood there was a usually small door in the slave yard wall, from which she heard the muffled sounds of barking. Every once in a while, when the door was opened and as the sound of the barking grew loud and furious, she'd notice a sudden hush amongst the slaves around her as their eyes turned toward the door with looks of fear and loathing.

By this door another group of slaves had gathered. Arliss noticed that most of the slaves in this group seemed elderly or looked sick or were maimed or injured in some way, but a good many of them looked perfectly fit and healthy.

She didn't have long to think about this as her attention was suddenly drawn away by a commotion in the slave yard. A young man, who Master Kopter had just finished examining, was protesting loudly about something.

The man was lean, muscular, and vigorous looking, with a chiseled face, and a military bearing that made her think that he may have been a soldier at one time. It was only when, Master Kopter gestured to the guards and they dragged the young man out of his group, that she noticed his wooden leg.

Suddenly for Arliss it seemed that time was standing still, as she watched, numb with horror as the young man grew more and more belligerent, as if he didn't realize the peril, he was in. She wanted to cry out to him to be silent but she had lost her voice.

Then she saw Master Kopter give an almost imperceptible nod to the guards beside him, and then as an unnatural hush fell over the slave yard, the guard beside Master Kopter, without the slightest hesitation, withdrew his sword from its sheath, and then in one smooth continuous movement, thrust it deep into the young man's chest.

There was a collective gasp from the crowd.

Taken by surprise the young man hadn't even cried out. For a long moment he just stood absolutely still, staring straight ahead, his eyes were wide with shocked surprise, both his hands clutching the blade of the sword as it entered his chest. Then for a brief moment comprehension dawned on him, as he rolled his eyes back hopelessly and sank to the ground.

Thunderstruck the crowd remained silent as the guard leaning over the fallen man, withdrew his sword, and coolly and fastidiously wiped it clean, with the edge of the man's own tunic, before returning it to his sheath.

Then as if on cue a rumble of normality began in a far off corner of the slave yard and in a moment or two completely encompassed the whole yard.

Stunned, Arliss stared in disbelief as the dead man's remains were shoveled efficiently into a cart that was a little larger than a wheelbarrow and wheeled right out the small door of the slave yard wall.

The crowd was thinning now as more and more wagons loaded with slaves rolled out of the slave yard. There was now quite a large group of slaves by the small door in the slave yard wall, but still Master Kopter continued relentlessly culling, all the while he was drawing closer to Arliss, and before long he had reached her group.

She watched anxiously from the corner of her eye as he moved along the row of female slaves toward her. Until at last Master Kopter stood in front of her. Glancing up at him she could feel her heart racing, and her knees shook. Then as Master Kopter took in her disheveled gaudy clothing with a look of distaste her face grew hot, at the same time as she realized with growing alarm what a fool she'd been to think that she could blend in with the other slaves.

"One of our slave merchants bought her from a couple of Gypsies," commented the guard at Kopter's side, by way of explanation.

Despite all her fear she couldn't help noticing that Master Kopter had the oddest complexion she had ever seen. His skin was smooth textured and very sallow, almost a translucent creamy yellow. It reminded her of candle wax. In fact if he were to have taken off that peculiar square cap he wore, she would not have been surprised at all to see a wick sticking out from the top of his head.

"A Gypsy. Hmm... "he said peering at her closely.

"Only half," she mumbled, her heart pounding as she heard the note of doubt in his voice.

"Aha." he said with a look of understanding as apparently satisfied with her answer, he wrote something down in his big black book.

With the book still in his hand, he stepped forward and took hold of her chin and turned her face roughly from side to side.

"She's rather attractive wouldn't you say." he said letting go of her chin.

"If you say so Master Kopter," answered the guard at his side. "She's not suitable for any of the breeding farms though, with that mixed blood." said Master Kopter regretfully.

"Makes it too difficult for us to refine desirable characteristics when the gene pool is enlarged willy-nilly." said Kopter aside, almost to himself.

Arliss swallowed hard as she thought about the people waiting by the small door in the keep wall.

He opened his book again and began leafing through it as she waited hardly breathing.

"Ahh, we haven't sent anyone to the Keep Garden yet," he said as his eyes scanned a page.

Looking up, his waxen brow furrowed as he glanced at her thoughtfully.

Arliss was focusing hard on a wart on his left ear, in an effort to not show her anxiety.

"Yes, I think she'll do nicely in the garden." he said at last as he glanced at Arliss once more as if to confirm his decision.

The euphoria of her near escape deadened the pain of branding, and as she glanced once more toward the small door in the slave yard wall, she Knew without a doubt that there were worse things in the Blackwillow Keep than branding.

Even as she was being led away to the Keep Garden, she was still unable to believe her good fortune. Despite the odds she had once again, at least for a while, cheated death.

Arliss soon got used to the long days and the constant physical toil of work in the Keep Garden. The work began everyday at dawn and ended well after sunset, when they would have to work by torch light.

Her manacles had been removed on her first day in the garden, but the leg irons were left on, eventually she got used to them, after a while, she barely noticing their weight upon her ankles.

The brand on her forearm was a crusty red lump for the first few days. She had been given some salve to put on it and after a week or two she could see that the brand was a circle within a circle. In the inner circle was a tiny willow tree and in the outer circle were several geometric shapes.

She detested the thought of having Urage's brand on her, feeling some kind inexplicable loss she would constantly trace its shape with her fingers, she knew no matter how long she lived, she would never get used it.

The first few days that she was in the garden, every time she saw a guard confer with one of the overseers, she was sure she'd been found out and expected to be called up to overseer's station on the ramparts, and to be put to death forthwith, but that never happened. It was strange really and it worked in her favor, it seemed that after she had become a slave no one except other slaves ever looked at her face or had eye contact with her.

On her first day in the Keep Garden, Ludkin the chief overseer, a big boned bristly haired man, set her to work in Urage's massive herb bed. She learned later from the other slaves, that Urage used these herbs in his various, medicines and potions.

There was a warm camaraderie among the slaves, she worked with. They talked to one another all day long to pass the time and lessen the tedium as they worked.

She knew that her knowledge of Eartheart was far too superficial for her to make up a believable background that would have passed any kind of close scrutiny. So she rebuffed any friendly overtures made to her by the other slaves and after a few days of making fruitless attempts to draw her out and include her in their conversations, they just gave up and ignored her.

In her effort to keep her distance from the other slaves, Arliss chose many times to work at the least liked jobs.

No one liked working with Urage's marigolds which were a special variety he cultivated to plant between rows of crops. They gave off a strange pungent odor that was many many times stronger than the normal flower and easily discouraged insects and animals from feeding on the crops before they were harvested. The marigolds were said to be singularly responsible for Maudland's reputation for producing the finest vegetables on Eartheart.

Urage was said to be working on developing a new variety that grew on a vine that could be used in fruit trees to keep the birds away. Arliss spent several days alone cutting and tying the flowers into bundles for drying so their seed could be harvested. Her eyes stung and teared with the odor so much at first, that she began to detest the sight of the pretty maroon and gold flowers. Eventually she didn't even notice their odor.

The first day or so in the garden, she had been simply referred to as the Gypsy. She'd taken Iver's advice and had Minera's name on the tip of her tongue in case she had been ask her name. But there was a slave girl called Minca, a young girl, who was a bit of a tomboy, and very outgoing, she had a nickname for everyone, and it was she who began referring to Arliss as the marigold girl and then just as Marigold.

Arliss was grateful as she had the chance to get used to hearing herself called Marigold, many times before she was "expected to respond to the name. She listened closely to all the slaves conversations and she learned quite a lot about the keep. To her relief, Urage and a few of his regiments were away from the keep and were not expected back for some time. She wondered just how long it would take him to track her back to his doorstep. She hoped with all her heart that by the time he did, she would've figured out a plan of escape.

She learned that the keep was able to subsist almost indefinitely without outside supplies. The garden which was located on the seaward side of the keep, completely enclosed by high walls, easily provided enough fruit and vegetables to feed all of it's inhabitants.

Also located on the seaward side, but walled off from the garden, was a pasture for grazing animals.

The ramparts were used by the keep guards as well as the garden overseers as a walkway to get from one side of the keep to another. Arliss had noticed on her very first day in the garden, that as soon as the sun had set and the torches were lit the conversation among the slaves suddenly died down as they rushed almost frantically to finish what was left of the day's chores.

When she heard a sudden intake of breath from the slave next to her she glanced up and her blood froze as she saw two of the Carnumbra on horseback riding side by side on top of ramparts.

They halted right at Ludkin's station and wheeled their horses around so that they were facing down into the garden. Their red eyes swept down over the slaves who now groveled fear silent and unmoving.

Arliss had instinctively lowered her head at the same moment as the other slaves and she kept it lowered as she listened the unearthly voices of the Carnumbra as they spoke to Ludkin. Their voice's sounded so hollow and distorted that she couldn't make out what they said. She didn't lift her head until she'd heard them ride off.

Arliss had been sent up to the ramparts several times with Ludkin's meals. The view was magnificent. The Fane Sea was a moving, churning carpet of gray stretching out to the horizon. On clear days she could see a dark land mass to the east of the horizon this she learned was the edge of the great wilderness.

The keep jutted out into the Fane Sea It's steep walls rose blackened with time out of the frothy water. The wind on top of the ramparts was strong and salty, and it was good deal colder than in the protected garden below. With her back to the sea the view looking down into the garden was also spectacular. The entire garden laid out before her like some massive handmade quilt. Everything in it was neat and symmetrical. A small orchard lay in the dead center of the garden, laid out in a perfect circle. The various fruit and vegetable beds with pathways, were fitted together tightly and efficiently. So as not a scrap of garden went to waste.

Many times when she had the occasion to be on top of the ramparts, she had considered the possibility of jumping but even if she survived the jump. She still had leg irons to contend with along with hampering her ability to swim they would probably take her straight to the bottom and without the Poseidon bands she would perish.

When Ludkin soporific after a heavy lunch dosed lightly each afternoon, stirring like a cat at the least odd noise, the other overseers relaxed their stances also, although not daring to nap they quietly talked amongst themselves.

Arliss was surprised to find that the favorite topic of conversation among the slaves at this time was the folly of escape.

In low somber voices they retold to one another many horror stories of slaves caught in the act of escaping.

There was almost a sacredness about these stories no detail was too small to be included, it was as if the slave was now remembered better for the way that he died, rather than the way he was forced to live.

Arliss didn't know whether they told each other these tales to discourage themselves from trying, or just to remind themselves that there would be one final escape from their life of servitude.

One day however the tale was different. They had been picking green tomatoes putting them into burlap sacks to ripen gradually over the fall and early winter. Ludkin up at his station, was as usual was dozing away, his face to the sun. The usual litany of failed escapes was going on when Minca, who had been feeling contrary all day, interrupted.

"What about Mercadin" she challenged.

"You know he drowned Minca! said Beleese a shy mousy girl who considered her self Minca's best friend.

"I don't know that at all," retorted Minca airily

"Your just being awkward," sighed Beleese

Then Minca glancing up at the still snoozing figure of Ludkin, said as she lowered her voice and widened her eyes for emphasis, "How is it that no one ever saw his body"

Expecting no reply she added, "And don't tell me it got washed away, when I know that around here everything gets washed up on the beaches."

Then waggling her finger at them she said, "And don't forget he was working in the Banquet Hall so he wasn't wearing any leg irons." The other slaves looked uncomfortably as they stared silently at Minca.

That had been the extent of the conversation because after that the slaves broke up into smaller groups and moved to other parts of the garden.

Arliss dared not ask any details about the slave Mercadin for fear of drawing attention to herself, besides that she was beginning to suspect that there was a spy amongst them, a slave named Bonren who didn't seem to work as hard as the others, yet was never bothered by any of the overseers. Once when she was bringing Ludkin's lunch up she met Bonren on the narrow rampart stairs, and as she stood against the wall, to let him pass, she was surprised to smell whiskey on his breath. She knew Ludkin kept a bottle of it under his desk at his station.

However she did later learn that slaves serving in Urage's banquet hall, did not wear shackles because, Urage could not stand the noise the shackles made or the way they scratched up his fine marble floors, but apparently the slaves were made to put the shackles back on as soon as soon as they left the banquet hall. No one seemed to know how Mercadin made it up to the ramparts without his shackles on.

Arliss was relieved that she'd never been ask to go up on the ramparts after sun set when the Carnumbra began their patrol. In fact none of the slaves ever went up after sunset. Only Ludkin remained up there at his post sending all the other overseers down into the garden.

When she was sent up to collect his supper things, she had noticed that he always did the same thing. He would set his pipe down, that he finished every meal with, and he'd reach into his pocket and take out a silver medallion and put it around his neck. It had caught Arliss's eye immediately, because it looked so much like the Glasstarr Amulet except instead of a crystal star in the center there was a silver willow tree set in the crystal.

She enjoyed working in the garden despite the circumstances, she found the work peaceful and satisfying. Time was passing by now very rapidly. She'd marked the wall above her cot in the slave quarters, so as to keep track of time, she'd been in the keep garden ten days.

The weather had turned colder and the days had grown shorter. The soil in the garden now was so cold to work with that she like many of the other slaves had developed painful chilblains on her hands.

On the eleventh day Arliss was horrified to hear word that Urage expected home in a couple of weeks. The slaves murmured to each other about the great flurry of activity that was taking place in the keep, as preparations were made for the Lord's return. Things in the garden however were slowing down. The work was nearly all done. Most of the harvest had been taken in and stored, most of the beds had been turned over and prepared for spring.

Some of the women were talking about wintering over at the great weaving sheds in up the Broduck Hills. The women were looking forward to the change. Arliss felt own spirits start to rise as she learned that they would be leaving for the Broduck Hills, several days before Urage was due home.

It was strange now that she knew she was leaving the garden, she began to feel claustrophobic. She eagerly looked forward to leaving the oppressiveness of the keep.

Most of the men would be leaving the garden too. Some would stay on all winter to help with clearing the snow of the ramparts and courtyards of the keep. The rest of the men would form crews and go into nearby forests and cut down wood to replenish the keep's fuel supply. The wood they cut down this year would be properly seasoned to use next year. The men seemed equally happy to be getting out of the garden.

The garden itself looked bleak and gray they had already had a frost and everything had that dying look. She still had not come up with a plan of escape, she was hoping that the weaving sheds wouldn't be as well guarded as the keep and that she would have more opportunity to escape.

She awoke on the morning of her departure feeling lighthearted about at last getting away from the garden and the bleakness of the slave quarters. She didn't even care at this point if the place she was going to was any better or not, just so long as it was different.

Finally the day arrived for them to leave the garden. She'd taken her place in line in front a double wooden door in garden wall that separated the garden from the main courtyard of the keep. At last the doors were flung opened and she began to move forward with the line of slaves when suddenly she felt a hand on her shoulder.

"Just step out of line."

She froze, so great was her terror, that she'd thought of bolting, but somehow reason still held its fine net over her emotions, so she just stepped out of line and turned and looked up into the face of Ludkin the overseer.

As the other garden slaves filed past her, they eyed her with a mixture of and pity and speculation. She watched numbly as the last of them passed through the door in the wall and out of the garden. Ludkin bolted the door behind them.

Then as he turned toward her, she searched his face wondering if she'd been found out But Ludkin gave no clue.

He had taken out his tobacco pouch and was diligently filling a bowl of a rough carved pipe with the damp brown flakes punching them down tightly with the pad of his thumb. It calmed her to watch him do the same thing, she watched him do many times before.

"Now girl I've had my eye on you for some time now, your not like the other girls. Yep I've seen you working away on, your own, minding your own business like,"

Here he paused to suck on his pipe. His grizzly face mellowing a little with satisfaction. With the initial fright of being pulled out of line wearing off her, Arliss felt a growing feeling of frustration rising in her, with her escape from the keep garden, and possibly from Urage and Maudland thwarted.

Ludkin misreading her expression said," There now girl don't take on so, I know that you've been probably looking forward to the jaunt up to the hills and the indoor work, but as I was saying previous like. Your not like those other girls and you don't belong with them. I 'I've seen the way you keep to your yourself real private like, and I've noticed the way you figure things out for yourself, not like the others, they have to be told over and over again, and they still don't understand it. I like the way I don't have to get after you all the time to finish a job, you just do it."

He paused here and took several more puffs on his pipe. "Now here's what's going to happen, "he said as he prodded something on the ground with his foot.

She was listening attentively and meekly.

"You're going to go and work in the kitchens and they'll watch you and if you play you cards right you could go far."

She was going to be working in Urage's Kitchen! Arliss had a hard time covering up her fear and disappointment. She thought about, trying to persuade Ludkin that she would be better suited to the weaving sheds, but decided this was too risky as it would only serve to bring her under closer scrutiny, and that she wanted to avoid at all cost.

Ludkin surprised by Arliss lack of enthusiasm began to get annoyed. "You know girl you don't know how lucky you have it and you'd better sort out your thinking right now."

All the pleasantness was gone from his manner and there was a definite hard edge to his voice. The only thing she couldn't get to smile was her eyes so she lowered those.

"That's better," growled Ludkin as he slapped her on the back and spun her around and began walking with her in the direction of the kitchen.

"You have to know which side your bread is buttered on in this life. Lord Urage is a fair man to work for, he runs Maudland smart like. That's why we're so prosperous. Oh sure I know that some people might not think all his method are right but I say they are for the common good, like."

Arliss listened without comment.

"I know you may have seen some unpretty sights in the slave yard. There always is, but don't let that upset you none. Urage is actually doing them a favor as well as folks like us. Those people who are sorted out for the chop like, you know the sick the weak and idiots and such."

Arliss listened numbly chilled to the soul, as Ludkin carried on oblivious to her reaction.

"It's just as I said to my wife like, they'd suffer worse if they were allowed to live. Like isn't that why they're killed They'd just bring the rest of us down with them like. Any farmer will tell you it never pays to raise a runt. Take the garden slaves now that Master Kopter you know the man in the slave yard he's the one who does the sorting. He's got a good eye and an instinct for the stock. I am a little surprised that you ended up in the garden, he usually picks the garden slaves young strong but not too bright, makes them easier to manage."

He paused here as if suddenly troubled by a thought he had. They had arrived at the steps to the great covered porch outside the entrance to the kitchen it was here that Ludkin left her, reminding her to work hard and think straight.

She had just raised her hand to knock on the green door when the door was suddenly ripped opened causing the curtains on the window of the door to fly up in a cloud of lace.

There before her stood the most remarkable looking man she had ever seen. As he stood looking at her still clenching the door, his whole body seemed to bristle. He was small and wiry and neatly wrapped in a starched apron that seemed to go around his compact body almost twice. He wore beneath the apron a starched white tunic that looked impeccably clean, the cuffs of the tunic shirt were crisply folded three quarters way up his sinewy arms. Perched on his head like a crown, was an impossibly tall sage green hat.

His strangely pliant face was seething with indignation as he spat out," A slave! They send me Bree Filowdie a slave! and a garden slave no less."

Arliss was relieved that he had at last spoken as she had been afraid he would burst. Then he did the strangest thing, he said, "No!... Go away I don't want you!" and slammed the door.

Arliss stood stunned on the doorstop not knowing what to do. She was afraid to knock on the door again, and afraid to return to the Keep garden for fear of incurring Ludkin's ire. She stood there for a few moments, trying to sum up the courage to knock again, when the door was again flung open.

"Well get in here stop wasting my time, its bad enough that I have to put up with the likes of you. without having my valuable time wasted as well."

Speechless, she followed him into the kitchen.

Bree Folowdie's eyes narrowed as he studied the young slave girl he had brought in with him. He watched as her eyes drank in the room. What a strange girl. What was it about her that was different Anyway she certainly was attractive. Her face held a reserve to it that out of place in a slave.

Even when he was yelling at her, he'd been struck by the way she didn't even flinch, but regarded him with a certain amount of curiosity even amusement.

Bree paused for a moment to consider whether or not, he should have been offended by this. Arliss had never been in the kitchen before as the food was always brought out by scullery maids and slavants. Her first impression was of cleanliness the huge kitchen was spotless, everything from the sparkling white crockery displayed on long shelves that lined the walls, to the huge scrubbed trestle table that stood in the middle of the kitchen.

A slavant stood by fireplace slowly turning a spit on which roasted a huge haunch of beef. There were brick ovens on either side of the fireplace from which came the sweet aroma of baking bread.

As he took in Arliss's appreciative gaze, Bree Filowdie took an instant liking to her. For a few days, Bree Flowdie kept her so busy that she almost forgot she was in the Blackwillow Keep. She'd never a spare moment to worry about her predicament. She now knew why Filowdie's kitchen was so clean. He was a tyrant, he kept her scrubbing and polishing all day long. If it was in the kitchen and it didn't move she was expected to scrub and polish it. Each night she'd collapse on her cot in the slave quarters and fall instantly to sleep. After a few days of this torture, she was beginning to remember her days out in the keep garden fondly.

Then he promoted her to peeling and scrubbing vegetables, this was a pleasant change as there were only so many vegetables he could ask her to peel and scrub. When her work was over he allowed her to watch him cook. She was not allowed to touch anything mind you, just to look.

Arliss had been in the kitchen only a few days when word came that Urage would be arriving home any day now. She had been until then working at Bree Filowdie side. The housekeeper who happened to be Ludkin's spinster sister was engaged what apparently an on going struggle with Flowdie over staff she said she would need help from the kitchen people to prepare the banquet hall and serve the meals as the keep was shorthanded because of Urage's long absence many of the female house slaves had been sent to the breeding farms and they wouldn't have there full complement of staff for a while.

Filowdie said it was already bad enough that they had to cook for the entire keep without having to do housekeeping's work for it, however much power Filowdie had in the end he gave in, albeit grudgingly.

When Arliss learned that she was being sent to work in the banquet hall she felt physically ill at the thought of being in the very same room as Urage. She knew that if she had to serve him that she would surely recognize her.

Chapter Seventeen
Urage Returns

The next morning Arliss had a partial reprieve as she prepared to leave the kitchen when Bree told her that after the banquet hall was made ready for Lord Urage's return, she would only be needed to serve supper as the Lord would be taking the rest of his meals in his suit. He reminded her that eventually when housekeeping had its full complement of slaves, she could return to the kitchen permanently. Arliss only hoped that she would live that long.

When Hassa Ludkin the housekeeper had first taken off Arliss's leg irons she had felt so incredibly light that for one mad instant she'd felt like pirouetting, but one look at Hassa Ludkin's dour face had persuaded her otherwise. It was a feminized version of her brother's, except Arliss didn't think it had been feminized enough.

As she glanced around her eyes got used to the dim light. She couldn't get over how gloomy the hall was, even now during the day with every chandelier lit, there was still not enough light to chase away the deep shadows that crouched in every corner. The only natural light that entered the immense hall filtered in through a large rose shaped stained glass window at the far end of the hall.

Underneath this window on a dais stood a massive baronial table and thirteen chairs. Hassa Ludkin set Arliss to work dusting and polishing it. As she polished diligently away, her face was reflected clearly in the soft black patina of the wood, and for a second or two, when she glanced down, she didn't recognize herself. She looked so different with the dark hair, but then when a moment later she happened to glanced down at the table again she recoiled in shock as the face of a hag leered back up at her. She caught her breath sharply as she stared wide eyed with disbelief as the crone's face slowly faded and her own reappeared.

Shaken, she glanced around and found that apparently no one else had noticed. Without daring to look down again, she finished polishing the table as quickly as possible.

Later that evening when she asked Bree about the table on the dais. He seemed surprised at her interest and glanced curiously at her as he told her that the table and thirteen chairs had been carved out of a single black willow tree that had grown over the grave of Urage's mother, Mardylla.

By late afternoon they had finished cleaning the banquet hall. Arliss lined up with the rest of the slaves to have her leg irons put back on, When Hassa Ludkin got to her she shook her head and grunted as she said irritably," Mr. Flowdie says your too important to him to be bound and fettered and the clatter of your chains offends his sensitive ears. So for now we'll leave these off."

Then Hassa Ludkin waved her bony finger at Arliss as she said, "But mind you girlie one false move from you and they'll be back on faster that you can say Bree Filowdie."

She was sent her back to the kitchen and told that she wouldn't be needed back in the banquet hall until tomorrow afternoon, when they would set up the tables for Lord Urage's welcoming home supper.

When she returned to the kitchen she found Bree Flowdie up to his elbows in flour, he was pleased to see her, he hadn't expected her back so soon. She helped him well into the evening peeling fruits and vegetables for his sweet and savory pies.

However something odd happened that she felt was of vital import but she just couldn't sort it all out. It all began very simply. Bree needed some more of the dried mushrooms that he was using in the preparation of a soup dish that he was going to serve on the first night of Urage's return.

These mushrooms were grown in nearby caves down by the water. They then were brought up and hung up on long strings from the rafters in a storage shed, located in a distant corner of the pasture, there they were dried and were used throughout the year.

Arliss had been to this shed a couple of times before with Bree to bring back preserved food to use in the kitchen but this was the first time she had ever gone alone. It was just dusk when she set off from the kitchen and Bree noticing for the first time how late it was, looked on the point of changing of changing his mind about sending her but seeing how anxious she was to go he relented. Before she went he called Hassa Ludkin's the housekeeper and explained the errand he was sending Arliss on. She looked at Arliss closely for a moment or two and then without a word drew a disk and chain off, of the heavy chatelaine that hung from her waist, and handed it to Bree saying as she walked away, "Be it on your head. Filowdie."

After making what Arliss was sure was a vulgar gesture, at the retreating form of Hassa Ludkin, Bree turned to her opening the hand that held the disk as he said, "This is your key to getting past the Carnumbra."

Mystified she took the thin silver disk from him

it was slightly smaller version of the one she'd seen Ludkin put on every night after supper. It was very plain except for the center which was of clear crystal with a silver willow tree set in the crystal.

"Marigold," said Bree watching her face very closely as always when he said the name as if he knew it wasn't her real name.

"Now you're a smart girl I can see that, but be careful after the sunsets till just before it rises, the ramparts are patrolled by the Carnumbra. You must go by way of the ramparts to get to the pasture shed, as the gates between the garden and the pasture are locked always at sundown, now if you are wearing this," he said as he plucked the disc out of her hand and dangled it front of her.

"They will know where you work in the keep, whether your male or female, slave or freeman."

"Now if you don't have this with you," he said gesturing to the disc. You will be killed on sight. "Bree paused and looked pointedly at Arliss."

"Take my advice and don't try anything clever. Even if you should survive the Carnumbra you will have wished you hadn't when Master Kopter gets a hold of you."

Bree seemed satisfied by Arliss's sobered attitude he nodded his approval as she placed the disc around her neck.

"That's good," he said, "If the disc is not worn it you may as well be carrying a shoe horn for all the good it will do you."

So albeit with much trepidation, she hurried out of the kitchen across the garden. Her footsteps had a strange hollow echo as she raced up the steep stairway in the keep wall to the top of the ramparts.

She stood catching her breath at the head of the stairs, there was no one in sight in either direction. The night had fallen dark and heavy and the wind had picked up, blowing cold and bitter. She shivered as she gathered her cloak around her and set off in the direction of the shed. She carried a basket in one hand as she walked along, she put her free hand over the silver disc, just to reassure herself that it was still there.

As gray mist began to roll in from the sea. She could see only a few feet in front of her. She felt like she was walking through clouds along a highway in the sky. She hadn't gone very far when she heard the sounds of hoof beats coming toward her.

She touched the disc again as the pounding of the hoofs drew near, her heart matched the rhythm of the hoof beats.

Then as if sensing her presence the hoof beats slowed to a trot then to a walk until finally the horse and rider emerged out of the mist before her.

Arliss brought herself up short, her courage draining away at the sight of the massive wraith-like horse and rider.

The creature came to a halt just a few feet in front of her she felt the wind die down as the air around her suddenly grew much colder.

The being sat still on his steed carefully regarding her.

Looking into the face of the Carnumbra was like looking into endless night.

In the quick furtive looks Arliss got of the creature she couldn't see a face beneath the shrouded hood, just fiery red eyes.

As the Carnumbra continued to observe her, she stood perfectly still, for what seemed like an eternity, her eyes downcast as she clutched at the disc so tightly that she was sure the chain would snap. Just when she thought the game was up and the creature was on to her, there was a sudden movement and she glanced up in time to see the creature pull back on the reins of his horse and started on his way again.

As Arliss turned to watch his retreating form, she relaxed her stance and at that moment something strange and frightening happened. She flashed back to Camden cove that predawn morning when she spotted Urage and the Carnumbra up on the rise behind her house and at the very moment the picture flashed into her head the Carnumbra on the rampart who was on the verge of disappearing into mist, stopped short and wheeled around toward her.

Instinctively as though she wore a Poseidon band she blocked her mind and as she did this, she was startled to see that the creature seemed suddenly confused, its red eyes looking right through her.

After a moment or two, it drew out it's sword, and began sweeping it to either side until it clanged against the rampart walls. In this manner horse and rider moved slowly toward her. Arliss's heart was in her throat, as she stood riveted to the spot unable to tear her eyes away from the advancing Carnumbra. there was no point running as she knew she could never out run the creature. Still clutching to her basket she crept quickly backwards, away from the advancing blade, all the while her hand groping along the wall. Feeling a gap in the wall she turned quickly and stepped up into the castelated notch of wall.

Arliss held her breath as the Carnumbra stopped in it's tracks and cocked it's head to one side, just then her basket scraped against the wall, the effect was immediate as the Carnumbra moved forward again with his blade held high his eyes fixed on the exact spot in the notch that Arliss stood.

She was so terrified that she was beyond thinking so there was no logic or reason to what she did.

It was a feeling rather than a thought that made her take off the disc while still blocking her thoughts and lay it on top of the wall beside her. Keeping her fear at bay she allowed her mind to become one with the elements.

She was the wind. She was that part of the wind that can be felt but not touched. She stood in the notch of the wall, her hair let loose from the kerchief blowing behind her, with her cape billowing out. Almost immediately the Carnumbra came to halt pausing only long enough to slip the blade back into its sheath before turning on its heel and riding briskly back into the mist.

It was many long moments before she had the courage to let down her control put the disc back on and continue on her errand. She retrieved the mushrooms from the shed and hurried back to the kitchen without further incident. She had not dared think about the significance of what had happened until she was safely back in her narrow cot of the slave quarters. Despite being unsure of exactly what had happened and why, she felt encouraged. This was the first time in all of the weeks of being held as a slave, did she see the possibility of escape. For the first time in a long while she fell asleep happy.

Arliss slept deeply she didn't hear the sound of urgent voices and running feet in the courtyard as Urage returned to the Blackwillow Keep in the dead of night.

"The Master is home." said Bree as she entered the kitchen that morning.

She was still reeling from this news when Bree a few moments later went on to tell her that they were all summoned to witness a public execution of a spy in the slave yard later that morning.

Sickened by the thought of having to watch someone executed, Arliss begged Bree Filowdie to let her remain behind and work.

Filowdie's face, took on a strange look as he said quietly, "We all must be there to bear witness so that the suffering will not be forgotten."

He had spoke in such a low voice that Arliss wasn't even sure she'd heard him right but she didn't dare ask him to repeat it.

It was the first time she had been back in the slave yard since the day that Master Kopter had sent her to the garden, the day she saw the man with the wooden leg struck down.

The sky was dark gray the air was thick and heavy it looked like it was going to rain soon. Arliss stood at the edge of the crowd next to Filowdie. She was standing near the doors, that she had been thrown out of, many weeks ago, when suddenly without warning they swung open and the guards lead the prisoner out. Arliss gasp in horror as she saw that the prisoner was none other than Iver Kedwick!

He spotted her immediately and a look of recognition flooded across his pale courtly face. His funny handlebar mustache seemed so pathetically cheerfully on his grave face. His eyes fluttered fearfully over the courtyard, coming to a rest at the gallows that had been erected in the center of the slave yard.

He glanced back at Arliss and gave a sad shrug of resignation.

Arliss watched helplessly as Iver bound in chains was led over to the gallows and up the steps of the platform.

From high up on a balcony on the keep wall there was the sound of doors opening and an unnatural hush came over the already quiet crowd.

Arliss gasped and as she recognized Urage this was the first time she had seen him since he pursued her down the slopes of the island of Thallassa. Arliss turned her eyes back to Iver. With a sense of unreality, she watched as they placed a sack over his head, and as they put the noose around his neck, she gasped and started forward. Filowdie grabbed her roughly and spoke angrily through clenched teeth, "Don't indulge yourself that will help no one. "

Iver was standing over the trap door now and before she had properly assimilated that information there was the sound of a latch being pulled, and a whooshing sound with a hollow clack as the trap door hit the underside of the platform and then a sickening thud and the sound of a cry cut short. At the same time Arliss felt a sudden rush of air and caught sight of a flash of metal leaving Filowdie's hand and a split second later a knife landed squarely in Iver's chest, buried to the hilt. The crowd was in an uproar.

Upset and confused Arliss turned to Filowdie his face had a weariness to it she had not seen before. His voice rough and cracking as he said, "The last one they hung took a very long time to die. He lay in a heap after they cut him down, his neck broken, his throat half collapsed, choking in his own blood. This won't happen this time I made sure of that."

On the balcony was Urage raised his hand for silence and got it. "Which of you did this?"

For a few moments the question just hung in the air, but everyone knew despite the coolness of the voice that this was not just a question but a command for the perpetrator to reveal himself.

Urage's face remained immobile but his eyes took on the look of a predator as they flicked back and forth over the crowd. In a sudden movement Bree Flowdie broke away from Arliss and sprang into the courtyard into the direct line of vision of Urage. Sweeping his green chef's hat off he swept the floor with it in a exaggerated bow.

"Sir, may I be among the first to welcome you home."

Urage, his face hard and unyielding ignored Filowdie's greeting.

Sir, if I had known that this would cause such a fuss, I would not have done it. I was merely trying to hasten things along. It's is not good for an artist like myself to witness a drawn out grizzly affair. It offends my sensibilities."

The guards by now stood on either side of Filowdie just waiting for orders.

Urage's face was implacable as he stared down at Filowdie then he let out a laugh that seemed to bounce of the keep walls.

The crowd giggled nervously.

Then he reigned in his laugh so suddenly that many didn't hear him some and some continued laughing in a way that was more frightening than crying, until Urage brought them up suddenly as his voice cracked through the air

"Oh Mr. Filowdie how unthinking of me not to think of your precious sensibilities. Any more of this nonsense I will take your sensibilities and roast them over a spit along with the rest of you."

There was a snicker from somewhere in the crowd.

"You silly little man you really think your irreplaceable."

Arliss could see Bree's body tremble, but his voice was strong. Gesturing up at balcony he said brazenly, "I'm sorry Sir, if I've made a little mistake. I'm a genius in the kitchen but out here I am not so smart."

For a moment Urage's lip curled as a look of annoyance crossed his face, as he said irritably "Let him go!"

Bree immediately began bowing and scraping as he said over and over again, "Oh thank you sir! Thank you, sir! You won't regret it. Tonight I will cook for you the finest meal you ever had."

Urage with a look of scorn turned on his heel and disappeared through the balcony doors. The sigh of relief was audible from the crowd.

As the slave yard began to empty a man came out of the small door in the wall with a barrow and Arliss still shocked, watched as the man cut Iver's gaunt lifeless body down from the noose that still held it and laid it in the barrow and wheeled it back through the door in the wall and as she heard the hellhounds began to howl, she wondered if she'd ever be able to cry again.

Arliss was dressed a white smocked apron over a long dark dress with a cap that fitted snugly on her head it was what all the slaves serving the banquet hall wore.

The hall was dimly lit with candles mounted in huge wheels that hung from the beams of the arched ceiling. Candles burned in all the candelabras on every table, but still there were still vast puddles of darkness throughout the great hall. Arliss was counting on this dimness to protect her from recognition.

The hall filled up very fast. From her place in the shadows, Arliss had a perfect a view of Urage. His face illuminated by the candelabra seemed to almost float in space as the rest of his body was swathed in black.

Her hackles rose as she noticed the unlit gallery overhead, filling up with the Carnumbra. All she could see was their red eyes glowing like coals in the dark. The Carnumbra from their vantage point could see everything in the hall.

Hassa Ludkin had giving her the job of clearing away the used plates and goblets and she was warned to intrude as little as possible. She was told that she should be like a shadow and flit from table to table and that suited her just fine..

The next few weeks were a blur to Arliss, she wasn't quite sure how she got through them. She worked in the kitchen from dawn to dusk and in the evenings she served in the banquet hall. At night back in the slave quarters she fell into a dead dreamless sleep.

Urage during this time had not once looked her way indeed as she studied him from afar he did not seem to notice anyone so engrossed in his own thoughts he was.

Many evening Urage would entertain guest some of these were very odd looking. She remembered vividly one guest in particular a very attractive woman with shiny black shoulder length hair who was served live suckling pig. It was a few moments before Arliss realized what was going on and as the pig began to squeal in agony Arliss bolted from the hall into the kitchen and promptly threw up.

One evening Urage was visited by three elderly men. They came in after the meal began and refused to take a seat at Urage's table despite Urage asking them numerous times. They delivered their message to Urage very quickly and were soon gone.

The rest of the evening Urage was in a foul mood. He punished several of the slaves and slavants for very small infractions and at one point he threw a silver goblet across the room hitting a hapless slavant and splitting open her head. Then as he got up from his chair he up turned the massive table, sending nervous diners scattering as they barely managed to avoid being crushed as the table toppled over.

Arliss helped Hassa Ludkin take the injured slavant, into a little service alcove between the hall and the kitchen. She watched as Hassa expertly sponged off the slavants wound with alcohol and took out what appeared to be an ordinary sewing needle except it was very fine and slightly curved and threaded it with a translucent cord like material. She told Arliss it was sheep's gut. Arliss watched as she drew the skin together with single stitches which she tied off one at a time until the wound was completely closed. The slavant with a dressing on her wound was able to return to immediately to work in the dining hall.

Hassa Ludkin could see that Arliss was impressed with her handiwork.

"If there's one thing I do know, it's how to take care of my stock," she said with a look of satisfaction as she returned her supplies to a small cupboard in the alcove.

One evening Hassa Ludkin had assigned her to tables up near the dais this was the closest she'd ever been to Urage's table in all her weeks in the banquet hall. This was a mixed blessing as on one hand she did not wish to get too close to Urage on the other hand she might over hear something that was useful.

The first few nights the conversation among Urage and his men seemed to be mostly about hunting and fishing and the running of the keep and goings on in the various towns and villages in Maudland. It was almost as though they avoided talking about the conflict with the Orchid Valley and the returning heir. Then one night Arliss heard a familiar voice at the table. Then glancing up at the dais Arliss was shocked to recognize Klick, the officer who had accosted her and Janos during the border search.

"My Lord you look distracted tonight may I inquire as to the cause," questioned Klick respectfully.

Urage at first did not acknowledge the question, instead he said, to himself more than to those gathered around the table, "Just the last one now Klick, and Mardylla will finally be avenged and the way will be clear for me to take my rightful place on the Orchid throne and rule Eartheart."

"My Lord," said Klick hesitantly, "Surely the last one is dead." Arliss's ears pricked up with interest at this.

"Why we haven't even laid eyes on her since the Island in the Cascall sea. She must be dead my lord surely..."

The question hung for several long moments in the air before Urage spoke again.

"She is very much alive and steadily gaining control and power I feel her very strongly."

Arliss instinctively brought up her mental shields this was a mistake she realized immediately as Urage's head shot up and he peered around the hall with the intensity of a predator. Arliss forced herself not to shrink back into the shadows instead she let go and became apart of everyone around her she let a little part of her go to this part of the hall and a little to another part and she began even to spread upwards and out of the great hall. At once she was all around the hall and outside of it. In the darkened part of the keep she felt all kinds of voices rise up and touch her core being which now was spread so thin, thinner than a film, thinner than a mood until she was no longer discernible. She felt herself spreading, still spreading. She was over ramparts and she was following the tide joyfully as it rolled back from the shore. It felt so sweet being elemental but she reached a point out in the Fane sea when she knew that if she went any further her body would grow cold and die back in the keep.

So back across the sea she went. The keep now lay a long way off at the shoreline, a massive square of blackness with flickering smoky lights. She flew back slowly and reluctantly over the ramparts. She felt Urage's searching presence like a thick black beam of light she thinned in parts of her being until she was sub elemental and the thick black beam passed through unhindered, but she grew weary as the dodging continued, then at long last the thick black beam began the fade until it finally disintegrated entirely.

She began to retreat back into the hall, from outside herself she saw Urage slumped over the table and all around him his officers waited anxiously for him to regain consciousness, they spoke in hushed voices.

The Carnumbra had cordoned off the dais from the rest of the hall, with their backs to the dias, their red eyes burned into the crowd in the hall.

With shock Arliss saw herself it took a few moments for her to actually believe it was her. She was standing off to the side in the shadows, looking straight ahead, a tray hung loosely from one of her hands the other rested on her chest and she could see her breathe rise slow and shallow in her chest. Her face was still dark from the henna her hair was completely tucked under the starched white cap not one hair was visible. Her gray eyes looked black in the shadows her face was not the same face that she saw each day in the mirror before coming through Shadow lake. It was thinner with deep shadows under her unfocussed eyes and somehow it looked younger.

Slowly she snaked her way in a little at a time reclaiming her physical being. All the while she strengthens her mental wall until she was at the core of a thick mental fortress. She felt very dizzy but kept her composure.

Urage was still out cold and now the ranks of Carnumbra broke to allow a chaise lounge to be carried in. A different mood had taken over the hall. There was confusion as people left there seats to catch a glimpse of Urage.

Klick seemed to be the highest ranking officer on the dais he was busy delegating various task to the other officers. Arliss knew this was it, her chance to make her move. When Urage awoke it would only be a matter of time before he figured out who she was, it was now or never.

Her eyes still on the dais she started to move backwards further out of the range of light deeper into the shadows. Klick's back was to her, when suddenly he spun around, his eyes immediately locking on to hers. The recognition was immediate.

Her heart sunk as she saw him grin as he took in her slave status and she was horrified when he beckoned to her.

Hesitantly, she made her way across the hall to where Klick stood, hoping against hope that she was mistaken and that he hadn't recognized her after all.

He waited until she was directly in front of him before reaching out and grasping her by the collar and all but lifting her off the ground.

"I seem to remember that you and I gypsy, have some unfinished business to take care of," he whispered between clenched teeth.

Just then someone from up on the dais called Klick's name.

Letting go of her reluctantly he said, "I'll settle with you latter," He glanced over his shoulder toward the dais before allowing himself a parting shot.

"We'll how defiant you are now that your one of Lord Urage's slaves. I may have to teach you some manners," he said touching the whip looped at his side, he left no doubt of his intentions.

Just then there was a disturbance on the dais. Klick spun around and left.

Momentarily transfixed with fear Arliss watched as Urage was being carried from the hall in the chaise lounge. At the same time she saw Klick standing with a soldier talking to him and pointing to her.

That was all it took to break the spell and impel Arliss into action, she knew that it was now or never. The instant Klick and the soldier turned away, she slipped down behind the table crouching out of sight she wove her way in and out of the tables, moments later a shout went up from the dais, as she reached the kitchen door she heard footstep running in the hall.

The kitchen was filled with slaves dressed exactly as she. She slipped unnoticed out the green door to the garden from the corner of her eye she saw soldiers enter the kitchen.

She ran across the garden toward the rampart steps breathless she reached the top of the stairs. Below her in the garden she heard the kitchen door open and sound of raised voices and running feet.

As she ran down the middle of the rampart she tore off her hat and apron. Her chest burned with exertion. She ran full out not once did not slow her pace.

By the time she had reached the corner where the ramparts ran parallel to the Fane sea, she heard footsteps running behind her. She clambered up on the rampart wall and looked down into the Fane sea it seemed an awful long way down, but she braced herself and prepared to launch herself off the ramparts and into the water.

Just as she was about to jump a black leather gloved hand clamped around her chest and she felt something hard on her arm and when she looked up all she saw was black leather and mail and then she was airborne the keep wall rose up as she spun through the black night her captor still held her.

When the Fane came up to greet them he did not let go He hit the water first absorbing the shock with his powerful legs bent deeply.

They plunged deep into the icy black water down down down, it was a few heartbeats before she realized that she wasn't drowning.

And still her captor still held her. She touched her forearm and traced the familiar outline of the jeweled fish of the Poseidon band and she reached up in the darkness of the water and felt the deep cleft in her captors chin and whispered, "Striker!"

Chapter Eighteen
With Old Friends Again

A few minutes later she made out the phosphorescent shape of Whapper swimming rapidly toward them. They greeted each other warmly but briefly.

"Come quickly we must hurry!" he urged them, "The Whisper is anchored, just over the horizon."

Lengths ahead of them, Whapper cut through the water with seemingly no effort. His form graceful in water, was adapted perfectly for swimming through the briny sea.

Arliss had taken Striker's knife and cut away most of the fabric of her skirt to free up her legs for swimming. With her eye on Whapper, she reached and pulled and kicked through the murky water. It always amazed her when she wore the Poseidon band, that although she was very aware at how cold the water was, she herself didn't feel cold.

There wasn't much time for conversation as she and Striker struggled to keep up with Whapper, but Striker did tell her that every one was safe and waiting anxiously on the ship to greet them.

Arliss was overjoyed to hear that no one had been lost. She was even looking forward to seeing Elsaroth. It wasn't long before they saw the outline of the Whisper above them. The moon was high overhead as Arliss surfaced next to the Whisper, almost immediately two pair of hands reached down and hauled her onto the ship.

"You're a sight for sore eyes!" exclaimed Farin giving her bear hug so strong that it lifted her clear off the deck. Then as he set her down she recognized the second man who had helped her aboard.

"Janos!" she cried in pleased surprise.

"It's a long story Gadja." said Janos shrugging shyly.

Elsaroth in a white ball gown and feathered cape that looked slightly disheveled and much out of place on the tiny sailing ship, swept Janos aside and descended on Arliss embracing her warmly. Then holding her at arm's length, she wrinkled her nose in distaste as she said, "What happened to your hair? It looks just awful. Why I hardly recognized you."

Arliss bit her lip to keep from smiling as Elsaroth gave a theatrical sigh as she muttered crossly, "I suppose I'll have to be the one to take care of this mess. You obviously, wouldn't care if your head was full of rat tails."

Then ignoring Arliss she turned to Whapper and began to list the aquatic plants she would need him to get her. Mallwynn appeared suddenly in front of Arliss in the moonlight. He looked tired and pale but his eyes as he met hers were twinkling.

"Slightly battered but none the worse for wear I hope?" he asked his voice gruff.

"Yes." she said simply.

Then he gave her one of his rare smiles as he said, "I'm very glad to see you. You gave us quite a scare"

By now Striker and Whapper were on board and everyone was talking at once. Mallwynn reminded them that there was little time to waste as it was only a matter of time before Urage realized what had happened. They would have to make haste as even now Urage could be launching a pursuit.

They weighed anchor and set off immediately. With the Whisper underway, they were all kept busy as they tacked rapidly across the Fane sea, trying to put as much distance between themselves and the keep.

They planned to put in, off the coast of the Great Wilderness to the north and west of Maudland. They would drop anchor there and wait till sunrise before sailing into one of the many coastal inlets. It would be far too risky to attempt this landing at night as the coast was riddled with sharp rocks that lay in shallow water off the shore. It would be very difficult avoiding scraping the keel and damaging or even sinking the boat. After several hours of hard sailing they finally dropped anchor a few miles off the coast of the great wilderness.

"Kipper," gasped Arliss with surprised pleasure as the cat sprang from out of the shadows of the foot of the companionway. He meowed at her reproachfully as she knelt to pick him up. He seemed to almost bristle at her touch.

"Oh come on Kipper! It wasn't my fault I left you." she said as she withdrew her hand from the cat's fur, smiling in spite of herself at the cat's touchy dignity

Then adopting the proper sober attitude she addressed the cat.

"Yes, I know it must have been a great worry for you, my being gone, without so much as by-your-leave," she consoled sympathetically. The cat responded with a frosty glare.

"And you not knowing where I was. I don't blame you for being miffed not one bit." she cooed softly

The cat was silent but now permitted Arliss to stroke it's fur.

"You must have worried yourself sick." she soothed, rubbing the cat between his ears.

"Well I'm back for good now."

Kipper let out suspicious yowl.

"Well yes, I know you have your doubts. I do too, but as far as I know I won't be leaving you anytime soon."

The cat appeared mollified moving closer to her.

"What a good cat you are," she said as she picked him up and continued to stroking him. The cat began to purr softly at first then no longer able to contain his pleasure at seeing her again his reserve gave way to a deep throaty purr that made Arliss's cheeks quiver as she held him close to her face.

As they gathered around the table in the alcove for supper the light from the gently swinging copper lamps overhead, caste a warm glow on all their faces. The mood during the meal was light and carefree, There was a lot bantering back and forth. It was as though everyone had secretly agreed that they would take this brief respite from their ordeals and the battle that was even now gathering. The ship for them that night was like a haven, one that they would have to leave in a short while.

Mallwynn was seated in the alcove sucking gently on an empty pipe watching Arliss. She was seated across from him absently stroking the cat. Elsaroth had given her dry clothes and helped dry and pin up her damp hair.

Mallwynn noticed a lot of change in Arliss. She looked very thin. Her hands and arms were deeply brown, scarred and callused from long hours of laboring in Urage's garden. That other world quality that he had always noticed in her eyes had deepened.

After dinner the laughter died down and the mood became serious as Arliss began to relate the tale of what had happened to her from her abduction till the moment she had decided to risk the leap off the ramparts.

Her face was grave and solemn as she spoke. She told them about the dungeon and meeting Iver Kedwick. She told them about the slave yard and the man with wooden leg and how they hung Iver Kedwick and about the bravery of Bree Filowdie how he had not let Iver suffer

Arliss told them about her experience on the ramparts with the Carnumbra and how she had removed the Black Willow disk and what had happened after that. Mallwynn's eyes widened and she heard several gasp when she recounted the incident in the dining hall when she fled out of the room the only way she could and how she eluded Urage in this manner and how he pursued her and she held on when he faded.

Janos nodded in recognition when she mentioned Klick.

Arliss told them how she finally managed to narrowly escape the hall while Urage was still unconscious.

They were silent for a few minutes and as Arliss's eyes rested on Janos, she thought of that day, that seemed almost another life time ago now, when he brought her the news that the Wizard and his party had plunged into Wenslydale gorge.

"You know I thought you were dead?" she said softly with wonder, still amazed at the recent turn of events.

Mallwynn smiled ironically as he lifted one eyebrow and said, "The same thing crossed our minds several times about you my dear. The way I remember it, you suddenly decided to chase after that cat of yours and that's the last we seen of you till now.

Kipper who was curled up on top of the bench behind Arliss opened his eyes a slit at the mention of the word cat and then unconcerned and guiltless went back to sleep.

Striker, who was seated across from Arliss stretched out his long legs and leaned back against the bench as he launched into the tale,"You disappeared so fast I remembered glancing back and seeing you myself not five minutes before I heard Whapper's cry. We searched well into the night, without finding a single clue as to your whereabouts. For days after that, we crisscrossed all the trails and pathways in the Mural forest without laying eyes on any sign off you. It was almost as if the forest had swallowed you up. We headed out of the forest along the Maudland road and came upon a place where a band of gypsies had recently camped. We were following their trail when Urage came upon us and pursued us to the bridge over Wenslydale Gorge. When he cut the anchor ropes and the bridge gave way, we were all plunged into the gorge. The gorge was so deep it seemed like we fell forever."

"You were lucky to have survived that fall, said Arliss with a shiver as even now she pushed back the vivid nightmare pictures her mind had conjured up, when she'd been told that they'd all plunged to their deaths.

"Through sorcery I was able save us all from certain death, but the effort took much out of me," said Mallwynn quietly as he began filling his pipe with what looked liked damp crushed flower petals.

"Mallwynn was unconscious for many weeks after the bridge collapsed," explained Striker.

"The magic comes from within me and my powers are limited. If I stretch beyond my limits I risk dangerously depleting myself, so much so that I can no longer sustain my own vital functions. I am also very old, so it takes me far longer than it used to, to recover, when I've been required to use an extraordinary amount of my power." he said as he lit his pipe and he inhaled deeply.

"Thanks to Mallwynn, we hit the water very gently and avoided the rocks, said Striker. "All of us, horses and all, managed to stay afloat as we drifted down the river for a mile or two, until the steep cliffs of the gorge disappeared and the river widened and we came to a bridge. The water had become shallow and slow moving so we were able to swim ashore. Mallwynn by this time was almost unconscious and had to be helped out of the water. We went up a grassy bank and headed down the road to get as far away as quickly as possible from Urage's troops. We stopped only long enough to construct a litter to carry Mallwynn who was by then deeply unconscious.

After traveling down the road for sometime we came to a village on a Lake, the town of Milltown on Muskrat lake. We went directly to the lumber mill at the head of the lake where we were taken in by the old man and his wife who ran the Mill.

Days passed and Mallwynn still showed no signs of waking. We were extremely worried and we were also concerned about not finding you and the trail was getting colder all the time. It was finally decided that we would leave and Elsaroth would stay with Mallwynn. I took Whapper with me to try and pick up your trail. Farin went off alone to some of the border towns and villages on the Orchidian side of the Spirit River to do some reconnoitering."

Farin broke in speaking for the first time, "Many of these people have close relatives that live over the border in Maudland. A lot of the people I talked too were very upset about the recent turns of event since the death of the old King. Urage had never before been so bold as to cross the borders in broad daylight, and now there was talk that he was closing down the borders, and soon no one would be permitted in or out of Maudland. I made some important contacts and I was able to find out a lot of useful information."

There was a slight pause in the conversation and Arliss was just about to ask Mallwynn, when it was that he finally woke, when Elsaroth cleared her throat.

As usual her timing was perfect and all eyes turned her way as they waited with bated breath for her to speak her piece. Her soft platinum hair was gathered in smooth sensible knot on the crown of her head only a few rebellious curls bounced softy on her forehead. She too had changed in the recent months, her face had thinned and lost its pampered look. She still looked feisty but a sense of caution had entered her demeanor.

As she began to speak and her eyes looked upwards as if she were visualizing and reliving the events that she related.

"Well naturally I didn't like being left on my own, with Mallwynn in the state he was in, but alas there was nothing else for it, so naturally I arose to the occasion,"

Here she slid her eyes over to Mallwynn, making sure he hadn't taken offense.

"We had told the miller and his wife who Mallwynn was. We didn't have to do much convincing as they recognized the famed Darrowglynn seal on his staff. They offered the mill as shelter and their services to aid us in any way they could. Striker told them of our need for secrecy. The miller's wife disguised me as a peasant woman. She told her neighbors that I had been traveling across the moor with my brothers, my husband and my father returning back home from the City of Orchids to the family farm on the Misty Downs, when my father took ill. Whapper believe or not was supposed to be my husband," she said glancing over at Whapper with a look of distaste.

Whapper just smiled serenely.

"Naturally he had to wear a hood over his face, people were told he wore it because his face was badly scarred from the pox."

Then looking sidelong at Whapper with a wicked gleam in her eye, she said, "Actually Whapper, it rather suited you."

Then she continued smoothly, "While the men were gone I worked at the mill, mostly helping out the miller's wife and I took care of Mallwynn. Not that he needed a lot of care. He lay in a very deep sleep. He had no need for food or other nourishment. His skin was cold to touch and the color of creamy alabaster. He didn't move hardly at all, he was like a statue. Only if you put your face close to his mouth could you actually be sure he was breathing. He just lay there like a stone carving on a cot in the front room of the miller's house.

The miller and his wife were good people but they had no life in them. Everyday they got up at the crack of dawn and worked till dusk. Then they would have their evening meal, after which they would sit on either side of the fire and snore away the evening. They had no children only a pet dog, who the miller's wife was always knitting sweaters for. Even the dog slept away the evening on a rug near the fire. This routine went on day in, day out for weeks. I thought I would die of boredom. At times I used to almost wish that Urage would discover where we were, just so that we would have an excuse to leave the mill.

So in order to entertain myself and not lose my social skills, for who knows I might need them again someday. I began to regale Mallwynn with tales of court life, some of them very naughty indeed, as a gentleman I'm sure he'll keep them to himself. However after a few weeks of this, I noticed that Mallwynn seemed to have a faint hint of color in his cheeks while I was telling him these stories.

At first I thought that I was imagining this, but I had the miller's wife watched with me one day and she noticed the same thing. It was she who had the idea to bring in the children of the village and have them sit with Mallwynn and tell him their stories. Then soon the adults of the village came and told their stories. Soon every one had a story to tell Mallwynn. Sometimes they whispered secrets in his ear that no one else knew. Sometimes they told him their saddest stories. Stories so sad they made me cry just listening to them. They also told him their happiest stories, the best things that ever happened to them these too sometimes made me sad."

Then Elsaroth's face took on an almost petulant look as if she expected someone to disagree, as glancing sidelong at Mallwynn, she said, "I like to think the stories that Mallwynn enjoyed the most were mine. I know my stories weren't particularly deep nor moving, but they were all very amusing."

Mallwynn made no comment but continued tamping out his pipe on the palm of his hand, but Arliss was certain she saw a smile cross his face when he thought Elsaroth wasn't looking.

"The strange thing was," continued Elsaroth, "That not only did Mallwynn look a little better after all the story telling but the people did too, even though they didn't even suspect that he was the Arch Mage, they seemed to feel better just telling him their stories."

Many days had past and I had almost given up hope that the men would ever return, when one morning just after dawn, I was in bed in my tiny room under the eaves of the house when heard a commotion outside. Naturally I thought it was Whapper, Striker, and Farin returning. I was so relieved as Mallwynn still hadn't awakened. I sprang out of bed and threw open the window and what should I see down on the grass under a tree but a gypsy struggling with a horse. At first I was so disappointed that I could have cried," said Elsaroth flashing Janos an apologetic look.

"Imagine then my surprise when I realized that the horse he was struggling with was none other than Targus, Arliss's Horse. I couldn't believe my eyes."

Janos smiled and nodded remembering the morning that he and Elsaroth had first met, he said, "I heard this strange screaming from a window high up in the millers house. I was so startled I nearly let go of the horse's reigns. I saw a woman in her night clothes at the window waving her arms around as she cried out something about the horse. I could not understand a word she was saying. Suddenly she slammed the window shut and I had not long to wait before the front door opened and out she came. I could see that she was very upset. The Gadja's cat, who was in a tree over near the front door, leapt immediately into Elsaroth's arms.'

"I was so startled I thought I'd faint." breathed Elsaroth as she fixed Kipper with a stern look and said, "You know its rude to drop in unannounced.'

The cat opened one eye briefly to stare at Elsaroth, then returned to sleep...

"But Gadja," said Janos looking at Arliss as he resumed the tale, "My part of the story really began the morning that we discovered you gone. Malcazar and a couple of the men along with Desmone were missing from the morning camp fire. When they returned I ask them about your disappearance. They said that they knew nothing. They were just out hunting and sure enough they had brought back a few braces of birds. But I did not believe them and I kept at them, asking them what they had done with you, and before long I got the truth out of them. I was so angry that I felt like killing Malcazar on the spot, but instead I sent him and Desmone away.

My mother Minera brooded for many days, about your disappearance, and when Kamishka spoke in her, she warned of dire things to come if Urage wasn't brought down. Kamishka said that if Urage gains the Eartheart throne, we Rom would be amongst the first to go.

Many weeks passed and we never heard word of you although we asked along the road of merchants who had recently been to the keep, but non remembered seeing you.

Then late one wet miserable night I look out when lo and behold what do I see but the Gadja's magnificent horse.

I called Minera and when she saw the horse she told me it was a sign for me to set out and see where the horse would lead me. She said it was my destiny.

Early the next morning the horse was still waiting just as I knew he would, even though I hadn't bothered to tie him up. He stood still while I mounted him and as I started to leave the camp Minera handed me this."

He paused in his tale and reached inside his shirt and pulled out the small blue velvet sack and handed it to Arliss. She held the unopened sack in her hands while Janos continued the tale.

Just as I was riding away from camp, the cat here, springs from the shadows on to the saddle." said Janos glancing at Kipper, who was still asleep on the bench behind Arliss. Hearing himself talked about again he raised his head briefly with his eyes half open, fixed them on Janos for moment before he nodded off again.

"I gave the horse his head," continued Janos, "He seemed to know just where he was going. We rode half the morning until we came to the bridge across a river. We crossed it and headed down the road I reached Milltown just after dusk.

I've often been to Milltown in fact the miller at the head of the lake is a friend of mine. It is he who builds any new vardos we need. But I had no need for a new vardo and no time for a social call, so I put the horse up in the livery stable and went directly over to the inn to listen to the local talk. This is something gypsies often do going into a new town. Some one is sent a day or two ahead to see the lay of the land. We avoid a lot of trouble that way. I ordered a pint of ale and a meat pastie and before long and I struck up a conversation with some of the locals. I told them that I was an itinerant cobbler and I showed them my tools. Then I settled in and listened to the town gossip and pretty soon I heard about strangers staying at the Watrane mill. My ears perked up as they made mention of a blonde woman and four large men, one who wears a hood over his face and smells strange and an old man who sleeps near death. It seems that half the town had been up to the mill to see the old man and to tell him a story to try and wake him, but so far he still sleeps. Well I made my way to the mill and I slept in the woods nearby, watching the house all the time with one eye. It's not easy, but I do it anyway. I watched and dozed all night long. The house had been dark when I arrived. All night long I watched, but no one came in or out of the house. Then just as the sun started to rise over Muskrat Lake, the horse broke loose from the branch I tethered him to, and ran out of the woods toward the house. I ran after the horse. I had just reached him, when Elsaroth threw open the window. As soon as I saw her face I knew I was at the right place. "said Janos.

"Janos had only been in the house a short while when Mallwynn woke up." said Elsaroth.

Mallwynn when he listened intently had a curious habit of looking like he was about to fall asleep. Arliss had noticed this time and time again, though she knew the contrary to be true. Instead he listened so completely he shut everything else out. Sometimes he would watch the speakers face more often than not he would either gaze off in the distance or close his eyes as though he did not want anything to distract him from what was being said.

Now as he took up the tale he was like a man awoke from deep slumber into alertness, except that the transition was almost immediate. His voice old and mellow and rich in resonance as he spoke, it waxed warmer and more vigorous.

"I had been greatly weakened by the sorcery at the gorge. It wasn't so much that my deeds at the gorge were so formidable, it is just that the nature of my power is such that I require some amount of preparation, no matter how small the task is to be cognizant of all the details. Instead I find myself plummeting down one of the deepest cracks in the entire of Eartheart. I had in fact to slow time, which I'm afraid taxes even the most gifted of us. Which was perhaps the reason that Urage was so certain that we had all perished and I am not afraid to tell you that he was very nearly right. But when at last I awoke I felt almost completely recovered,"

Glancing at Elsaroth with a look of gratitude Mallwynn muttered, "Her ways are surely strange, but sometimes she does just the right thing, even if it's by accident."

Then focusing his attention once more on Arliss, he said, "We knew what had happened to you from what Janos told us, but until Striker, Farin and Whapper returned we suspected that you might have been dead and if perchance you had been lucky enough to succeed at staying alive the chances of you getting out of the keep were next to none."

"Whapper and myself," said Striker had been searching in the woods along the Maudland road for only a couple of days. We were fairly certain that you were with the gypsies and we were hopeful of getting you back. We traveled up the Maudland road taking cover in the woods to avoid the steady stream of Urage soldiers on the road going and coming from the keep. We made inquiries of the many people on the road and they gave us much important information.

Urage was still searching for you. He was back tracking over land past the Orchid Valley clear through the Glasston moors back down through the deep and ancient Drudic forest, all the way into the Umbrial Valley and the Krippner caverns. He'd even dispatched ships from the keep harbor to search the seas for any signs of the Whisper.

There was great alarm amongst the peasants we talked to some of them were from border towns Many who we talked to were very frightened and alarmed by Urage's increasing boldness which had escalated to new heights. Some of the people we met along the road carried their possessions on their backs and in barrows and carts any means they could they were leaving their towns and villages as they feared they would soon turn into a battlefield.

They were angry and frightened about Urage's strange night forays across the borders with his Carnumbra, the likes of which were rarely seen outside of Maudland . They were concerned about the people gone missing from their beds at night, whole crops trampled in the field on the night of the eve before their harvest. All these and even more devious crimes where blamed on Urage.

Here Striker paused and after a moments consideration he continued. " My guess is," said Striker, "At this point Urage believed that except for Arliss we were all dead."

Mallwynn was nodding in agreement.

Then Striker continued," He saw this as a signal to start being a larger presence over the border and he was going to see how far the Council of Twelve would go to avoid war. He knew that any strong retaliation from the them would be a sign that Arliss had made it to the palace, but he was very certain she hadn't.

He was blocking her only escape through the well in the Krippner caverns. So he was confident that in time he would run her to ground. I expect this thought gave him a lot of pleasure.

All the travelers on the road into and out of and away from Maudland made it easier for us to escape the notice of Urage and his soldiers. There was no sign at all of the band of gypsies till the evening of the third day when we spotted a lone caravan on the road. We rode up to the caravan introduced ourselves. The man and woman up on the back board didn't look very happy to see us. They were very cagey about answering my questions saying they knew nothing about a blonde girl traveling alone on the road. I could tell that they were lying and I saw the look of greed in the girl's eyes when I drew out a silver coin. Then she gave herself away when she asked suddenly if I was traveling with the Arch Mage 's party. I pretended not to notice her mistake and just said that we were.

She was quick to seize an opportunity as the next thing she said was, "You'll have to do a lot better than one piece of silver if you hope to find the girl."

Her brother tried to silence her but she would have none off it. She silenced him, with a look that could freeze the tale of a donkey. Then she said, "Give me ten gold pieces and I will tell you about the girl."

I didn't trust her not even a little bit, but I couldn't risk not playing the game on the off chance that she would know your whereabouts. So I gave her the gold, and she said that you were camped with a band of gypsies, just outside of Blackheath. I knew by the fear on Malcazar's face that she was lying. I would have preferred to question her at length and eventually prize the truth out of her but we had no time to waste so I reached over and pulled Whapper's hood off and said, "Women used to think him handsome before he lied to the Arch Mage!" She screamed bloody murder, then she talked. "

If Whapper was offended he did not show it he laughed as heartily as the rest of them.

"That was all the encouragement she needed. She told us the worst. Arliss was in the keep as a slave. How she got there she said she had no idea. She said it was just a rumor that she heard in the camp, that was all she knew," said Striker as he tried to smother a yawn.

The copper lamps in the alcove were burning low. The evening was growing late.

"Striker," said Arliss asking the question that she'd been burning to ask all evening, "How is it you happened to appear at my side just as I was about to risk the leap from the keep ramparts?"

"Well I might ask a similar question of you Arliss," said Striker his tone differential, "How is it you appear right before my eyes running straight for the ramparts just as if you knew the plan?"

Confused they both looked at Mallwynn who shrugged and muttered something under his breath that sounded like "Grace."

There were not many hours left before dawn so Mallwynn suggested that they turn in and that call it a night and continue the tale on land when they made camp the following evening.

Chapter Nineteen
Into The Spirit Valley

The entire party was out of bed and on deck long before the first rays of sunlight glanced over the sea. There was much to do to prepare to go ashore, the little ship fairly hummed with activity. Just after dawn they weighed anchor and ran up the sails. Striker took the helm and maneuvered the ship safely through the rocky shoals to the distant shore.

They put in at the sheltered cove of Looking Glass Bay at Kesick, a remote fishing village on the Great Wilderness Coast.

Before they left the ship they gathered once again in the salon.

Mallwynn was hunched intently over an ancient map, he drew his eyes away only for a moment to announce, "We'll enter the Orchid Valley through the Western Fairy Gates."

Farin's eyes widened in surprise.

"Fairy Gates?" murmured Arliss frowning, the name was familiar.

"It can't be done," declared Striker, "They've been locked for hundreds of years." but even as he spoke, his hard green eyes were fixed on the wizard expectantly.

Mallwynn looked up from the map and said quietly, "That's exactly why we should do it. Urage won't be expecting it."

"The fairy gates are the only entrance to the Orchid valley on the western side," explained Mallwynn answering Arliss's inquiring look.

"The gates were said to be built in ancient times for the Glasstarr family by Fairy folk, before they too, along with the old ones and many of the more sensitive races left to live in the great wilderness. The gates have remained firmly closed for centuries despite many recent and past efforts to open them,"

They all gathered around the table as the wizard began pouring over the map again. With his boney finger tracing out the route they would take he said, "We'll head in a Southeasterly direction away from the coast. We'll cross over the fifth Demon bridge on the River Nightshade."

"That's a day and a half away," said Striker.

"Exactly," agreed Mallwynn,

Then a look of loathing crossed the wizard's face as he said, "We'll have to hurry to make sure we get there before night fall. If it's at all possible I'd like to avoid those miserable slithering creatures."

"Yes," agreed Farin with a shudder, "I've heard that they swarm over the Demon bridges at night.

Cringing inwardly at the mere thought of the "slithering creatures", Arliss wanted to ask more about them, but the moment was past, Mallwynn had already turned back to the map.

"If we follow the River Nightshade to the Spirit River," said Mallwynn, "And travel along the river pathway, which is all that remains of the old Fairy road, all the way down into the Valley of Spirits. We'll eventually reach the stairs to the Fairy gates.

It was then that Striker voiced all their fears when he said quietly, "What if we can't get the gates opened?"

"Let's not worry about that now, we could all be dead by then," observed Mallwynn tucking the folded map inside his cloak. Only his penetrating glance gave weight to the seriousness of the remark.

They hurried getting horses and supplies quickly off the ship and before long they were ready to begin the next leg of their journey. Earlier that morning Mallwynn had sent the Whisper on its way. They had all stood by the shore and watched it head out to sea. It was quite a sight to see, that pretty little ship skimming rapidly across the water with all its sails unfurled, with the figurehead of the Whispering lady leaning so low over the water that it looked to Arliss as though she kissed the sea. Watching the ship disappear over the horizon Arliss wondered with a pang of regret if they'd ever see it again.

The Village of Kesick was oddly quiet. The only sound they could hear as they stood on the shore was the pounding surf. The simple open boats of the local village fishermen, lay in neat rows along the beach. The row of gray stone houses and shops that lined the shore was curiously still. They encountered no one as they made their way through the town, even the town square was empty, but as they passed by some houses on their way out of town, Arliss had an odd feeling of disquiet as she noticed an occasional curtain twitch.

Striker sitting very straight in his saddle, rested his right hand casually on the hilt of his sword. Farin drew an arrow out of his quiver, his long bow rested lightly on his right arm. Striker nodded to Farin as wordlessly they flanked either side of the party. They left the village without incident.

They were traveling along a road known as the Wilderness Road it would eventually take them straight across the fifth demon bridge over the River Nightshade.

On the Wilderness Road they wended their way through many small towns and villages. In these too, they found silent empty streets with that quality of having just been deserted and always there the feeling that they were being watched.

As they drew further away from the coast the road became more remote, passing into what seemed like barren wasteland. On and On they traveled stopping only briefly to water the horses.

The pale winter sun sparkled briefly before sinking down behind the trees. As the gathering dusk deepened into night the moon rose high in the sky, a silvery and luminescent disc beneath a thin veil of dark clouds.

The velvet blackness of the forest on either side of them hemmed them in as they rode along the narrow road lit only by pale moonlight

The wind had picked up from the west, blowing hard and bitter. Arliss shivered and bowed her hooded head as the road curved upwards and they headed right into the face of the harsh biting wind.

For Arliss the warm and pleasant evening aboard the Whisper, now seemed like just a dream, as relentlessly they journeyed into the night. Mile after mile along the endless dark road they traveled. The harsh cold wind beat against her until her face stung and her eyes watered. The wind crept a like thief into her cloak and snaked up her sleeves robbing all the heat from her body until it seemed like she would never be warm again. Her body ached all over. She fantasized constantly about getting down of Targus and laying down by the side of the road and going to sleep for a few hours. Once in while she would drift off to sleep and awake with sudden jerk as she felt herself begin to slip off Targus. It was only sheer will power and providence that kept her in the saddle.

On and on they traveled. The road narrowed and twisted treacherously upward through densely forested land. They were all silent as they rode along, conserving their strength just to keep going. Then abruptly and mercifully the wind died down. It was suddenly so quiet that

Arliss was filled with disquiet. There was no other sound to be heard except for the steady hoof beats of the horses. Then suddenly without warning Mallwynn pulled Leonis up short.

"There it is at last!" he cried pointing upwards to where the road disappeared into the trees.

"I see it!" exclaimed Farin with excitement, "A light!"

Near the very pinnacle of the hill, a small yellow light could be seen flickering in the darkness.

"Yes," said Mallwynn, "That's the Wilderness Inn. We'll spend the night there."

The spirits of the entire party rose and the weary mood of a short while ago was replaced by excited anticipation. Even the horses seem to step a little quicker as if they too, sensed their long journey was near it's end.

Whapper began to worry out loud what he was going to eat this far from the sea.

"I'll be all right if they keep goldfish or any kind of carp, perhaps in a small ornamental pond," Whapper mused.

"Carp can be perfectly delicious especially when they're tiny." he said wistfully his hunger getting the better of him.

"That should keep me going until I have the chance to catch something from a brook or stream tomorrow."

"No doubt that should endear you no end to our hosts," observed Mallwynn dryly.

"I am sure they look forward with unmitigated glee to guest who gobble up their pets." said the wizard as he shook his head in disapproval.

Whapper could feel the heat as he blushed red beneath his green skin at the same time as he pulled his head further under his hood and tried to look very small.

Mallwynn eyeing him this time more kindly said, "We're all cold and hungry Whapper, but rest assured our host are very special people and they'll have something for every one of us, and if they don't have something for you, I myself will conjure you up a salmon fresh or smoked, your choice."

Whapper brightened at Mallwynn's words.

In truth at this point salmon fresh or smoked sounded pretty good to everyone.

When they reached the top of the hill Mallwynn lead them off the road and into the woods toward the glimmering yellow light. They followed a footpath that was practically obscured by trees from the road.

After walking about a mile into woods they came to a large clearing. In the middle of the clearing stood what looked like an old country manor covered with ivy. It was built of fieldstone and had a steep roof and many gables.

"The Wilderness Inn?" asked Arliss unable to hide her disappointment because except for the lit lamp hanging by the front door, which appeared as though it had been only recently placed there, the inn appeared otherwise deserted, and by the looks of things, had been that way for some time."

As they crossed the clearing toward the inn the moonlight overhead cast long shadows giving the old inn what Arliss thought was a rather forbidding look.

As Arliss got closer she could see that the ivy that clung to the old inn was so overgrown that the outline of the windows could barely be seen.

Arliss felt her face fall as already the happy prospect of a warm bed and a hot meal were fast fading, and she started to feel depressed as she began to think of how bleak it would be to pass the night in this desolate place.

Striker and Farin had remained on their horses alert and wary as the rest of the party dismounted and approached the inn.

Stepping on to the porch of inn Arliss glanced up warily as a sudden gust of wind caught a sign suspended on chains above their heads causing it to creak dangerously. In meticulous gold lettering the cracked and peeling sign proclaimed: THE WIlDERNESS INN and beneath it in tiny black letters so small that Arliss could barely read was written, A Traveler's Respite.

As Mallwynn rapped on the oversize inn door, Arliss could hear the hollow sound of the brass knocker as it reverberated and echoed within. She recognized the sound of emptiness, but to her surprise even as the last echo still bounced through the inn the huge door was flung open and there stood a tall stout rosy cheeked red head man.

"Tharrel you do look well," exclaimed Mallwynn smiling broadly one of his rare smiles. Arliss had only seen him smile on one or two occasions and each time she was struck by how much the smile lit up his face.

Tharrel broke out in a wide grin and laughed.

"Well my word aren't you a sight for sore eyes? Its been far far too long Wynnie." he cried.

"Wynnie!" Arliss could hardly believe her ears. Of one thing she was certain off, she would never ever be allowed to call Mallwynn "Wynnie, not in a thousand years."

Tharrel turning his attention away from Mallwynn for a moment took them all in with a swift sweeping glance. He said, "Please step inside all of you. Gramiel is out in the kitchen. Leave your horses. We'll take care of them."

These were the best words they'd heard all day.

With their spirits rising once more in happy anticipation, they followed Tharrel down a dark hallway to the back of the Inn. He showed them into a dimly lit room filled with an odd assortment of formal looking furniture. Even though a small fire glowed in the hearth the room looked as though it was seldom used. Tharrel ask them to wait as he would be back shortly.

In a short while he returned with his wife Gramiel who was still smoothing her crisp white apron and patting a few stray chestnut hairs into place. She had that same ageless look that Tharrel had. Her merry blue eyes twinkled as Mallwynn introduced her to every member of the party. But at the mention of Arliss's name, a flicker of recognition touched her face and her merry eyes took on a thoughtful measuring look as she scrutinized Arliss and finally she smiled at Arliss, openly and warmly.

After a few pleasantries had been exchanged, Gramiel beckoned all of them as she said," The horses have been fed and stabled, so come lets have supper."

They ate at a long trestle table in Gramial's kitchen in front of an open hearth. The meal consisted of little half moon shaped pies filled with savory minced meat and finely chopped carrots, onions and potatoes wrapped in crisp pastry. The pies were hot steamy and delicious. They washed them down with pint mugs of cold ale and cider.

Gramiel seemed to have an unlimited supply of pies. She would see to it that their plates were never empty. She regularly appears at the table with her apron gathered up in front of her filled with little pies which despite their polite protest, she expertly slid out on to their plates. Neither was Whapper forgotten as he sat at the table with child-like patience, confident that the empty plate in front of him would soon be filled with something good to eat. Gramiel appeared at his side carrying a platter with two huge salmon, which she set down in front of him with a flourish as she said, "Salmon fresh or smoked your choice."

Just as if she'd overheard Mallwynn's promise.

Whapper keeping to his avowed preference of fresh live food passed the smoked salmon around the table for everyone to sample. He then scooped the remaining still jumping fish off the platter, and ate it with about as much dignity as one can eat a live fish. Fastidiously dabbing himself between bites with a linen napkin.

They all ate their fill, even Kipper who feasted on fish heads and a bowl of milk. For dessert they contented themselves with the large bowl of perfectly ripe pears and apples and plums that Gramiel had put on the table.

The fire burned brightly and Arliss luxuriated in its warmth as she felt the cold dampness leave her bones. The meal had made her soporific she felt her eyes grow heavy and her head nodded onto her chest a few times.

She caught only snatches of the conversation between Mallwynn and Tharrel and Gramiel. They were talking about the Great Wilderness and about the old ones. The next thing she knew she was in a bed in a small room. She didn't remember how she got there. Across the room she spied Elsaroth snoring gently. She drifted back to sleep again.

The whole party was up at dawn and they were quickly ready to leave. Arliss couldn't help but notice everyone of them looked at least five years younger and thoroughly rested.

There was a feeling of exhilaration in air as they mounted their horses. A stiff wind had swept away all the grayness and damp from the previous day leaving the skies deep blue and the air scented with hemlocks and yews.

They thanked Tharrel and Gramiel for their hospitality and bade them farewell. Just as they were ready to go Gramiel handed them a basket laden with her savory meat pies and fruits for the journey.

Then Gramiel reached out and took hold of both of Arliss's hands.

"Take care now." she said Her twinkling blue eyes for once serious. "We all are depending on you more than you will ever know." Then she reached into the pocket of her apron and slipped a small blue and gold satin pouch into Arliss's hands.

Arliss glanced up at Gramiel in surprise and confusion.

"Go ahead open it," encouraged Gramiel.

As Arliss opened the pouch. There was a sudden glint of gold as she poured the contents out into her hand.

"Thank you," she murmured softly as she held the necklace in her hands. It was a miniature hunting horn on a thin gold chain.

"Wear it at all times," cautioned Gramiel.

"If you are in need of any help from us, blow the horn three times."

And then added gravely, "Use the horn wisely and only when its absolutely necessary."

Arliss thanked Gramiel and slipped the necklace over her head. The little golden horn clinked softly against the Glasstarr medallion.

Kipper had become adept at riding in front of the saddle and some how managed to relax even to the point of apparently nodding off to sleep. Farin had taken the precaution to constructed a harness for the cat to wear, to discourage any more sudden departures. The tiny harness attached very neatly to a ring on the saddle.

As they rode along toward the River Nightshade Arliss ask Mallwynn about the charms she had been given, the Glasstarr medallion, the opening bracelet from the maze, and now the hunting horn.

"Each one is an alliance."

He said, "We'll be in great need of them all before long. Be honored they were not given lightly.

As they rode along Mallwynn got his pipe and filled it with pungent smelling herbs as he said, "Tharrel and Gramiel are valued allies and make no mistake about it they would make desperate enemies. It is a rare cause that has them participating in the affairs of mortal man. They are the last of the old ones still living in our land, the rest of their kind have long since passed over far into the Great Wilderness."

Arliss had hoped that Mallwynn would say more about Gramiel and Tharrel, the old ones, the Great Wilderness and the charms, but apparently Mallwynn had decided he'd said enough about it for today.

So desperate were they to cross the Demon bridge before dark that they made the entire journey to the banks of the river Nightshade without stopping once.

It was late afternoon when they arrived at the river side. Before them lay the fifth of the ancient demon bridges, it's zig-zaging shape almost hidden in the mist.

The River Nightshade was just like the Spirit River except not as wide. The mist hung over it in either direction as far as the eye could see. In truth it seemed to Arliss that the mist some how emanated from the river itself.

The horses wanted no part of the river or the strange bridge, they whinnied and snorted with flattened ears and eyes flicking back and forth nervously. Arliss thought that she'd have to get down and lead Targus across, but she nudged him gently one more time and he reluctantly stepped on to the Demon Bridge.

The party crossed quickly over the bridge and started along the river pathway. The mist from river overflowed its banks and flowed onto the pathway.

Arliss could barely make out Striker's form a few feet in front of her. She was aware of strange creatures moving in the mist. She couldn't see the creatures, but none the less, she knew they were they were there. Mile after mile they continued along the pathway. Then as darkness descended it became almost impossible to see anything in the mist. They kept track of each other by keeping a running conversation going. They had been riding along the river path for some time without incident when suddenly without warning a cold rubbery hand clamped down hard on Arliss's ankle. She was so petrified that her scream became soundless as it left her lips. Instantly she regretted not having battle singer in her hand as desperately she tried to wrest the cold slithery flesh from her ankle. She was afraid if she took time to get the sword out of its sheath the creature would pull her right off Targus. She could feel the icy coldness penetrating right through her leather boot.

Suddenly she heard a sword whistle through the air, immediately followed by an inhuman cry as instantly the hand let go, and she heard the sound of a creature scuttling away.

Moments later when she emerged from the mist into the pale moonlight she could still feel the coldness where the hand had touched her ankle.

Farin's sword was still out of its sheath as he emerged behind her from the mist and there was a frank look of loathing on his face as he for a moment continued to brandish the sword it in the air. He glanced sidelong at her acknowledging her thanks, while at the same time remaining alert and watchful.

Finally the pathway pulled away from the river and the going was now easier. They made camp at sundown, and had a satisfying supper of Gramial's cold pies and ales. Whapper relied on Mallwynn producing a couple large silvery fish out of thin air rather risk anything out of the fetid waters of the deadly River Nightshade.

Arliss thought wistfully of the hospitality they had all enjoyed the night before at the Wilderness Inn. This was a different night entirely. It was decided that they would take watch in shifts by pairs. The night passed uneventfully except for an occasional ear splitting yowl from Kipper when he wandered too close to the river. After a few of these outbursts to every ones relief the cat contained his nocturnal activities to patrolling within the borders of the camp. The rest of the night passed peacefully. Mallwynn had told them that with an early start they should reach the source of the river Nightshade, the Spirit river late tomorrow morning.

They were ready to go by the first light. They made faster progress than the day before. Somehow the mist the mist was easier to cope with in the morning light. They reached the rivers source at high noon, the place where the River Nightshade's waters mixed with the Spirit River.

The Spirit River, Mallwynn explained was the natural border that ran between Maudland and the Orchid mountain range. The river itself was very unusual in that it flowed both into the Fane Sea and the Cascall Sea. It severed the land mass from end to end leaving Maudland an Island separated off from the rest of the land. It arose somewhere midway in its length from an underground river deep within heart of the Orchid mountains.

The heavy thick mist hung that over the river and its tributaries at all times, flowed down it's length in both directions, and even for a short distance after it joined the waters of the Fane Sea and the Cascall Sea, a high column of mist, it snaked persistently out to sea.

It had grown cooler and the mist was deepening as the afternoon sun began to wane. The little party had been traveling for several hours along Spirit River, when Mallwynn warned them that they would be soon within sight of the fourth Demon Bridge and the Great Maudland Road.

Leaving the river pathway they rode into the mist to escape detection. The mist was now their friend as it swaddled them and kept them from sight and muffling their sounds. As they embraced the mist it became less formidable and threatening.

Putting his finger to his lips Mallwynn cautioned them to be quiet. "Careful!" he warned, "Urage has posted guards on the bridge."

A myriad of hooves and feet passed overhead and every once in a while, a carriage or wagon would roll like thunder across the bridge pausing at each acute angle then finally rumbling off the bridge. The brief moments that they were under the bridge Arliss had to choke back a claustrophobic feeling that started to envelop her. She shuddered and drew her cloak tighter around her. The sound of water echoed against the curious stone of the bridge as all around them they felt the presence of nameless creatures moving just out of reach. Above them they could hear the guards, with hollow sounding voices checking travelers entering and leaving Maudland.

As she heard snatches of conversation from people crossing the bridge Arliss remembered back when she and Janos and the gypsy caravan had crossed into Maudland here at this Demon Bridge, so much had happened since then, it seemed like a life time ago now.

She knew Janos was thinking the same thing as their eyes met briefly.

Avoiding the river pathway Mallwynn lead them through the mist so close to the river that Arliss was certain at any moment she would be pitched headlong into the Spirit river. Not until the Second Demon Bridge was far behind did they risk traveling on the river pathway again.

The pathway widened and pulled away from the river and they left the mist. Arliss squinted in the red gold light of the setting sun in the Western Horizon.

The land around them began to change dramatically as they entered into wide chasm that lead into the Spirit Valley. To the left of them was sheer rock rising up thousands of feet in the air to high cliffs. The rock face was smooth as a glass and stratified with broad strokes of pastel color that were imbedded with debris and sediment of ages past, layered one on top another.

The river had broadened considerably and the water was faster moving.

They could hear it's constant rush as they followed the path down into the Spirit Valley. The mist still prevailed on top of the river but the atmosphere had changed. The river itself was more active less stagnant. There still was the feeling that they were being watched from the mist but the watching was more curious than anything else.

On their way down into the Valley they came upon one more of demon bridges. It loomed in the mist like some kind of mystical conundrum. Even though it appeared to be deserted they stayed out of sight in the mist until they were well past it.

Nightfall had dropped like a heavy curtain as they reached the bottom of the valley. The Fairy road was changing. Large Urns of well tended flowers cascaded over the pathway in the moonlight. Every mile or so there was a statue of a woodland animal or fairy or nymph. There were lots of water fountains along the road but Mallwynn warned them against drinking the water.

"I will mention no names because I know well they are listening but there are some creatures of the nether world who while definitely are not evil are confoundingly annoying. They think it great fun to play tricks with the water.

They may give you a waking dream or a voice that sounds like silver bells or make a statue out of you for a few hours, so don't drink the water!"

Ever since Mallwynn had warned them of the water from the many fountains along the way, the water looked more and more inviting to Arliss. The sound of the water bubbling up in a fountain and falling back in a short water fall was music to her ears. Oh for one glass of that water she thought ruefully. Then she got distracted from her strange craving as ahead the road seemed to fizzle out in front of a wall of solid rock interrupted by what at first looked some haphazard boulders piled on top of each other. But when she took a second look as the air shimmered briefly she could see that these were indeed the fairy stairs. Along side of the stairs carved into the rock was a fountain in the shape of a pixie face the water spewed out through the pixie's pursed lips into a basin held in his hands. As Arliss stared wistfully at the water she gasped as for a moment she could have sworn the pixie winked at her.

She turned quickly as she heard Strikers soft low whistle. He and Farin had an unpleasant surprise when they noticed directly opposite the Fairy Stairs almost hidden in the mist was the second demon bridge! They hadn't seen it at first because it was so dark and the bridge was almost completely enveloped in the mist. Mallwynn alone showed no surprise.

"Well make camp here," he announced without comment.

With their backs against the cliff wall facing the Demon Bridge they huddled together eating the last of the Gramiel pies fruit and ale. Arliss shivered as she tried to ward of the feeling that they were being watched, which was stronger than ever.

Despite their tiredness they had agreed to rest a few hours and then begin the long climb to the Fairy Gates.

Hunched against the wall, Arliss's thin arms drew her cloak tight around her as she sheltered from the cutting wind that whipped down the Spirit valley. As she dozed off and on, she was aware of the almost musical bubbling of the pixie fountain in the background. She had to contented herself with a drink of rather flat tasting water from Mallwynn's flask instead. As she drank the water from the flask she happened to glance over at the pixie fountain, the little face look very disappointed in her.

She must have finally fallen asleep for when she awoke there was a golden three quarter moon hanging in a navy sky. The rest of the party were already up, silently moving around, casting strange shadows in the moonlight as they packed up the horses and prepared for the journey up the fairy stairs. Arliss felt surprisingly refreshed as she sprang to her feet to prepare to leave.

With only the moonlight to light their way. They went single file leading their horses up the steep and narrow stairway. Sometimes the Fairy Stairs would switch back but mostly they rose steeply digging deeper into the mountain.

The calves of Arliss's legs ached, she longed to stop the upward climb, but she ignored the pain as she continued on, her natural ebullience buoying her up as she wondered with excitement if the Fairy Gates would actually open for her! In a few hours she could actually be in the Orchid Valley!

Elsaroth was doing a lot of complaining under her breath about the awful climb. Mallwynn had shushed and once or twice tapped her on the head with his staff. But she still kept on complaining in loud whispers to Whapper who was just behind her carrying her gear as well as his own.

Arliss couldn't help but notice when she glanced back, Janos didn't look in the least bothered by Elsaroth's shenanigans. Instead he kept his eyes fixed on her with a very odd look on his face.

Up and up they continued climbing until even Elsaroth was silent as she no longer had the strength to complain. Just when Arliss was sure they would never reach the top they did. There was a collective gasp as they turned the corner and before them lay the Fairy Gates.

In the moonlight the massive silver gates scintillated with tiny flashes of blue and white light. Arliss took it all in with wonder. Letting Targus's reins slip from her hands she moved forward to take a closer look.

"The gates are bound in many complex fairy spells making them impregnable." explained Mallwynn as he joined her. He reached out and gave the gates a good shake as if to prove his point.

Arliss ran her hand tentatively over the still tremoring gates and felt the energy travel up her arm and into her chest. It felt warm and pleasing. Suddenly she looked up as she heard the far off sound of trumpets and there appeared a large glowing light coming down the pathway on the other side of the gate. It was a curious light it looked the way gold would look if it were on fire, a soft brilliant shimmering. Now above the sound of trumpets she could hear laughter and the silvery sylvan sound of flute music.

She could make out figures in the light. At the head of them was a tall beautiful woman with hair like burnished gold woven into thick plaits that she wore around her head beneath a simple crown of gold. She wore a simple white gown cinched at the waist with a broad gold girdle.

She was at the front of what appeared to be her retinue of fairies and elves. When she reached the gate she and all her retinue disappeared into thin air.

"Arliss, What is it? What did you see?" demanded Mallwynn. As Arliss related the vision to Mallwynn he nodded knowingly as he said,

"That would be Gaelin the Keeper of the Crown. She's been probably waiting for you."

"Too bad Gaelin didn't open the gates for you." said Elsaroth her voice laden with sarcasm, but if truth be known she only made the remark to cover up the excitement she felt when she heard Arliss tell of her vision as she herself had been able to see faint shadows of Gaelin and her retinue! Even though curiosity burned inside as to what the others saw she was at loath to disclose what she'd seen. "Interesting that you should mention Gaelin unlocking the gates." said Mallwynn giving Elsaroth a piercing look. "These gates are so ensorcelled that any attempt to break the spell other than the way it was meant to be broken could have disastrous effects for all of Eartheart. The Fairy Gates will open when they are meant to open and not a moment sooner."

"I don't suppose we can climb over the gates," asked Farin dubiously as he gazed up at the twelve foot high still scintillating gates.

Mallwynn just shook his head.

"Isn't their another way into the Valley," asked Janos as helped Elsaroth make a little makeshift seat to sit on out of saddle bags.

"There is no other way into the Orchid Valley on this side of the Orchid mountain range except through those gates answered Striker.

The little party sat around most of the night and watched as Mallwynn tried spell after spell to unbind the gates but they still held after every failure they were certain that the next would surely work. Elsaroth grew bored of listening to spell after spell and started to make herself a cup of tea on a little campfire she'd built and just as she lit the fire under the kettle there was a brief flash and she let out a sharp cry as light shot from Mallwynn's hands and turned the kettle into a blackened molten mess.

Looking at the Wizard in amazement she cried plaintively," Why? I was only making myself a cup of tea I would have offered you...." Arliss stopped mid sentence as she caught sight of Mallwynn's face.

The wizard said in a voice barely above a whisper, "The Carnumbra are upon us. They've just crossed over the second Demon Bridge!"

Everyone was immediately on their feet racing to pack up the horses quickly. "Everyone on their mount now!" cried Striker. Then he and Farin disappeared back down the Fairy stairs to scout out the whereabouts of the Carnumbra. Arliss had overheard Striker muttered under his breath to

Mallwynn, "If they find the stairway entrance we're trapped like pigs in a barrel."

Arliss's heart thudded hard in her chest as she scrambled onto Targus and waited with the rest of the party. There eyes were fixed on the gates as Mallwynn continued to try spell after spell. It seemed the longest time but actually it had been only a moment or two until Striker and Farin reappeared. As soon as they saw Farin's face they knew the news was bad.

"They've found the stairway they're coming up very fast almost as though they were flying!" Farin said in shocked disbelief.

"It won't belong before they're here." warned Striker grimly as he mounted his steed. The Wizard continued to try spell after spell. Weapons were drawn, faces were strained, eyes remained nervously fixed on the gates. Then from somewhere down the stairway they heard that awful hollow soulless sound of the Carnumbrian chant! Arliss felt her skin begin to crawl as she suddenly realized how close the Carnumbra were.

All eyes flicked nervously back and forth between the gates and the stairs. Then as the first hell hound bounded around the corner an arrow from Farin's bow caught it full in the chest quickly downing the beast.

Mallwynn swore under his breath as yet another spell failed to budge the gates. Then as he glanced Arliss's way his face took on a look of sudden comprehension. He drew Leonis next to her as he said, "Its all so obvious I was foolish not to think of it before."

He handed her his staff as he said, "I want you to repeat after me the words of the incantation, and at the same time visualize these gates opening up."

As Arliss struggled with the strange words she could hear the thunder of the of the Carnumbra as they neared the gates. A hell hound let out a blood curdling scream as Jano's airborne dagger hit it's mark.

Arliss's mouth and throat were suddenly so dry that the words of the incantation came out as barely a whisper, but still she didn't pause or hesitate even when over Mallwynn's shoulder she saw the hellhounds and Carnumbra bearing down on them in the murky predawn light. With the last word of the spell the silver gates sprang opened and from somewhere far off there was the sound of trumpets.

Chapter Twenty
Into the Valley of Orchids

As the little party surged through, the gates clanged closed behind them but not before one of the hell hounds slipped through and launched its self at Whapper nipping cruelly at his delicate fin like feet. Sword in hand Whapper desperately fought off the beast. Striker came to his aid swiftly dispatching the beast in one fell blow.

Breathless, Arliss watched as the hellhounds in a frenzy threw themselves repeatedly against the gates. The Carnumbra had started to toss their war axes over the gates. One just barely missed Mallwynn. Janos picked it up and flung it back over the gate where it lodged in one of the hellhounds stopping it dead in it's tracks.

Then suddenly from out of nowhere again there was the sound of a single trumpet, it was fulsome and sweet and plaintive.

"Come quickly Arliss, Gaelin heralds your arrival!" cried Mallwynn his voice exultant as the whole party set off at a swift cantor, leaving the Fairy Gates far behind.

As they rode down the road into the valley the morning sun was just crowning the Orchid Mountains, casting a dazzling honey colored light across the land. A fine mist hung in the air, causing it to sparkle and somehow making colors and textures somehow seem richer and more vibrant.

The West Road wound steeply down through a dense emerald swale into a valley so steep and narrow that Arliss felt as though she could have reached out and touched the other side. Tiny wisps of steam arose from numerous nooks and crannies throughout the valley. These were the famous Orchidian hot springs. It was from these springs the land got it's name, for in them grew rare wild orchids found no where else on Eartheart.

From far down in the valley they could hear the tentative sound of an answering trumpet. Arliss's heart did a curious flip as Gaelin's trumpet sounded again. Then suddenly the whole valley was filled with the sound of trumpets.

Mallwynn, with Arliss beside him led the way. Arliss had Kipper tucked under her cape. Striker followed close behind them. Farin, Janos, and Elsaroth followed behind Striker. Whapper hooded and almost completely covered up brought up the rear.

The sound of trumpets still resounded as they rode swiftly down the road toward the ancient City of Orchids. Many people had began gather along the road leading into the city, they watched with awe as the party rode by. They didn't fail to notice the slight flaxen haired girl who rode beside the Arch Mage, nor did they miss the familial resemblance between the two.

When the little party came within sight of the city they were met by an escort of guards from the palace of Orchids who fell in around them. The crowds were getting thicker, the closer they drew to the city. Just outside the city walls the road was jam packed with people. The crowds cheered and roared as the party entered the city. Arliss was overwhelmed by the crowds but at the same time she was oddly moved and she felt her spirits rise up in response to their support.

"What do you think?" asked Mallwynn sometime later after the little party had finally made its way through the crowded city streets arriving at last in front of the palace of Orchids.

"Well?" he prompted again, smiling at Arliss expectantly, as he drew Leonis up along side of her and began studying the three thousand year old Palace of Orchids, as if for the first time.

"I think its amazing," breathed Arliss as she stared with awe at the palace.

"Really truly...amazing." she repeated searching vainly for a more appropriate word.

"Yes, I thought you'd feel that way." said Mallwynn with more than a hint of pride in his voice.

"I myself am bored by the ordinary."

The palace not only surprised Arliss because it was so different from the palace in Poseidon but also because it was not nearly as grand. It was a sprawling structure with deeply pitched roofs and many gable ends. There were it seemed an uncountable number of turrets and leaded latticed windows. Doors and windows were hung in the most unusual places. Odd balconies were strung here and there, with seemingly no rhyme nor reason. The palace was set off by the thick masses of leafy ivy that bound the whole hodgepodge pleasantly together.

Outside of the palace was a small crowd of excited but restrained palace officials and staff waiting anxiously to greet the long lost heir and her party. A man was introduced to her as Theo Depper, the late King's steward. Only when Mallwynn mentioned that Theo Depper was his second cousin did she notice that he resembled Mallwynn but at the same time he had a more steely pragmatic look to him. Theo Depper made the introductions. Arliss was soon awash in a sea of faces as she a struggled valiantly to acknowledge every greeting, and touch every hand that reached out to her.

The entire party was warmly greeted. Mallwynn in particular was quickly surrounded by a small group of serious looking young people all dressed in long gray robes. These he explained were his acolytes, young people, hand-picked by him from all over Eartheart, to be schooled in the mystical arts. They had not only the gift but also the special heart that was required.

That first day for Arliss sped by as fast as quicksilver. It wasn't until the wee hours of the morning that she retired to what had been the old King's royal suit. She hardly noticed her surroundings so preoccupied was she by what lay ahead and despite the soft feather bed she slept fitful. She dreamt that she was standing in a pool of silver moonlight in the middle of a huge frozen lake. She knew the ice was going to break at any moment. She could hear it groan like a wounded animal and feel it tremble beneath her feet. Gaelin, the keeper of the crown was standing in front of her in the moonlight, seemly oblivious to the treachery of the ice, holding out the Orchid crown to Arliss. Arliss reached out to accept the crown, but found that it was so heavy that she couldn't even lift it out of Gaelin's hands. When Gaelin moved to put the crown on Arliss's head, Arliss protested but then from behind Gaelin a woman appeared. Arliss stared at the woman in surprise, she looked very like herself except her face was rounder and her hair a lighter shade of flaxen. Immediately Arliss felt her throat thicken as she realized this was her mother, Kyrianna.

"Arliss, my dear one," whispered Kyrianna so softly that Arliss could barely hear her. "Take the crown." Even as she spoke Kyrianna was fast fading, but that look of urgent supplication Arliss would never forget. Without hesitation she gestured to Gaelin that she was ready to receive the crown. Just as Gaelin was about to set the it on her head she awoke in a cold sweat.

EARTHEART

At Mallwynn's insistence the coronation was set to take place at sunrise of the following week in the grand Hall of Hallows at the palace. This was where Eartheart monarchs had been crowned for the past two millenniums.

"It's one thing to try hunt down and kill a pretender," said Mallwynn, "it's quite another thing to try to kill the Queen of Eartheart, even for Urage. This may be our last chance to avert the impending war that even as we speak is drawing near. Once you are firmly installed on the throne there is a slight chance that Urage might give up his claim to the throne, but I really think that he's gone too far to stop" sighed the Wizard.

The next few days at the palace were a whirlwind of activity. There was a lot of comings and goings as kings and queens and other noblemen began to arrive at the palace from the many small kingdoms spread throughout Eartheart. They were drawn into the valley by the sound of Gaelin's trumpet, which had not been heard in many a life time. For Arliss it meant introduction after introduction.

As Arliss entered the Hall of Hallows to the sound of heralding trumpets the crowd turned to watch her walk up the aisle on the Arch Wizard's arm. She was dressed in garments of gold thread encrusted with sapphires, rubies and diamonds. Her flaxen hair was thickly braided and caught up in a net of gold thread studded with even more gemstones.

Arliss had hardly recognized Mallwynn, when she first seen him in his elaborate ceremonial robes. Only the twisted crook neck staff was familiar, it was the same one the wizard had pulled out of the copper beech tree in the Krippner Caverns when they came through the well between the worlds. That seemed a life time ago now to Arliss.

Gaelin, who was waiting on the dais, even though she was completely visible, she still continued to scintillate. When Arliss looked up Gaelin, she was smiling at her and Arliss was surprised to notice that she too, bore a striking resemblance to Mallwynn. When she ask the mage later about it he just shrugged and said, "Yes I suppose she is related to me in a distant way on the Darrowglynn side of the family, but Gaelin is not of this world so in that way she not related to anyone in it."

Arliss felt comforted by presence of Striker and Farin in the shadows of the throne. They both looked every inch the aristocrats in their formal court attire. Striker, vigilant as always, his hard bottle green eyes missing nothing as they swept across the hall. His right hand within easy reach of his sword's hilt. Although Farin looked more relaxed with a smile not far from his lips, Arliss knew he too, was ready to spring into action at a moments notice.

Whapper, Elsaroth and Janos watched Arliss solemnly as they stood at the edge of the dais next to Theo Depper and other dignitaries. Whapper no longer hid his face and although Theo Depper had special shoes and gloves made for him, they were not meant to conceal his hands and feet but rather to provide a measure of comfort and protection for them.

Kipper was curled up outside on a narrow parapet, that connected the hall of hallows from the rest of the Palace of Orchids, with his eyes narrowed and his face was inscrutable he watched and waited for the coronation to be over.

Arliss had an odd sense of unreality as she sat on the Orchid throne in middle of the immense Hall of Hallows. The huge ornate throne diminished her size and made her feel childlike. Then as she felt the sun's warmth on her face, she smiled as strange sense of peacefulness overcame her, and suddenly she knew beyond any doubt at this moment was fulfilling her destiny.

From outside, Arliss could still hear the trumpeters, as they heralded the upcoming coronation. Gaelin the keeper of the crown was now surrounded by an aura of dazzling light. Everyone waited for her to decide the exact moment to begin the ceremony. Despite the earliness of the hour the hall was packed. It was traditional Arliss had been told for coronations to take place at dawn.

Suddenly Gaelin was ready and a hush fell over the hall as she murmured an invocation as she began to anointed Arliss, first with oil from oak blossoms gathered in the Druid's forest for wisdom, truth and justice, and then with oil from the silver aureole tree for love and compassion, and lastly with sacred amaranth oil for power beyond imagination.

Then Gaelin crowned Arliss, Queen and Empress of Eartheart. As the crown was set on Arliss's head she felt a sudden sensation like wind rushing from her head to her toes and in that moment Arliss knew that she was forever changed.

The heads of the Eartheart military had been gathering at the palace since when Gaelin's trumpet first sounded the palace drawing room had been dubbed the war room. There was almost a jubilant air among those gathered despite what might lay ahead. One grizzled faced general told

Arliss, "At least if we are defeated which I fear we might be. We will have our swords in our hands not just our hoes and shovels.

The Orchid Valley was extremely vulnerable to attack and although the Western fairy gates were again closed and the gates to the other three passes could also be closed, only the mountains on the western side of the Valley were truly impassable. If Urage marched on the valley in any other direction, it would be only a matter of days before the mountains were scaled. The walls of the City of Orchids would only hold Urage back another few days.

The war council decided early on that their only hope of winning the battle with Urage was to be on the offensive. It was decided that they would move the troops out of the valley through the north gate down past the Mural Forest and advance on Maudland in that direction.

Whapper left the Orchid Valley to return to Poseidon with a formal request for Amarin from Arliss to send aid and troops for battle. Farin left with him to go as far the coast to organize a coastal defense from the tiny Orchidian navy.

Janos left to join his band of gypsies, which were camped on the slopes of the valley up near the eastern gate. He would then set out with some of his best scouts to bring a decree from the Queen declaring war on Maudland to all the towns, villages, and kingdoms of Eartheart. The decree was also a call to arms to raise men and supplies to join and reinforce the advance on Maudland.

Janos was confident that he and his scouts could cover the territory faster than anyone else on Eartheart, but he was concerned that his or his men's authority would be challenged. Mallwynn reassured him that the decree with the Orchid seal would be received and recognized without question. Janos planned to send the rest of his band of Gypsies and their caravans into the city where they would be safer.

Arliss released Elsaroth to travel back to Poseidon with Whapper, but to her surprise Elsaroth refused to go, with her eyes flashing with passion and her voice quivering with emotion, she said, "I no longer covet my sisters throne. I would rather live under the stars and blue skies, than while away my time with idle pursuits in a palace under glass at the bottom of the sea. I know that if this war is not won, I will either be dead or back under the sea awaiting the day that Urage comes for me and my people. I want to fight now so that I may live tomorrow."

Elsaroth had spent many years learning martial skills as Poseidon's princess she had her own regiment. The general of the Ochidian army quickly put her to work training the new recruits who had been streaming into the city daily since Gaelin's trumpet was first heard.

Mallwynn set out with a couple of his acolytes to secure the four roads into the city with a protective spell. He and his acolytes would cover every inch of the perimeter of the city with a similar enchantment. Word had already been sent all over the valley for the women and children, elderly and infirm to come into the city.

It was long before dawn and the valley was still cloaked in darkness as the Orchidian army left the silent somnolent City of Orchids and advanced up the valley road toward the north gate. The road was empty and except for an occasional light twinkling from a far off cottage high up on the slopes, the valley slept on, unaware of their leave taking.

Arliss's alert face was solemn and her eyes strangely bright as she rode at the head of the Orchidian Army. She was dressed completely in light chain mail. On her head she wore a close fitting cowl of mail that was draped like a veil around her shoulders, on top of which she wore the Orchid Crown. At her side rode Mallwynn and Striker. Elsaroth had insisted on be put in charge of her own squad. She rode at their head further down the ranks. Kipper, had been left despite his protest in the care of Theo Depper.

Janos promised to catch up with the Orchidian army as soon as he could. He promised to bring with him as many reinforcements as he could find. Whapper and Farin planned to form fleet with the Orchidian navy, fishing boats, merchant ships and any and all Children of Poseidon that Amarin would send. They intended to descend on Maudland by way of the Fane sea.

The regular army of Eartheart was very small even augmented by reinforcements, they would still find themselves hopelessly outnumbered by more than two to one. Arliss had expressed her concern about this to Mallwynn, but he only shook his head seeming uninterested in the details of numbers, saying softly. "Its always fallen on the brave and good in times of crisis, to lean heavily on faith. "Be still in your heart." he advised her, "for the answers will unfold as you're ready to receive them." But Mallwynn's words did little to comfort Arliss, her heart still felt heavy.

Leaving the valley they moved quickly and quietly up the North Road. It was late afternoon by the time they'd reached the Mural forest. As they entered the cool muskiness of the dense woods a silence descended upon them. Angles of light filtered through the overhead canopy illuminating the trail with patches of dappled golden light. Arliss, was again struck by the enormity of the trees. The trek through the rows and rows of endless giant evergreens seemed endless. All the pathways still looked the same to her; she could never in a thousand years have found the place, where she had gotten lost, the first time she was in these woods.

The sun set onto a moonless night and the woods had become so dark that they couldn't even see the person in front of them. The little army spent the night camped among the trees. It was odd really, and Arliss couldn't quite put her finger on exactly why it was, but she felt strangely safe and protected in the forest that night, it was as if the forest knew they were there and welcomed them. It spread its bows low over them as they slept. Wafting its lovely balsam perfume through their hair and clothing. They found edible pine nuts and hives full of honey all along the trail enough to turn the little Orchidian army's spartan supper of dry crackers into a feast and as incredible as it seemed everyone seem to have enough. That night as Arliss fell asleep in velvet darkness of the Mural Forest she thought she heard Gramial and Tharrel voices approaching but some how she drifted off to sleep before she could check to see if it was really them.

It was dusk the following day when they arrived at the western most edge of Mural Forest. Ahead of them lay the Spirit River. They were only a half a mile south of the Great Maudland Road and the Third Demon Bridge. The scouts who had been sent out, brought back the disquieting news that so far all of Maudland's borders were quiet. The usual border patrols were no where to be seen.

They spent an uneasy night camped on a rise. As the darkness deepened, a sharp keening wind arose whipping up the bottoms of their tents and blowing grit in their eye, scattering their belongings and supplies and stirring up fear and anxiety in the hearts of the little Orchidian army. Sometime after midnight there was a flurry of excitement as lookouts signaled a sighting of the Carnumbra on the other side of the river. It was several agonizingly long moments before they finally drifted away. A sense of relief was felt throughout the camp when dawn finally came.

"Surely they know we are here," said Arliss mystified as she sat atop Targus looking across the Spirit river into Maudland. There were no guards at the border in fact there were no guards anywhere to be seen. Beyond the river, the Maudland road stretched out, empty and desolate for miles. The Third Demon bridge enshrouded in a thin mist was completely deserted.

"Step right in," said, the spider to the fly." said Striker with long low whistle."

Mallwynn, who was sucking on an empty pipe nodded in agreement at the same time as he muttered under his breath, "But where else is there a more ideal place to catch a hunter than near his trap?"

"We shall soon see," sighed Striker ruefully, "We should reach the keep by the end of the day."

The wind was blowing now out of the northwest, Arliss shivered as she gathered her cloak around her. She was standing by the side of the road, on the Maudland side of the river, with Mallwynn and Striker, and Elsaroth. They watched nervously as the Orchidian army, bottlenecking at the Third Demon bridge, filed slowly by.

"He's got nothing to lose by bringing the battle to his door step and everything to gain," commented Striker. "All the crops have been harvested from the fields. The keep is virtually self sufficient. Urage could easily hold off a siege for six months or more."

Arliss nodded in agreement with Striker. Then as she turned and looked down the road wondering what lay ahead of them, and at that very moment something cold touched her heart, and she was suddenly overwhelmed with the feeling of sadness. So suddenly and strongly did this feeling overtake her that she began to swoon. Mallwynn frowned with concern and reached over and touched her. His touch immediately infused her with warmth and she felt her head begin to clear. The Wizard's usual expression of genial mysticism was gone as he gave her a look of such intensity, that Arliss felt suddenly afraid.

"You will have to be vigilant against moments like this," the wizard warned. "Even now Urage is doing battle with you with his dark magic on another plane. Use the Glasstarr amulet to help you fight against him. The Amulet represents the base element of goodness, the source, the one, and you as the Orchid Queen are its vessel, it's servant and its symbol."

"And Urage?" asked Arliss still reeling from the strength of his attack.

"Urage has made himself the vessel of the no one. said Mallwynn as a look of revulsion crossed his face."

"The no one?" repeated Arliss not sure she heard correctly.

"You know him Arliss, by other names, but by any name he is the same. He is the hole through which all light is sucked. He is the height and breadth of emptiness. He is the one who is everlasting despair squared to the infinite power. He is the one who even if he so much as lays his smallest finger on you, he would sully your being forever."

Then with the look of an avenging angel, Mallwynn admonished, "Be vigilant and fierce Arliss, much depends on you."

Arliss mutely nodded her understanding as she fingered the amulet, it was warm beneath her touch.

The harsh bone chilling wind intensified as it swept over Maudland's flat bleak terrain whipping through the ranks of the little army as it advanced along the road in a slow almost mournful march toward the keep. Late in the afternoon a rumble of thunder began and the skies overhead began to darken ominously. Lightening flashed and thunder boomed vibrating against their faces and chests as the sky was suddenly torn open and a steady downpour of rain began.

It was long after dark when they at last came upon the keep at the edge of the Fane sea, the massive structure loomed large against the night sky, its narrow windows lit from within by smoky torch light. A feeling of dread swept over Arliss as she stared at the keep, remembering too vividly the horrors of the slave yard.

There was no one on the ramparts, and except for the smoking torch lights, there was no other signs of life around the keep. The little army left the road and with a wary eye on the keep, began to make camp on a hill across from the gates of the keep. It wasn't long however before the Carnumbra suddenly appeared in great numbers on top of the ramparts. Arliss drew back at the sight of them. With Striker beside her she waited and watched uneasily, fully expecting at any moment for a volley of fiery arrows to rain down on them from the ramparts, but instead the Carnumbra disappeared from sight.

When the dawn finally came the sun rose up from the Fane sea colouring the sky an unnatural shade of fiery red. The atmosphere in the Orchidian encampment was very tense those who had managed to get some sleep, had done so with one eye opened and it didn't help that the night watch reported an uneventful night as many found this particularly unnerving wondering what Urage had up his sleeve. Arliss had spent the night at Mallwynn's side watching the silent keep. She paid little attention when the wizard protested telling her that she would need to conserve her strength for what lay ahead.

An odd heaviness and silence pervaded the early morning air as the Orchidians watched and waited. Then suddenly from the keep there rose a thunderous roll of drums. Immediately Striker gave the signal and the Orchidian fell into their ranks. Their heartbeats quickened with the beat of the drums as if somehow the drums themselves heralded impending doom. The peace loving Orchidians were ill prepared for war, in fact there was no one alive on Eartheart who could remember a real war, because for as long as the Glasstarrs had reigned, there had been peace. Disputes between the various kingdoms of Eartheart had nearly always been settled without strife in the Orchid Court. There of course had been small skirmishes with bloodshed and even loss of life but these incidents were rare and isolated incidents that most Orchidians disapproved of. Orchidian justice was seen by most of Eartheart as the only acceptable way to settle a dispute as the incessant drumming continued the Orchidians swiftly readied themselves for battle although there was still no one to be seen on the ramparts.

Suddenly, without warning, a murmur arose from the ranks as Urage's black guard soldiers suddenly appeared, filing along three sides of the ramparts their movements keeping pace with the beat of the drums.

Arliss mounted on Targus, rode with the Orchidian army down from the rise, closer to the keep. Striker gave the command and the little army flanked the keep on it's three land sides. Arliss with Mallwynn and Striker at her side, positioned herself in front the entrance to the keep. The little Orchidian army tense and battle ready awaited the signal to commence fighting. Arliss swallowed hard as she scanned the faces of the ranks noticing for the first time that many of the faces were even younger than her own.

Suddenly without warning Arliss broke out of rank, urging Targus forward, as from the corner of her eye she saw Striker's hand reaching out to restrain her, evading his grasp she stopped just a few feet short of the keep gateway. There was a sudden hush as the drumming stopped abruptly. She felt rather than saw the arrows aimed in her direction. She waited for a couple of heart beats and when there still was no twang of a launched arrow, she dared look up and she caught a brief glance of Urage's face. His expression was one of mild interest.

Urage smiled down at the slight figure on horseback. But then as he recognized the legendary Orchid crown on her head his smile hardened slightly. While she still had the courage and the breath Arliss, called out, "Urage I command you as Queen of the Orchid Valley and Empress of Eartheart to come out and surrender."

Then as Urage locked eyes with the young girl he was momentarily taken back by the awareness in her clear gray eyes and suddenly an uncharacteristic wave of doubt assailed him, but Urage swept it from him as he took a second look at the girl. She was so young especially considering her life span if she were allowed to live it would be at least as long as his. He clenched his hands in excitement. She was so close to him, he'd half a mind to give the order to bring her into the keep, but the risk of her being injured or killed in the ensuing fracas was too great. He smiled to himself in delicious anticipation. He would wait and bide his time as he had big plans for the pawn who would be Queen.

"Sire why not take her now and be done with the nuisance," asked Klick interrupting Urage's thoughts.

"Don't be so impatient Klick," muttered Urage irritably, annoyed by Klick's usual lack of timing Klicks' stupidity never failed to get on his nerves and besides that the man had no sense of form. He was a peasant really. I should have fed him to the hellhounds a long time ago, but then of course his blind obedience and loyalty were so useful, mused Urage to himself as he let a small sigh of resignation escape him.

Urage smiled patting Klick on the back as he said, "You don't know how much I depend on your incisive mind.

"Klick beamed under the glow of the praise and hoped that those within earshot had heard the Lord Urage's words. Maybe this was a good time to ask the Lord to spare a prisoner or two so that he could practice some of the new methods of torture he'd learned from Master Kopter. It just wasn't the same practicing on the slavants, he might as well torture a dog. Klick decided restrain himself and wait and ask for this favor another time as he didn't want to incur the masters wrath by seeming like an advantage seeker.

Arliss drew back until she was again next to Striker and Mallwynn.

"What you think" she asked wheeling the horse around so that her back was covered.

"I think," said Striker with unnatural coolness," If I might be so bold as to say so Madam, you're very lucky to be alive."

"Yes I am," agreed Arliss, but not to be deterred by Striker's disapproval she said, "but it was reasonable to believe that Urage had no notion of moving on us right away. Why else would he let us get this far into Maudland and right up to the doors of the keep without offering any resistance? They out number us almost three to one. They could have easily have crushed us long before now. He's toying with us he has no intentions of fighting a battle at least not a physical battle."

Mallwynn nodded, agreeing with Arliss's words.

"What you mean?" asked Striker doubtfully his eyes still fixed on the keep.

"I've been in the keep and I know that Urage probably thinks of our small Orchidians army as valuable slave stock. Valuable slave stock that he has no wish to destroy unnecessarily."

"So what do you propose?" asked Striker carefully his smooth gold face a mask of calm only his hard glittering green eyes revealed understanding and foreknowledge of her reply.

"You know ...," she murmured, her voice throaty and barely above a whisper as she leveled her steady gray eyes at him and said with much more conviction than she felt, "We're going to have to go in."

A short while later Striker stood out of sight in the shadows of the royal tent. His eyes were fixed on the gates of the keep, as he muttered to Arliss, "There must be another way in from the seaward side of the keep. It wouldn't make sense having almost a third of the keep is on the water not to have a dock to land and launch boats from and not to be able to get to that dock from the keep. I'm loath to send the men out into the water to scout out the rear of the keep because if they are spotted they will give away any element of surprise we have."

Arliss started to shake her head then she caught her breath and her eyes grew wide. "There is a dock!" she exclaimed. "I remember one night when I was working in the kitchens and Bree sent me for fish which he said would be outside the kitchen door off the central passageway of the keep. When I opened the door onto the passageway there was no fish to be seen, but in a distance I could see two men approaching from the rear of the keep, each of them carrying a bushel basket of fish. I didn't think much about this at time as I was told that all of the store rooms were in the back of the keep, but then I noticed that the men were dressed in oilskins like fishermen and when I looked at the fish they were very fresh as if they'd just been caught, some of the fish were still quivering.

They men helped me bring the fish into the kitchen and when they left I didn't notice in what direction they went and I thought no more about it until now," finished Arliss breathlessly. "

"That's it then" grinned Striker "Tonight, as soon as it's dark we're going for a swim."

The plans were quickly made. The royal tent which was the military headquarters for the battle, had been positioned in plain view of the of the keep. A rear entrance was made in the large tent and Elsaroth and a young lieutenant named Drue who bore a strong resemblance to Striker were brought in to masquerade as Striker and Arliss. Arliss gave Elsaroth her cloak and chain mail and Mallwynn conjured up an exact likeness of the Orchid crown as he said it would be disrespectful for anyone but Arliss to wear the real crown. Striker gave his cloak and his suit of armor to Drue.

It was decided that while Arliss and Striker tried to find the seaward entrance to the keep, Mallwynn, Elsaroth and Drue would provide plenty of distraction for Urage. Mallwynn planned to use his magic to assault the main keep door with all kinds of opening spells. He had no real hope of opening the door but he counted on Urage not knowing that. Elsaroth and Drue would make sure they were seen at Mallwynn's side carrying on much as Arliss and Striker did. Mallwynn said it was important that they not get too close to the keep because Urage would know it wasn't the real crown. At a distance it would fool him but close up he would notice the absence of the powerful spells and charms that the real one had. It was planned that when darkness came the Orchidian bowmen would try their hand at picking off some of the Carnumbra from the ramparts who because of there red eyes would be visible.

Arliss had wondered if they would even be vulnerable to the arrows. Mallwynn said that most certainly the carnal part of them would be.

When nightfall came Arliss and Striker and set off. A small squad of soldiers and two acolytes Anni and Ancil stood by the shore ready to launch skiffs if a seaward entrance was found. Dressed completely in black and under the cover of darkness Arliss and Striker quietly made their way to the shore. Stripping down to just their tunics they silently entered the water. It was high tide and the water was black and cold and if not for the magic of the Poseidon bands they would have froze in the water, as it was their bodies adjusted quickly to the cold and they were quite comfortably despite the frigid temperature.

It was a perilous swim to the keep, as they had to cope with the surf buffeting them up against razor sharp rocks that were strewn in the shallow water near the shore. They had some relief from the treacherous rocks when the water became precipitously deep where the keep jutted out into the Fane Sea. The surf pounded against them mercilessly as blindly they felt their way along the outside of the keep, hoping to find a break in the wall. They were in luck about midway along the wall of the keep Striker, who was in the lead reached out and touched nothingness. Then his hand touched metal grating. Quickly he and Arliss surfaced and before them was an entrance to a mostly submerged chamber. It was covered with a portcullis. Looking through the grating they could see into the chamber, it was lit by torches mounted on the walls. At the far end was a dock, along which several small boats rocked and swayed at anchor. The place was unguarded there was no sign that anyone had recently been there.

Arliss and Striker dove beneath the surface once again and found that the portcullis closed off the archway all the way down to the bedrock of the submerged promontory upon which the keep had been built on.

Arliss and Striker heaved up on, and shook the portcullis, hoping to raise the heavy curtain just enough to let them slip under, but to no avail, the portcullis remained firmly fixed in place. Arliss refusing to believe that there was no way in, looked around in the dim light. Her pulse quickened as she noticed that the sea floor around the piling which supported the wall of the arch had eroded and there was just enough room for a small person to slip through. Without giving Striker a chance to stop her she slipped quickly through the small opening.

From the other side of the portcullis Striker grimaced at her and she could hear his loud protestations as he spoke to her through the Poseidon bands. Putting her finger to her lips she reminded him that Urage was sensitive enough to pick up their presence. Striker continued to glare at her as he struggled to squeeze his large frame through the tiny opening between the portcullis and the archway wall. A few moments later disgusted and annoyed he finally gave up and surfaced with Arliss on opposite side of the portcullis.

Arliss tried not to think of the fact that if she were discovered in the keep this time it would mean a certain and tortuous death. In near panic she searched for a way to raise the portcullis. Striker who waited on the other side was chalked as his eyes darted this way and that, searching for the device to raise the portcullis.

Arliss caught her breath as she thought she heard footsteps but it was only the echo of the lapping water. Her eyes followed the pulleys, ropes, and chains as they led from the portcullis up over the ceiling of the chamber and down to the far wall off the dock. She gasped, as she spotted the wheel to open the portcullis. She swam quickly to the dock and pulled herself out of the water and ran across the landing and then cringing with every creak and groan, certain that the noise would bring the Carnumbra down upon them, she turned the wheel and raised the portcullis.

Once Striker was through, he gave a low hooting call that sounded remarkably like an owl to signal the others on shore.

In a short time, the loaded skiffs glided swiftly and silently under the archway with all on board bowing their heads low just get through. The little crafts skimmed across the water to the dock. They hid the skiffs within the shadows of the dock and closed the portcullis. Arliss and Striker changed into dry clothes and then they along with the two acolytes Anni and Ancil and handful of Orchidian soldiers headed quietly up a flight of stairs that Arliss hoped led to the central passageway of the keep.

Chapter Twenty-One
Into the Lion's Lair

"This way!" whispered Striker beckoning Arliss, the soldiers and acolytes, to follow him. Like shadows they crept along the dim dank passageway until Striker raised his hand to stay them. For a moment they all stood still listening intently as Striker disappeared out of sight around a corner. A short time later he reappeared and gestured for them to follow him. They pulled their hoods low over their faces and slipped silently into the dimly lit passageway. Taking cover in the numerous doorways they edged their way up toward the front of the keep.

Arliss didn't know exactly where Urage's quarters were, but she had overheard Hassa Ludkin from time to time mention "the master's tower". Urage's tower would most likely be one of the two towers located in the inner bailey.

They passed silently out through the doors at the end of the corridor into the moonlit courtyard of the inner bailey. Just as they crossed into the shadows of the bailey wall there was a terrific booming noise, so loud that the ground shook.

"Mallwynn has begun the attack." murmured Arliss knowing now there was no turning back.

Striker nodded saying, "Let's hope that it's enough to keep them distracted, at least until we're ready for them."

If we'll ever be ready for them thought Arliss grimly as her hand touched the Glasstarr Amulet just beneath her tunic, suddenly the whole party crouched low in the shadows as a series of bloodcurdling screams ripped the night air.

"Sounds like they've felled a few Carnumbra," whispered Striker in surprise, and then as an afterthought he added "It must be some spell Mallwynn's putting on the arrows."

Cautiously they crept along the courtyard wall until they reached the first tower door. It was firmly locked so they continued on until they reached the second tower. She held her breath, as Striker tried the door, and didn't let herself dare think of what may happen if this door was also locked. To her relief the door creaked open and they and found themselves in a large square room.

Torches flickered from the wall sconces. The fire in the large hearth had burned low lending the room a warm glow but did little to take the chill out of the air. "Officers quarters," muttered, Striker as he glanced around the room. Suits of armor stood gleaming on stands. Various small heraldic shields decorated the walls of the room. Prominently displayed above the fireplace was the unmistakable Black Willow coat of arms. The room was furnished with benches chairs and tables.

Striker took a couple of Orchidian soldiers up the stairway to check out the rest of the tower. He returned quickly and reported that the officers dormitory, which was deserted, took up two floors of the tower. On the second floor, there was a connecting corridor between the two towers. They had gotten almost to the top of the second tower when they encountered a locked door.

"Urage's lair could be behind this locked door" suggested Striker. At the thought of a direct confrontation with Urage, Arliss's knees grew weak and her heart beat fast, but she knew she could no longer avoid facing Urage. But, come what may she knew, she was finished with running away.

They were just about to turn into the passage that connected the two towers when before them out of nowhere appeared six or seven Carnumbra. It all happened so fast there wasn't time to think; yet at the same time the action seem to slow and unfold with a chilling deliberateness. Arliss was separated out from the rest of her the party as Striker struggled desperately to draw the Carnumbra away from her, but he was set upon by two Carnumbra in rapid succession. Striker was battling just to stay alive.

Arliss drew battle singer out of it's sheath realizing bitterly it was far too late to regret not having had more experience with the sword. She held it the way Farin had shown her like an extension of her arm. As she thrusted the beast casually parried her every move with a large broad sword. Maybe because the Carnumbri didn't feel threatened by her skill with a sword and so was less on it's guard, she actually managed to get past the broad sword a few times. She was sickened to realize that the tip of the her blade had actually cut into the flesh of the Cunumbri. The Carnumbri seemed oblivious to it. She felt tears come to her eyes as realized that the Carnumbri was already dead! She was hacking away at some poor pitiful corpse that had been dragged from it's grave and turned into wraith-like creature by the real monster, Urage!

The Cunumbri seem to tire of toying with her as it raised it's broadsword as if to bring it crashing down on her head. Arliss scrambled to move out of range but she couldn't move fast enough. The broadsword hit her so hard she fell backwards. She felt no pain at first, just a warm sticky trickle down her arm. For a moment she just lay there, stunned, just looking up at the red eyed beast. She caught sight of the creature's flesh beneath it's torn garment. She could still see the random stab marks that her blade singer had left, but an amazing thing seemed to be happening with the wounds. They were sealing up and disappearing, without even a scar to mar the bluish white flesh! Suddenly Arliss started and rolled out of the way as she realized that the beast was preparing to raise his blade again. Then for some reason Arliss remembered Strikers words about Mallwynn putting a spell on the arrows. That would do her little good she thought ruefully as she knew no spells.

Then with a sudden flash of intuition Arliss springing to her feet and raised battle singer to her lips and kissed the blade as she said in a clear commanding voice, "As Empress of Eartheart I release you from this worm eaten flesh and command your soul to move on the way that natural law intended it to. "

The Carnumbra stopped dead in its tracks and stared at Arliss for a moment as if it was trying to fathom out what she had just said. And then suddenly quick as lightening the Carnumbra raised it blade again and prepared to bring it down upon Arliss's head, Arliss was quicker still as she took battle singer and launched herself at the creature spearing him in the heart. There was a sudden silence in the narrow corridor as the fighting suddenly halted as every one stared at Arliss and the Carnumbri in disbelief as the creature let out ear splitting shriek and fell away from Arliss's blade and crumpled into a dark loose heap on the floor which flamed up briefly. The creature, in a matter of moments it was totally consumed by the flame except for a dark cloud of smoke that dissipated out through the window. Arliss, Striker and the two acolytes Ansil and Anni competently dispatched the rest of the Carnumbra in much the same manner as Arliss had the first one.

Cautiously the Orchidian party continued on down the connecting hallway to the second tower. Rapidly they mounted the stairs of the second tower as they neared the top they found that the locked door was now wide open as if someone had left in a hurry,

"The Carnumbra that attacked us, must have been guarding these chambers when they heard us coming, "murmured Striker as he leaned through the doorway and glanced nervously around the chamber.

The room was a drawing room with an enormous fireplace. There was a door on either side of the fire place.

"Yes, these must be Urage's chambers" said Striker as he and an Orchidian soldier crossed quickly to either side of the room and threw open the doors on either side of the fireplace. Both rooms appeared empty. The room to the right of the fire place was a sleep chamber. The room to the left of the fireplace was a large study. All the walls of the study were lined with bookcases. The room had a writing desk. There was an easy chair in front of yet another smaller fireplace. Arliss and the acolytes and the rest of the Orchidian soldiers followed Striker into the study.

There was a book on the desk opened. Arliss's eyes widened as she looked at the title. She wrinkled her nose in distaste as she said "Necromancy?"

"Just one of Urage's many interest," Striker said in disgust.

A door in the study opened into a narrow hallway. They filed through the hallway which turned out to be a kind of portrait gallery. The paintings were illuminated by candle lit sconces on either side of the oil paintings. Dark shadows to flitted across the faces in the portraits making Arliss think for a moment that the faces actually moved but then she could see that it was merely a trick of the candle light. Arliss recognized the subject of most of the paintings as Urage at various ages. The small gallery opened up to a large white room. There were windows on three of the walls. The room was brightly lit with many candle and torches. Awestruck, Arliss followed Striker into the room. The walls were hung with incredible detailed human anatomy charts and water color drawings of plants and small animals. There were detailed drawings of generations of cross and line breeding of animal and plant species.

There was even a niche devoted purely to alchemy. There were jars of powders and dried leaves, there were jars of strange and weird flower heads that had been dried and a large collection of dried fungi and mold. There were jars of animal extracts and venom everything was neatly organized and labeled. But it was in the small room of the larger room, that they had a real shocker. At first glance it looked like a record room. There was shelf after shelf of log books in chronological order. There was a large central table with two books opened one for births and one for deaths. On the walls again Arliss saw the pretty water color pictures except there was something different about these she took a closer look and to her surprise and horror they were indeed breeding charts but the pictures were of people. Despite her horror she walked around the room compelled to look at the pictures one after the other. In some families he had managed to breed as many eight generations in a little over a hundred years. Arliss turned away numbed. In another corner of the room there was a map of the Orchid valley with shelves of books on the genealogy of the valley. He had charts with family names and each member was categorized by sex, coloring, height weight, temperament, intelligence, level of industry and many other characteristics. Arliss felt shaken as the full significance of what she was seeing began to dawn on her.

"Come on," said Striker, "We've got hurry, if we are going to be prepared for when Urage returns to his quarters. The look out will alert us, when he sees Urage coming. Striker went ahead of Arliss back out through the portrait gallery. Arliss was just taking a last glance around the record room when Striker called out, "Come and have a look here."

He was standing in Urage's sleep chamber in front of what appeared to be a large closet. Striker had pushed the clothes aside to reveal a hidden panel in the back that swung outward.

"Its another stairway." said Striker, his voice rising in excitement. Leaving a few guards and an Anni behind they mounted the steep spiral stairs.

Arliss, and Striker threw open the door at the top of the stairs and stepped into a strange kind of chapel. With Ancil and the Orchidians following them they filed down the narrow aisle between the rows of pews. Arliss shivered both from fear and the cold as the temperature seemed to drop as soon as she stepped over the chapel threshold. At the front of the chapel there was a stone altar covered with a black altar cloth. On the floor in front of the altar was a mosaic pentagram. Enormous black candles flickered from heavy silver candle stands on either side of the altar. She narrowed her eyes and looked at the altar more closely. Draped over the it was what appeared to be a black organza dress and veil and a bouquet of white lilies. The lilies were so perfect they looked waxen and they gave off an unnatural sickly sweet odor. Behind the altar was large dark oil

painting. It was a picture of a woman standing in a cope of black willows. Arliss knew the woman in the picture had to be Mardylla.

Arliss gasped with horror as suddenly she felt Urage's presence.

Striker jerked to a halt as he heard Arliss let out a moan and as he glanced sidelong at her he saw his own worst fears reflected in her face. Then from out of the shadows behind the altar stepped Urage. He was wearing a long dark robe. His eyes glinted like steel. Arliss felt him begin to draw her in as he looked deep into her eyes. Then his lips curled into an almost sensuous smile as he said" I expected you a little earlier, but what is it they say back where you come from? Better late than never?"

Then Urage's smile suddenly died on his face as he said, "It won't be that easy for you to slip away from the Blackwillow Keep with not even one fond fare well this time my sweet. You can depend on that."

And then as if to prove his point he crossed the room and came up to her as she stood paralyzed, frozen in place.

"Unhand the Empress cried Striker raising his sword to strike out at Urage.

Leveling his gaze at Striker, Urage stopped him in his tracks. Striker's face was contorted into look of agonized frustration as he struggled vainly to break through the thrall. At the same time, Urage with a sweep of his hands cast the same thrall over the rest of the Orchidian party. The Orchidian soldiers tried desperately to raise their arms as the spell overtook them, but they were as helpless as Arliss and Striker under Urage's thrall. Only the acolyte Anni didn't struggle instead she stood where she was still at the bottom of the spiral stairway for she had been the last one. Her body limp like a rag doll her eyes - looking into the next world.

Then Urage turned his attention again on Arliss. He gripped her shoulders and she thought he was going to shake her. She tried to look away from him but she was compelled to look him in the eye. His dark eyes were endlessly deep and she felt her self sinking and then without warning his face hovered close to hers. She could feel his breath on her face as his lips drew back in an angry grimace.

"You absurd foolish woman. Don't you realize that the only thing greater than your strength is your weakness,"

His words stung as intended somehow now everything she had done seemed trivial and not for the first time did she wish herself back in Camden Cove. She should have done the Orchidians and the rest of Eartheart a big favor and not come. Satisfied with the reaction he had engendered in her. He turned away and looked around the room speculatively as if to check that everything was in order. He turned back to her as if nothing happened and said solicitously, "Now that you are here we won't delay the wedding another moment, "Arliss was stunned.

Urage clapped his hands and Klick and Og with some of the black guard appeared at a doorway to the right side of the altar.

"Come gentlemen please disarm and seat our guest for the wedding." Arliss stood helpless while Striker was seated in the pew to the right of the altar. Strikers face was immobile his gold skin looked pale and had lost its glow, and on his brow beneath his sleek dark hair, trickled cold sweat. Urage laughed and said , "My dear I saved the pews on the right for your side of the family although he laughed again, "Strictly speaking Strongforth is not a family member even if he is a sixth cousin. My dear did he ever tell you that he was next in line for the crown that is if you couldn't have been found or I suppose if something happened to you or if you had refused the Orchid crown. I must admit I was really nervous about that one but I suppose I who must know genealogy better than anyone alive knew that I could count on your Glasstarr sense of honor, and devotion to duty after all you are also are a product of my breeding program.

As Arliss gasped, Urage laughed, "Surely you didn't think it an accident that the kings son and the Arch Wizards daughter should wed. How convenient. Well, it was and desirable that is why I arranged it. I even arranged that Mallwynn a confirmed bachelor wed, it was I who arranged for his accidental meeting with the beautiful Destell the half druid a perfect mother for Kyrianna."

"I don't believe it!" cried Arliss unable to bear it any more. "Oh believe it, my dear because its all deliciously true." Then ignoring her horrified moans Urage went on, "Why you might ask would I be interested in who Mallwynn married. Its really quite simple. I wanted to breed for myself the perfect bride. You Arliss you are my perfect bride."

Urage paused with a malicious smile to gauge the effect of his words. "Don't swoon my dear. Klick support the dear girl. Now isn't that better you really mustn't get emotional about all this. I want you to look beautiful for the ceremony we must hurry because that old man is getting very annoying. Klick send down for a woman to dress my bride."

"Right sire do you want the rest of the Orchidians and the other acolyte brought up."

"By all means Klick and please seat them on the bride side. Mistress Ludkin appeared at Arliss's side she still wore her familiar lemon sucking expression. She hustled Arliss off toward a small room to left of the altar, over her arms she carried the black veil and gown.

A distraught Striker watched as Arliss was led off by the grim faced Ludkin woman. His face rendered immobile by the thrall his eyes none the less had a wild frantic look. Arliss, just needed to have the advantage of surprise to take Urage on. She had already defeated Urage in the upper plane once he thought ran thought as he watched the door closed on a Arliss. As Striker caught a glimpse of Arliss's face. He knew all the fight had gone out of her. She looked on the point of collapse. Striker was angry with himself. He had been lulled into a false sense of security by the ease in which they were able to enter the keep. He had led them blindly led into a trap. He should have known better. Striker watched grimly as Urage conferred with his household staff. he seemed very excited and his voice was raised.

"Hah! there's no danger at all of losing the battle they don't need me to hold their hand out there. I am not going to worry about a few Orchidians and walking fish breaching the walls. The Orchidians and their friends the fish people will all be defeated all in good time. Why should I worry about an army whose reinforcements carry picks and shovels. Klick, you disappoint me. I thought you understood things. Just send word out to the captains that we will be delayed in the tower sanctuary only a little while longer and when I do emerge it will as according to Drudic law as the King of Orchidia and Emperor of Eartheart. The war will end the moment and the Black Willow Dynasty begins on its first Millennium of the rule of Eartheart. Until then keep the Orchidians and their allies busy, try to keep casualties low as we will need all the breeding stock we can get our hands on. My new Dynasty will have many frontiers to conquer purge and settle and I'll will need as many genetically bred settlers as possible. Then Urage's face darken as he said, "Tell your captains if my wedding is frivolously interrupted, I will waste good flesh and have all their heads.

Striker felt hope like a faint glimmer start to rise, protectively he pushed it down inside. He looked toward the tower stairs the black guard was just bringing the acolyte Ancil and the rest of the Queens Guard. Ancil looked deeply shaken his eyes sought out his sister Anni. She was seated in the pew behind Striker with the rest of the Orchidians. Ancil slid up next to Striker.

Urage had disappeared from the sanctuary. The pews opposite Striker had started to fill up with Black guard notables and their wives as well as those women and men who could be spared from the battle. Suddenly Urage appeared out of no where in front of him. By his side was a tall sallow faced intellectual looking man.

"Lord Strongforth may I introduce, Master Kopter our learned triage master. I know you have been wondering if I am going to do this thing right and proper so I am just hear to set your mind at easily. Kopter here is bonified marriage officiator. Sworn in and registered with the imperial office in The city of Orchids."

Striker blanched. Urage leered and said, "Thought I was bluffing," He paused here and said, "Excuse me my bride awaits. "

A grotesquely large woman dressed completely in black rose from the pews opposite and went up the side of left side of the altar and began a mournful dirge. Striker couldn't make out the words to her song and thought it just as well as the melody alone made him feel hollow and alone. Then out from the side room came Arliss her skin a translucent white beneath a cloud of black organza. The black net veil held in place on her head by a crown of diamonds and jet that resembled a large spider. Striker was stricken by the haunted look on Arliss's face and the deep shadows beneath her glassy eyes.

The song was hurting Arliss's head. She looked around to try and distract herself from the discordant sound. The first person she noticed was Striker. He looked pale and shaken, and as their eyes met briefly, she desperately wished they could awake from this nightmare. Arliss noticed with surprise that the acolyte Anni, who was seated behind Striker looked as if she were in a deep trance.

A moment later as Arliss stood in front of the altar another wave of shock and revulsion hit her as she recognized the man who was presiding over the ceremony as none other than Master Kopter. As Urage, took his place beside her, he looked highly excited and pleased with himself. He reached for her hand saying softly. "My bride."

Arliss shrunk away in disgust. Then Master Kopter began to drone out the terms of the marriage and had gotten a fair way along when a voice at the back of the sanctuary interrupted them. Arliss and Urage turned in accord.

"Mother!", gasped Urage, his eyes wide and staring with disbelief. It was Anni but not really Anni. She was filled up inside with Mardylla. Her face was strangely contorted. Her voice was not her own and she looked at least thirty years older.

"Urage is this the way you betray me! I, who have given you my life's blood? You consort with my enemies and plan a dynasty who's roots will be from this vipers womb!" Mardylla snarled as she glared at Arliss with a malevolent look.

Mardylla rose and pointed an accusing finger at Urage.

"You would suffer a Glasstarr to live? Urage, you promised me before I died that you would revenge me and the Black Willow house and that not a single Glasstarr would be left living. And now this." She said gesturing toward Arliss.

Urage had recovered himself, his shock had turned to annoyance. "Mardylla please don't hold us up any longer. Time is of the essence if I am to be Emperor of Eartheart. Please take a seat and enjoy the wedding."

Mardylla's voice took on a shrill quality as she said "I will not be dismissed this easily Urage."

Urage struggled to control his impatience as he moderated his voice and he said with great equanimity, "Now mother that was long time ago and our revenge will be all the greater to condemn the last Glasstarr to sire a whole new BlackWillow line. Mardylla cut him off as she cried out, "That is not revenge enough for me! They took my flesh, Urage! I was only your age when they killed me. I could have lived easily another five hundred years. Urage! do you know what its like to have not flesh?

What happened next, happened so fast that Arliss could hardly believe her eyes. There was a glint of steel in Mardylla's hand. Arliss recognized Anni's dagger. Mardylla quickly covered the distance between herself and Urage and stood over him with the dagger poised over his heart. For a second Mardylla lost her grip on Anni's body. In a sudden quick flash Anni's face was back to normal. Just as suddenly Anni was gone as Mardylla once was again infested her body . All this was not lost on Urage as Mardylla drew back on the dagger that she still held in her hand and prepared to plunge it into his chest. As she taunted, "Come Urage join my fleshless life," a shadow of disappointment crossed Urage's face. Quick as lightening Urage raised his hand to deflect the blade.

"I remembered you as being much smarter, mother." said Urage as he dropped the thrall that gripped the Orchidians. The effect was immediate the knife clanged out of the acolyte Anni's hand she looked around confused. At that very moment the doors of the of the sanctuary burst opened revealing Mallwynn. The wizard appeared radiant. His staff emitted a bright white light that lit up every nook and cranny of the sanctuary.

For half heartbeat Urage, and his blackguard and their captive Orchidians, just froze, as the wizard with the armies of Eartheart behind him entered the sanctuary. Arliss saw Janos and Elsaroth and Whapper and Farin in the front ranks. Suddenly as if awakened from a sleep, Urage and his men sprung into action. In the resulting melee Arliss found herself roughly dragged across the sanctuary by Urage to the room that she had dressed in. Master Kopter was at their heels. Klick who followed closely by Striker, who had leaped from the pews to the altar steps in a single bound. Klick was having a trouble fending Striker off as he expertly sliced and parried and lunged at Klick. Then as Klick reached the dressing room he struggled to squeeze the door shut between him and Striker.

Urage let go of Arliss for a moment while he and Master Kopter went to help Klick. Arliss quickly looking around the room spotted battle singer on top of the pile of her clothes. Crossing the room quickly she then grabbed the sword and hid it in the folds of her skirt. Then spying the Glasstarr Amulet which lay beside her clothes on impulse she snatched it up and looped it around her neck, stuffing it out of sight down the bodice of her black wedding gown, just in the nick of time before Urage returned to her side.

As Striker pounded at the door, Urage grabbed Arliss's arm. His dark eyes glittered as he said hoarsly, "Soon Arliss, you and I will unite this mob and end forever this infernal din."

Urage dragged roughly Arliss through a small door in the corner of the room up another flight of spiral stairs. The tower stairs. Arliss managed to keep battle singer to concealed it in her skirts. Urage had his arm around Arliss's neck so tightly that she was sure she would suffocate but still she held on tightly to battle singer.

"Klick stands guard." said Urage as they reached the top of the stairs.

"Kopter, You may begin the wedding ceremony now." Urage's veneer of nonchalance suddenly slipped as he glanced toward the stairs and added, "And be quick about it!"

Master Kopter took only a moment to compose him self clearing his throat before he opening the book he held in his hands. Urage turned to Arliss catching her eye he suddenly released her from his grasp. For a moment as Urage held her in his gaze she stood stock still not knowing quite what to do. His brows spread like eagles over his dark fringed eyes. She saw a softness in his eyes that she hadn't noticed before and strangely enough she was struck by a feeling of pity as she regarded him and for a crazy moment she was certain she could end the bloodshed of the Orchidia and Maudland by just sitting down with Urage and talking things out with him. They would do that after the wedding she supposed. Just then she felt the Glasstarr medallion burn beneath her breast.

Brought suddenly to her senses, Arliss was shocked at the power Urage had over her. How could she possibly ever give in to this beast who so heartlessly killed Iver in front of her very eyes, not to mention her parents. How could she ever forget the slave yard. Arliss, knew that if she gave into Urage he would destroy her. She knew she would never be free of him, not even in death. Urage, smiled encouragingly at Arliss unaware that she was no longer under his thrall, he extended his hand out to her. With lightning speed, and the battle singer still in her hands Arliss sprang onto the low parapet wall.

Urage gasped, and cried out, "Don't jump!"

"What's the matter Urage, are you afraid that the only hope of you ever being emperor is about to leap out of your grasp." Arliss taunted to cover up her fear.

Arliss felt kind of dizzy. The wall wasn't exactly easy to stand on, it sloped in both directions to allow rainwater to flow off of it. The slave yard was right under her. She could see Master Kopters brazier cart with it's branding irons right below her. The Fane sea was on the other side of the tower. Arliss's black wedding gown billowed like a sail against the wind and the wind buffeted her catching her veiled flaxen hair in the breeze. Her eyes were fixed on Urage, as she removed her veil and watched it drift like a black cloud down to the slave yard.

EARTHEART

"One step closer Urage, and I will jump." said Arliss decisively, already her eyes had begun to take on a faraway look as if part of her had already left her body. Suddenly, there was a commotion from the below as there was the sound of axes splitting the tower door and Striker, Mallwynn, and Farin appeared at the head of the stairs. They froze in their tracks staring transfixed at Arliss balanced precariously on the parapet wall. Arliss appeared not to have seen them. Then as Wizard called her name sofly, Arliss turned and smiled with relief at the sight of Mallwynn Striker and Farin. Seizing his chance, Urage lunged at Arliss while she was momentarily distracted. Grasping her ankle he held it firm.

"Not a step closer Mallwynn, or I'll toss the girl over the wall. Alright Kopter, you may continue with the wedding ceremony." Master Kopter nodded and opened his book once again.

But before he could even find his place in the book Arliss leaned over and grabbed Urage by the hair thrusting battle singer in under his chin she as she cried," Urage let go, or I will be forced to make you let me go."

Quick as lightening Urage reached back and before Arliss knew what happened, he grabbed both her arms and toppled her off the parapet on to the floor of the tower knocking battle singer out of her hands. She heard it clang to the floor of the tower. Don't even think of moving Wizard, cried out Urage as already his own sword was poised over Arliss's heart.

Mallwynn, Striker and Farin watched helplessly on as once again the wedding ceremony began. Arliss paler than ever had a faraway look in her eyes as she stood at Urage's side. Klick was behind Arliss his sword drawn and held at her back.

"But surely this can't be legitimate, muttered Striker under his breath to Mallwynn." She's been held at knife point. she has no free will."

"Unfortunately, I'm afraid it's just as legitimate as any other way of being bound to another human being for life", said Mallwynn vacantly.

Just as Master Kopter was about to pronounce Urage and Arliss husband and wife, Mardylla's voice rang out from the tower stairs.

"Urage, you didn't invite me to the wedding. I'm disappointed."

It was the acolyte Anni filled again with the spirit of Mardylla. Her sweet childlike face contorted to resemble the hag Mardylla. She brushed by Mallwynn Striker and Farin. As Urage turned to look at Mardylla, there was fear in his face. It was as if somehow, he knew what was about to happen but was helpless to do anything about it.

"Urage you disappoint me. I gave life for you so that you might one day rule Eartheart. By marrying this descendant of Darl, you make my sacrifice insignificant, my life forgettable. Here son," said Mardylla bending and picking up Arliss's battle singer. "This used to be Darl's sword. Take it and behead her with it the way he had me beheaded. Do it now!" begged Mardylla with venom in her eyes.

Arliss blanched at Mardylla's words somehow sensing that she wasn't going to back down in her demand for Arliss's head. Urages face was implacable. Arliss's heart thudded, she could feel her own breath coming in short little gasps. Arliss had never seen Mallwynns face look as grave. Striker's green eyes glittered in his stoic face. An uncharacteristic hardness played upon Farin's face as he watched and listened.

"Please Urage, take the sword and kill that Glasstarr viper." whined Mardylla with tears running down her sunken face." No mother, I've told you that I have other plans. I think that you should leave now. I have some important things to do."

"But, you promised me a lovely young body, Urage." pleaded Mardylla peevishly giving Urage a sly look.

"Please Urage, give me a body like this one." coaxed Mardylla, her shrill voice taking on a little girl quality as she caressed young Anni's arms. "This one will do nicely. Help me drive this silly child out of it so I can begin living my life again with you. Please, Urage, you're the only one who can't do it. Help me drive her out now."

Urage's face darkened as at it became clear to him that Mardylla had no intentions of leaving and was enjoying his obvious discomfort. "Go back to your grave old hag," spat Urage. "I have no further use for you. I will never give you a body. Why would I put a decrepit crone like you in a young body? Your time is over now it's my turn," said Urage coldly.

Mardylla looked stunned as if she had just been slapped. Her reptilian eyes narrowed and her smile became a grimace as she dropped the ingratiating veneer as snarling, she spat" If I'm going back to my grave, I 'm taking you with me,"

Mardylla's anger gave her super human strength as she lunged at Urage spearing him in the heart with battle singer. Klick with reflex action turned his blade on Mardylla — Anni, but Farin had already tossed his axe which landed squarely in Klicks chest. With a sort of surprised look Klick staggered and slid to the floor dying almost instantly which was a whole lot sooner than most of his victims. Mardylla at the first sight of Klicks sword had left Anni's body. Anni collapsed on to the floor in a stupor exhausted by the ordeal of Mardylla. Master Kopter had dropped his book and was in the act of picking up Klick's sword when Strikers battle axe came whizzing through the air cleaning slicing off his arm just below the elbow. For a moment Kopter looked at the remembered arm. Looking wildly around Master Kopter spotted Arliss by the parapet wall. He sprung at her with the idea of using her as a shield but she moved out of the at the last moment and Kopter went toppling over the parapet wall. A second later they heard an agonizing scream as Kopter impaled himself on the branding irons of the brazier cart. Its over said Mallwynn quietly.

"I buried them here together in this grove of oak because Kyriana loved the forest so much. I knew Balsarian would be happy anywhere Kyriana was." The old wizard knelt down stiffly and began pulling up the undergrowth that had begun to encroached on the grave.

Arliss stared at the simple headstone. An old gnarly oak had begun to grow around the granite stone. In few years the tree would probably swallow the stone up entirely. A feeling of sadness came over Arliss as she realized that in time there would be nothing on Eartheart to even suggest that her parents had ever even lived. She'd go back to Camden Cove. The thousand-year reign of the Glasstarrs would end. The Glasstarr throne would be no more. Mallwynn would pass on and in time there would be no one here on Eartheart to remember Kyriana and Balsarian. Arliss took a sharp breath inward and knelt down beside Malllwynn and began attacking the weeds.

The sun was setting as they walked down the valley slope. They walked in companionable silence, but as they drew near the city of Orchids. Mallwynn looked at her sidelong as said, "So when are you going home?"

Caught off guard Arliss looked blankly at him and said in slowly, "Well soon I suppose. Urage's dead and the crown can be passed on to another family. Meanwhile the royal council with Striker and Farin can manage very well indefinitely."

Mallwynn nodded in agreement with her. Arliss glancing at the old man's pensive face said suddenly, Well you know I could stay." Then watching Mallwynn closely as he tried to hold back a pleased smile, she said "but of course if you really think there's no need for me here I'll go."

"No, no, not at all," said Mallwyn hastily, "There is plenty for you to do."

Mallwynn his face beaming picked up the pace and said, "Come on let's hurry. That old coot Depper will give our supper to the dogs if we're the least bit late."

Chapter Twenty-Two
The Wedding

It had been years since the palace had looked so festive. Theo Depper had been busy for weeks preparing for tomorrow's celebration. But even efficient Depper couldn't keep up with all the details of a royal wedding. Theo Depper couldn't believe that it had been over a year since the battle of the Black Willow Keep. It had been a peaceful prosperous year for all of Eartheart. For Theo Depper it had been particularly happy year as once again he was serving a Glasstarr scion. The young Queen had proven to be a good and wise ruler belove by the people of Eartheart. Theo Depper was very proud to be her steward. Suddenly Theo Depper frowned he remembered the fly in ointment. The Wedding.

It seemed as though there were hundreds of those queer sea people all around the city. A score or more of them were bivouacked in the palace itself. Theo Depper sincerely hoped that the palace wells would hold up to all the bathes the sea folk were taking, The palace had been in a state of chaos for days . And what with those gypsies camped out on the palace lawn the whole place was in an uproar.

Theo Depper expression of unhappiness deepened as he thought about the Gypsies. Since the Gypsies were in the Queen's graces they could do exactly as they pleased and Theo Depper was certain they were the ones responsible for the disappearance of the royal linen from the clothes line in the palace kitchen garden. The gypsies were a bad influence on the palace staff. Their nightly singing and dancing was keeping the staff up half the night. Last night, he'd actually caught a few of the house maids and footmen dancing with the Gypsies. The nerve of those scoundrels sending his royal footmen running in an out of the palace wine cellar well into the wee hours of the morning. And to make matters worse every time Theo Depper happened to pass the kitchen he'd spy some Gypsies carting off, a whole hog or a brace of pheasant to roast over their camp fires. The baked goods, fruit, and confectioneries the Gypsies ate, were enough to sink a ship. The sooner they left palace the better. When ever he brought any of this up to the young Queen, she would just smile sweetly and say, "But, they are our guest."

It was going to take the royal gardeners weeks to get the lawn back to normal after the Gypsies left. It was a good job that the queen hired that chef Bree Flowdie. He's the only one who could keep up with the Gypsy's appetites. And even Theo Depper had to admit that the cake Bree Flowdie baked for the wedding was truly magnificent. But Bree in his own way was just as bad as the rest of them. He was probably out there now with the gypsies sitting around a camp fire with Mallwynn, that fish man Whapper, and that mangy cat of the Queen's. Even that nice couple the Drumners with their two small were out there dancing with the Gypsys. You'd think parents of small children would be more careful of bad influences. Though the ones that Theo Depper was most surprised at were the acolytes Annie and Anson. Theo Depper had always considered Mallwynn's acolytes to be of an ascetic nature. However Annies and Anson seemed to be reveling with the best of them. He even seen Annie dancing with a handsome young Gypsy.

Theo Depper had overheard the Sea Queen Amarin, tell Bree Flowdie's if he needed a job, Poseidon Palace could use a chef like him. Theo had been pleased to note the Bree had politely declined.

It seemed to Theo that the large gypsy woman Minera, had been given the whole run of the palace. She'd already fleeced half of his staff out umpteen pieces of silver. Telling their fortunes of all things. Depper wouldn't found out about this only he caught Minera in the act. And he made Minera give back the money she took. But that nice Miss Stimson, the palace seamstress refused to take back the piece of silver. She said Minera earned it. Theo, thought that Minera's language was a bit strong when she confronted him and told him to mind his own business. He was so taken back by how her black eyes flashed when she was angry, that he forgot to remind her that it was indeed his business.

Even a steady person like Striker Strongforth had been taken by these Gypsies. If Theo hadn't seen him dance that strange Gypsy dance with the Queen no less. He wouldn't have believed it possible. And as for Lord Farin, racing those Gypsy ponies just like he was born in a caravan. One would think that the nobility would know how to conduct oneself.

This state of affairs couldn't continue for much longer. Fortunately the Gypsies would be leaving immediately after the wedding. Theo Depper would be glad when the palace was back to normal.

Just then there was a knock on Theo Depper's door. He opened the door to a smiling Mallwynn. "Its a beautiful night out, Theo. The moon is full the sky is clear and the stars are bright. Come on out and join the wedding eve party."

Theo Depper shook his long serious face. " I really couldn't Arch Mage I have far too much to do in the morning to prepare for the wedding. I really do need my sleep, Arch Mage." Mallwynn's blue eyes twinkled as he eyed Depper. "The Queen is well aware of all the work you've have done for their wedding. They wish to thank you personally.

Why the young Queen insisted on hosting this wedding of Elsaroth of Poseidon and the Gypsy King, Theo Depper would never understand."

Depper for a brief moment looked pleased but then he shook his head and said, "I really shouldn't Arch Mage. "Oh Depper, don't be such a stuffed shirt," declared Mallwynn," Besides you've got to come. The groom's mother Minera is even saving you a dance. With that Theo's face broke out in a wide grin which looked strangely out of place on his usual dour countenance as he said, "Give me a few moments while I grab my cloak."

The Mage and the Theo Depper headed out into the palace garden toward the large party jubilant of revelers gathered around the Gypsy Caravan.

The End

www.ingramcontent.com/pod-product-compliance
Lightning Source LLC
LaVergne TN
LVHW021233080526
838199LV00088B/4334